FROM GENERATIO
ONE FIRE BURNS

RENNO—A noble warrior and leader of his people, he is the proud namesake of the legendary White Indian. He has fought many bold battles, but now he faces his fiercest challenge as he risks everything to stop a conspiracy that could destroy the magnificent land he calls home.

LITTLE HAWK—Like his fearless father, this proud Seneca soldier possesses the sacred vision and courageous spirit of a true warrior. But his mettle will be put to the harshest tests of all in the wilderness, on the open seas—and in the treacherous country of the heart.

NAOMI BURNS—She has never forgotten the magnificent young Seneca who won her heart, and she dreams of belonging to him forever. But that is before a terrifying stranger murders her parents and takes her captive, before her world explodes in a nightmare of violence, brutality—and shame.

BEARCLAW MORGAN—Towering, rifle-toting, and deadly, he takes what he wants, does what he will, and kills those who stand in his way. So when his oldest son is slain and his captive stolen, he rides into the Seneca village bent on a terrible revenge: savage, cold-blooded murder.

AARON BURR—Former vice president of the United States, he barely escaped imprisonment for killing Alexander Hamilton. Now he has hatched a plot to conquer Mexico, create a new empire, and lead a revolt against the nation that has given him up for mad.

GENERAL JAMES WILKINSON—A traitor to both kin and country, he is a man whose twisted loyalties lie with the Spanish government. Unless he is stopped, America and Spain could be embroiled in a war resulting in the worst bloodshed either nation has ever seen.

The White Indian Series
Ask your bookseller for the books you
have missed

The White Indian Series
Book XXIII

HAWK'S JOURNEY

Donald Clayton Porter

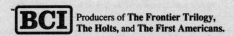

BCI Producers of **The Frontier Trilogy,**
The Holts, and **The First Americans.**

Book Creations Inc., Canaan, NY • Lyle Kenyon Engel, Founder

BANTAM BOOKS
NEW YORK • TORONTO • LONDON • SYDNEY • AUCKLAND

HAWK'S JOURNEY

*A Bantam Domain Book / published by arrangement with
Book Creations Inc.*

Bantam edition / September 1992

*Produced by Book Creations Inc.
Lyle Kenyon Engel, Founder*

DOMAIN *and the portrayal of a boxed ''d'' are trademarks of Bantam
Books, a division of Bantam Doubleday Dell Publishing Group, Inc.*

ISBN 0-553-29218-8

Published simultaneously in the United States and Canada

*Bantam Books are published by Bantam Books, a division of Bantam
Doubleday Dell Publishing Group, Inc. Its trademark, consisting of the
words ''Bantam Books'' and the portrayal of a rooster, is Registered
in U.S. Patent and Trademark Office and in other countries. Marca
Registrada. Bantam Books, 666 Fifth Avenue, New York, New York
10103.*

PRINTED IN THE UNITED STATES OF AMERICA

OPM   0 9 8 7 6 5 4 3 2 1

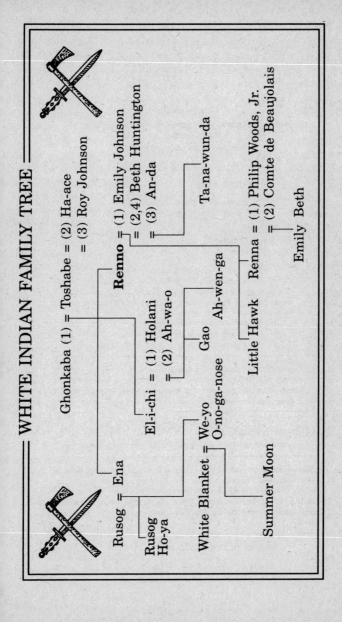

WHITE INDIAN FAMILY TREE

Ghonkaba (1) = Toshabe = (2) Ha-ace
                        = (3) Roy Johnson

Rusog = Ena

Rusog
Ho-ya

Renno = (1) Emily Johnson
         = (2,4) Beth Huntington
         = (3) An-da

El-i-chi = (1) Holani
         = (2) Ah-wa-o

White Blanket = We-yo
O-no-ga-nose

Gao   Ah-wen-ga

Summer Moon

Ta-na-wun-da

Little Hawk   Renna = (1) Philip Woods, Jr.
                     = (2) Comte de Beaujolais

Emily Beth

HAWK'S
JOURNEY

Chapter One

March 4, 1805

Thomas Jefferson left the big house that sat in an open field on Pennsylvania Avenue and walked to the Capitol Building to be sworn in for the second time as president of the United States. He was a tall man, dressed warmly against the lingering winter. His auburn hair was going gray, but his sharp, patrician face was as lineless and serene as it had been when he took the same stroll in 1801. As he walked, his eyes held their usual alertness. He glanced from side to side, nodding and speaking to those who had chosen to brave the weather and go with him.

Beside Jefferson was the stern-faced James Madison, fellow Virginian, friend of the president's, and secretary of state. Behind him a small band of militia marched in ragged files.

"You whupped 'em good, didn't you, Tom?" a

1

gray-bearded oldster yelled at him from the side of the avenue.

"That we did, sir," Jefferson called back.

Indeed, Madison thought, his friend's election victory of the previous fall had been so overwhelming as to be a mandate. Jefferson had carried every state except Connecticut and Delaware, with a vote of 162 to 14 in the electoral college. The Yankee Federalists' threat to take the New England states plus New York and New Jersey out of the Union was no longer a concern. Aaron Burr, a man never trusted by Jefferson, had, along with the Federalists, gone down to political defeat in New York. That outcome completed the inevitable process of ruin that had begun for Burr on the heights overlooking Weehawken, New Jersey, on July 11, 1804, when he mortally wounded Alexander Hamilton in a duel.

Jefferson had been pragmatic enough to admit to Madison that Burr, in killing Hamilton, had relieved him of two potent political opponents with one shot from his pistol.

George Clinton, ex-governor of New York, old and becoming senile, was to take Burr's place as vice president during Jefferson's second term. Jefferson anticipated no trouble with the old man unless, when Clinton presided over the Senate, he should forget both the business and the question before that body.

The audience at the inauguration ceremonies soon realized that Jefferson's public-speaking skills had not improved during the previous four years. In a half-audible voice, heard by only those nearest him, he reviewed the accomplishments of his first term in office. He was justly proud that "the suppression of unnecessary offices, of useless establishments and expenses, enabled us to discontinue our internal taxes."

"What farmer," he asked, "what mechanic, what laborer, ever sees a tax gatherer of the United States?"

He stated as a goal the elimination of the public debt, at which time federal revenues would be meted out to the states for the building of "rivers, canals, roads" and for "arts, manufactures, education, and other great objects *within* the states." Tax and revenue money was not to be used by the federal government for any other purpose.

"Some," he said, "feared the acquisition of Louisiana by my administration on the grounds that undue extension of territory would endanger the Union, but who can limit the extent to which the federative principle may operate effectively? The larger our association, the less it will be shaken by local passion."

Such as, Madison thought, *the desire of Burr and the New England Federalists to break up our union.*

Almost in passing, the president touched on the "Indian Problem." He avowed himself to be in sympathy with the tribes who were being overwhelmed by the irresistible tide of white expansion. He said it would be necessary, however, to accustom the Indian to "narrower limits" by promoting agriculture and the domestic arts among them, a worthy effort often stymied by Indian pride, ignorance, and prejudice.

James Madison let a tiny smile twitch on his lips. While looking over Jefferson's draft of the second inaugural address he had commented wryly, "I wonder, Mr. President, if you should mention the fact that fifty million acres of Indian lands were transferred to the United States for the very favorable price of one hundred forty-two thousand dollars?"

But nothing was to be allowed to darken Jefferson's day of triumph. He went on to predict a period of national tranquillity and prosperity. He spoke of cordial friendship with England, and Madison's lips twitched again. Even as Jefferson spoke, British warships were standing off the New York harbor, where, at will, they halted American ships to impress seamen on the pretense that they were deserters from the Royal Navy and, therefore, British subjects.

Nor, Madison knew, were things so peaceful elsewhere. In Spain, James Monroe was trying to soothe feelings inflamed when the inept diplomat Charles

Pinckney spat out an ultimatum regarding American rights to navigate the rivers of western Florida; and there was a small war brewing in North Africa against the Barbary pirate nations.

The young United States seemed to be surrounded by ill will. France was showing signs of regretting the cession of Louisiana. Spain was angry with everyone for having been forced by Napoleon to give up huge areas of her American empire. Great Britain was . . . well, she was Great Britain—arrogant, unpredictable, and, it seemed, always poised on the brink of belligerency toward her former colonies.

That night, Madison had the opportunity to speak with the president during a subdued celebration at the White House.

"A bit optimistic, weren't we, Mr. President?" he asked with an admonishing smile. His dark hair was turning gray. His eyes were beginning to take on a sunken look that promised to make his face ever more dour as he aged.

Jefferson laughed. "It's a day for optimism, James."

"Old Spain feels that she's been robbed by a secret agreement between France and the United States. Our agent threatens them with war, and the reply is: 'You may choose either peace or war. 'Tis the same thing to me.' And you taste the wine—"

"French wine," Jefferson said with a wide smile, lifting his glass.

"—and speak rosy platitudes."

Jefferson waved off Madison's chiding. "Have I told you, James, that I am going to have Dr. Benjamin Waterhouse of Massachusetts inoculate me and all the members of my family against the smallpox?"

Madison shuddered. "It literally makes my flesh crawl to think of having the juices of the sores of a victim of that disease injected into my body."

"Results, James! Results! It has been proven by

the scientific process that the recipient of this treatment is thereafter immune to the disease."

"I shall take my chances with the pox," Madison said. "Isn't it odd that you work so closely with a man—and I mean Dr. Waterhouse—who writes violent blasts against tobacco?" He chuckled. "Last I heard, Mr. President, you had a rather large crop of the vile weed on your place."

Jefferson nodded and was sobered for a moment.

Madison realized that the mere mention of the president's largest cash crop had reminded him of his always burdensome debts.

"Four years, James," Jefferson said. "Four more years, and then I'll be free to go home to Monticello and straighten out my affairs once and for all."

"Sorry to touch on a sore subject, my friend." Madison lifted his glass and brightened. "To the next four years, Mr. President. May they be great ones for you and for our country."

Jefferson touched his crystal wine glass to his friend's. "Indeed, James, I pray so, and I am quite optimistic that it will be so."

But toward the end of an eventful year, on December 3, 1805, when the president delivered his annual message to the Congress, events seemed to be mocking Madison's toast. Aside from a somewhat muddled resolution of the war against the Barbary pirates in North Africa, Jefferson had little reason for optimism. France and England, the two great powers of Europe, had revived their seemingly endless war and, in protecting their own individual interests, were, Jefferson said, "threatening our peaceable country."

The American coast was plagued with piratical armed vessels, including French and British ships of war, which were plundering, capturing, and sinking American shipping. Spain continued to refuse to define the boundary of the Louisiana Territory and was raiding into Orleans and Mississippi to seize American citizens and property. Finally, the Lewis and Clark expedition, ordered to march to the Pacific, had not returned, so Jefferson was still in the dark about the extent of his purchase.

Jefferson's soaring dreams for the future of the United States sounded hollow to the members of the Congress who were losing constituents to Spanish incursions and being constantly besieged by merchants and shipowners for relief from the virtual state of war that existed at sea.

Toshabe, senior matron of the Ghonkabanese band of Seneca, used her left hand to turn her granddaughter's face toward the light sifting down through the smoke hole in the roof of her traditional longhouse. The forefinger of her right hand was reddened by a mixture of iron oxide and lard.

We-yo, daughter of Toshabe's eldest child, the matron Ena, was sixteen. In profile she had the strong nose of her mother and the brow of her father, Rusog, the principal chief of the Cherokee. The shape of her face spoke of the small amount of white blood—one-quarter—that ran in her veins. She was dressed warmly in a fashion shared by her father's Cherokee and her mother's Seneca. A one-piece bleached doe-skin dress reached almost to her ankles to cover leggings of the same material. A large, round, skin collar was decorated with ancient circular and triangular symbols to match the band of like patterns on the lower portion of her skirt. We-yo's dark hair was in braids, which hung down over her firm, pointed breasts. She looked altogether too young to be the mother of the sixteen-month-old girl who sat on a blanket and played with gourd rattles.

"Red, you see," Toshabe explained as she carefully applied the iron-oxide dye to We-yo's cheek, "is the color of pride." She wiped her finger on a cloth, then applied a design of round dots and wavy lines across We-yo's forehead. "Yellow is for love and happiness. Green for vigilance and wisdom."

Little Summer Moon put aside her rattles, pushed herself to her feet, and toddled over to tug at her great-grandmother's skirts. "Me, me," she said.

"So, little one," Toshabe said. She applied red spots to Summer Moon's chubby cheeks. Looking at We-yo's daughter, no one would have guessed that she was a descendant of the original white Indian; the blood of her father, the Mingo warrior White Blanket, had been one hundred percent Seneca. Summer Moon held still for all of five seconds and then wiped her hand across her cheeks, smearing the red dots.

"It seems that the baby does not appreciate the spiritual value of the paints," said Beth Huntington, the flame-haired English wife of Toshabe's son Renno.

Beth, dressed in Scottish woolens, sat on an unused bed close to the fire and wiped away tears. Smoke from the fire often detoured on its way through the smoke hole and stung her eyes. Cold air crept around her ankles. Beside her lay a bearskin robe of daunting weight, which she used only in the coldest weather. Her autumn-leaf hair was gathered into a neat bun on the nape of her neck.

"Summer Moon will learn to appreciate our customs all in good time," Toshabe said confidently.

Once again the older woman cleaned her fingers. "And now," she said to We-yo, "we accent the complexion that is given to you by the sun, the shade that the first Europeans called red." She glanced toward Beth and had spoken loudly enough to ensure that her daughter-in-law heard. "The powder that I now use to enrich the beautiful shade of your skin is made of the red dry rot from the heart of a pine tree, mixed with the red earth that our learned friend Se-quo-i calls iron oxide."

Beth's summer tan had faded during the winter, leaving the smooth, creamy perfection that is most often seen in those of pure English descent. She smiled at Toshabe's obvious intention to inform her, not for the first time, that Indian red, the color given to Seneca women by the sun, was the only truly beautiful skin tone.

"But is it not true, Toshabe," Beth reminded, "that many Seneca and Cherokee women use the same white powder for their faces that is used on a baby's bottom to prevent chafing?"

Toshabe nodded. "True. Some use the finely powdered corn . . . but not on important occasions."

We-yo was smiling as she watched her daughter play on the blanket. She had heard her grandmother and her aunt Beth exchange friendly barbs before. Toshabe's first husband, the great Ghonkaba, had been half-white, and she was now married to Roy Johnson, a man of European extraction. But We-yo knew that deep in her heart Toshabe would have preferred that Renno have a good, Seneca wife, like his deceased An-da had been, instead of the regal Englishwoman Beth Huntington.

One thing about her aunt Beth, We-yo thought. She was always the lady but did not hesitate to acknowledge and return any small slight. Beth could be counted on to stand up for herself, her family, and her beliefs.

We-yo knew her aunt also to be a most generous woman. Many times Beth had begged Toshabe to allow her to have a house built for the mother of her husband—a real house with a fireplace and windows and chinked log walls to keep out the knife breath of winter. But the senior matron of the tribe always refused. Her justification was based on her personal custodianship of Seneca customs. She steadfastly refused to give up the longhouse in which she had lived with three husbands.

Toshabe did not refuse all gifts from her daughter-by-marriage. There were luxuries in the Seneca longhouse: a set of fine bone china from faraway Prussia; cooking utensils of cast iron; and woolen blankets, feather pillows, and silken and woolen garments purchased by Beth during a stay in New Orleans. Toshabe had welcomed the cook pots and the feather pillows. She did not, however, care to wear white-woman's clothing. And the woolen blankets were, in her opinion, not as warm as cured hides. She did use the blankets on the bed she shared with Roy Johnson because he had complained one morning, "My God, woman, these hides are so heavy I feel as if the varmints have not been skinned out of them."

With a rush of cold wind the door opened. Ena, Toshabe's only daughter, entered, then hurriedly slammed the door behind her.

"So," Ena said, smiling at Beth, "are you getting another lesson in how to be a good Seneca wife?"

"Master of Life," Toshabe implored, lifting her hands toward the smoky ceiling of the longhouse, "why did I not have a daughter to respect my gray hair and the wisdom that I have accumulated with such difficulty?"

Ena was no longer as slim as a girl, but when she threw off her buffalo robe she revealed a shapely body in man's buckskins. She ignored Toshabe's complaint, swooped down on her granddaughter, and whispered Summer Moon's Seneca name, Ga-ha-neh So-a-ka-ga-gwa.

"So here we gather, all of the hunting widows," Beth said good-naturedly. "If Ah-wa-o were here, the circle would be complete."

"One thing I learned long ago," Ena said. "Never try to keep a man out of the woods, especially when the weather is so terrible that no sensible being would venture away from his fire."

"Not long ago," Toshabe remarked tartly, "you would have been with them."

Ena laughed. "Well, I suppose that even I have a capacity for learning."

The conversation was conducted, for the main part, in English. Now and then Toshabe would interject a phrase in French. In Beth's makeshift classrooms, We-yo had been among the youngsters exposed to Spanish and Beth's classic English. In addition, We-yo spoke both Cherokee and Seneca and had picked up a bit of French from her grandmother.

"And what have you learned today?" Toshabe asked the girl.

We-yo recited the spiritual meaning of the colors, the facial paints that had for so long been a part of Indian life. Satisfied, Toshabe nodded.

Beth and Ena sat side by side on the bed and played with Summer Moon. The little girl laughed happily. Like all Seneca and Cherokee babies, she was spoiled and accepted the attention as her due.

We-yo was the first to hear the high, warbling trill that came from the edge of the village. "Home are the hunters," she said with a smile that faded quickly. The pleasure of knowing that her father and her uncles had returned was killed by a swift rush of memories of the brief time she had had with the man she loved.

"Mine will be ravenous," Ena said, rising, handing Summer Moon to We-yo, then going out the door.

"Men are always ravenous," Toshabe said, trying to hide her happy smile as she recognized Roy's voice among those warbling out the song of a successful hunt. "And they'll have skins for the working."

"That's why I like woolen blankets," Beth said. "Because someone else has already done the work."

We-yo was gathering up Summer Moon's playthings. A cold blast arrived just ahead of a skin-bundled Roy Johnson. Toshabe met him with gladness as he walked in, but she avoided his attempt to embrace her. She was of the old school. Affection between husband and wife was not for public display.

"Hi there, pumpkin," Roy said to Summer Moon. "Hey, don't run off, We-yo."

"I must," We-yo said, although, unlike her mother and her aunt Beth, who was gathering her bearskin around her preparatory to going out into the late December blast, she had no husband to arrive at the log cabin that her twin brother, Rusog Ho-ya, and Se-quo-i's nephews had built for her and the baby.

"Beth," Roy said in greeting.

"You look frozen," she said.

"Only half," Roy replied, grinning.

Then they were alone—a graying, stringy, tough old bird of a white man and his sassy, sixtyish squaw. He had shed his skins down to a buckskin tunic and trousers. He moved toward her and took her in his arms.

"The cold of the forests is still with you," she said.

He kissed her on the cheek. "Feels good in here. I think about a week of sitting by the fire will warm me up."

She would not release him. "I will warm you more quickly than the fire."

He winked at her. She had put on a little weight since their marriage, and it was becoming to her. Her face was fuller, and the fullness had erased her age wrinkles. She smelled of wood smoke and Beth's English soap.

"You know, wife of mine, you are one hundred percent right in that."

"Come," she said, loosening the rawhide thongs that laced his tunic.

When all of her family was gathered, Toshabe was grateful for the wide expanse of the traditional longhouse. The sons and the daughter of Ghonkaba were there with their respective mates: Renno and Beth, El-i-chi and Ah-wa-o, Ena and stoic Rusog. The grandchildren included Renno's Little Hawk and Ta-na-wun-da, An-da's son; Ena's twins, Rusog Ho-ya and We-yo; El-i-chi and Ah-wa-o's Gao; and the one member of the fourth generation, Summer Moon. The only absent one was Renno's daughter, Renna, who lived in faraway France with her royal husband, the comte de Beaujolais. Roy Johnson, the patriarch, had been father-by-marriage to Renno by the white Indian's first wife, Emily, and was now father-by-marriage to Toshabe's brood.

The senior matron was content. She had enjoyed the help of Ah-wa-o and We-yo—not to mention Summer Moon—in the preparation of the meal, which had been reduced to a small residue of stew in the bottom of an iron pot, a few bread crumbs, and a pile of well-gnawed bones. In looking around the table she saw all of those, save Renna, who were near and dear to her. The silent and dependable Rusog seemed to grow broader and more dignified with each passing year. His handsome son, Ho-ya, had apparently given up his romantic and misguided plan to leave the cojoining Seneca-Cherokee villages and join the Shawnee Tecumseh's long-touted but so far abortive Indian Confederation. We-yo was, at least on the surface, recovered from the sorrow of seeing her husband killed before her eyes by her mother and her brother.

She is strong, that one, Toshabe thought. White Blanket had tried to murder both Ena and Rusog Ho-ya, only to perish himself. Toshabe nodded to herself with pride in We-yo's stamina.

All of her family were in health. Ah-wa-o and El-i-chi were glowing, for they were expecting a second child. Gao and Ta-na, thirteen and twelve, were whispering between themselves—complicated plots in the making, no doubt, to confound all adults. Twenty-one-year-old Little Hawk, in the winter garb of a Seneca warrior, was showing maturity in his young face; and Toshabe's own two sons, Renno and El-i-chi, were in their prime, a sachem and a shaman, men to make any mother proud.

Toshabe put wood on the fire. El-i-chi leaned over to pull Ah-wa-o's blanket closer around her neck.

"Tell us a story, Uncle El-i-chi," said We-yo.

As the shaman composed himself, he took a stick and punched sparks from the fire with it, then watched the sparks as they were carried toward the smoke hole. "There was a time," he began, "when the great

Seneca sachem Cornplanter was asked by a European how the Indians came to be so reduced in number." He looked around, letting his eyes fall on each of the younger ones in turn. "Have you heard?"

"I know, Father," said Ta-na, who called both his uncle El-i-chi and Renno by that title, "that the white man breeds like the mice of the fields, while the Indian is less prolific. Witness the fact that my brother Gao only now has a brother or a sister in his mother's womb."

The adults at the table suppressed grins at the youngster's impressive vocabulary.

"So your answer would be that the white men's women are more fecund?" El-i-chi asked.

"So," Ta-na said, looking at Gao for approval.

"That may be," El-i-chi said, "but that was not Cornplanter's answer."

"You knew the sachem Cornplanter, did you not, Uncle Renno?" Gao asked.

"I have held council with him, as has your father," Renno replied.

At forty-one years of age, Renno was mature in all ways and was at the height of his physical powers. He was proud of his family, especially of his two sons, Little Hawk and Ta-na, the one so bronzed and fair, the other the perfect dark-haired, black-eyed Seneca boy.

"And what was Cornplanter's answer to the European's question?" Ho-ya asked.

"Cornplanter said that the white man used deceit. He sent an army of bald-headed men against the Iroquois. The Iroquois won the battle, true; but they were unable to take any scalp locks to prove it, and so, in total frustration, many of them jumped off Niagara Falls."

It took a few slow seconds for Ta-na and Gao to realize that El-i-chi had been indulging in some gentle leg pulling. They and We-yo laughed as one.

"Perhaps our sachem should do the story telling tonight," We-yo said, still laughing.

Renno smiled back at his comely niece. His words were in the ancient language of the Seneca. "Overhead is the baby moon," he said, his tone of voice indicating that he was reciting poetry. "A canoe, a papoose canoe, it sails and sails into the Indian West. A ring of silver foxes, a mist of silver foxes, sit and sit around the Indian moon with one yellow star for a runner, and rows of blue stars for more runners."

Renno looked at Beth. She joined her voice to his on the last lines. "O, foxes, baby moon, runners, you are fire white, writing tonight of the red man's dreams."

In the hush came the mournful moaning of the late December winds, a far-off wolf's call.

It was Toshabe who broke the silence. "Long ago, when the white faces were fewer, a great Seneca chieftain, fighting white incursions into the sacred hunting grounds of the Ho-de-no-sau-nee, burned a white settler's cabin to the ground. His warriors killed the white faces in the cabin, save only one small boy."

"She speaks of Ghonka," Ta-na intoned reverently.

"I speak of the great sachem Ghonka," Toshabe said, "who, hearing the wails of the small white boy, prevented his warriors from killing the infant. You see, for many years he had wanted a son. His first woman gave birth to a daughter, but mother and child both died when a fever swept across the land. His second woman, many years his junior, gave birth to a son, but this infant died before Ghonka could rejoice. So he said to the small white-face boy, 'You will be my son.' And he took the baby from the cabin on the banks of the Connecticut River west of Lake Winnipesaukee in the Seneca homelands. Ghonka gave the baby a name to honor the manitou of fertility."

"Renno," Gao whispered, his eyes wide.

"They called Renno the white Indian," Ta-na said.

"The boy grew and learned the ways of the Seneca and became a great warrior—tall, blond, blue eyed. His deeds were many; his strength was legend. He married Betsy, a woman of Virginia, with blond hair and green eyes, and she gave him a son whom he called Ja-gonh.

"Ja-gonh was also a white Seneca. He married the beautiful Ah-wen-ga, who was half-Seneca and half-Biloxi. Renno went to the Place across the River to join his father, Ghonka, in the West. Ah-wen-ga was kidnapped by Frenchmen and taken to France to be the mistress of a king—"

"My sister, Renna, is in France," Ta-na said.

"—but Ja-gonh went after them and rescued her. Their son was Ghonkaba, whom I loved, who was the father of my children. He led the Seneca to fight with the American white faces in the great white man's war. He led the American allies among the Seneca here, to live with the Cherokee." Toshabe paused to look at the two boys. "In your veins runs the blood of great warriors and sachems of the Seneca. Now you play, and hunt, and learn. When you enter manhood your duties will not be easy. It will be well, then, to remember those who have gone before you and how they fought and did honor to themselves and to the Seneca. You must always remember that you are the heirs to Ghonka, Renno, Ja-gonh, Ghonkaba, and to your own fathers, Renno and El-i-chi."

"We will, Grandmother," Ta-na and Gao said simultaneously.

When the stolid Rusog spoke, they all looked at him in surprise, for he usually left the story telling to the others. Ho-ya glanced at his sister, and We-yo winked at her twin as Rusog began. The siblings recognized the story as their father's favorite and only tale.

"Sun," Rusog began ponderously, "lived on the other side of the sky. But Sun's daughter lived directly above the earth, so each time Sun rose she stopped at her daughter's house for dinner. Sun hated all men because when men looked up at her they squinted their eyes and looked hateful. Sun said to her brother, Moon, 'My grandchildren are ugly. They make faces at me.'

"Moon said, 'I like my younger brothers, for they are handsome when they smile at me in the night. My rays are kinder than yours.'

"Sun was jealous and wanted to kill all of the people. She sent down rays so fierce that men fainted and had fevers and died by the hundreds, and it was feared that soon no one would be left. So the men of the earth went to the Little Men, who made medicine. The Little Men turned two warriors into snakes, a spreading adder and a copperhead, which would bite Sun. The poisonous snakes went to Sun's daughter's house to lie in wait. But Sun's fierce light scared the spreading adder so badly that he could not bite. He could only spew yellow slime, as he does to this day. Copperhead, also frightened, slithered away. But still men died from Sun's heat.

"So the Little Men made medicine again, this time changing one man into a great uktena and another into a rattlesnake."

Rusog looked around, waiting.

Dutifully Ho-ya asked, "What is a uktena, Father?"

"A huge bird monster," Rusog continued, "with feathers of fire and horns on its head. The Little Men were sure that it would do the job and kill Sun, but Rattlesnake was too quick. He bit Sun's daughter, and she fell dead. Then, in great fear of reprisal, Rattlesnake ran away. This angered Uktena, the fire-feathered one, and he became so dangerous that a man had only to look upon him to die.

"When Sun found her daughter dead, she went to her house and grieved, leaving the world in darkness. Now men no longer died of her rays. But now there was no light. The Little Men were told that Sun would never come back until Sun's daughter was brought back from Tsusginai, the land of ghosts. The land of ghosts is located in Usunhiyi, the darkening land in the west. The Little Men gave seven warriors

sourwood rods and one box. They were told to bring
the daughter home without fail and not to fall for any
tricks. The warriors traveled seven days, until they
came to the darkening land where the ghosts were
dancing. They saw Sun's daughter, and one of the
men struck her with his rod. But she kept on dancing
with the other ghosts. So the seven warriors formed a
circle around her. Each time she danced around the
circle, one of the men struck her with his magic rod
until, after seven times, she was weak. The warriors
were able to put her into the box.

"On the way home the girl woke and begged to
be let out of the box. She claimed that she was hungry. She begged and begged for food and asked for
water also. And then, when the group was near her
home, she rasped out that she was dying from lack of
air. The warriors took pity on her and lifted the lid
to give her air. Suddenly there was a rush of sound,
and a redbird appeared on a bush nearby. The warriors quickly closed the lid, only to find at their journey's end that the box was empty. They knew then
that the daughter of Sun was Redbird."

Rusog paused and let his dark brown eyes look
into every face. "And so it is," he said solemnly, "that
we cannot bring our loved ones home when they travel
to the West. Those warriors should have listened more
closely to the Little Men. If they had not heeded the
daughter of Sun's piteous pleas, they would have succeeded in bringing her home. And they—and we—
would have been able to bring back our friends and
family from the ghost country. But now when our
loved ones go to the West, they do not come back.
Ever."

"What happened to Sun, Uncle Rusog?" Ta-na
asked.

"Poor Sun wept until her tears made a flood on
the earth," Rusog answered. "The world was drown-
ing, so the people held council and decided to make
Sun laugh. Only then would she stop weeping. They
danced to Sun, and they sang to Sun. At last Sun

lifted her face and was so pleased by the singing and
the dancing that she smiled."

Renno nodded. "A good story," he commended.

"Soon *we* will sing and dance," Ta-na said.

"To the Master of Life," Toshabe added. "To the
powers of good, asking them to renew life, to bring
once again the new beginning."

"But the effect will be to make the sun smile
again," Beth Huntington said, speaking for the first
time.

"So," Toshabe said.

In the connecting villages of Rusog's Cherokee
and Renno's Seneca the old women had worn down
their teeth severely by chewing on deerskin to soften
it. Toshabe still liked to prepare skins in the old way,
but her tender mouth would not allow it. Instead she
moistened the cured deer hide with water and kneaded
it gently with a smooth stone. Roy, watching, seeing
for the first time the process used by Toshabe, wondered why any woman would ruin her teeth when it
was possible to achieve the same effect with stones.

"There is a difference," Toshabe told him.

"Can't prove it by me," Roy said.

"Oh, you. You are too easily pleased."

He grinned. "I don't know 'bout that. I had to
look a long time before I found a woman who pleased
me."

She felt a flush of pleasure. She had outlived two
husbands—good men both—and she considered herself very lucky to have been allowed a third.

"Toshabe," he said, "we've got skins a-plenty.
We have no children who need skins. Why don't you
leave that work to those who need clothing?"

"And let the fruits of your kill go to waste?" She
shook her head. "The spirit of the deer would mourn
if his hide were allowed to rot or to be chewed upon
by the scavengers."

"Well, the answer to that, I guess, is that I won't
shoot any more deer," Roy said.

"And eat no more venison?"

"I reckon I wouldn't miss it too much," Roy said without hesitation. "I can always buy us a hog from Beth or one of the Cherokee farmers. Little bit of bacon, a cured ham . . . beats dry deer meat any time."

"White faces," Toshabe said in disgust.

"Didn't see you pushing away from the table last ham I brought in," Roy said.

"That, you see, is the trouble," Toshabe explained. "You white men have an infinite capacity to beguile the poor Indian into your decadent ways."

Roy laughed. "But that's what your son advocates, isn't it? Doesn't he want the Seneca and the Cherokee to become more like the white man?"

Toshabe remained thoughtfully silent. The old ways were changing. In her opinion, she had seen too much change in her sixty-plus years. As a young girl she had lived in Quebec. After her father died, she and her mother went to live among the Erie, her mother's people. At eighteen, she was captured by the Seneca and forced to stay with them. The League of the Ho-de-no-sau-nee, the tribes of the Iroquois, lived in peace with one another and were strong. In those days a girl, or a woman, knew what to expect out of life, for the wise old men and women guarded traditions as a tribal treasure. But she had lived to see her people desert their homeland, having followed her husband to the South. Now she was sometimes afraid that she would live to see the southern Seneca lose all identity, just as those who left the lands of the lakes for the western areas now called themselves not Seneca or Mohawk or Cayuga or Oneida but Mingo.

The little band of Seneca of which her son was sachem was an isolated island in the midst of the great Cherokee Nation. Intermarriage was accepted, and because there were many more Cherokee than Seneca, each intertribal marriage further strengthened the larger group at the expense of the smaller. Her younger son, El-i-chi, had broken tradition by marrying Ah-wa-o; she was his sister-by-marriage, but in the old traditions, she was considered his sister. The marriage was taboo. Toshabe shook her head now as she remembered all the trouble he had caused in the tribe as a result of falling in love with the wrong woman.

And her other son was married to an English milady. Throughout the settlement both Cherokee and Seneca were abandoning the old ways to build log cabins, to use the white man's plow—an accident involving that invention of the evil spirits had broken poor Se-quo-i's leg—and to raise the disgusting but admittedly good-tasting swine, an animal of the white settlers.

She did not answer Roy's rhetorical question, nor did he ask for an answer. In truth, Renno believed that the Indian's very survival depended upon his ability to assimilate quickly and smoothly in the unstoppable tide of white civilization. But at what cost? Toshabe wondered sadly.

Roy went out for wood, something an Indian warrior would never do, and came back in smelling of fresh air and the year-end cold that had brought snow and heavy skies.

At the large wooden house that Roy Johnson had facetiously named Huntington Castle, Renno and Beth sat before a roaring fire and listened to the pleasant sound of corn popping in a covered iron pan. When the din inside the receptacle quieted, Renno used cloths to remove it from the fire. Beth poured freshly melted butter over it, sprinkled salt, and divided the white richness into two portions, the larger of which she handed to Renno.

The Seneca sighed as he sat back and began to nibble on the popped corn. "To become a legend among one's own people, a man would have only to invent a new way to eat corn," he said.

"Or a woman?"

"Or a woman," he agreed. "Any ideas?"

"Aside from corn bread," Beth said, "I think the best use for corn is as a fattener for pigs and cows." Beth was, in fact, experimenting with feed lots for swine, and she had installed a small herd of cattle on her property.

"Perhaps some rich French sauce?" Renno suggested idly.

She laughed. "I'll ask Renna for advice the next time I write."

Thinking of Renna put an ache in Renno's heart. His daughter's last letter had informed them that she was again with child. Her last pregnancy had ended in a miscarriage, as had the first, so the family was very concerned that things go right this time for her and Beau. There was little the family could do but wait; she was a world away among strangers. Sadly, the child who would be only one small part Seneca, might well never know her grandfather.

Beth, very familiar with her husband's moods in spite of Renno's attempts at being as stoic as Rusog, smiled at him affectionately. "You need not worry about her. There are excellent doctors in Paris. The child will be born sometime this month, and soon we'll have a letter telling us that he or she looks exactly like his or her grandfather."

"So," Renno said, smiling wanly.

"Or are you moody because Renna is going to make you a grandfather?" Beth teased. "Is that it? Do you fear growing old?"

Renno shot a kernel of popcorn at her. It landed in her lap. "You have found me out."

"Well, old man," she said, sending the kernel back whence it came, "I don't know whether or not I'll like sleeping with a grandfather."

Renno refrained from pointing out that she would be a grandmother. Beth's barrenness was one of the few regrets she had.

"I will try not to creak when I crawl into your bed," he promised. Then, he fell silent, his thoughts far away, across the Atlantic.

*   *   *

Renno was already a grandparent, for the child Renna named Emily Beth after her natural mother and her stepmother had come as a Christmas gift, entering an uncertain world on December 25, 1805. The doctors in attendance were favorites of the emperor's court. Josephine herself stopped in at the Beaujolais estate on the Ile de la Cité to offer her congratulations and to coo at the squirming, mewling infant.

When Renna was able to sit up—and that was well before the doctors said it was permissible to do so—she wrote immediately to William and Estrela in England, with enclosed letters to be forwarded to Renno and Beth.

"For shame," one of the doctors scolded, coming into the room to see her sitting propped up against her pillows, a lap desk in place, pen busy. "You must rest, madam."

"Thank you for your concern," Renna said, "but I am almost fully recovered, M'sieur le Docteur."

"No, no," the good man protested. "You will strain the delicate membranes and—"

"Don't worry," Renna said. "I come from sturdy stock." Mischief shone in her cornflower blue eyes. "During the time my people traveled hundreds of miles, from the northern lakes to the land of the Cherokee, when a woman's time came, she squatted beside the trail, gave birth to her child, handed it to a female relative, and within an hour or two was back on the march."

The doctor's face turned white. Renna was still chuckling when he rushed out the door.

Knowing her father's interest in the affairs of the world, especially when they might have an effect on the United States, she endeavored to write a summary of the eventful year that was coming to a close.

> The little Englishman Nelson has put an
> end to our emperor's hope of ending this in-
> cessant war by an invasion of 'perfidious Al-

bion.' It's difficult to find a man in Paris who
will admit it, but I can assure you that the
naval battle of Trafalgar ended any chance
of an invasion of England. But on land our
emperor is supreme. You must have read by
now that French armies have been victorious
over the combined Austrian and Russian armies at Ulm and at Austerlitz. There are rumors now, Beau tells me, that the Prussians
regret not having joined the fighting at Austerlitz and may very well challenge the emperor again. God help us all. Here in Paris,
however, one might never guess that war
continues, so gay are the social gatherings.

She wrote more pages describing her daughter,
her home, her life. And a piece of her heart went with
the packet when she entrusted it to Beau. The letter
would be sent by military pouch to a channel port.

Soon Renna was on her feet, nursing little Emily
Beth, to the consternation of her doctors, who advised
madam to avail herself of a wet nurse, lest the constant tugging at her breasts weaken the muscles and
make her look old before her time.

Again she laughed at them. To nurse her child
was a mother's duty and her joy. She was a comtesse,
and her husband was in favor with Napoleon. She was
nineteen years old. In the end she did much as she
pleased.

Chapter Two

In the days when the allied tribes of the Iroquois ruled the forests and fertile fields of their extensive northern homeland, every young warrior knew that he had, and would always have, a home and a meaningful place in life. His prestige and stature within the tribe depended upon his own personal physical and mental gifts. He could advance himself by acts of bravery and by skill with weapons, but one thing would never change: his proud identity and heritage. He had been born Seneca or Cayuga, Onondaga, Oneida, or Mohawk. Each tribe had its own hunting grounds, but the individual areas made up the whole, which was the land of the League of the Iroquois. And there, somewhere within the boundaries of that territory, the young man would make his home. When he married, he would leave the home of his father to become a part of his bride's clan; but his new home would be

Seneca or Cayuga, Onondaga, Oneida, or Mohawk, and the same customs and rules would apply.

Occasionally a young warrior would emulate ancient Hiawatha and go a-journeying. He might well count coup against some tribe whose hunting grounds adjoined the territory of the league, then come home to tell of his adventures over the fire in the council house. If he were a Seneca, in the fullness of time he would become a Pine Tree of the tribe or even a war chief, and as a senior warrior he would live out his life among his children and his grandchildren and, without regret, pass to the Place across the River to join his ancestors who had made that last trip before him.

The coming of the white man and his insatiable gluttony for land began to erode Iroquois tradition long before Ghonkaba led a portion of the Seneca tribe to fight at the side of George Washington's colonials in the great white man's war. For those Seneca who survived the war and followed Ghonkaba to the South, change became the rule.

Without being able to define the basic enigma, there were young men in Renno's village—such as his nephew, Rusog Ho-ya—who lived with nagging discontent. Not even the wisest of matrons could put a finger on the problem and say, "The restlessness of our young men is due to a lack of permanence. There can be no security in the mind of a young man whose beliefs are not based firmly on tradition."

Some young Seneca had, and would in the future, put daunting distances between themselves and the fires of home. Little Hawk, son of the sachem, had left home at a very early age to travel to Philadelphia, where he became a page in the United States Senate. Although he often returned to his father's village, never could he recapture the old, comfortable feeling of being in a place where everything and everyone, including himself, had a station.

He had seen North Africa and the islands of the Mediterranean Sea. He had traveled far, and now that he was among his family again he wondered why he could not find contentment. He had celebrated Christmas in his stepmother's house, had stuffed himself with a score of dishes cooked in both the English and the Indian way. He had exchanged gifts with his father and Beth. In that well furnished, luxurious home English was spoken with an upper-class accent. He dressed for dinner in the constraining garments of the white man, and he found himself missing something . . . the blazing, hard-edged glare of the lights in the sky over the desert? the stretch of unknown distances before him? Something . . .

For a brief and gratifying period he had almost recaptured the timeless, smug timbre of his youth, of the days before he left the Cherokee Nation to ride east and north with his father to the capital of the United States. In the virgin forests with Renno, his uncle El-i-chi, his grandfather Roy, and his cousin Ho-ya, he wore buckskin and spoke only Seneca. He brought down his deer not with a long rifle but with a Seneca bow. There in the December chill, with a campfire blazing and a cut of venison roasting over the flames and dripping savory juices to sizzle and hiss before sending their essences toward the lights in the sky, he was Os-sweh-ga-da-ah Ne-wa-ah, Little Hawk of the Seneca. Wrapped in the cured skin of a panther, the animal's open mouth, teeth, and false eyes looking alive atop his head, he joked with his uncle, bit into the half-cooked meat to taste hot blood.

The warm sands of North Africa seemed impossibly far away. Even when, at the request of one or another of his companions, he retold the taking of the fort at Derna and how the small band of United States Marines marched from Egypt through the trackless wastes, the story seemed as lost in time as the legends of the beginning, which El-i-chi related. Not even Roy tired of hearing him recount the battle of the step pyramid, where he had been joined by the manitous of the pharaohs and by the spirit of his ancestor the original white Indian.

It was a good life in the forest. His six-foot height matched that of his father, but his coloring was fairer than Renno's. He was a throwback, he had been told, to the first white Indian. In the winter his skin lost some of its sun-bronzed hue. His sun-bleached blond hair darkened just slightly, and his blue eyes deepened. He was almost as strong as his father and could beat everyone in the family but Renno at arm wrestling. In the forest he was content. It was when the hunting party returned to the village that the restlessness returned. His life settled into that dull, uneventful period of midwinter prior to the time when the False Face Society, of which he was long a member, donned their masks and made mischief in celebration of the new beginning. The members of his family were busy with their own lives.

He visited the man whom he called Uncle Se-quo-i. The gifted Cherokee scholar was sitting by the fire in the small cabin he shared with his mother.

"So, my young warrior," Se-quo-i said, carving a sprightly little wren from a piece of soft pine.

"How goes it?" Little Hawk asked.

"The quarter of venison you brought to me— thank you very much—is gone."

Little Hawk reached over and patted his friend on the back. "You are a wise man."

Se-quo-i raised his eyebrows. "What makes you say that?"

"You have just given me the excuse I need."

"Ah, you are like your father," Se-quo-i remarked. "Since when does a son of the white Indian need an excuse to lose himself in the forest?"

"Can you hunt no more?"

Se-quo-i made one final adjustment around the wren's beak and extended the carving toward Little Hawk. "I have captured this."

Little Hawk accepted the sculpture. "You have

indeed captured Miss Wren. If she begins to fuss at me for disturbing her, I will not be surprised." He smiled. "A fair trade, Uncle? Miss Wren for a young and tender doe?"

"I am overwhelmed," Se-quo-i said, inclining his head in agreement.

They sat in congenial silence for a while. A log settled in the fireplace, sending a reverse cascade of sparks up the chimney.

"The disease you have, my young friend, is curable," Se-quo-i said.

Little Hawk looked startled. "But I am in perfect health."

"Your body, yes. But your heart?"

"Not you too, Uncle," Little Hawk protested. "You are an unlikely matchmaker."

"You are—how old?" He mused for a moment, then snapped his fingers. "Twenty. You are twenty."

"Twenty-one."

"And without a woman."

Little Hawk shrugged. He had known two women, one with exquisite and youthful pleasure—the daughter of his commander at West Point—and one with eerie and ominous lust, the witch Melisande.

"So you think you are not ready to marry," Se-quo-i said, "which, I must state, I consider to be a mistake. The Master of Life intended babies to be gifts for those just past being children themselves. Otherwise childish enthusiasm drives parents mad."

Little Hawk shrugged.

"Since you choose to ignore good advice—"

"You sound like my grandmother," Little Hawk moaned.

"—and refuse to claim a wife, there are willing young widows who are lovely and lonely and quite eager to have a handsome young man on a temporary basis." Se-quo-i grinned at Little Hawk. "If not in your own village, then in mine."

"Thank you for your concern, Uncle," Little Hawk said, getting up to escape the lecture.

*   *   *

He did not think of Se-quo-i's advice again until he sat alone, miles from the village, his back to a rock overhang and his hands and face being warmed by a small fire. He had run, walked, and climbed the ridges to the northwest, then finally took down a deer. He thought of a girl named Lillie. He could remember her body well, but for the moment he had forgotten her first name. So much, he told himself, for true love. At West Point, when he was risking his commission and perhaps his life by sneaking through the bedroom window of the daughter of the commanding officer, he had thought that his love for the slim, amorous, pale-skinned girl was eternal.

When the fire died down, he arranged his bedding—pine boughs, one blanket, the skin cloak he wore—and slept. Into his dreams came a young, freckled, smiling face, a visage that seemed to live only in the night. Naomi Burns . . .

With the morning he ate warmed-over meat and looked upward at the sky. The weather was holding cold and clear, perfect for traveling. The Tennessee state line was only a few miles to the north. On an impulse inspired by his dream, he turned his back toward the south and began a journey into the past.

It seemed longer than the few years that had passed since he had left Philadelphia and his position as Senate page to make the long trek southwestward to his home. Not far north of the boundary between Tennessee and the Cherokee Nation he had spent one night in the barn of a friendly farmer named Frank Burns, and there he had been given his first kiss by a taffy-haired girl in a faded calico dress.

Naomi had not been all that beautiful—certainly not as striking as Beth Huntington—but her smile had stayed with him for a long time. The freckled face of Naomi Burns had come into his dreams under the clear-skied stars of North Africa and again in cramped quarters aboard ships crossing the Atlantic.

"You're being foolish, Os-sweh-ga-da-ah Ne-wa-ah," he told himself more than once as he crossed the invisible boundary into white man's lands and continued northward. "You are trying to visit a memory that is gone, like last year's fallen leaves." But still he continued, even though he did not recognize a single landmark.

After two days' travel he hailed the log cabin of a farmstead and made polite inquiry about the location of the Burns place. "I came this way several years ago," he said, laughing, "but now I don't seem to be able to remember exactly where my friend Frank Burns lives."

"Things change."

"Indeed, they do."

"Old man Burns, he's dead," said the farmer, after lancing the air with a spurt of tobacco juice.

Little Hawk felt a rush of foreboding. "There was a young girl. Her name was Naomi?"

"Yep. She's still around c'here."

Little Hawk waited while the farmer bunched loose tobacco leaves from a leather pouch and replenished his chaw.

"She's married to that no 'count Bearclaw Morgan."

Ah, well.

"Still livin' on her pappy's place with that passel of white trash. You wanta see her, you jest missed the trail. Them white trash has let it growed up. You go back cross the crick and look for it, you'll see it leadin' up and over the ridge."

"Yes, I remember now," Little Hawk said. "I am obliged."

"Old woman's got vittles ready, iffen you be hungry."

"Thank you, sir. That's kind, but I have to move on."

"You go to the Burns place, keep your rifle handy. That's my advice."

"Thank you again," Little Hawk said.

Ah, well, he had fully expected her to be married. He was not saddened, he told himself, because he had been prepared for it. She was, after all, no longer a girl. She was every bit as old as he, maybe older, and on the frontier a girl didn't get to be twenty or twenty-one and remain single.

He did not even turn his head to look when the weed-grown track branched off the rocky road toward the ridge. His face was toward home—not his home, the home of his father. He himself felt rootless, and that feeling grew into self-doubt when he made a dry camp, built a fire for warmth and light, and made his meal of jerky and *canutchie,* the delicious sweet and chewy Cherokee hickory nut and honey ball that his aunt Ena made so well. He bundled himself in his skins and blanket and watched the fire burn down to embers.

He tried to shake off a feeling of loss and tried instead to concentrate on what good might come in his life. Thomas Jefferson had told him to take an extended leave, at least until the hearings into William Eaton's war in North Africa were over. He had seen few newspapers—none for weeks, but it had seemed that the interest in the capture of Derna had faded. The newspapers he'd seen held no mention of the war against the Barbary pirates or of "General" William Eaton. Perhaps, Little Hawk was thinking as sleep began to gnaw at his consciousness, it was time to report for duty. Then there would be the sea, for he was a marine. He had requested that the president allow him to keep his commission in the corps, and that meant that he would, in all probability, be in charge of a marine detachment aboard a U.S. ship of war. Whatever . . .

There was, after all, no permanence. He would let the Marine Corps decide his future, at least for the next few years.

He dozed.

A face formed in the glowing embers of his dying fire and became three dimensional. He started and cried out "Naomi," but then he saw that the pale-haired vision was not the girl who had haunted his

dreams for so long. He stiffened in shock, then gratitude, and began to chant an old Seneca hymn of praise
to the manitous, for it was his mother's face that grew
and floated above the fire.

"Ah," he whispered, "you were so beautiful,
Mother."

Emily wore a dress that he vaguely remembered,
her best, the one she donned when she was going into
Knoxville to visit her parents.

"I thank thee, manitous, for this gift," Little
Hawk whispered as his heart filled with pride and
love.

The manitou smiled.

"Will you speak to me, Mother?"

"I will speak."

He waited. The manitou's smile faded, and her
eyes narrowed in concern. "You are lonely."

"Yes, oh, yes."

"And still you passed the turning?"

He cocked his head. "Do you speak of the track
to her house?"

The manitou was smiling again, and as she began
to fade, Little Hawk held out his hands, pleading for
more. It came. The soft voice did not disturb the quiet
of the night, nor did it startle a whippoorwill that had
begun its mournful song from a nearby copse of trees.

"Love is not to be discarded so lightly," the manitou said. And then she was gone.

The smell of a young girl from the past was in his
nostrils—lye soap and fresh bread, the clean sweetness
of her hair.

An irresistible exhaustion overwhelmed him, and
he fell into a deep, dreamless sleep. The sun was high
when he awoke.

Little Hawk got up and, remembering the manitou's visit with vivid clarity, set off along his back
trail. He reached the track to the Burns place, climbed
the ridge, and followed it for at least five miles. The
Seneca remembered now that he had crossed the little
valley below at a point to the west.

He saw the smoke from the Burns cabin and slowed his pace. Second-growth brush had been allowed to clog Frank Burns's laboriously cleared fields. In the dooryard, where once Naomi and her mother had planted roses and wildflowers, hog weeds grew rank and dense. The cedar shake roof of the cabin had accumulated a thick coating of moss. A broken window was covered by larded brown paper. The log and cedar shake outbuildings were caving in on themselves, and the ruins were choked by leafy vines. If smoke had not been issuing from the chimney, he would have thought the place to be deserted.

He halted a hundred feet from the cabin and called out, "Hello, the house!"

With a barely heard movement, a hulking man-boy stepped out from behind dense bushes.

"What'chu want?" the surly boy demanded. He was no older, Little Hawk guessed, than sixteen. His eyes were the color of river sand, and there was a haze over them, as if he looked on the world from deep within a dark cavern. His mouth sagged open. His eyes did not blink as he stared at Little Hawk.

"I'm an old friend of the Burns family," Little Hawk said, noting that the large boy had his finger inside the trigger guard of an old musket.

"Yeah? So?"

"I was passing," Little Hawk said. "I thought I'd stop by and see them."

"Ain't no Burnses here no more."

"You don't mean it," Little Hawk said, feigning shock.

His response puzzled the boy. It was clear to Little Hawk that this one, obviously a member of the Morgan family, had been, in Indian terms, blessed by the spirits. There was a definite look of madness about him, and a slightly intimidating aura of barely controlled violence.

"Are you saying that the whole Burns family is dead?"

"Yeah."

"All of them? Frank Burns?"

"Yeah."

"His wife?"

"Yeah."

"The daughter, Naomi?"

A long pause. The unblinking eyes shifted, then came back. "Yeah."

Little Hawk knew that the boy was lying. As the Seneca moved toward the well, which was just inside the broken-down rail fence, there was nothing slow about the boy's movements. He leaped to block Little Hawk's path.

"Thought I'd have a drink of water before I move on," Little Hawk explained, wondering if he could lift his rifle and cock it in time to counter what he feared were the boy's intentions.

"Huh?"

"A drink of water?"

"Oh. Yeah."

Little Hawk slowly lowered the wooden bucket, drew it up, filled the metal dipper, sipped.

"I likes hog killin' time," the boy said, leaning close, thrusting his face to within inches of Little Hawk's.

"Yes, that's a good time," Little Hawk agreed, sneaking a look toward the house.

"I does the killin'."

"Ummm?"

The boy drew a long knife from his belt with one hand and held it under Little Hawk's nose. "I kills 'em with this. I likes to hear 'em squeal. I likes to open they bellies 'fore I slits they throats."

"Yes," Little Hawk said, chilled by the look in the boy's pale eyes. Fear of death had never caused him to deviate from his planned course of action—neither in facing enemies in the frontier wilderness nor when he was charging into Arab guns in North Africa. But he felt the skin on the back of his neck begin to crawl as he was faced by the demented stare of the Morgan boy and heard threatening words spoken in monotone. Once he had seen a rabid wolf in the forest. His father, who did not know the meaning of fear, found swift safety in the branch of a tree, dragging Little Hawk up with him. Looking down on the slobbering, suffering, maddened wolf, he had felt the same dread that he experienced now as he looked into the mad, sand-colored eyes.

"Well, I'll be going," he said, easing his rifle into position.

"Maybe you better stay," the boy said.

The noise came from the cabin. He allowed himself a quick glance. Naomi was standing in the doorway. The boy backed off; her presence seemed to confuse him. He stood beside the well, his musket in one hand and the long knife in the other, his unblinking eyes following Little Hawk's movements.

"Naomi?" Little Hawk asked, stepping over the fallen fence and walking toward the porch.

The girl had become a woman. Her burnished gold hair hung in stringy disarray to unevenly cut ends touching her shoulders. She was wearing a thin cotton dress, and as Little Hawk halted at the steps, he realized that there was nothing else—just the thin dress that showed her apple-sized breasts against the loose material. Her legs were bare and exposed from just below the knees. To Little Hawk's surprise there was soil on her face and legs. He remembered her as being such a clean girl.

"Naomi?" Little Hawk repeated.

Her sable-brown eyes widened, and for a moment, her mouth seemed to spread across her face, upper lip wide and sensuous, in a glad smile. Then the smile died. She looked over her shoulder fearfully in response to a question in a harsh, deep voice.

Little Hawk moved closer.

"Go away, quickly," she whispered at Little Hawk.

Suddenly she was pushed roughly aside. A huge man armed with a rifle stood in the doorway. His black hair was long and tangled. His dark eyes nar-

rowed with suspicion and threat. His nose protruded
from a massive beard that was as stiff and as black as
bear's fur.

"What in the name of Satan you want, boy?" the
big man rumbled.

From behind the black-bearded man Naomi made
a frantic motion: go away.

"I knew Frank Burns," Little Hawk said mildly.
Out of the corner of his eye he was watching the boy
by the well and adjusting his grip on his rifle. "I was
passing by and thought I'd stop and see the family."

The huge man showed rotting teeth in a wide
grin. "Gal," he said, turning toward Naomi, "this one
of your old beaus?"

Naomi did not speak, but she shook her head
sharply in negation. Little Hawk felt a surge of anger
as he realized that what he had thought to be dirt on
her legs and on her face was bruises—some fresh, others in the final stages of lividity.

"Well, boy," the big man said, "you see what's
left of the Burnses. Just my gal here. But any friend
of the Burnses is a friend of Bearclaw Morgan's." He
put a hand on Naomi's shoulder, turned her around,
and slapped her not at all gently on the rump. "Git
in that kitchen and rustle up some vittles."

A craggy-faced, beardless junior edition of Bearclaw Morgan came out the door, pushing past Naomi
as she went in.

"This here's my boy Jimbo," Bearclaw said.
"Reckon you done met my t'other son, Tommy.
Come on up and set. Won't take the woman long to
get us some grub. Jimbo, fetch that there jug."

Jimbo went into the house and came back with a
gallon crock jug. Bearclaw extended it to Little Hawk.

"Thank you, Mr. Morgan, but I don't drink,"
Little Hawk said, coming to sit on the edge of the
porch. He positioned himself to be able to see the
three Morgan men.

Jimbo's small, close-set eyes narrowed. "You re-
fusin' to accept my pa's hospitality?"

Tommy had moved to stand just inside the broken fence, his musket cradled in his arms.

"Now see here, Jimbo," Bearclaw Morgan said. "Iffen a man don't take whiskey, that's his ownself's concern."

"Never did trust a feller what wouldn't take a drink," Jimbo muttered, tilting the jug.

"Set down and shut up," Bearclaw said.

While Tommy drank he kept his sand-colored eyes on Little Hawk's face. Whiskey spilled and ran down his chin.

"So you knowed my friend Frank Burns?" Bearclaw asked.

"Yes, sir," Little Hawk said. He was thinking of the neighboring settler's warning to keep his rifle at the ready around the Morgans. Little Hawk had decided that he'd take out Jimbo Morgan with his rifle, try to get Bearclaw with his knife, and then, if he was still alive, turn to Tommy in the yard with his tomahawk.

"Me and my boys, we come out west here from Georgia just to take up some land close by old Frank," Bearclaw said. "Soon after we'uns got c'here, Frank and his missus died off. Frank's dyin' words was that I look after his little Naomi. I tole him, I said, 'Frank, now don't you worry none, because I find it my bounden duty to holp you out in this here matter.' " He looked at Little Hawk and grinned. "Now it warn't that I was dead set on takin' another wife, mind you. It was my duty to my old friend, so I holped him out as best I could and still try to do my duty by his youngun."

Tommy Morgan was snickering. "What I done," he said, "was throw ole Frank's body to the hogs."

"Shut up, Tommy!" Bearclaw said harshly. Then he grinned and winked at Little Hawk and made a circular motion with his finger at his temple. "Never mind the boy."

"Yawl can come on to supper," Naomi said from the doorway.

The once pristine house stank of tobacco, old
sweat, dirty feet, and spoiled food. Naomi was standing nervously beside the table, where she had set a
steaming tureen. Bearclaw seated Little Hawk at one
end of the table. The two boys plopped down on the
sides, and Bearclaw took his place at the other end.
Naomi ladled beans onto Bearclaw's plate first.

"I threw Frank's old woman to the hogs, too,"
Tommy said, showing a broken tooth in a smirk.

Naomi's head jerked toward Little Hawk, her
eyes wide with terror.

"After we'uns got through with her," Tommy
said, chortling.

"Shut up, boy!" Bearclaw shouted. He winked at
Little Hawk again. "Don't mind the boy. He makes
up things."

"Mama, dear," Jimbo said, putting his hand on
Naomi's arm, "yore old beau here, he don't like whiskey. I say any man won't take a drink ain't much of
a man. What 'chu say?"

"I say this here boy is a guest in my house!"
Bearclaw snarled. "Now you shet yore mouth 'fore I
shet it fer you."

Naomi moved around the table to serve Little
Hawk. She had to bend over to reach his plate. "Go
away quick," she whispered.

"What we done," Bearclaw said, "was to put
Frank and his missus in the ground with all due respect. Ain't that right, gal?"

"Yes," Naomi said dully.

"I still says that iffen a man won't drink, he ain't
much a man," Jimbo said.

Bearclaw chuckled when he saw the glint of Little
Hawk's blue eyes. "Jimbo, if it's a fight yer lookin'
for, I bet this here boy can give you more'n you would
ever want. Was I you, I'd keep my fly trap shut."

"Reckon we might go outside now?" Jimbo asked
Little Hawk, standing.

The Seneca started to rise, but Bearclaw jerked

Jimbo back into his seat. "Not on an empty stomach, boy. Not 'fore we extend the hospitality of this here house to our guest."

Naomi leaned over to spoon beans into Tommy's plate. With the quickness of a snake the boy ran his hand up her dress, all the way, and grabbed female softness. Naomi jumped and cried out, and hot beans spilled down Tommy's front and into his lap. He screamed and leaped up, holding his crotch.

"She ruint me, Pa!" he yelled. "The bitch done it a-purpose."

Bearclaw jumped to his feet and backhanded Naomi across the face. She crashed into the wall.

"Now you git crackin' and clean up this mess," Bearclaw growled as she put her hand up to her cheek.

Little Hawk's rifle was leaning against the wall just inside the front door, but his hand was on his knife. Naomi looked at him pleadingly, shaking her head. Bearclaw, meanwhile, was wiping the beans off Tommy's overalls and muttering solicitously to the boy. Jimbo, grinning widely, watched the cleanup.

"Burn it off, little brother?" Jimbo asked.

"The bitch is puttin' on airs fer her company," Tommy complained.

Naomi edged close to Little Hawk and hissed, "Leave now or they'll kill you."

Terror was bright in her eyes. Little Hawk nodded. He stood. "Mr. Morgan, I want to thank you very kindly for the meal and for your hospitality." He stepped quickly to the door, took his rifle in one hand, his tomahawk in the other. "Yes, sir, I want to thank you very much. I enjoyed the meal, Miz Morgan. I'll be on my way now."

"Now see here, boy, it ain't fittin' to leave a man's house in the night. We got a warm place fer you out in the barn. Lots of clean straw. You don't want to go traipsin' around out in them hills in the dark."

"I'll make a few miles by the light of the moon," Little Hawk said. "Then I'll sleep a couple of hours and get an early start."

"You got any money?" Tommy mumbled around a mouthful of beans. Juice was running down his chin.

"Afraid not," Little Hawk lied. Having lived in the white man's world, he had acquired the habit of carrying a few coins just in case of emergency.

"Too bad," Tommy said, " 'cause iffen you had two dollars, you could have company out there in the barn." He looked at Naomi and snickered.

Little Hawk was able to hide his anger and disgust only with great effort. He glanced at Naomi, and she nodded almost imperceptibly. The look in her eyes, the flowering new bruise on her face, and his own feeling of anger combined to make his decision. He opened a small leather pouch that he wore around his neck and poured five Spanish gold coins into his hand, making sure that the Morgans saw the gleam of the yellow metal. He tossed a coin onto the table.

It rang, bounced, and was snatched expertly from midair by Bearclaw. "Send her out, then," he said, biting the coin.

"After the bitch is done cleanin' up the kitchen," Tommy said.

Little Hawk walked out to the barn, alert for the sounds of being followed. He went inside. A full moon sent its beams through the windows and the cracks in the wall. The straw there was far from fresh, but it was dry. He bunched some straw into a roll the size and shape of a sleeping man, then covered it with his blanket. He took up position in shadows, rifle cocked, tomahawk and knife ready. He was counting on the gleam of avarice in Bearclaw Morgan's eyes upon seeing the four gold coins go back into the leather pouch to bring the Morgans to him. He was ready and more than willing to kill them all. There had been the ring of truth in Tommy's voice when he spoke of throwing Frank Burns and his wife to the hogs. The razorback hogs of the frontier settlements would eat anything. Almost every settlement had its horror story about someone, usually a child, falling into the hog pen and being consumed. It was not a pretty picture.

As Little Hawk waited he remembered a young girl, her taffy-colored hair in pigtails. She had stood on tiptoes to give him the first kiss he had ever shared. A cold fury built within his gut as he reviewed the events at the table.

At last the soft movements outside the door told him to be ready to do battle; but when the door creaked open on its leather hinges, Naomi stepped inside.

Little Hawk emerged from the shadows. "Where are they?" he whispered.

She took a deep breath. "In the house. They'll wait until you're asleep."

"He sent you to me for one coin?"

"Yes, and you must go now, Little Hawk. They'll kill you for the gold. They'd kill you for your rifle and your clothing or for the fun of it."

"They murdered your parents?"

"Yes," she said quietly through a constricted throat.

"And threw the bodies into the hog pen?"

Moonlight reflected off her wet cheeks as she nodded confirmation, but her weeping was silent. Her voice was a mere croak. "They made me watch."

"In a few minutes you will go back to the house and tell them that I—that I—uh, have finished with you and was asleep when you left me."

"No! Oh, no, please. You don't know them. They're very strong, and there are three of them." She moved toward him and put her hands on his arms. "All I have left are my memories, Little Hawk, and I do think of you often. If I were the cause of your death—"

"Some will die," he said. "But not I, manitous willing."

"Go," she begged. "Please go."

He nodded. "All right, then. *We* will go."

She jerked away from him. The heat of her hands lingered on his arms. "No!"

"I will not leave you here with those animals."

"It's too late for me," she said, turning away. Then she whirled to face him again. "Please," she implored hoarsely, "time is running out. Jimbo said that he was going to cut your throat while—while you were—"

Little Hawk felt heartsick. He remembered her sweet innocence and openness and the soft, warm mouth that he had kissed so many years before; but now he was alienated and disgusted by this woman who smelled of old clothes and kitchen grease, whose thin dress bulged with her apple-sized breasts. She had allowed Tommy to run his hand up her skirt. Obviously she wore nothing underneath. What else had she allowed? he wondered, repulsed.

"Tell me quickly how they killed your father."

"Mother was ill, and we were tending her—you know, washing her, trying to give her some broth. They came riding up and were inside the house before we even realized they were around. Ordinarily we would have been more aware, but they came at just the time we were so occupied with Mama."

"Yes, yes," he said impatiently.

"Daddy told them that, as they could see, he wasn't in a position to offer hospitality. Bearclaw just laughed and hit him in the face with his rifle butt. Then Tommy dragged him outside and cut his throat so that he wouldn't bleed in the house. Mama started screaming, and her heart gave out. Bearclaw told Jimbo to take my mother's body out and bury it. But then Tommy came in and said he'd take care of it. He threw her over his shoulder like a sack of grain and carried her out to the barn. Bearclaw and Tommy ate the food I'd cooked and then—" She paused and swallowed hard. "And then they—"

"You don't have to tell that part of it."

"After they finished, I slipped out. I went to see

what Tommy had done with my mother's body. He had her in the barn and was—" She started to choke and gag. Little Hawk took her into his arms and patted her on the back. "I lost my head and leaped on his back, and he hurt me. And then he tied me up to a stall gate and made me watch while he—used my dead mother's body. And then he threw her into the hog pen and went and got my father's body and did the same. He took me there and held me, making me watch while—"

"Enough," Little Hawk said. He lifted her face. "Listen to me. Here's what you are going to do."

He led her to his blanket, on the straw, helped her lie down, then lay atop her. He could feel the sharpness of her hipbones protruding through a thin layer of flesh. Her breath was sour, as if she had been sick. Her hair stank of neglect. Even with his weight on her, he felt nothing other than anger. His every sense was alert.

He heard the door as it was eased open, felt the intruder's presence, and waited as Jimbo Morgan took a deep breath as he lifted a chopping ax. Little Hawk could see the gleam of moonlight on the blade. He rolled away, driving his foot up hard into Jimbo's genitals. The man screamed and dropped the ax, then bent to cup his pain in both hands. Little Hawk's tomahawk made a sound like a ripe watermelon falling on stone as he slammed it through Jimbo's skull.

"You'll have to kill Bearclaw and Tommy, too," Naomi quavered. She rolled Jimbo over and spit into his face.

"Perhaps," Little Hawk allowed. "But first I'm going to get you away from here."

"They'll follow."

"So," he said.

"I can't go," she said. "Not until both of them are dead."

"Get up," he said.

"No."

He bent and scooped her into his arms. He was

amazed by her frailty—she weighed no more than a child. She began to struggle, but he held her tightly as he went out into the moonlight and trotted away from the house. She was weeping when he slowed to a walk and put her feet on the ground.

"I'm going to take you to my home," he said. "Then I'll come back."

"Maybe you're right. They might have killed you."

He left a confused trail. When the full moon was creeping down the western sky he led her along the bed of a shallow stream until the icy water had numbed his feet. Then he made a careful emergence.

"We'll sleep awhile now," he said, covering her with the blanket. "Until dawn."

"I'm so cold." Her teeth chattered.

He got under the blanket with her and cupped his body to hers from behind, his arm around her for warmth. She began to sob.

"It's over," he soothed.

"It can never be over," she moaned. "Not after what they did to me."

He didn't really want to hear the details, but she seemed to have a need to tell him everything. He cringed and tensed as she described beatings and cruelties and perversions beyond a normal man's imagination. Once, as she moved, he accidentally touched one of her nipples, warm, large, soft. Repulsed, he jerked his hand away. All three of the Morgans had used her whenever it suited them, and in his mind she was irrevocably soiled.

When at last she fell silent and her even breathing indicated that she was asleep, he stayed beside her, for the night was cold and they were alone in the wilderness. She felt so fragile and thin in his arms. He prayed to the manitous that Bearclaw and Tommy Morgan *would* follow them. He hated himself for not having killed them while he had the opportunity.

Naomi would need clothing, he knew. This was borne out with the next day's trek. Even with the exertion and Little Hawk's blanket wrapped around her, she shivered. He decided to go to Knoxville, and at the end of the second day's march they were inside Roy Johnson's cabin. Little Hawk was grateful to find that some of his grandmother Nora's old clothes were still there. He dragged out a washtub for bathing, fetched icy water from the well, and built a fire in the iron cookstove on which to heat the water.

Little Hawk slept in the loft and left the lower floor to Naomi. As he tried to sleep, he could not help but think that downstairs, in the bed where the young woman slept, his grandfather had known two wives, the dead Nora and Little Hawk's other grandmother, Toshabe. All lovemaking that had taken place in that feather bed had been based in mutual desire and consent. He shuddered, thinking of Naomi's far different experiences.

Sleep continued to evade him, replaced by the persistent description of what the young woman had endured. Once during the night he heard her moan and then cry out. "Naomi?" he called.

"It's nothing," she said, her voice thick with sleep. "Only a dream."

At last he slept. When he awoke at sunrise he smelled biscuits cooking. Naomi was in the kitchen. Her silken, taffy hair was clean and worn in a single neat braid that hung over one shoulder. Her faded dress smelled slightly of cedar chips; but it was clean, and it was obvious that she wore underthings.

"I'm afraid there was no milk," she apologized. "So they're water biscuits. And the fatback I rendered down was pretty high."

"That's all right," he said. "They smell wonderful." For just a moment, seeing her there clean, neat, and smiling in his grandfather's house, he had forgotten what she had become.

Chapter Three

Thomas Jefferson glanced up in irritation when his secretary opened the door to his office and cleared his throat for attention.

"Sorry, Mr. President," the young man said.

At that moment Jefferson was thinking nostalgically of his former secretary, Meriwether Clark. Meriwether would not have interrupted him after being ordered specifically not to do so. With some difficulty he conquered his momentary chagrin and nodded to give the secretary permission to speak.

"Sir, you could never guess who is in the reception hall asking to see you."

"Nor would I try," Jefferson murmured.

"It's Aaron Burr himself."

"I'll be damned," Jefferson said. He put aside a report from James Monroe, who was in London, and rose. "Did he give you a reason for wanting to see me?"

"He did not, sir."

Jefferson rubbed his chin and pondered. His former vice president, the elegant Mr. Burr, had come upon hard times. One could almost believe that the Fates had deserted Burr at the moment his pistol discharged on the Weehawken heights, for when Alexander Hamilton fell before Burr's dueling piece, his fortunes followed. He had lost his bid for election as governor of New York, and the weakened Federalist party had deserted him.

Burr had left Washington after the inaugural ceremony that began Jefferson's second term in the White House. The former vice president had done a lot of traveling. He had taken several trips to various western points and, once, had gone all the way south to New Orleans. And wherever Burr went, rumors sprang up and eventually found their way back to Washington.

"Please show Mr. Burr in," Jefferson said.

The dapper New Yorker was smiling as he entered the office. The man, Jefferson had to admit, looked good. He was dressed somberly in black. His broad forehead, formed by a receding hairline, was browned by the sun. His hair had been recently trimmed. From his temples a thin sideburn connected with whiskers that were cut close to his face. On the other hand, Jefferson had always felt that Burr's sharp nose and chin made him look rapacious.

He stood and came around his desk to meet his visitor and take Burr's hand. "Will you sit, sir?" Jefferson asked.

Burr sat, crossing one leg over the other. Jefferson chose a chair opposite him and tented his fingers under his chin in speculation and expectation.

"As you know, Mr. President," Burr began, "I have long been in the service of my country."

Jefferson nodded coldly.

"It has been said," Burr continued, "that my service with the Continental Army was creditable but not distinguished. I will accept that analysis, with one qualification. I did my best, within the limits of my health and strength." He smiled. "Some have faulted me for being with General Benedict Arnold against Quebec; but I submit, sir, that I was a mere captain and that I was following orders. Moreover, at that time and as far as anyone knew, General Arnold was a loyal soldier of the new nation."

Jefferson still had his fingers tented under his chin. As he watched Burr closely, he wondered where the man was leading with this telling of the story of his life.

"I have always felt that it was my having been with Arnold that caused General Washington to discriminate against me. But that no longer matters, does it?"

Jefferson shrugged.

"I entered public life as a member of the New York legislature in 1784 and later became attorney general. In 1791 I defeated General Philip Schuyler for a seat in the Senate of the United States." He spread his hands and smiled wryly. "That General Schuyler happened to be the father-in-law of the late Alexander Hamilton may have had some bearing on subsequent events."

Burr paused to use a gleaming white handkerchief to mop his face and forehead, then continued. "I came to New York State as a stranger and found it to be under the control of the Livingstons and the Clintons. I will admit that there was a certain amount of self-interest involved when I became a part of their power structure, but whatever my motive, good came of my actions, for I was given the opportunity to accept the vice presidency and to promote the fame and advancement of a great man—yourself."

Jefferson nodded, unmoved by the obvious flattery.

"I had always had a desire to work with you, Mr. President. Your company and your conversation always fascinated me."

"You flatter me," Jefferson said.

"I am merely trying to establish the truth that my attachment to you was and is strong and sincere."

"Thank you."

"Of course, attachments must be reciprocal, or they cease to exist. I retired without a fight at the end of my first term in order to prevent a schism in the party."

Jefferson controlled his desire to tell his guest that he "retired" because he, Jefferson, would not have Burr on the ticket with him again.

"My enemies used your name, sir, to ruin me. They spread the calumnies that led to my defeat in the New York election. They claimed that you had found me unworthy."

Jefferson shifted his weight in the chair.

"If you would say publicly, Mr. President, that you always found Aaron Burr to be willing to work for the common cause—"

"I do not give political endorsements," Jefferson interrupted.

Burr's face darkened.

"Further," Jefferson said, "if you have any hope of a position in my administration, I must disavow you immediately."

Burr's voice was shaking when he spoke. "You speak harshly to a man who can do you much good or much harm."

"I speak," Jefferson said icily, "to a man who has lost the confidence of the public, as indicated by your defeat in New York. As for any potential harm, I fear no injury that any man could do me." He stood. "And now, Mr. Burr, I bid you good day. I think, sir, that you and I are done with each other."

It took mere hours for word to spread from the president's secretary to two junior congressmen, then beyond, that Jefferson had held a long, private conference with Aaron Burr. In truth, Jefferson was not done with Aaron Burr at all.

* * *

Oddly, Burr left the presidential house with a little smile on his face. Jefferson's cold rejection had not been a surprise, nor had it angered Burr. The primary purpose of the visit had been accomplished. Actually, there had never been much chance of a presidential appointment. Had Jefferson relented in his old antagonism for Burr and offered, say, the position of minister to one of the more important European nations, or Russia, Burr might or might not have accepted it.

Quite soon he made it evident why he had gone to Washington to ask for an audience with his holiness, the president. At home, he went into his library and pulled a piece of paper and quill pen from his desk drawer.

"Dear General Jackson," he wrote. "I have recently talked with the president. . . ."

He spent two days over his letters, for he had an impressive list of correspondents. Shortly after he had been dumped as vice president he had taken a grand tour down the Ohio River, stopping off to chat with men of importance. During that excursion and now, in the letters, he discussed a particular project that he had in mind. He was very careful in choosing his words and never spelled out his plans completely. He made it clear, however, that they involved an expedition in force against the Spaniards. Now, after Burr's visit to Jefferson in Washington, the time had come to make his final plans.

While the attention of Jefferson and the Congress was directed largely toward foreign affairs—the war in North Africa, the piracy on the high seas of England and France, the rancor of old Spain—not much had changed in the vast western territories of the United States. There the pioneers had been stonewalled by the Spanish presence. For decades the commerce of the West had been controlled by the Spanish in New Orleans and along the Mississippi. For decades the frontier's leaders had begged Washington to do something to ease the intolerable situation, even if war was necessary. They got no satisfaction from Washington, and many of them were ready to go to war on their own against Spain. That situation had changed, of course, with the purchase of Louisiana, but the old fears and hatred of Spain still existed in the hearts of the frontiersmen.

Burr's grand tour had met with interest from an impressive list of western leaders, including senators John Brown and John Adair of Kentucky, senators John Smith of Ohio and Jonathan Dayton of New Jersey, a few congressmen, General Andrew Jackson of Tennessee, Governor William Henry Harrison of the Indiana Territory, and General James Wilkinson, governor of Louisiana. Burr's smooth tongue and personal magnetism had fascinated these politicians and had made a convert of Harman Blennerhassett, a man who was most important to Burr's plans.

Near Marietta, on an island in the Ohio River, Burr met Blennerhassett and his youthful wife, Margaret. An Irishman of great wealth and questionable culture, Blennerhassett had come to America with his wife to seek solitude. He wanted to build an estate, perform chemical experiments, and play his violin. Burr turned his charm on the impressionable young wife and, through her, bemused Blennerhassett as well. It would be Blennerhassett who financed Burr's army.

Once again Burr traveled to the west. When he arrived by boat at Blennerhassett's island, Margaret, in traditional Irish costume, met him at the dock and could scarcely contain her excitement until they were alone in her bedroom.

"I think, my dear," Burr said as Margaret loosed her black hair and began to unlace her bodice, "that I should see your husband."

"He's busy," she told him. "He's involved in one of his infernal experiments and would not be disturbed by the Second Coming."

She bared her youthful breasts and was soon Venus emerging from a sea of feminine linen. Burr sighed. He was about fifty years old, virile, and not at all unmoved by Margaret's beauty. So, once again a common purpose was joined.

Later, when Blennerhassett had finished his experiment and emerged smelling of vile, chemical things from his laboratory, he embraced Burr and willingly handed over cash to advance the cause, which, for Burr, was to travel farther down the Ohio and the Mississippi.

Burr was greeted warmly by his principal ally, James Wilkinson, at Natchitoches on the Sabine River, the frontier with Spain's Mexican possessions. The two men were old friends; their relationship went back to the days of the Revolution. Wilkinson quickly secluded himself with Burr.

"The time has come, James," Burr said.

Wilkinson nodded. Although it had been he who first suggested to Burr the glorious opportunity in the Southwest, he, like many others, had fallen under the spell of Burr's personality. Now Wilkinson was nothing more than a partner in Burr's machinations.

"In spite of what you might hear," Burr began, "the United States and Spain are on the verge of war. The people of Mexico have risen up against their masters. In the western territories the discontent with Washington is deep-seated. New Orleans is not taking kindly to having been ceded to the United States. Every American pioneer west of the mountains is eager to join us."

"What have you heard from the British?" Wilkinson asked.

Burr frowned. "As you know," he said, "I offered Merry the prospect of having the western states separated from the United States."

"Yes, yes," Wilkinson said. The British minister, Anthony Merry, had been enthusiastic about a military expedition against Spanish America. Merry hated Jefferson *and* the United States and was eager to see both president and country humiliated or diminished in size and importance. "But have you received money from the Bank of England?"

"Not as yet," Burr admitted. He raised his hand, asking for patience. "I expect to hear from them soon. We must remember that England has been preoccupied with Napoleon's threat of invasion. In the meantime, we have Blennerhassett."

"Can he provide weapons for an army?"

"My dear general," Burr said with a disarming smile, "we already have a well-equipped army. All of the American troops along the border are under your command."

Even though Wilkinson was a man who had vast experience in intrigue, there were times when he suffered doubts. While he was plotting invasion of Spanish territories, he was known to the Spanish government as Agent 13, a spy against his own country. He had been on the Spanish payroll for years. Still, Burr's optimism was contagious. Wilkinson settled back and listened to the enthralling visions of the man from New York. How could things go wrong when they had people like Jackson and Harrison on their side?

For an hour Burr expounded on his plans and his dreams. His face burned with his intensity. Suddenly he fell silent, wilting visibly. "I am quite tired," he said.

Wilkinson showed him to a room and assigned a Spanish maid to tend to his needs. He, meanwhile, hurried to his own room. The woman who ruled his passions awaited. She was dressed in black Spanish lace. She held out her arms to him, and he went to her.

"Burr is well?" asked Melisande, the Witch of the Pyrenean Woods.

"He is well, my dear."

"And the financing from England?"

"He has heard nothing yet."

She stroked his hair. Had another person been

standing behind Wilkinson to look into her face, Melisande would have seemed parched and wrinkled, with gleaming, eerie eyes. And when she spoke, her teeth would have gleamed with a blackness not of decay but a shining blackness, a sheen, like darkest pearls. To Wilkinson, however, when he looked into her eyes and lifted his face to place his lips on hers, she appeared young and vibrant, smooth skinned, and ultimately sensuous.

"My love," she said, "we must proceed with great caution."

"There is nothing to worry about," Wilkinson assured her. "Burr has powerful friends."

"Any man can mouth names," Melisande warned. "Before we march, my love, be sure that at our side are more than mere names mentioned in passing."

Water biscuits and beans . . . Little Hawk had made meals on less. Across his grandfather's table from him, Naomi Burns watched him eat. Her face was expressionless, but warmth glowed in her hazel eyes. In repose her full lips looked so soft that to avoid tasting them in his imagination he had to turn his eyes away.

"I have some money," he said. "I'll go to the store and buy provisions for you."

"For *me? . . .*"

"Naomi, I'm in the marines. My leave has expired. I have to go back on duty."

Her voice was strained. "You're going to *leave* me here?"

"It's my grandfather's cabin," he said. "You're welcome to use it for as long as you like. Until—"

"Until Bearclaw or Tommy comes for me," she said bitterly. She stood up. Her thigh hit the table, and dishes rattled. She ran to stand before a window, arms clasped over her breasts, shoulders trembling.

Little Hawk felt a rush of irrational anger. What more did she expect from him? He had rescued her from the Morgans, for heaven's sake! He could not help but believe that if she really wanted to, she could have left the Morgans behind long since. There must have been a way! The innocent girl who had given Little Hawk his first kiss was no more. In her place was a young woman who, in spite of her freshly washed and braided hair and her clean clothing, seemed soiled. He was angry with her, for she had ruined something for him—something that had been dear to him for a long time.

He thought at first that she was weeping. He rose from the table and approached her. She glanced at him. There were no tears. Her lips were set in an expression of terror. Her arms and shoulders were trembling uncontrollably.

"I'll tell the authorities to keep an eye on you," Little Hawk said. "Is there anyplace you can go? Do you have relatives back east?"

"N-no." She shuddered.

"You're being silly," he said, all out of patience. "They won't come into a civilized town and kill you."

"You don't know them. Th-th-they'll come. They might not kill me, but if they take me back, I'll kill myself, I swear it."

He could not find tenderness for her. He could not bring himself to care for a creature who had allowed all three of the Morgan animals, including the idiot, Tommy, to use her. On his tongue were the words *Then why didn't you?* He did not say them. He wondered how many more men, traveling past the Burns house, had been offered a companion in the straw for two dollars—or less.

"What do you expect me to do?" he asked angrily.

"I don't know."

Her upper lip pulled back. She moaned. It was a low sound of desperation and hopelessness. She turned away, and now her entire body shook with her sobbing. He put his arms around her from the rear and said awkwardly, "All right. All right."

*   *   *

They left Knoxville at midmorning. Soon the sounds and sights of the white man's culture were behind them and the well-traveled track, so familiar to Little Hawk, drove southward through virgin forest. The young man had brought extra blankets from Roy's cabin, for the weather had turned more chill, and judging from the troubled sky to the northwest, worse was coming.

Slight as Naomi was, nothing more than skin and bones, Little Hawk thought, she kept up the pace. Late in the day, with dusk coming quickly due to the dark, turgid roiling of lowering clouds, Little Hawk picked his campsite carefully. The smell of snow was strong in the frigid air. He cut pine boughs and laced them over the dead branches of a fallen forest giant, to form a lean-to with the horizontal bole of the tree to the back. More pine boughs covered the frozen ground, and the blankets were laid atop. The roof was just high enough to allow Naomi and him to sit inside. A fire snapped and crackled under the outer edge of the shelter. As the first fat flakes of snow swirled down on confused winds, smoke eddied into the shelter and caused Naomi to cough.

"It'll be a long night," Little Hawk said, offering her strips of jerky that he'd taken from Roy's kitchen.

A stray wisp of wind blew flakes of snow into the fire, where they sizzled and disappeared. The ground outside began to turn white. At last the winds passed. The snow thickened until it was a white curtain beyond the glow of the fire, a barrier against the world. The shelter became the center of the universe for Naomi and Little Hawk as they chewed on the tough, dried meat. Naomi scooped up a handful of snow and ate it. Little Hawk shook snow from two pieces of the wood he had gathered and added them to the fire.

"You'd better get some sleep," he suggested.

"All right." She curled up within the blankets and tucked them around her ears.

"Cold?"

"Not terribly."

"There won't be enough wood to keep the fire going all night."

"I'm fine," she said.

He lifted the top blankets and lay beside her. The fire burned down, and the snow continued to pile up in front of the entrance. He sat up and massed the dry, soft snow to make a wall that reached to the top of the shelter. The embers of the fire lit the interior of their sanctuary with a red glow. He lay back down and was thoroughly chilled after having his hands in the snow.

"You're shivering," Naomi said. She put her arm across his chest and pulled herself to press against his side.

"It will warm up soon," he said. "At least for as long as the fire lasts."

He could feel the softness of her breasts and the hardness of her thighs. He closed his eyes, and sleep came. In his dream she was there—young, virginal, fresh. She was with him in his dream as his hand went down to touch the womanly flesh of her bare leg.

He awoke to find himself aroused. She had curled up beside him, and in her sleep she had thrown one leg across his loins so that her inner thigh was pressed against his manhood. She was breathing deeply and evenly. The fire was nothing more than embers, but the interior of the shelter was warm and cozy. The snow had filled all of its chinks and openings. He was still half asleep, and his touch roused her from sleep. Her skirt was bunched high on her thigh. She was painfully thin, but warm and soft. When his hand ventured higher, higher, an incredible heat touched his fingers. The tip of his index finger invaded moistness and then he froze, coming wide awake. He had seen the imbecile Tommy Morgan thrust his hand into that same heated softness.

He jerked his hand away.

"You didn't have to stop," she whispered, her voice vibrating with sadness.

She's been awake all the time, he thought angrily.

She pressed her thigh against me deliberately. He said, "I'm sorry. I was dreaming."

"It's all right. Whatever you want."

For a few moments he wavered, his hand aching to touch that warmed softness again. He turned her over somewhat roughly, pulled down her dress, and cupped himself to her back because they would have to share body warmth for the remainder of the night.

"I can't blame you for not wanting me," she whispered.

"Go to sleep," he said gruffly.

She was stiff in his arms.

He closed his eyes and, hating himself, tried to will sleep.

"In the morning would you please take me back to Knoxville?" she asked.

"Why?" he asked in exasperation.

"Never mind," she said, then lay quietly until her savior had dropped off to sleep. . . .

It took hours, but Naomi's desire to go back to Knoxville and die at the hands of Bearclaw or Tommy did pass. She knew that it had been a mistake to pretend to be asleep, to let Little Hawk place his hand on her womanhood, and then to offer herself to him. She would never make that mistake again.

In that moment she accepted herself and her condition. Only she could ever know the full extent of her degradation, the terror of living at the whims of the three Morgan men. Naomi accepted also that people she would meet would question why she was still alive, why she had not killed herself in preference to living in shame and with humiliation. But anyone who would even ask such a question surely had never faced the choice of an existence that was less than honorable, less than comfortable, less than desirable . . . or having no life at all.

Little Hawk's rejection of her, his obvious distaste for her, was a punishment that ranked with her

first terror-filled days as a captive of Bearclaw Morgan
and his two sons. The shame she felt when Little
Hawk jerked his hand away in disgust was every bit
as painful to her as the shame she suffered under the
perversions of Tommy Morgan. Now Little Hawk
would never know that he had given her her first kiss
and had filled her life with dreams and longings. Her
love for him had remained with her to the very day
that she walked out onto the porch to see him standing
in the yard. Her hope for a normal life died in the
red glow of embers, in a shelter beside a deadfall in
the forest. With that absolute pain, with that absolute
deprivation, Naomi felt something akin to relief, for
she knew that the future could not hold anything
worse than what life had shown her already. Not even
death itself could lance her heart as profoundly as the
demise of her dreams had done. But still there was
life, and whatever came, she would continue to cling
to it.

The snow that had overtaken Naomi and Little
Hawk on the trail drifted with the wind to depths of
four feet and more on the grounds of Huntington Castle. Smoke issued from four of the house's eight chim-
neys. Lounging in front of the fire from which one
column of smoke originated was Renno, on a rug that
had been woven by dark-skinned women in a land far
away in Asia Minor. He lay on his stomach, chin resting on his hands. He was dressed comfortably in loose-
legged pantaloons, woolen stockings, carpet slippers,
and a baggy, coarsely woven sweater of Scottish wool.
Beth sat beside him, in a rocking chair that had
made the long voyage across the Atlantic in one of
her own ships and the overland trek from Wilmington,
North Carolina, by ox cart. She, too, was dressed
warmly, although the room was cozy. The feeling of
chill was engendered by a glance out the large-paned
window to see the trees burdened by snow. The world
was brilliant and brittle under the winter sun. The

unbroken field of whiteness seemed to extend end-
lessly, making the big house feel snug and giving Beth
a sense of isolation.

It was with regret that she saw two figures dark
against the purity of the snow, for they spoiled the
empty unity of the scene, and their labored steps left
dark, ugly holes in the pristine whiteness. Bundled as
they were in blankets and skins, she could tell only
that they were male and female as they entered the
long, pecan-tree-lined lane leading to the front garden
of the house.

"Company, my dear," she said.

"*Unnnn*," Renno groaned in protest. His lids
were heavy. A pleasant lethargy engulfed him. "Tell
them we're not at home."

"It's Little Hawk!" Beth said as the couple came
nearer. "With a girl."

When a loved one is far away, one's thoughts turn
to her without regard for logic. The face of his daughter, Renna, leaped into Renno's mind, and although
his reason told him that Renna was in France, he came
to his feet and walked swiftly to the window. He was
not even disappointed when he saw that the thin,
slight girl walking beside his tall son could not possibly
be his daughter, for there had been no real reason for
him to think that it might be.

Renno opened the front door while Little Hawk
and the girl were still tramping through the deep snow
in the lane. The white Indian walked gingerly on the
slick, icy boards. He had cleared the snow from the
porch three times, but it was impossible to remove
the coating of ice that had accumulated. The cold air,
clean and bracing, touched his face. He took a deep
breath.

"*Kou-ee*," Little Hawk called out, lifting one
hand.

"*Ha-oh*," Renno said, waving back to his son.

Beth, bundled into her favorite extreme-weather
garment, a bearskin cape, joined Renno on the porch.

"*Nyah-weh ska-noh*," Renno said as Little Hawk

and the girl reached the steps and began to mount them carefully.

"*Do-ges,*" Little Hawk said. "*Ska-noh nai?*"

Father and son clasped arms. Beth, seeing that Little Hawk's companion was a white woman, stepped forward and said, "How do you do? I'm Beth Huntington. You look as if you're half-frozen."

"Maybe more than half," Naomi admitted through numbed lips.

"Come inside," Beth invited. "We'll get you some dry, warm clothing and put some hot tea into you."

"Thank you," Naomi said, smiling as Beth opened the front door.

"Father, Mother," Little Hawk said, "this is Naomi Burns." His father's look demanded explanation. "She's—an old friend."

"Are you two going to stand here in the cold?" Beth demanded, holding the door ajar.

"No longer than necessary," Little Hawk said.

Beth and the girl disappeared upstairs.

Renno led Little Hawk into the cozy room where he had been lounging, punched up the fire, added a piece of wood, dipped a red-hot poker into a mug of apple cider, and let the steam rise while he sprinkled in spices.

Little Hawk sipped the hot drink gratefully. "It's belly deep to a boar bear out in the woods," he said.

"You have come far?"

"Beyond Knoxville," Little Hawk said.

"So." He would not ask, although his curiosity was strong.

"I know her from a long time ago," Little Hawk explained. "When I was coming home from Philadelphia, I slept one night in her father's barn."

"So." Renno did not point out that his son had never mentioned such an event, especially not one that concerned an attractive golden-blond girl.

"She was, uh, she was in trouble," Little Hawk said. "I thought maybe you and Mother—"

"Yes?" Renno asked, when Little Hawk hesitated for long seconds.

"Well, I thought maybe you could let her stay here for a while, until she, well, gets on her feet—"

"Of course," Renno said. When the time was right, his son would explain. In the meantime, he would not make Little Hawk uncomfortable with questions.

Upstairs, Beth supplied Naomi with dry hose, warm underthings, and a woolen gown that had been Renna's. Beth's own clothing would have been far too large. When Beth saw how white and damp-looking Naomi's feet were, she said, "Sit down in that chair and put your feet on the stool."

"I'll be all right," Naomi said. "The hose will warm them."

"Child," Beth said, smiling, "you are too young to argue with me." She forced Naomi down into the chair and, taking a towel in hand, began vigorously to massage Naomi's feet. "Can you feel this?" she asked.

"Very much so," Naomi said, wincing.

"Good. They're not frozen, then."

"Please, I'm all right now."

"Yes, I'm sure you are. Let's get you out of those wet clothes."

Naomi made no protest as Beth helped her remove Nora Johnson's dress. "After you're dressed, come downstairs to the room on the left," Beth told her. Then, out of deference to her guest's modesty, Beth left Naomi alone in the room so she could change into the dry, clean underthings.

As Beth walked into the downstairs study, Little Hawk was describing the route of his hunt to Renno, who nodded at the mention of landmarks. Beth listened patiently. Because she was curious about Naomi, Beth's interest soared when Little Hawk said, "So since I was so close to the Tennessee border and after that it was only one or two days to the Burns farm—"

"Only one or two days?" Beth asked.

"Well, I couldn't remember exactly," Little Hawk said, "but Frank Burns had been very hospitable when he let me stay in his barn on the way home from Philadelphia."

"Ah," Beth said. "Let me see . . . the girl would have been what, about twelve? Thirteen?"

"She was quite young, then," Little Hawk admitted, blushing.

"She is wasted away," Beth said. "She has no more flesh on her than a sparrow."

"I'm not sure you want to hear about this, Mother," Little Hawk warned.

"If it gets too awful, I'll faint like a proper English lady," Beth said with rich sarcasm.

"I'm sorry. I didn't mean—"

"Oh, go on," Beth urged.

Then, as Little Hawk talked, she told herself, *No, I didn't want to hear this.* Hearing the story as it related to someone she did not know and had never seen would have been terrible enough. Hearing it with the knowledge that the atrocities described by Little Hawk had been endured by the girl upstairs, the girl with the wide, smiling mouth, the girl with two freckles on the tip of her nose, made it almost unbearable.

Beth could sense Little Hawk's anger, his resentment, and his strong passions. As a result, she could guess at the rest of the story. For years she had looked forward to the day when her stepson would bring home the girl of his choice. Seeing them walk up the porch steps together, the tall young man and the thin girl, she had imagined pleasant things: trousseaus and wedding cakes and the house full of company. She was weeping when she got up from the chair and waited out in the hallway.

Little Hawk watched Beth leave, then looked unhappily at his father. "And I left out some of the details. I saw Tommy Morgan run his hand up Naomi's dress. I know for certain that Naomi had been used for the perversions of all three men, but she might have been sold to travelers, too." He paused. "There is a chance that Bearclaw and Tommy might follow us here."

"So," Renno said, his blue eyes narrowed menacingly, his hand on the haft of his Spanish stiletto, the weapon that never left his belt. "I hope that they do."

Beth and Naomi entered the room, the younger woman walking with shy deference. Renno sprang to his feet and heated a dram of cider for her.

"Sit here by me," Beth invited.

"If you don't mind," Naomi said, "I'll stand by the fire for a few minutes. The cold seems to have penetrated right through me."

"Of course, dear," Beth said.

"My father and my mother have invited you to stay here with them," Little Hawk told her.

"Thank you." Naomi looked at the floor. "If you will have me just until the weather gets a bit warmer—"

"We will put no time limit on it, my dear," Beth said.

"I can help around the house," Naomi offered. "I'm not afraid of work. I'm not a fancy cook, but I can make bread. And if I have the makings, I can do a real good chocolate cake—"

"We will take you up on that last offer soon," Renno said. "Chocolate cake is one of my favorites."

"I fear that I might bring you trouble," Naomi said with a sudden change of mood. She glanced nervously toward the door.

"Little Hawk told us about the man who killed your father," Renno said. "You have no need to concern yourself about him as long as you are in this house."

Naomi looked at Little Hawk, her face burning. It was obvious that she was wondering how much more he had told his parents. Wishing to ease her discomfort, Little Hawk said, "No one blames you for anything."

"Don't they?" she asked pointedly, her eyes boring directly into his.

The young man looked ill at ease, and Beth did not miss the significance. "It seems to me that I heard someone mention food," she said brightly. "Naomi, would you like to help me in the kitchen?"

"Yes," she said. "I'd be glad to."

Little Hawk announced his decision at the dinner table. "Since I am a marine officer on active duty, I think it's time I reported to my superiors."

"Can't you wait for better weather?" Beth asked.

"There could well be impassable drifts in the passes of the mountains," Renno pointed out.

"Please don't leave until the snow melts," Beth urged.

"It will be gone soon," Little Hawk said.

"True," Renno allowed. "In this land the snows do not stay as did the snows of the northern lakes."

In fact, within two days nothing was left of the storm but darkened, coarse-grained blobs of snow in the deepest shadows of the forest. The temperatures had warmed to a false balminess. The skies were clean, blue, windless.

Little Hawk made his farewells to his father in privacy.

"When your duty as an officer of the United States is finished," Renno said, "there will remain your duty to your people."

"My people will not need me as long as they have my father, the great sachem."

"That will not be forever."

Little Hawk laughed, embraced Renno, and pounded him affectionately on the back. "You're a young man, Father. And you are indestructible."

"I pray that you will be the same," Renno said, ushering Little Hawk into the hallway. "May the manitous watch over you wherever you travel."

Beth wept a little bit as she gave Little Hawk a

hug, then a kiss on each cheek. Naomi stood in the background, small and thin in Renna's dress, her hair gleaming with brushing and piled attractively atop her head in a style arranged by Beth. She was in partial shadow, and when Little Hawk turned to look at her, his heart leaped, for he saw an image of his dead mother—the manitou who had sent him to the Frank Burns house. Then the moment was past.

"God go with you," Naomi said.

"And you."

"I will be gone when you next return," she said. He nodded.

"I'm grateful to you and to your parents."

"Good-bye," he said as he turned away.

It would all be for the best, he thought, taking long strides down the lane, that she be gone from his father's house as quickly as possible.

Chapter Four

It took Beth fewer than two days after Little Hawk's departure to get the details of her adopted son's first meeting with Naomi Burns. Naomi responded to Beth's compassion and gentleness, and Beth's heart went out to the girl as she spoke of the time when Little Hawk, a young boy traveling alone, spent the night at the Burns farm. A wide smile lighted Naomi's face and made her look as if she'd never had a care.

"I thought he was so brave," Naomi said, "coming all that distance alone." She blushed, making the two freckles on the tip of her nose stand out. "And so handsome."

Later, alone with Renno, Beth said, "She was just a girl when she fell in love with our handsome son. Isn't it odd that he never mentioned her?"

Renno had not been blind to his son's emotional distress, and he was certain that Naomi's presence had, in fact, prompted Little Hawk to leave for Washington in midwinter. Already Renno was missing his son. Nothing else would have sent the young man away before the traditional Seneca midwinter celebration of the time of the new beginning.

"In his own time," the sachem said, "he will reveal the reason why he returned to the Burns farm after so many years."

"She's a lovely girl," Beth mused. "One would think that the horrible things done to her would have coarsened her, but she's so sweet, so eager to please."

Renno nodded, keeping his thoughts to himself. Little Hawk had warned that two surviving Morgan men might follow Naomi to Knoxville, then on to Huntington Castle. He had no respect for men who would abuse a woman. Again he hoped that Bearclaw Morgan and his son would come.

Beth's enjoyment of Naomi's company continued to grow. The two women had much in common. For example, Beth liked sewing. When she discovered that her houseguest shared that interest, they spent pleasant days making up new dresses for Naomi. Other members of the family extended friendship to the girl. Ah-wa-o came to visit and reported with a knowing smile that the women of the villages were beginning to see abominable detached heads floating in the shadows of the woodlands.

Naomi's eyes were wide with interest. Beth explained that the members of the False Face Society were just trying out their carved masks. Prior to the formal beginning of the ceremonies, Ah-wa-o said, the False Face Society would initiate two new members. Ta-na and Gao, sons of the tribe's sachem and its shaman, were following in the footsteps of Little Hawk, who had thoroughly enjoyed donning the grotesque mask of the society. Because Naomi looked befuddled, the three women went upstairs to Little Hawk's room to see the false faces that had been worn by the sachem's son. The mask that had been carved for Little Hawk by Se-quo-i was especially bizarre with its wide, staring eyes and tresses of horse hair.

"With such horrors," Beth said, "the men and boys frighten away evil spirits."

Naomi laughed. "They would certainly frighten me." She smiled at Beth. "You know so much about Seneca customs."

"Do such things interest you?"

"Oh, yes."

Beth nodded. "So." She laughed at herself for sounding so much like Renno. "Then it is time to put aside our sewing."

Beth had been making extensive notes on the traditions of the Seneca and, to a lesser extent, the Cherokee. Her ultimate goal was to compile her notes, elaborate upon them, then write a book about her husband's people. In her growing library Beth had volumes about the Indian, but they were written mostly by traveling Europeans who, in their haste, often misinterpreted what they saw and heard. She had read to Renno an account of a traveler who visited an Oneida village. There he was greeted with friendly touches on the shoulders and the word *se-go-li*. Everywhere he went in the village he heard the same thing, "Se-go-li, we are honored by your visit. Se-go-li, you have come far to see us." In his book the traveler wrote that he had·been so well liked by the Oneida that they immediately gave him a name and that wherever he went he was recognized and greeted by that name. What he did not know was that *se-go-li* was the Oneida word of greeting, an Iroquois equivalent of *howdy*.

"I suppose," Renno had said dryly, "that those who know the Indian best are too busy killing him and stealing his land to write books about him."

Beth was pleased now to learn that in addition to liking to sew, her guest shared another common interest. She helped Naomi dress in Seneca costume, again from the wardrobe left behind by Renna, and together they joined the Seneca women in the council longhouse for a ceremony that was an informal beginning of the celebration of the new beginning.

As the senior matron of the tribe, Renno's mother presided at the rite of the Naming of the Babies. In a clear, loud, solemn voice Toshabe called out the names of all of the babies who had been born since the green corn festival, four months before. Even though Toshabe included the names of several babies born to Cherokee women who had, over the years, come to take part in the Seneca festival, the number of names was still quite small. It did not take long for Toshabe to finish.

"Now it begins," Beth said, leading Naomi out of the longhouse and onto the village commons. All of the Seneca were gathered there. Fires lent warmth and cheer. Children ran among the adults, laughing and, in general, being very noisy. To the happy sounds of the young was added the excited barking of at least two dozen dogs who followed their young masters and occasionally banged into the legs of an adult.

Then a silence fell over the assembly. Even the youngsters were still, for out of the council longhouse stepped two Pine-Tree senior warriors dressed in baggy buffalo robes adorned with corn husks. They wore huge constructions of corn husks over their heads and were, quite understandably, called Big Heads. When one of them spoke, Naomi recognized the voice of the shaman, El-i-chi. She could not understand the Seneca words.

Beth said, "It's difficult to give an exact translation. He's chanting an ancient Seneca prayer to the Master of Life and the good manitous."

El-i-chi lifted both hands, and his voice rose.

" 'Let us begin,' " Beth translated, " 'with the prayer that the Master of Life once again will grant us not only the renewal of the world but of our dreams.' "

A group of young men began to sing in eerie falsetto voices. They danced, but their stomping moccasined feet made only small sounds on the hard, packed earth of the commons.

"Spring is still weeks and weeks away," Naomi said.

"We wouldn't want it *not* to come, though, would we?" Beth asked, smiling.

"Do they really believe that it wouldn't come if they didn't go through the ceremonies?" Naomi asked.

Beth continued to smile. "All I can tell you, dear, is that from the beginning of time the Seneca have praised the Master of Life at the time of the new beginning, and so far, spring has always come."

Naomi laughed. "I suppose it's best not to take any chances."

To the delight of all, a new winter storm deposited twelve inches of snow that night, allowing the young men to observe the time of the new beginning with the snow-snake game. A pine tree was cut down and trimmed. The bark was then removed from the log, and ropes were attached. The log was hauled through the snow by several strong men to make a furrow. By pulling the log back and forth carefully, the sides and bottom of the narrow trench were compacted into a smooth, slick surface. Meanwhile, a nine foot long, straight stick had been tipped with lead to make a conical head. The long stick, the snow snake, was flexible. When it was cast down the furrow, it undulated like a snake and sped along the smooth, hard track with the speed of an arrow. To the pride of his mother, Rusog Ho-ya, son of Rusog and Ena, sent the snow snake speeding to the greatest distance. He was named the winner.

Inside the council longhouse El-i-chi taught the new False Face Society members secrets of the ancient art of healing. He noted wryly that two of the members, whose masks were painted with glaring white and reds, were not concentrating overly hard. As quickly as possible he released all the initiates, including the inattentive Gao and Ta-na, to the outdoors.

During the festival, the food was good and plentiful. Roy Johnson and Toshabe's longhouse became the unofficial gathering place for the sachem's family, his friends, and Cherokee leaders who came from outlying villages. The war chiefs and elders came to renew alliances with Rusog and the white-skinned sachem of the Seneca and to witness such wild events as the dream renewal dances, during which the False Faces led dozens of yelping, happy Seneca and Cherokee youngsters through the village. The children demanded that they be given presents—or else. Presents, of course, were duly offered.

One event lessened Beth's enjoyment of the celebration. No one had mentioned beforehand that some of the Seneca matrons had decided to revive the white-dog tradition. The first hint came when, with fires burning in the village commons, a matron called for quiet and, standing in front of a fire with her arms outstretched, cried out, "Who has an old dream?"

There was much talk of dreams during the ceremonies, so Beth did not realize what was about to happen.

"Who has a new dream?" the matron asked. "Who has a white dog?"

"Renno?" Beth asked, turning to her husband.

Renno's face was expressionless.

"Renno," Beth repeated urgently.

Renno was himself not overly fond of the white-dog tradition, but he had been forewarned by his mother that some of the old ones were going to bring back the practice. "It is tradition," he said to Beth.

Three matrons used besoms to scatter the ashes of the symbolic old year fire. An older boy lifted a small, white dog to allow it to be seen by all and then, with one solid blow with his war club, killed the pup. Matrons quickly daubed the body of the dog with red paint and garlanded it with white wampum. After several boys hung the body of the dog from a pole, the dancing and singing began.

"Do you mind if I go back to the house now?" Naomi asked in a small voice.

One look at the girl's face told Beth everything. It was as if that act of senseless cruelty summed up all of the violence poor Naomi had suffered. The Morgans, Beth thought, probably had killed Mr. Burns as quickly and with as little regard for his life. "I'll go with you, dear," Beth offered, and put an arm around Naomi's waist.

At the castle, Naomi went directly to her room. Beth, meanwhile, built up the fire in the cozy little room that Renno and she used as a sitting room and a retreat. There she waited for her husband to come home. She was writing down her impressions of the night's events when she heard a faint scream from upstairs.

Beth, lifting her skirts, ran up the stairs, her moccasined feet flashing. When she flung open Naomi's door, the girl was sitting up in bed. Her chest was heaving. A candle burned on the table beside her, and there was the smell of a lucifer match in the air.

"Are you all right?" Beth asked.

"Yes. I'm sorry if I startled you."

Beth sat on the side of the bed and took Naomi's hand. "Bad dreams?"

Naomi nodded. "The death of that little dog affected me more than I admitted."

"Sometimes it helps if you talk about your dreams," Beth said. "By giving voice to them, you lessen them."

"It was the way they killed the dog."

Beth was silent.

"In the dream the dog became my father." She was unable to continue. Tears ran down her cheeks. "Oh, Beth," she moaned, "will I ever get over this?"

Beth gathered her into a comforting hug. "It's all right," she whispered and kissed the top of Naomi's head. "It's perfectly all right to cry."

As if she had been given permission for the first time, Naomi broke into harsh, racking sobs that continued for a long, long time. At last, hiccuping, she whispered, "They dragged him out onto the porch so that when Tommy cut his throat he wouldn't bleed in the house."

More words tumbled out. Beth held her close, close, and made encouraging sounds when she faltered. Eventually all of it came out. Naomi made no effort to sanitize her account of brutality, the sexual slavery, or the crudity of the three men who had held her prisoner for one eternal year. And Beth cried, too, just as she had when Little Hawk described Naomi's personal hell.

The telling was cathartic. Naomi fell asleep in Beth's arms and was resting peacefully when Beth eased the girl down on the pillow, then quietly tiptoed out the door.

The next morning, when Naomi came downstairs to breakfast, she looked pale and felt drained. She had revealed everything to the elegant Englishwoman, and she was sure that Beth, now knowing what Naomi had become while she was in the Morgans' hands, would look upon her as dirt.

But Beth came to her, took both of her hands, and said brightly, "Good morning, dear. You'll have to eat quickly, so we can get over to the village for the day's activities."

Naomi, relieved, disbelieving, managed a wan smile.

Even when Beth hurried her into dressing in doeskin with a buffalo robe atop and led her out into the crisp, winter air, Naomi could not believe that her hostess could know what had happened and still be so kind to her.

It was the fifth day of the time of the new beginning. The unfortunate white dog was taken down from the pole and burned so that his spirit could go to the Place across the River to join the Seneca—and the Seneca dogs—who had gone before him. First there was good food in Toshabe's longhouse, then singing.

On the sixth day El-i-chi performed the graceful

sacred feather dance. By the light of fires on the common, other men joined the shaman in the thanksgiving dance. Afterward, in the hush of a cold night, each individual who chose to do so was given an opportunity to sing his own song for all of the people. Then it was over. A new year had begun. The renewal of all things good and green and fruitful was, once again, guaranteed by the Master of Life as a reward for the devotion of his people.

Rusog Ho-ya, seed of Rusog, had not participated in the singing and dancing. Instead, with his sister, We-yo, and his niece, Summer Moon, he had sat quietly in his grandmother's longhouse to hear the old Seneca tales, the laughter, the friendly bantering that went on among Rusog and Rusog's brothers-by-marriage. Ho-ya was nearly seventeen. He was built like his father—broad, thick chested, and strong of arm. He was the son of Ena and, thus, the great-great-grandson of the original white Indian. The Cherokee and Seneca blood that ran in his veins was, in his opinion, contaminated by the one-quarter of it that was white. He had joined the Mingo White Blanket on the journey to join Tecumseh's army, which was committed to fighting white expansion on the frontier. After Ho-ya and Ena had killed White Blanket in self-defense and come back to the villages, the young Cherokee had been discontent.

The Seneca midwinter celebration had, if anything, exacerbated his restlessness, for the events of the six days had been exclusively of the Indian civilization, unsullied by the cultural impact of the white faces who bred like the mice of the field. The purity of the ceremony contrasted sharply with the white influences that affected every aspect of life in the villages, and that made him sad.

On a day of wind and steely cold rain, Ho-ya entered his twin sister's log cabin to find We-yo and Summer Moon picking the meat from hickory nut shells for honey-and-nut balls.

"Don't just stand there," We-yo said in English. "Crack nuts for us."

"Speak your own language," Ho-ya said harshly.

"My brother is so charming," We-yo said in French.

Ho-ya glowered. "If I am to be treated with disrespect, I will go."

"I used the language of my grandmother's father," We-yo said in Cherokee. "I spoke in jest. Seat yourself. Talk to us."

Ho-ya threw himself down on a cushion. "Would you hear me say that I am sick to death of the language of my grandmother's father? And of my mother's white ancestors and of this white man's log cabin and everything—" He paused. His face was congested with anger.

We-yo put aside the bowl of nuts and walked to stand beside him. She put her hand on his shoulder. "Don't," she said.

"I have stayed here too long," he grumbled. "I put my faith in false prophets, and I wait. I hear and I hear that Tecumseh will fight, that he will bring all of the nations together against the white faces, but I see no action. I think, Sister, that it is too late even to dream of driving the white faces back across the mountains."

"So says our uncle Renno."

"Our uncle," Ho-ya seethed in distaste.

"He is wise."

"He fought for the white generals against his own blood at Fallen Timbers."

"Please do not speak badly of our uncle," We-yo said.

"No one can fault his courage," Ho-ya said, "only his conviction that we—Cherokee, Seneca, all of us—must become white."

"Please?" she begged, kneeling beside him.

He relented, seeing the pain he was causing her. He blew out a deep breath. "Come, then. I will crack the nuts for you."

Summer Moon, intimidated by the anger in her uncle's voice, had been very, very quiet, but when Ho-ya began to crack the hard little hickory nuts with stone on stone, she smiled brightly and said, "Ho-ya. Ho-ya."

He patted his niece on the head and looked as if his mood was lifting.

We-yo began to pick the small bits of meat from the broken shells. Summer Moon played with a corn-husk doll. The fire crackled and sent a puff of smoke from the fireplace. We-yo got up to put on more wood.

Ho-ya, still thinking about his life and future, said, "It is too late to change that which is. But there must be lands where there are no white settlers."

"Lands of warlike and fierce tribes," We-yo said.

"West of the Father of Waters, our uncles were greeted in peace by the Quapaw and by others. You have heard the stories. The lands of Arkansas were rich, they said, and there were virgin forests and mountains and hot springs that bubbled up from beneath the earth."

"And these rich, wooded lands are the hunting grounds of those who live there," We-yo said.

"A small group could find space to live and to hunt without disturbing those already there," Ho-ya said. "I have considered this. I think that Indian brothers would accept us, just as the Cherokee accepted Ghonkaba's Seneca."

We-yo was silent for a while, then she said quietly, "I know that it has long been on your mind. If your decision is to go to the west of the Father of Waters, then Summer Moon and I will go with you, of course."

Ho-ya nodded and reached out to touch his sister's hand lightly.

When Little Hawk arrived in Washington City, he weighed a few pounds less, for the winter journey had been a difficult one. In the upper passes of the

Great Smoky Mountains he had battled snow and ice. At times, exhausted, he almost lost the will to continue. He had ridden coaches from Charlotte, in North Carolina, and the long, uncomfortable ride over roads made treacherous by winter gave him plenty of time to purge himself of his doubts. By the time he reached his destination, he could forget Naomi Burns for hours at a time.

He found that the nation's capital still had the raw look of a new city. The wide boulevards were muddy and rutted. Water stood in shallow pools in the fields near the president's house.

Little Hawk, dressed in his marine uniform, went to the White House, but the new secretary needed some convincing before he agreed to tell Mr. Jefferson that Lieutenant Hawk Harper was in the waiting room.

"Well, my young Hawk," Jefferson said in greeting, his hand outthrust. "You look as if your leave did you good."

"It's always good to be at home, sir," Little Hawk said.

"You have timed your return well," the president said, motioning Little Hawk to a chair. "The Congress is involved with matters other than the late war in North Africa. Your former commander seems intent upon making an ass of himself, but he is, I fear, yesterday's hero. Have you been in touch with the news?"

"I've seen newspapers for the last few weeks," Little Hawk answered.

"You know, then, that nothing has been heard from Mr. Lewis and Captain Clark?"

"I've seen no mention at all of the expedition, sir."

"Understandably," Jefferson said. "They've been gone for over a year."

"Well, sir," Little Hawk said, "it is a big country. I've seen only a bit of it, but it would be daunting to me to have to walk from the Mississippi River to the Pacific."

"Yes, I asked much of them, didn't I?"

Little Hawk remained silent. Jefferson's keen eyes bored deeply into his before the older man spoke. "Why do I feel that I can rely on you, Hawk?"

Little Hawk spread his hands and smiled. "I have no answer, sir, but you do me honor."

Jefferson became all business. "A private vessel, the *Orient*, is sailing from Baltimore within the week. She'll round Cape Horn and proceed to the northwestern Pacific Coast. The purpose of this expedition is to trade for furs with the Pacific Coast Indian tribes who live to the north of the Spanish possessions. Once this goal is achieved, the *Orient* will then sail westward to China to sell the furs. It will be a voyage of two to three years' duration."

"Yes, sir," Little Hawk said.

"It is my hope, and I pray not a vain one, that when the *Orient* reaches the northwest Pacific Coast it might there encounter some word of my former secretary's expedition." He sighed. "I don't often make decisions based on hunch or intuition, Hawk, but somehow I feel—and it haunts me—that my friends have reached the Pacific. I wake in the night with a feeling of dread, thinking that they are there, that they are in desperate need of help." He pounded a fist into his palm. "I must know. I must know."

"I am at your command," Little Hawk said, but he was thinking, *Ah, two to three years*. It was an eternity when measured in absence from his family; but it also gave him time to forget Naomi.

"It will be a long and hazardous journey," Jefferson warned. "I will not order you to make it."

"Then, sir, I will volunteer."

"Spoken like a marine," Jefferson replied with a smile. "You'll need gear and money. Make a list of your requirements and present it to my secretary. I will have letters for you to the ship's captain, to Mr.

Lewis, and to Whom It May Concern, stating that you are my personal envoy. You'll have to make haste, my young friend, although I will send a message to the captain of the *Orient* to delay his departure until you are safely aboard."

The *Orient* was a three-master. With her sails furled at dockside in Baltimore, she showed the racy lines of the new family of frigates being built for the U.S. Navy, a class of ship well-known to a lad who had sailed to Tripoli to take part in the war against the Barbary pirates. Private vessel she was, for the president had said so; but frigate she was as well, at least in outline. When Little Hawk boarded he soon saw that her lines were misleading, for she did not mount the guns of a ship of the line. Her gun decks had been converted to storage areas. The living quarters for the crew were more spacious than those on a naval ship, and the cabins for the officers—and for a personal envoy of the president—were almost luxurious.

Little Hawk presented his letter of introduction to Captain Micah Davidson. The captain wore a uniform-cut tunic with a double row of brass buttons, a wide sash with rosettes of silver, and a sword at his waist. His white, high-collared shirt was accented by a bow tie of startling size, and his black, thick hair was topped by a high-crowned hat. He was clean shaven and looked to Little Hawk to be no older than his middle thirties. His mouth was set permanently in a half smile.

"We've been expecting you, Lieutenant," Davidson said. "Welcome aboard. I'll have a boy show you to your cabin."

"Thank you, sir," Little Hawk said.

"Since this is a merchantman, and since this is not a military expedition," Davidson said, "I must ask you, sir, to put away your uniform. In fact, it would be wise to leave it ashore."

"Yes, sir," Little Hawk said. He had been told by the president that this would probably be the case, so he had used some of the gold from the U.S. Treasury to outfit himself for the trip and to purchase a cold-weather wardrobe that would serve during the long voyage.

"If you'll excuse me, then," the captain said.

From inside his cabin Little Hawk heard the shouted orders on deck. As he stowed his gear and belongings, he realized that words that would befuddle a landsman were familiar to him from his tour with the marines in the Mediterranean and North Africa.

"Cant her, Mr. Wellman. You there, grapple the buoy."

The captain's voice carried well.

"You may cat and fish the anchor, Mr. Wellman."

When Little Hawk went on deck, *Orient* was under way and the first mate, Horace Wellman, a Boston man, was shouting his orders. The captain, high beaver hat pushed back, was on the bridge, watching alertly as Wellman called, "Lively now, square the headyards. Brail up the jib."

She left Baltimore on a crisp, cold winter day but would sail into summer off the coast of South America. The *Orient* rode a small, fast sea with her topgallant and royals stiff with a favorable wind.

In contrast to getting about on land by foot, on horseback, or in a wheeled, horse- or ox-drawn vehicle, sea travel was swift, clean, and relatively quiet. Before the cold stars of winter became visible in the unblemished sky, land had fallen below the horizon. Little Hawk stood at the stern of the ship, allowing himself to become one with the rhythmic rise and fall of the deck. Although he was aboard a small ship with more than three dozen companions, he felt very much alone and, as it happened, rather sorry for himself as he whispered to cold sea air, "Good-bye. Good-bye, then."

He was bidding farewell to a girl he had once known, not to the soiled and repellent young woman who had stolen her place. His adieu was for the taffy-haired girl who had placed her soft, wide mouth on

his so sweetly, so tenderly, so warmly, and so long
before.

Many a man who went west with the object of
making his fortune ended up facing disappointment.
Andy Jackson understood that full well in the winter
of 1805–1806, for his financial affairs were less than
satisfactory. He had retired from the unprofitable life
of public servant, keeping only his association with the
Tennessee Militia, although, mainly by correspon-
dence, he maintained his contacts with former associ-
ates, Aaron Burr among them.

Now Jackson found himself stuck in Knoxville.
While he waited for the outcome of a court case in
which he represented the claimant in a civil action, he
inquired about his old friend, Colonel Roy Johnson.
He knew that Roy had married a senior matron of
the Seneca; now he learned that his old friend had
abandoned Knoxville in favor of living with his wife's
people. Nothing would do but for Jackson to go see
for himself how the old warhorse was enjoying life.

He rented a horse, rode out to Renno's village,
and there asked for Roy. He was directed by young
boys to Toshabe's longhouse, where he found Roy
helping Toshabe prepare supper.

Word was spread through the village that Roy
and Toshabe had distinguished company. First El-i-chi
and then Renno and Beth appeared, just in time for
supper. The talk was light during the meal. Afterward,
when the men moved to one end of the longhouse to
smoke, Jackson asked about Renno's son, and that
brought up the subject of the war that William Eaton
had conducted in North Africa.

"Trouble is," Jackson grumbled, "the politicians
and the navy didn't allow Eaton to finish it. We never
seem to finish our wars, my friends. We signed an
unfavorable peace treaty with England at a time when
we had them so thoroughly whupped that we could
have called our own tune. We've swallowed insult
after insult from Spain over the decades when they

weren't strong enough on this continent to whup a company of good militia. Hells bells, Roy, you and I should have gone on with old John Sevier and George Rogers Clark and kicked the Spaniards off the Mississippi River and south of the Rio Grande years ago."

"There was a time when I was ready," Roy said.

"This ain't why I came out here," Jackson said, "but since I'm here, I might as well mention it, knowing as how you folks can keep a confidence. I'm considering taking a little romp down Mexico way. I won't go into it any more'n that, but if I decide to go kick a few Spanish backsides, would you fellows want to go along? I don't know of anyone I'd rather have fighting at my side, Renno, except maybe you *and* your brother, here."

"Now, General, who's going to conquer New Spain this time?" Roy drawled. "Clark and Sevier are too damned old."

"I'd rather not mention names, not at this time," Jackson said.

Roy snorted. "Things that dull in Nashboro?"

"They're calling it Nashville these days," Jackson said. "But it's still dull."

"General Jackson," Renno said, "might one of the men involved in this new venture be General James Wilkinson?"

Jackson puffed on his corncob pipe for a few moments. "Maybe," he said.

Renno looked at Roy. Roy shook his head.

"What's wrong?" Jackson asked, eyebrows raised. "I've always thought Wilkinson was a good man. He knows a slew of people, and he can gather a lot of men with rifles to his side when and if."

"Andy," Roy said, "I hate to tell you this because I hate to disillusion a man who believes in fairy tales—"

Jackson made a rude sound deep in his throat.

"—but James Wilkinson has been in the pay of the Spaniards for as long as I've known him or known about him."

"The devil you say!" Jackson scoffed.

"Know it to be a fact—me *and* Renno," Roy said. "We caught him selling Anthony Wayne's munitions and supplies to the Spanish. And one time Renno and his brother-in-law intercepted a shipment of Spanish silver coins that were meant for Wilkinson."

"If this is true," Jackson said darkly, "I will, of course, reconsider my participation in this Mexico venture. But why on God's great, green earth would Jefferson appoint a Spanish spy to be governor of Louisiana?"

"I once asked George Washington a similar question," Renno replied. "He said Wilkinson was given his commission in the army to keep him out of mischief."

"Good Lord, the politician's mind," Jackson fumed. "God deliver me from politics for the rest of my life."

"Wilkinson did his best to sabotage General Wayne's campaign in the Ohio country," Roy continued. "Wayne just ignored him, even after Renno and I showed what Wilkinson was doing with the supplies that weren't getting to the American Legion. I reckon, though, that what Renno and I did stayed on the general's mind, because he gave orders to have us killed awhile back."

"Oh, my God, I thank you for telling me this," Jackson murmured. He shuddered. "Of course I'm forced to believe what you and Renno have told him, but I wondered how a man like Aaron Burr could be so wrong. . . . I mean, Burr is no idiot, and he has the friendship of such solid men as William Henry Harrison and Henry Clay." He puffed furiously on his pipe. "I take it, then, that you gentlemen would not be interested in venturing down the big river to fight Spaniards."

"Not with James Wilkinson, that's for sure," Roy answered.

"Since you knew about Wilkinson," Jackson said, "do you know others who are involved?"

"Well, I could guess at a lot of small fish," Roy answered.

"And what's your opinion of Mr. Burr?" Jackson asked.

"Since the ex-vice president was willing to betray the United States once," Renno said, "I would question his intentions closely."

"What did you say?" Jackson stormed, thoroughly startled. "You're not talking about his duel with Hamilton! That was not treason. I myself have fought duels. I see nothing wrong in a man defending his honor, even against a man as famous and as prominent as Alexander Hamilton."

"No, I am talking about his efforts, along with New England Federalists, to take the northern states, including New York and New Jersey, out of the union," Renno explained.

Jackson was stunned. "Roy," he said weakly, "if you happen to have a jug, I wouldn't turn down a swig or two."

Roy just happened to have a jug, and Jackson had more than one or two swigs. After a late evening of talk he slept soundly in a guest room at Huntington Castle. With the morning he made his good-byes.

Roy sought out Renno after Jackson's departure. The sachem was in the garden behind the big house, practicing with his English longbow. The current bow was the third in its line, the original one having been given to him as a gift by Beth's brother, William. Even though Renno had been inactive of late, his aim was still true, his arm strong.

"Been thinking, Renno, 'bout what Andy was saying."

"So have I," Renno admitted.

"We knew that Wilkinson was trying to resurrect the old dream about an independent empire in Spanish America. As I recall, you wrote a letter to Mr. Jefferson, saying as much."

"I remember," Renno said.

"El-i-chi and I were wondering if it wouldn't be a good idea if you wrote again and mentioned Aaron Burr's name this time."

"But not the others'?" Renno said.

"No, I'd bet my life on William Henry Harrison's being a true patriot."

All three of them had known Harrison when he was a young aide to Mad Anthony Wayne before Fallen Timbers. Renno concurred that Harrison would do nothing to harm the United States, that if Harrison had given support to Burr's scheme, it was because he had no idea that Wilkinson was involved.

So it was that Renno sat down at his desk that night and penned a letter to Thomas Jefferson, in which he said that he had it on good authority that Aaron Burr was conspiring with a known traitor, a man who had been in the pay of the Spanish government for decades, to foment trouble on the western frontier of the United States in an effort to wrest territory from the Spanish provinces.

The letter was sent off to Knoxville. For a while Renno was content. It was Roy Johnson who caused him to doubt.

"I wonder if we've done enough," Roy said.

"You *have* done enough," Beth said heatedly, for she did not want to see the wanderlust gleam in Renno's eyes. Things had been so good, so peaceful, with her husband living at home and tending to his light duties as sachem.

"Well, if Burr and the others start a war with Spain, it might not go the way they plan it," Roy said. "It just might be that old Spain might say, 'Hey, lookee here, these boys fighting us are Americans. Now how could citizens of the United States go to war against us without the knowledge and consent of their country?' And then first thing you know we'd be in a big war with Spain here in North America and at sea, and I think we've already got enough trouble what with French pirates and the damned English impressing our sailors."

"Now you listen to me," Beth said, glaring first at Roy and then at Renno. "Just because you haven't been on a long hunt lately—"

"I have not expressed any desire to leave you," Renno said.

"But you're working up to it, aren't you?"

"I have only heard the words of my father-by-marriage," Renno said, his face Indian stoic.

"I know that look," Beth said accusingly. "Go hunt. Go for a run. You've been cooped up here at home since before the time of the new beginning."

"I don't reckon El-i-chi would want to go, what with Ah-wa-o expecting? . . ." Roy said.

"Roy Johnson!" Beth wailed.

"I expect not," Renno answered.

"Last I read, Wilkinson had moved his headquarters south from St. Louis to Natchitoches."

"Damn you, Roy!" Beth seethed.

"Shame on you," Roy said, shaking his finger at her.

"I think the thing to do would be to go north," Renno put in. "If Burr is gathering an army, he will have to be somewhere on the Ohio."

"Well," Beth said, "if that's the way it's going to be, I'll go start getting my kit together."

Renno looked at her with a smile, and in his eyes she saw the expression that she knew so well—the curiosity, the desire to climb the next ridge and peer beyond.

"I hardly think, my dear," Renno said, "that you could pass yourself off as a likely recruit for Mr. Burr's army."

Chapter Five

Although being left alone was nothing new for Beth Huntington Harper, that didn't mean she had to like it. She was on excellent terms with Renno's family. Beth respected Toshabe as a wise, strong woman; loved Ah-wa-o dearly; and considered Ena to be not only a relative-by-marriage but a good friend. Of course the cultural gulf that separated her from Indian life was not always successfully bridged, so she was grateful that she had Naomi for company. True, Naomi's background differed greatly from Beth's. A hardscrabble dirt farmer's daughter could hardly claim equality of opportunity with the daughter of an English peer; but both the country girl and the Englishwoman took their main beliefs from the King James version of the Bible, spoke a common language that had been with them from their earliest childhood, and took their attitudes from a shared background of Anglo-European ancestry. Actually Naomi and Beth had more common ground for a relationship than Beth and her husband's relatives shared.

Early on, Naomi demonstrated an insatiable interest in reading. Awed by the extent of Beth's library, she handled the leather-bound books as if they were among the world's greatest treasures. Now and then Naomi would come to Beth to ask shyly the meaning of a word and, later, to discuss the author's intent in making this or that assertion. It was evident that Naomi's mother, who had been her sole mentor, had been an educated woman who taught Naomi well.

Naomi started each morning with a prayer to God for having sent Little Hawk to deliver her from her life of shame and horror. Many times during the day she prayed that somehow God would arrange for her to stay for just a little while longer—for another day, another week, another month—with the lovely and gentle woman she had come to love. She made a great effort to forget the year that followed the murder of her parents, and since one of mankind's most blessed gifts is the ability to forget the bad and remember the good, she seemed to succeed. But far back in the recesses of her mind the terror still lurked, evidencing itself in odd ways. For no reason she would begin to tremble, and the dread of having to leave Beth Huntington's house would expand inside her like a ball of overleavened dough until she felt that she would burst with it.

In her dreams Bearclaw Morgan and his idiot son would come calling, and she would awake with her nightdress soaked with perspiration and with her heart pounding. Huntington Castle was on a hillside not far from the Seneca village. But still the house was isolated, separated from the settlement of longhouses and cabins both by a tree-lined creek and a meadow. At the lea's edge began a long lane, planted on each side with pecan trees. Although Renno had assured Naomi and Beth that El-i-chi and others would keep an eye on the place, it seemed to the girl that the two surviving Morgans could easily reach the

house without alerting anyone in the village. She had
been told that El-i-chi was a great warrior; but he was
preoccupied with the coming birth of his second child,
and he also had his duties as shaman.

"Do you really know how to use that weapon?"
Naomi asked Beth one day, indicating the woman's
own English longbow and a quiver of arrows, which
hung over the fireplace in the sitting room.

"With fatal accuracy. When I was young I wanted
to be a boy," Beth explained. "I felt a need to com-
pete with my brother, so I learned how to use the
bow."

"Is it difficult to master?"

"It takes a certain amount of strength to bend the
bow, yes," Beth said. "Would you like to try?"

The first lesson in the back garden was a disaster.
Naomi's left hand slipped off the bow as she was trying to pull the string, and the bow jerked back to slam
into her face. For a moment, as bright flashes of pain
filled her vision, she feared that she had badly damaged her eye. Beth, making soothing noises, looked
at her and said, "You are going to have a very spec-
tacular black eye."

Naomi gamely insisted on trying again. The arrow
left the bow and dropped to the ground a few feet in
front of her, for the drawstring had been held too
close to her cheek and had caught behind her ear,
causing a jolt of excruciating pain. She lifted one hand
timidly. Her ear was numb; she had been afraid that
the bowstring had severed it.

Beth burst out laughing. She tried to stop but
couldn't. Naomi, hurt, looked at her. "Oh, my dear,"
Beth said, gasping, "I know it isn't funny, not really,
but you should have seen the look on your face." She
controlled her laughter and took Naomi's hand. "I
think it's time to admit that the longbow is just not
your weapon of choice."

"Once I killed a rabid wolf with my father's musket," Naomi said.

With the musket Naomi was more effective. She

would have had to put in a lot of practice to win a turkey shoot, but she could hit a large pine tree's trunk at a distance of one hundred feet.

Beth, perceiving the reason for Naomi's interest in weapons, showed her how to load a pistol and had her practice in the back garden until El-i-chi and Gao and Ta-na came to see what war was being fought at the castle. Then El-i-chi took over the teaching and advised Naomi to keep *both* eyes open, confusing her to the point where she missed the target tree entirely. Soon, however, she was hitting the pine with regularity. She was satisfied. Beth told her that the pistol and its adjuncts were a gift. Naomi put it on the table beside her bed, and there it stayed.

Quite often Beth took Naomi to the Seneca village to have tea with Toshabe and Ah-wa-o and, less often, on to the Cherokee town to see Ena and We-yo. Flame Hair, as Beth was called, was loved and respected by everyone, and her young friend was shown the utmost courtesy. Slowly Naomi began to acquire Seneca and Cherokee words, but she often confused the two languages. She learned the names of Renno's people and exchanged the Seneca greetings as she and Beth walked through the town.

"Isn't it odd?" Naomi asked Beth one day. "I grew up fearing three things—God, Indians, and mad dogs. Every time settlers got together they told stories about Indian massacres. But these people are not savages. Toshabe's longhouse is as warm and comfortable as my mother's cabin. My father hunted for our meat, just as El-i-chi does for his family. My father and mother grew vegetables, just as the Indian women do. We prayed to God and read the Bible. The Seneca don't have a Bible, but they pray to the Master of Life. Since God is all-powerful and is everywhere, in everything, and since we and the Seneca speak a different language, isn't it possible that God and the Master of Life are the same thing?"

"That's how Renno and I look at it," Beth said. "But don't make the mistake of thinking that the Indian is just a white man in a red skin. He's not. He comes from a totally different culture. You speak of massacres. Well, there have been many. The Indian can be a cruel enemy. Not too long ago it was customary among the Iroquois, a warlike people, to turn a captured enemy over to the women and girls of the tribe. This was a fate that enemy warriors dreaded most, for the women were capable of thinking up exquisite tortures."

"In Spain the Catholic church tortured those who deviated from what the authorities decreed to be the true belief," Naomi said.

Beth pondered a moment. "If you want to discuss the fine points of difference between the European and the Indian, I know just the person for it. Come with me."

Se-quo-i was in another of his jewelry-making phases. He welcomed Beth and Naomi and escorted them to his workshop in a log building, where he was molding tiny, beautiful animals of molten silver by the lost-wax method. When he had finished pouring the sizzling streams into the molds, he chose two finished creations strung on thin, rawhide thongs.

"Beautiful things for two beautiful ladies," he said. "A deer for you, Miss Beth, and for the young lady a dancing bear."

"You mustn't, Se-quo-i," Beth protested.

"My pleasure."

"At least let me pay you the worth of the silver."

Se-quo-i walked to a window and looked up at the sky. "By the sun," he said, "it is midday. Throughout the entire morning I have not been insulted, and then, Flame Hair, you spoil this day by offering me money in exchange for a gift given freely."

"I am sorry," Beth said sincerely.

"My heart is healed," Se-quo-i told her. "Mine is a small gift compared to the books and materials you have given to the children of my village."

"It's such a beautiful little bear, Mr. Se-quo-i," Naomi said. "I am so very grateful."

"Name one of your sons for me," Se-quo-i said, causing Naomi to blush mightily.

The Cherokee turned and limped toward the house. "Come. We will indulge in that vile English drink that you white faces have used to pervert the poor Indian."

Inside Sequoi's house, a pretty Indian woman smiled at them. "This is my niece Wynona," Se-quo-i said.

Amused, Beth smiled back at the young woman. Almost every time she came to Se-quo-i's home, a different niece was there. Once she had asked Se-quo-i how many brothers and sisters he had, for while he was working on a project he seemed to have scads of nephews to help him. And there never seemed to be a shortage of nieces around his house. Se-quo-i's answer had been: "But, Flame Hair, are not we all brothers and sisters?"

Now, over tea, Beth asked, "And how goes the great work?"

"If you are not truly interested," Se-quo-i said with a wide smile, "it is best not to ask." Without waiting for further comment from Beth, he reached for a stack of papers.

For Naomi's benefit he explained, "It is not my opinion alone that one of the main reasons for the European's superiority in science and knowledge is the ability to store his discoveries in the written word. For a long time now I have been making an effort to formulate an alphabet for the Cherokee language." He laughed. "I often think that I have set myself an impossible task." He looked at Naomi appraisingly. "Do you know the difference between an alphabetic written language and a syllabic written language?"

"I'm afraid I don't," Naomi said.

"English is alphabetic. Just twenty-six symbols are used to indicate all of the sounds of the spoken language." He spread his hands. "One letter can be sounded in several different ways, depending on context, but that variability simply makes the language more interesting. Chinese, on the other hand, uses many more characters because each sign represents not a single letter but a syllable, or a sound." He sighed. "At first I decided to keep written Cherokee as simple as possible. But there were just too many sounds. I have, at the moment"—he extended a sheet of paper toward Beth, another to Naomi—"no fewer than eighty-six characters. If you'll follow along with me, the sequence begins with *e, a, la, tsi, nah.* The difficulty is that the language has such sounds as *dble, dba,* and *gwv.* The *v* is like the *u* in the English word *but.* Therefore it is a vowel. The Cherokee *d* represents nearly the same sound as in English but approximates the English *t.*"

Naomi's wide, sensuous mouth had dropped open in puzzlement. Beth threw up her hands. "Enough! I surrender."

"Really," Se-quo-i said, "it's very simple. You speak English, French, Spanish, Seneca, Cherokee, and a smattering of other Indian dialects. You should have no trouble at all learning to read and write in Cherokee."

Beth, eyes sparkling, turned to Naomi. "You see why I have brought you and your questions to this man?"

Naomi closed her mouth and nodded.

"You have questions, Naomi?" Se-quo-i asked.

"I can't think of any at the moment," she said weakly.

"Perhaps," Se-quo-i said, "Flame Hair will leave you with me, and we will discuss any questions you might care to ask."

"Another time," Beth said, rising. "I'm sure Naomi wouldn't want to interfere with your visit with your niece."

Se-quo-i smiled and nodded. "How considerate of you, Flame Hair."

* * *

Little Hawk first saw Captain Micah Davidson's seven-year-old daughter while the *Orient* was struggling against contrary winds past the Cape of Storms on the northern North Carolina coast. He had taken his exercise on the pitching, rolling deck in spite of a rain that lanced his face with icy needles and a wind that penetrated his oilskin weather gear.

The ship was a tiny, insignificant mote on the great, roiling sea. Once, the dark, churning clouds overhead parted, and he saw a winter moon, pale and lonely, causing his heart to leap with memories of home. He went to his cabin, which seemed dank and small, and welcomed the call to evening mess in officer's quarters.

Esther Davidson was seated to the left of her father, at table in the chair usually reserved for First Mate Horace Wellman.

"Hawk," Davidson said, "this is my daughter, Esther."

"How do you do, Mr. Hawk?" the little girl said, rising, making a graceful curtsy. "My father has told me about you."

"How do you do, Miss Esther?" Little Hawk said, smiling and bowing. "May I ask when you learned how to fly?"

Esther laughed. The sound was a silvery tinkle that made the hardened men of the sea at the captain's mess smile. "I can't fly, silly."

"Then how on earth did you get aboard a ship in the middle of the ocean?" Little Hawk asked.

"You haven't seen Esther because she has been confined to our cabin. She has been unwell," Davidson explained.

"But I'm all better now," Esther said.

A messman came in with a large, silver tureen.

"We're having lentil soup tonight, Mr. Hawk," Esther said. "It's my favorite, and Cook said that he would make it for me since this is the first night I've been able to leave our cabin."

Esther Davidson had her father's dark, thick hair.

It was cut quite short, not at all in a girlish style, obviously for ease of care aboard ship. She had a thin, pale little face in which black eyes burned like coals with a cheerful intensity that belied the dark, sunken circles underneath.

"My father says that you walk on deck every day, even in bad weather," Esther said as Little Hawk took his seat.

"That I do," he confirmed. "Perhaps you'll feel well enough tomorrow to join me?"

"May I, Father?" she asked brightly, an expectant smile lighting her face.

"If you feel well enough, yes," Davidson said.

"Before my mother went to heaven, we sailed to England with my father," Esther told Little Hawk as the messman began to ladle soup into her bowl. "Have you been to England?"

"I've been to Egypt," he said.

"Oh! Did you see the pyramids?"

"Yes, they were quite impressive."

"Well, I haven't been to Egypt," she said with resignation, "but we're going to China, aren't we, Father?"

"That we are," the captain said with a fond smile.

"It's very far," Esther said with great seriousness. "And the voyage will take us ever so long. We'll have a lot of time to get acquainted."

"I won't be going to China with you," Little Hawk said, "but I wonder how many miles we can walk on the deck of this old ship before you go on without me."

"A million," she answered immediately, and Little Hawk told her she was exactly correct.

With the morning the weather was somewhat improved. The *Orient* was thundering from crest to crest of a running sea as she flew before a north wind. Little Hawk found Captain Davidson with the steersman.

"And how is the fair miss Esther?" Little Hawk

asked after an exchange of morning greetings. "Is she up to a stroll on deck?"

Davidson shook his head and looked up at the leaden skies. "Let's wait for better weather, Hawk. She's been quite ill."

"I'm sorry."

"She'll improve when we reach warmer waters. The physicians said that the sea air would be good for her." He clasped his hands behind his back and walked to the rail. Little Hawk joined him there. "When her mother was alive, they lived aboard with me," Davidson said. "They said that if my wife had stayed ashore in Boston, she would have died sooner."

"Again, I'm sorry," Little Hawk said.

"She knew, poor dear, that she was living on borrowed time." The captain took a deep breath, then let it out slowly. "Consumption. It came on her suddenly just after we were married. When we were in warm waters, she felt better. Except for one trip to Europe, I sailed only the Caribbean. After she died I had only my daughter—no other family left on either side. And little Esther, curse it, has developed her mother's disease. There are those who criticize me for keeping a young girl aboard ship, but, by God, I intend to be with her for as long as He wills it."

The *Orient* sailed into the fair skies of summer between the islands of the Bahamas and Spanish Florida. Laughing dolphins paced her racing prow as she drove through azure swells. All sails billowed at their fullest. Captain Davidson reported that the ship would be making the Windward Passage between the eastern end of Cuba and Hispaniola in a few days if the favorable winds continued.

Esther was eating her meals regularly at the captain's table, and on one fine day, with a gentle wind pushing the ship along at a sedate, gently rocking pace, the child joined Little Hawk on deck and walked beside him. Two sleek, bullet-swift dolphins were ri-

ding the small swell pushed up by the ship's bow.
Little Hawk paused, leaned on the rail, and looked
down.

"They don't eat people," Esther said.

"No, I 'spect not."

"Sharks and whales do."

"Whales, too?"

"Oh, yes, 'cause they're so big."

"They *are* big."

"I hate 'em."

"Why do you hate whales?"

"It was probably whales that ate my mother."
She clung to the rail as the ship pitched. Her knuckles
went white, and her shoulders shuddered. "I hate the
ocean, too."

Unnoticed, Captain Davidson had walked up behind them in time to hear Esther's last words. He
picked his daughter up and held her close for a moment. "I think it's time for a rest for a certain little
missy."

"When I die, Papa, you won't put me in the
ocean. You promised. Do you remember?"

"We'll have no talk of dying. You and I are going
to live forever, little miss."

She hugged him hard around the neck. "Yes,"
she said, resting her cheek against his shoulder. "Forever. But you promised, remember?"

"I remember," he said.

"I want to be buried in the earth, like my grandmother and my grandfather," she said, her thin, pale
face quite serious, her black eyes burning. "If we're
in China, or somewhere like that, you maybe can't
take me all the way back to Boston—"

"Hush now. You hush," Davidson said, his face
full of pain.

Little Hawk turned his eyes away, watching the
sporting dolphins. In a book in the library of his stepmother there had been a Greek legend about a boy
on a dolphin—a naked, smiling boy riding the shining

black water beast. His chubby little legs were clamped
to the dolphin's gleaming sides.

Davidson cleared his throat. The noise drew Little Hawk's eyes. There were tears on the captain's
cheek.

"You run along now. Chin-chin will help you get
ready for your nap." Chin-Chin, a fifty-year-old Chinese man called Boy by the crew, was in charge of
the girl's day-to-day needs—tending her wardrobe,
keeping her little room off the captain's cabin clean
and neat, and fussing when she did not eat enough to
please him.

"I'll see you at dinner, Mr. Hawk," Esther called
as she walked toward the captain's cabin.

"I had to bury her mother at sea," Davidson said,
his voice heavy with emotion.

Little Hawk nodded. That explained not only Esther's hatred and fear of the sea but her statement
that the whales probably ate her mother.

"Thank you for putting up with her," Davidson
said.

"Not at all, Captain," Little Hawk said truthfully.
"It's my pleasure."

As the *Orient* skirted the coast of the former
French colony of St. Domingue, Little Hawk gazed
with some interest at the land low on the horizon, for
Renna had lived there with Beau and had narrowly
escaped death at the hands of the Negro rebels who
now controlled the land and called it Haiti. Esther's
health did improve in the warm Caribbean. The sun
first pinked and then browned her face. Her laughter
rippled throughout the ship, and the officers and men
spoiled her thoroughly with gifts and attentions.

But Little Hawk was clearly Esther's favorite. "I
have decided, Mr. Hawk," she announced when *Orient* was approaching the island of Trinidad, where she
would stop for stores and water, "that I'll marry you
when I grow up."

Off the northern coast of Brazil the *Orient* sailed
for days in a freshwater sea, although there was no
land in sight. This phenomenon, which had puzzled
early Portuguese and Spanish explorers of the eastern
South American coast, was created by the discharge
of the Amazon River. *Orient*'s steersman turned her
more to the east to round the pointed shoulder of
Brazil. Davidson took on fresh water and stores at
Recife, then bypassed Rio de Janeiro in favor of Mon-
tevideo, where Little Hawk took Esther ashore and
purchased her a rainbow-colored shawl. When they
were once again sailing south, she wore the garment
by day and used it as a top coverlet by night until
Chin-Chin stole it away for a badly needed wash while
she was sleeping.

The storms that blew off the great Antarctic ice
mass slammed into the *Orient* with frightening force
in the Gulf of St. George when the captain's sextant
measured the latitude as forty-five degrees eight minutes south. The frigid blasts drove Esther quickly to
her cabin, where she fussed at Chin-Chin until he had
returned her shawl, freshly washed, to spread over her
legs while she sat in her bed, holding on tightly as the
ship slammed her way southward through a rising sea.

Roy Johnson pulled his buffalo-skin coat more
tightly around him and shivered. "I don't know whose
crazy idea this was," he grumbled.

Renno had built a fire under a rock overhang
near a frozen creek. Sleet sizzled on ice-coated, dead,
brown grass and the dead, fallen leaves of summer
outside the protection of the protruding rock ledge. A
sound as sharp as a pistol shot told of the sudden
surrender of a tree branch to the weight of encasing
ice.

"I myself was wondering if this trip could not
have been postponed for a month or two," Renno
confessed. He took jerky from his kit and offered a
strip to Roy.

"My teeth won't take any more jerky," Roy said.

"If you were any kind of a son, you'd go get us some fresh meat."

"I admit failure," Renno said with a grin. "Perhaps age and experience would care to teach me how to find game in this storm?"

"Oh, go to sleep," Roy said.

The ice storm that forced Renno and Roy to waste a full day in shelter did not reach as far south as the sachem's village. There was, in contrast, a feeling almost of spring in the air when Naomi looked up from her sewing. Her eyes were wide, her white teeth pressed into her full, lower lip.

"Is something wrong?" Beth asked.

"I don't know," Naomi said. "I just have the strangest feeling that we should go to the village."

"Ah-wa-o?" Beth asked.

"I can't say."

"Well, it's nice out," Beth said. "Shall we take a stroll and find out?"

Beth had lived for a number of years with a man who talked to ghosts. As a result, she was not one to question the unexplained. If Naomi had a feeling that something was wrong in the village, it was worth the time to walk over and see.

There was no need for heavy, warm furs. Light doeskin jackets served the women quite comfortably. As they walked down the pecan-tree lined lane, Beth checked to see if the leaf buds were showing yet, but the tree limbs were still bare in spite of the blue sky and pleasant temperature. There had not been ice on the creek for weeks, but the water still looked cold as Beth and Naomi leaped across on stepping stones. Up ahead the smokes of the village were rising in perfectly straight columns in the windless air. A dog, barking and wagging a greeting, ran toward the women.

El-i-chi was standing in front of his longhouse. When he saw them coming, he ran to meet them. "I was just going to send the boys," he said.

"It has begun?" Beth asked.

El-i-chi nodded. He looked pale and nervous.

Beth took his arm and smiled up at him. "Don't worry, Brother. You survived this ordeal once before."

He laughed in spite of himself. "I have, without fear, faced armed enemies in the snows of the North, in the deep forests of Ohio, and in the jungles of Africa; but when my wife tenses with pain, there is nothing my weapons can do, and I become a craven coward."

"Go hunting?" Beth suggested. "Take the boys for a run in the woods? Leave this matter to those of us who can handle it."

"I have not yet sent for Ena. My mother is here, though," El-i-chi said. He looked up at the sky, his handsome face drawn with concern. Then he looked suspiciously at Beth. "How did you know?"

"Just a lucky guess," Beth said, glancing at Naomi.

The women went inside. Only Ah-wa-o and Tosh-abe were there. "It is early yet," Toshabe said.

In fact, Ah-wa-o was at work preparing the evening meal, a corn and venison stew. She was using her largest pot because as soon as word spread that her labor had begun, relatives and friends would begin to gather. The birth of a child was an important event, something to be shared with all. If a Seneca woman had found herself locked in the pains of prebirth in an empty house, she would have wept in sadness, thinking that she was not liked, that she had no one who cared for her. It was, Beth thought, one of the more bothersome customs of her in-laws, but she had long since learned that a mere Englishwoman had no say when it came to ancient and honored mores among the Seneca.

Ah-wa-o stiffened, pulled her lips tight, and put one hand on her distended stomach. Beth watched. She had helped Toshabe and the midwives at several births, and she was always amazed by the courage of the Indian women. She was sometimes thankful, sometimes regretful that she herself had not been blessed with children. But she imagined that it would not be at all pleasant to have a watermelon-sized object with sharp knees and elbows emerge from one's loins.

Weeks before, in preparation for this day, Beth had brought clean sheets and towels to El-i-chi's long-house. Now she set about heating water. Giving birth was a messy business both for the mother and the midwives, and there would be considerable cleaning up to do, not to mention sponging the birth-canal fluids off the newborn.

"What can I do?" Naomi asked.

"Find the boys and have them bring in some more wood," Toshabe suggested.

Gao and Ta-na looked wide-eyed at Ah-wa-o as they replenished the pile of firewood against one wall of the longhouse. A contraction seized Ah-wa-o while they were in the house. Gao took his mother's hand and told her to squeeze. He was very brave, not wincing at all when her fingernails cut his palm; but his dilated pupils and open mouth revealed his concern for Ah-wa-o.

"Run along," Toshabe told the boys. She patted Gao on the head. "Your mother will be all right. In a few hours she will give you a new brother or a new sister."

"A sister," Naomi blurted with certainty. She lifted her hand to her mouth quickly. "I'm sorry—"

"A sister?" Beth asked.

Naomi flushed, then nodded. "Yes. It will be a girl."

"Does this one speak with the manitous?" Toshabe wanted to know.

"Oh, no," Naomi said. "It's just—"

"Just what, dear?" Beth asked.

"It's just that somehow I know that it's going to be a girl and that El-i-chi has decided to name her after his grandmother Ah-wen-ga."

"That is so," Ah-wa-o said wonderingly. "We *have* agreed that it will be so."

Beth saw Toshabe look with squinted eyes at Naomi. The Englishwoman had to stifle a laugh. Toshabe obviously knew that there were some who could see certain events in the future. Beth suspected that Toshabe would resent the manitous' giving such a gift to the white woman who had come to the village under questionable circumstances. Toshabe must have wondered why her grandson would deliver the girl to Beth Huntington and then flee as fast as his feet would carry him. Beth had not told Toshabe why Naomi was living with her and Renno. Beth felt that was Renno's or Little Hawk's responsibility.

Ena and We-yo arrived. We-yo took Ah-wa-o by the arms and forced her to sit down, then took over the cooking chores.

At the time of the evening meal there was only family in El-i-chi's longhouse. Word had spread, though, and soon after the meal was finished, others came to pay their respects to the mother-to-be, to lay friendly hands on Ah-wa-o's swollen stomach, and to nod in satisfaction at the force of the contractions. Women brought food and sewing projects. The men gathered in one end of the longhouse to smoke and tell tales of other births. El-i-chi looked nervous. One senior warrior held the floor for a full half hour as he told of the births of the sachem and the shaman in the Seneca homeland far to the north.

"Is it always like this?" Naomi whispered to Beth. "I've never seen anything like it."

The house was filled with laughing, chattering, smoking, talking, eating people. Ah-wa-o reclined on a bed against the wall, with relatives and friends spread out in a fan shape from that place of honor. Gao and Ta-na had taken responsibility for entertaining little Summer Moon, and the three of them were playing a noisy game of catch-me-if-you-can, with Summer Moon sometimes taking shortcuts between the legs of a standing man.

"The more people, the more noise, the more

laughter, the more honor for the mother," Beth explained.

"Lord deliver me from marrying an Indian then," Naomi said. When the import of what she had said sank in, she blushed and lowered her eyes.

At last Ah-wa-o assumed the birthing position, squatting on the bed with Beth on one side and Ena on the other holding her arms. Toshabe bent in front of her, hands out to catch the drop of the baby. Naomi turned her head away in embarrassment, for it seemed to her that modesty had been totally abandoned. The longhouse had fallen quiet. Smoke curled up from the pipes of the men. Summer Moon was sleeping in Gao's lap. The two boys were watching with awe and some fear when Ah-wa-o made a long, grating grunt of effort.

With a splashing sound like the fall of hot entrails from a gutted deer, the child plopped into Toshabe's cupped hands. Ena snipped the natal cord with one quick motion. Toshabe inserted a finger into the baby's mouth and cleared mucus. To her great pleasure Beth was given the honor of holding the infant upside down by the legs. She slapped the wet, red little rump with the flat of her hand.

"So," said a senior warrior as the sound of the slap rang throughout the longhouse.

"Again," Toshabe whispered.

Naomi's heart seemed to stop. Why didn't the baby cry?

And then the sound of Beth's second slap was followed by a delightfully strong wail of protest from the baby.

An old woman chanted a prayer of thanksgiving in a quavering voice while Beth assisted Toshabe in cleaning the baby. Ena worked with the now-recumbent Ah-wa-o.

"It is a girl," Toshabe announced, holding the squalling child high. She glanced quickly at Naomi.

Beth wrapped the baby in a clean, warm, soft

blanket and handed her to El-i-chi, who handled the little bundle as if it might break. The child's wailing stopped.

"Ah, she knows her father," Beth said, smiling at him.

El-i-chi sat on the side of the bed and showed the baby to Ah-wa-o. "She is complete, Little Rose," he said.

"I praise the manitous," Ah-wa-o said.

El-i-chi rose, lifted the child high. "This is my daughter, Ah-wen-ga. She is Seneca, and she is named for the wife and mother of Seneca sachems. When she is old enough to understand, I will tell her the names of all of you who honored her at her birth."

There was a murmur of approval. One by one the onlookers came forward to admire the child, and then, once more, there was only family.

Ena embraced Beth. "So you have seen the birth now of two members of our family." She was recalling that Beth had been present at the birth of Summer Moon.

"I am grateful to have been allowed to help," Beth said.

"My flame-haired sister," Ena said, tightening the embrace.

Beth felt genuine pleasure. Never before had Ena called her sister. Never before had her husband's sister embraced her.

"We will tell our little Ah-wen-ga," Ah-wa-o said, "that it was her aunt Beth who spanked life into her."

It was the privilege of the father to tend the new one and the mother through the first night, which, as Beth and Naomi walked out of the longhouse, was waning. The moon had completed her journey, and there was only the glow of the lights in the sky to guide them.

"Well?" Beth asked when they were clear of the village. She was interested in hearing Naomi's reaction.

"At first I thought it was awful, shameless," the young woman said. "But when El-i-chi said that he would tell his daughter the names of all those who honored her at her birth, I began to understand."

"Nakedness, among the Indians, is not the evil it is considered to be by most of our people," Beth explained. "There's modesty enough in the villages. In the summer the young boys and girls use different swimming holes in the creek; but if there happens to be a spillover, no one takes much notice. And as for giving birth, the Seneca consider it to be a natural thing, a gift from the Master of Life, and, thus, an event of beauty."

The women had reached the creek. In the shadows it was difficult to see the stepping stones. Beth, more familiar than Naomi with the configuration, went first. Naomi's foot slipped, and her moccasin sank into frigid water. She let out a little yelp.

"Yes," Beth said, "it's cold, and it will be as cold tomorrow when El-i-chi, as shaman, dips his daughter in the creek during the water ceremony."

"Heavens, no!"

"Yes. It's similar to a baptism, but it has a different meaning." The women were back on terra firma. "The Seneca believe that water gives life and that introducing the newly born to it immediately protects them from evil, makes them strong, and prepares them for the hardships of life."

"My goodness, if they survive being dunked into ice water they have to be strong," Naomi said. "That poor little girl. Can't you stop them?"

"My dear, I wouldn't even try," Beth said. "My husband has spent his life in an effort to encourage change among the Seneca, to convince them that the days of roaming wide areas and hunting their meat are almost at an end. You see how little he has swayed them, and he's a strong man, a sachem, a direct descendant of the greatest Seneca sachems."

"Dunking that tiny thing seems like senseless cruelty."

As they gained the steps to the porch, Beth put her arm around Naomi. "Don't worry about little Ah-wen-ga. Babies are tough."

Upstairs, in her room, Naomi peeled off her wet moccasin and hose. Her foot was pink with cold. She sat in a rosewood slipper chair and rubbed warmth into her toes. As she finished undressing and put on her nightgown, she thought about the events of the night and decided that yes, it had been a beautiful thing, seeing a new life come into the world. And, in the warmth of her bed, as sleep crept over her, she wondered if she would ever give birth. During her year with the three Morgan men, there had been ample opportunity for her to conceive. Had her failure to do so been God's blessing, or was she, like Beth, barren?

"Little fool," she said to herself. "What does it matter? No decent man would ever want to marry you."

Chapter Six

As the *Orient* rounded the Cape of the Virgins on Argentina's southeastern coast, her sails were close hauled and her crew was exhausted from battling the constant storms. There, in the shelter of glowering, barren ridges rising from the cold, clear water, the ship found temporary relief from the roaring, westerly winds. A small, cold sun was a welcome change from the days of stormy darkness. Esther, bundled in furs and mittens, came out onto the deck.

Before the *Orient* began to be battered by the low-latitude storms, Little Hawk had become a student of the art of navigation. During the long, boring watches both Captain Davidson and First Mate Horace Wellman had worked with the young marine. The most difficult thing, Little Hawk had found, was bracing himself against the constant rolling and pitching of the ship in order to get an accurate sextant reading of the sun or, in the night, of certain stars. Now and

then, when he applied his sun and star sights to the
charts, he would find that he had put the ship within
five hundred miles of her position as calculated by
Davidson and Wellman.

The storms and the continuing leaden skies put
an end to his work with the sextant. As the *Orient*
made landfall on the Cape of the Virgins he learned
how to match the visible contours of a point of land
with the charts. After that lesson he decided that he was
not cut out to be a master mariner; he would leave
navigation to men like the captain and the first mate.
Indeed, Captain Davidson brought the ship safely into
the eastern entrance of the Strait of Magellan, a winding, treacherous passage between three hundred sixty
miles of rockbound shores that sometimes narrowed to
two miles.

Little Hawk's decision, however, did not prevent
him from studying the charts showing the crooks and
turns of the passage into which the Portuguese Fernão
de Magalhães had led five ships on October 21, 1520—
almost three hundred years prior to the *Orient*'s entry.
Magalhães, called Magellan by his patron, King Charles
I of Spain, had lost only two ships during the traverse,
and Little Hawk, studying the charts with great thor-
oughness, considered that to be a miracle.

The winds moderated. The *Orient* made her way
through wonderfully calm waters, her sails backing
and filling in the slight breezes. The sun warmed the
seamen as they scampered aloft to obey the bellowed
orders of the captain or the first mate. Esther fed bits
of stale biscuits to the birds that the seamen called
"stinkers." Horace Wellman told Little Hawk that
they were actually giant petrels. They were called
stinkers for two reasons: first, since they were scavengers of sea carrion, they carried with them a smell of
death. Secondly, if they were disturbed while on their
nests they spat a stinking, foul liquid at the intruder.
It delighted Esther when the big birds with their
heavy, tube-nosed beaks came driving down the wind
on stiffly held wings to seize a tidbit from her hand.

The *Orient* emerged into the Pacific, and the captain set a northward course to carry them along the coast of Chile. "Never," he said as the *Orient* sailed sedately into a rolling swell, "has a ship had a better passage through the strait."

The *Orient*'s luck ran out as the light began to fail. Darkness was hastened by the sudden rise of writhing, blue-black clouds, which hid the setting sun. A storm front raced toward the ship with a speed that caused even the seasoned sailors to watch the onslaught in awe. Clouds hid the emerging stars, and a thousand evil spirits howled and moaned in the rigging. Suddenly a wind like a moving wall hit the ship—a steady, roaring blast of hurricane strength. *Orient* creaked at all of her joints and heeled under the strain.

Davidson, thrown out of his chair at the table during the evening meal, struggled against the wild, erratic movements of the ship to join Horace Wellman on deck. Little Hawk was left to soothe Esther, who was frightened by the storm's explosive attack. It took Little Hawk over an hour to convince the girl that in spite of the violent rocking of the ship she had to go to sleep.

"I watch," Chin-Chin offered.

Esther was tucked into her bunk. The Chinaman had placed pillows under the front side of the mattress, raising it so that the child would not be thrown out as the *Orient* rolled.

Once his small friend was settled in, Little Hawk put on his weather gear and went out on deck. Wind-blown sleet like needles stung his face. In the roaring blackness a white-crested wave slammed into the bow quarter and sent tons of frigid water surging across the deck. He clung to the hatchway for his life, then made his way aft with great difficulty. A film of ice was forming on all exposed surfaces. The deck was constantly washed by the waves that thundered up from the awful darkness of the night to crash down onto the ship's port quarter. Horace Wellman was helping the steersman with the wheel. Davidson was shouting orders to seamen aloft who were clinging precariously to the rigging. He had to yell at the top of his voice to be heard over the wind.

"Mr. Hawk, sir," Wellman said, "I believe that you would find it more comfortable below."

"Is there anything I can do to help?" Little Hawk asked.

"If you insist on staying on deck," Wellman said, "then grab hold of the wheel. Do as the steersman says."

Little Hawk seized the spokes of the wheel with both hands and felt ice against his palms.The steersman's arms were straining. The wheel pulled hard as *Orient* quartered over a wave, and Little Hawk had to use all of his strength to help the steersman hold the rudder in the desired position.

"Mr. Wellman!" the captain bellowed.

"Aye, sir."

"We're going to have to come about and run with the storm," Davidson shouted.

"Aye, aye." Wellman leaped toward the midmast, pulling his way through a wash of white water to cling to the spar and shout his orders upward.

Davidson's decision made sense. Having just cleared the Strait of Magellan, the *Orient* was caught close to a rocky, desolate coast with both the storm winds and the prevailing currents pushing her eastward toward the rocks and disaster. To beat northward against the westerly storm had proven to be impossible. The only course of action was to run with the storm, steering to the west of south to gain open water for maneuvering room.

It was as if all of the winds of the world were being sucked down, down, into the Antarctic. The *Orient* bucked and struggled against the cutting, hurricane-force westerly winds. As the seaman fought to free the ice-bound rigging, they tore their fingers open. Canvas sails were frozen into iron-hard rolls that defied manipulation as the captain gave the orders that brought the *Orient*'s bow up into the howling wind. Now the sharp prow knifed into the oncoming rollers, and with each impact tons of water surged onto the ship's deck, immersing the first mate to his waist in swirling whiteness.

For long, terrifying moments the ship rolled in a trough between two great walls of water. Then her reefed sails filled with wind. There was a sharp report as the ice-shrouded canvas burst free of its frozen coating. Shards of ice showered the deck. The *Orient* flew before the winds with only enough sail to give steerage. Seamen fought their way to the stern and loosed a sea anchor, and soon the wild motion of the ship moderated slightly.

No man felt secure. Many times a ship had reached what seemed to be safety, well to the north of Cape Horn, only to be driven back. It had happened to Sir Frances Drake in 1578, when the *Golden Hind* was blown southward to below fifty-seven degrees latitude into the strait that was given his name, the Drake Passage. It was the most terrible of all seas, the wide stretch between the South Shetland Islands and Tierra del Fuego.

There terror and deadly peril begin with a wind that blows around the globe without hindrance, building waves that can circle the world without obstruction of shore or island. Nowhere else on Earth does the sea circle the globe unfettered. Chilled by ice-covered Antarctica, the winds reach the highest velocities known to man and create the Cape Horn Rollers, the graybeards that are one mile from crest to crest. The cold, heavy water stacks itself to heights of eighty to one hundred feet.

Day by day as the thundering winds from the west continued, the *Orient* was driven southward. She was running with the mountainous waves so that once every ninety seconds the small areas of sail she was carrying went slack as the wind was blocked by the towering wave building behind her. To look upward was to see a wall of gray. The icy water seemed to tower to the sky, from which it took its color. To look upward was to feel that soon the ship and all those aboard her were to be buried without hope under an

impossible weight of water; but then the *Orient* would
bestir herself, and with popping rigging and creaking
ribs she would soar upward, flying as if she had grown
wings. The crest of the wave would jerk her forward
at an immediate speed of thirty to fifty miles per hour.
Then, her sails filling, she would suddenly fall off the
crest and sink down into the deep trough, where nothing was visible but the walls of water to the fore and
aft and the leaden sky overhead.

On the seventh day, when it seemed that she was
to be driven all the way to the ice packs of the Antarctic Peninsula, the *Orient* lifted a tentative sail in a
lessening gale and began the long, arduous task of
beating northwestward against the winds and the cold
currents that moved southeastward past the southern
tip of South America. It had been impossible for Davidson to get an accurate sighting with the sextant.
But when a low, dark mass of land appeared to the
northeast, he studied it with his glass and said grimly,
"Well, Hawk, now you've seen Cape Horn herself."

The cape, contrary to Little Hawk's anticipation,
was not at all impressive. It was just a lump of low,
gray rock on the horizon.

Freezing rain helped to calm the agitated seas and
made life a misery for the mariners who climbed icy-
coated shrouds to battle the frozen sails. But little by
little, gaining ground on one tack, losing it on the
other, the *Orient* once again drew past Tierra del
Fuego and the gray cape to head northward.

Storms continued to beset them in the Roaring
Forties, but now the *Orient* had the Nazco current
to help her struggle northward. When the sun finally
reappeared, an air of elation grew among the crew, for
with each tack the ship was moving farther from the
Southern Sea. When the peaks of the Juan Fernández
Islands appeared, a spontaneous cheer went up.

Little Hawk went into Esther's cabin. The little
girl's strength had been sapped by the long weeks of
storm. Even when one is lying in bed the wild movements of a ship in a severe storm require the tensing

and relaxing of muscles. Moreover, damp, icy air had penetrated the cabins. Esther was running a fever. The dark circles under her eyes were more pronounced, and her eyes seemed to glow.

"You remember, don't you, my favorite cure for seasickness?" Little Hawk asked her.

"Yes," she said, attempting to smile. "Sit under a tree."

"Which you and I will be doing very, very soon," he said.

Her lips managed a little smile. "Land?"

"Your father says that the islands ahead have huge, beautiful trees and a lot of streams with waterfalls. We'll have fresh beef and pork. And Mr. Wellman says he'll have the boys gather palm cabbage so that we'll have fresh greens."

"Yum," Esther said, sitting up. "I want to see."

"Later," Little Hawk said. "We're still quite far out."

"Please?"

Little Hawk looked at Chin-Chin questioningly.

"You wrap her good in blanket," the Chinaman said. "She see."

"Agreed."

"You're smothering me," Esther complained as Little Hawk carried her out onto the deck. She freed one hand and moved the blanket away from her face. Little Hawk carried her to where the captain stood by the railing. Davidson held out his arms and accepted Esther's weight.

"The higher mountain is Más Afuera," he told them. "It's over five thousand feet high. We'll moor the ship in Cumberland Bay, on the north side."

"May we please go ashore?" Esther asked.

"I think that can be arranged," Davidson said, smiling fondly at his daughter. "Do you remember my reading to you Mr. Daniel Defoe's story about Robinson Crusoe?"

"Oh, yes," Esther said.

"The man who is thought to have been the pattern for Mr. Defoe's character spent four years alone on that island ahead of us."

Esther peered out of her blanket with interest, but lines of strain were appearing around her lips.

"All right, young lady," her father told her, "it's back to bed for you. After we are anchored in the bay we'll go ashore, you and Mr. Hawk and I."

When at last the ship was motionless on calm waters in Cumberland Bay, Little Hawk lowered Esther from the deck to a longboat. Chin-Chin took the child into his arms. The lush smell of growing vegetation seemed to invigorate her. She was able to walk a bit on shore. She was pleased into vibrant laughter by a flying host of colorful hummingbirds. She drank from a clear, cold spring and rinsed her face in the sparkling water.

The ship's foragers found no cattle but captured several goats and pigs. Goat meat, little Hawk found, was excellent, so long as those who prepared it knew what they were about. Cook explained that the goat's hair must never be allowed to touch any portion of the meat that is to be eaten. This is accomplished by carefully rolling back the goat's pelt as it is being removed.

Under way again, the ship well stocked with fresh water and provisions, the crew of the *Orient* warded off any hint of that dread mariners' disease, scurvy, by eating prodigious quantities of cabbage palm with stewed goat and fresh roasted ham. With favoring winds and the cold, Peru current adding its increment of motion to the *Orient*'s speed, Davidson decided to bypass the ports of Peru and drive straight toward the latitudes of Baja California. The next opportunity for taking on water or food would be in the lands to the north of Spain's possession in California. It would be a long haul, but there was no alternative—entering one of the Spanish ports in California would invite seizure of the ship and prison for all of those aboard her.

Ray Johnson had already lived longer than most men, especially those who had spent their years on the troubled frontier. The psalmist had said: *The days of our years are threescore years and ten; and if by reason of strength they be fourscore . . . it is soon cut off and we fly away.* King David—if, indeed, he had been the author of that particular psalm—had not lived in a raw, new country where, if a wild Indian didn't scalp you or a wild animal mangle you, there were the fever in all of its varieties and consumption and canker and half a dozen other ailments that could, at any moment, put the lie to a biblical life span.

The psalmist had also said: *We spent our years as a tale that is told.* Roy's tale had been a violent one, so he was very thankful for having been allowed to reach his sixty-fifth year and still be able to keep up with a young buck like Renno, who was a sprout of only forty-one.

True, Renno didn't hold to a fast warrior's pace as the men passed through Kentucky, but Roy suspected that Renno wouldn't have been all that eager to do so even if he'd been alone. When it came right down to it, there wasn't much urgency about getting to the Ohio. There were times when Roy wondered why they'd ever left the comfort of two pretty good homes and two damned fine women to go traipsing off through the woods, looking for a big-city galoot who was allegedly forming an army to go adventuring in Mexico. True, it was good to be out in God's great outdoors and to see a lot of new country. *But, hell,* Roy thought, *once you've seen one batch of woods, you've got a pretty good idea about the rest of 'em.* When you've seen the Ohio once, seeing it again doesn't change the fact that it's a wide, muddy old river that flows through a big country with only a few people living along the banks.

She was still there, the Ohio. There were scattered homesteads on the Kentucky and Virginia side, where Roy and Renno traveled. The Kentuckians were hospitable to the two traveling white men. They slept now and then in barns on a good bed of hay and had woman-cooked meals during which they asked

pertinent questions. The answers led them to believe
that no man in Kentucky had ever heard of Aaron
Burr or a new attempt to organize an army to march
down into Spanish territory. Some of the old–timers
remembered how George Rogers Clark and John Sevier used to spout such nonsense now and then; but
nothing had ever come of it before, and nothing would
come of it now.

Renno and Roy got their first direct information
about Aaron Burr from the crew of a flatboat drifting
down the Ohio toward St. Louis. The flatboat had
tied up for the night when the two travelers approached the camp, hailing it first, then exchanging a
couple of freshly killed turkeys for hot coffee and a
share of a pot of beans.

"Yes, sir, I hearn about this eastern feller wantin'
men fer an army," said the homespun-clad owner of
the flatboat. "You got a ways to go iffen you're bound
and determined to git up with him, though. I hearn
his army was gatherin' on what they call Blennerhassett Island, just below Marietta."

"Lord, Lord," Roy moaned, for Marietta was up
beyond the big bends of the Ohio.

"I notice you fellows didn't join up," Renno said.

The boatman laughed. "My mama didn't raise no
idiots."

The boatman's son, a strapping young fellow with
big, hard hands and a bemused expression, grinned,
spat tobacco juice, and said, "Reckon I'd a'jined up
iffen that Margaret Blennerhassett asked me."

"Wal, you was not even next in line there, boy,"
the boatman said.

"Ole Burr didn't look to me like he could put up
any kind of fight fer her," the boy said.

"Harmless. Kilt that feller Hamilton dead, that's
all," the boatman said sarcastically.

Roy asked, "This Margaret you're talking about—
she's the wife of this feller they named the island after?"

"Yep. She's a pip. And they calls the island after
Blennerhassett 'cause he owns it lock, stock, and bar-

rel. Got armed guards to keep off the riffraff. He's older than his wife, somewhere between you too." He looked at Roy, then Renno. "Wife's a pretty little thing. Sings like a bird. Occasionally we'uns ties up on the south end of his island fer the night. Ole Blennerhassett, he don't like it none. But we kin hear that woman singin' all the way down from his house—songs from the old country."

Roy was finding it interesting to hear the gossip about Blennerhassett's pretty wife, but he was more concerned about other things. "This army," he said. "Any sign of it?"

"Not so's you could tell it," the boatman said.

Two days later Renno and Roy swam the river, pushing their kits ahead of them on little rafts. The river bent back to the south upstream from the point where they had landed.

"Renno, dadgum it, I'm just about ready to find me a big log, push it into the river, and start floating back toward home."

"Don't tempt me," Renno said with a grin.

The way to the northeast led through virgin wilderness. Renno had been in the Ohio Territory before, of course, but it was such a wide stretch of country that until he saw the burial mounds rising before him he had no idea he was traveling familiar ground. The hair on the back of his neck prickled, for he realized that he had stumbled upon the sacred site of the ancient ones. In this place, in a hollow formed by the coils of a great serpent, he fought against the evil Seneca shaman, Hodano.

Roy and Renno camped there for the night, and the sachem retold the details of the fight, about Hodano's spirit monsters, and how it had ended. Roy walked the great, long mound and got a sense of the extent of the earthen construction. Renno could tell that he was impressed.

A meeting with another Ohio River flatboat gave them the news that rough-looking men armed with long rifles were gathering on Blennerhassett Island.

"Still want to go home?" Renno asked.

"Since we've come this far, I suppose I ought to have a look at this here little Irish girl," Roy said. "Maybe she can cook better than you."

North of the Tropic of Cancer, where the great, whirling storms come bellowing out of the Mexican jungles to go spinning off into the emptiness of the Pacific, the *Orient* lazed along on a balmy wind with all sails set. Little Hawk had carried Esther out onto the deck, where she sat on a blanket and watched the blowings of a great, gray whale. The whale was pacing the slow-moving ship, showing his great hump now and again and sending spumes of spray into the air from his blowhole.

"Mr. Hawk," Esther quavered, "make it go away."

Little Hawk sat down beside the pale child and put his arm around her protectively. "Honey, it's a little bit bigger than I am, and I don't speak its language."

"You could shoot it with your rifle."

"Well, I don't ordinarily shoot something unless I am going to eat it," he said.

She shuddered. He frowned, upset with himself for having mentioned eating. She still believed that a whale had eaten her mother's body when it was consigned to the sea.

"Tell you what," he said. "I'll do an old Seneca stomp dance that was designed to keep bears away. You never can tell—it just might keep whales away."

"Yes, do," she said.

He pranced around her blanket and chanted a little song of spring and hope.

"If that there is a rain dance, you can stop it," a crewman yelled.

"You hush," Esther called out in a weak, shrill voice. "Mr. Hawk is making a dance to scare the whale away."

Curious seamen gathered round. Little Hawk was feeling more and more foolish, but he broke into a dance from the False Faces ceremony and sang a winter song designed to drive away the spirits of evil.

"It's going, it's going!" Esther cried out.

And, sure enough, the big, gray whale had turned and was rushing away from the gracefully dipping ship at full speed.

"Any comments, gentlemen?" Little Hawk asked with a grin. "If you ever want any whales chased away, don't hesitate to call on me."

"You are wonderful, Mr. Hawk," Esther cried as Little Hawk sat down beside her. A fit of coughing came over her.

Little Hawk reached quickly for a handkerchief and held it to her mouth. When she subsided and lay back weakly, the handkerchief was flecked with blood. His heart lurched when he saw it.

A shadow fell over the deck, bringing with it a touch of coolness. Little Hawk looked up. A small, black cloud neatly covered the sun.

"Time for a rest?" he asked.

"Not yet, please," she begged, clinging to his hand. "It's so stuffy in the cabin."

"Well, soon we'll be back on land," Little Hawk said, "and while your father is trading with the Indians, you and I will build a house. Then you'll be able to sleep on solid land and have the breeze blow right through the open windows."

"Will you, really?"

"What did I say?" Little Hawk asked with mock severity.

"You said—"

"Yes, I know." He drew himself up, crossed his arms, and fancied his face to be as stern as that of old Ghonka. "Injun never lie to little white squaw."

"I don't think you're really an Indian," she said.

He gave the cry of a hunting hawk, answered with the roar of a great bear looking for a fight. "Can *you* speak like the hawk, like the bear?"

She shook her head.

"Can any white man you know make the call of the wolf?" He lifted his head and howled.

She giggled with delight.

"Of course not, for they are not Indian."

But the laughter caused her to cough again. When the spasm was over, she made no protest as he carried her to her bed.

Once again the longitudinal position of the *Orient* was expressed in the forties, but the north forties were, at least at first, a far cry from the Roaring Forties of the south. The Pacific was living up to the name given to it by Magellan. The ship rocked northward on a quartering sea with a wind at her stern. Micah Davidson left the running of the ship to the first mate and spent his time with his weakening daughter in the cabin. She could not control her coughing, and she was having difficulty breathing. Each racking, painful spasm bloodied a cloth held to her lips.

Little Hawk helped Chin-Chin carry two trays of food to the cabin—one for Esther, one for Davidson. Neither of them was hungry. The child's thin, ravaged little face burned with fever. The grief in Micah Davidson's reddened eyes made Little Hawk feel bereft.

"Mr. Hawk," Esther whispered.

He bent over her. "I'm here, honey."

"I won't be able to walk with you anymore."

"Oh, but you will," Little Hawk said quickly. "You'll be well again before you know it."

"Chest . . . hurts," she whispered. Her eyes closed, then she was still.

Little Hawk took a deep, shuddering breath. Micah Davidson leaped to his side and looked down at the quiet face. The eyelids were sooty, almost black.

"Well, she's with her mother," the captain whispered.

Little Hawk wanted to strike out at something. He longed to have his tomahawk in his hand and Death, that evil who would steal a precious seven-year-old girl, before him to suffer the blow.

Davidson put out his hand and smoothed Esther's hair. "Stay with her? I have to be alone."

"Of course," Little Hawk said.

Alone with her he prayed. He prayed to the Master of Life, but Esther was not Indian. She would not go to the Place across the River. So he prayed to his mother's God, to Esther's God. The prayer eased his spirit, and he was feeling calmer when Captain Davidson returned.

Chin-Chin came into the cabin behind the captain. He, too, had been weeping. "Chin-Chin will prepare her," Davidson said.

Little Hawk came to his feet and looked into the captain's eyes. "She feared being buried at sea."

"I know," Davidson said. He put his hand on Little Hawk's shoulder. "It's all right."

Little Hawk wanted to join Chin-Chin in weeping. They were days, perhaps weeks from landfall. There was no way of keeping a dead body aboard the ship. She would have to go into the water, and the thought of it was more than he could bear. "We can't—" he said brokenly. "We can't—"

"It's all right," Davidson said, turning away. "The whales will not have her."

Services were held on the open deck. It was a perfect day, warm and sunny. A small breeze kept the ship loafing along on her course. The way Davidson handled the funeral service showed that he had buried others at sea. His voice was steady until the very end. The crew sang a hymn and then dispersed to gather in small groups, where they talked in low voices. They stole glances now and then at the little girl in her best dress, laid out with her hands folded over her thin chest.

"Will you please help me, Mr. Hawk?" Davidson asked.

"Yes, surely."

To Little Hawk's puzzlement they carried her to the carpenter's shop, a little room below the decks, where a rum cask sat in the middle of the deck. The ship's carpenter stood beside the cask. He had removed the top. The cask was half-full. The dark, aro-

matic rum sloshed back and forth with the gentle
rocking of the ship.

"Cap'n, if I may speak?" said the carpenter.

"Not now," Davidson said brusquely.

"Sir, it ain't right."

Davidson gave the carpenter a withering look.

"I'm bound to speak, sir," the carpenter said.
"Some of the men said it was bad luck, having a girl-
child on board in the first place, sir. But to have a
corpse—"

"I will not give her to the sea," Davidson said.

"If I may say something?" Little Hawk asked.

"Of course." The captain nodded.

The Seneca turned to the carpenter. "Once, my
father had to return the body of a dear friend to his
homeland for burial according to that man's beliefs.
His body was also stored in a cask. No harm came to
the ship or the crew. In fact, if you're a religious
man"—the carpenter drew himself up and nodded a
vigorous response—"you might say the ship enjoyed
some special protection. After all, the crew willingly
set aside a superstition out of respect for the man's
religious beliefs. Can we not do the same for an innocent child?"

Subdued, the carpenter agreed. "I'll spread the
word."

With her knees up in a fetal position, Esther was
lowered into the cask. The rum that was displaced by
her weight swirled and covered her head. The carpenter poured more rum into the open cask until it was
full. The top was put on, an iron hoop pounded into
place. Hot wax sealed the lid, and the three men ma-
neuvered the heavy cask into a corner of the carpenter's
shop, where it was lashed securely.

When Margaret Farrell, at the age of fifteen, married Harman Blennerhassett in Dublin, everyone agreed
it was a splendid match for her. He was much older
than she, but he had more than twice as much money
as all of the Farrell clan put together. Everyone was

certain that young Margaret would have a good life.
No one, including Margaret, expected Harman Blen-
nerhasset to sell everything he owned in Dublin and
move to the New World.

So it was that Margaret was still a young woman
when she found herself enisled, literally, in the middle of a muddy river miles from the nearest point of
what the Americans, in their naïve isolation, called
civilization.

Blennerhassett had enough money to make almost anything possible, so Margaret was not surprised
when her husband had all of the comforts of gracious
living shipped downriver to his island. Some goods
came all the way from London. He imported masons
from Philadelphia and carpenters from Pittsburgh to
build a manor house that would have done credit to
the old sod. Ornate and comfortable furniture was
floated on rafts and flatboats down the Ohio. Hired
hands worked the soil of the island to put new potatoes and other fresh vegetables on the table. The
kitchen staff could butcher a cow or a pig in the morning and have roasted beef or baked ham for the evening meal.

Many women would have envied Margaret. She
had only to ask, and a selection of dresses would be
sent to her from Marietta and Pittsburgh. More time
was needed to fulfill her desires than, say, a woman
living in a more conventional location, but anything
she wanted could be brought to her by ship, wagon,
and flatboat from the merchants of Baltimore, New
York, or London. Margaret was given a free hand in
running the Blennerhassett household, for Harman
was consumed by his own work. Just exactly what
constituted Harman's "work" was difficult for Margaret to explain.

"Well, you see," she told her husband's elegant
friend, Mr. Aaron Burr, "it has to do with, ah, *experiments* . . . with chemicals and all? . . ."

Blennerhassett had installed a complete laboratory in one wing of the house. He spent most of his

time there, often working far into the night to create,
it seemed to Margaret, nothing more than foul smells
and odd stains on his clothing. The stains often de-
voured cloth to leave a gaping hole in a perfectly good
pair of trousers or a shirt.

"Your husband, madam," Burr said, "is a vision-
ary, just as I am."

Margaret was small of waist and large of bosom.
She was a pretty little Irish wren, black-haired, black-
eyed. Her lips needed no coloring agent. Her cheeks
glowed with a rose-cream softness. She was lonely. It
pleased her to bring out the finest Irish crystal, the
best English china, and the snowiest linens, for it was
obvious that Mr. Aaron Burr was a gentleman.

She couldn't imagine what Burr and her husband
had in common, for their conversations were held in
privacy. She knew only that they had to do with some
venture in the Southwest and that her husband was so
taken with Burr's enthusiasm, he handed over large
amounts of money to Mr. Burr during his frequent
visits. None of that concerned Margaret. She was just
very happy that Aaron and her husband had business
together, for although Burr was the perfect gentleman
as long as he was dressed, he was a playful rogue
when he joined Margaret in her bedroom while her
husband bent over his experiments in the laboratory.

If Harman Blennerhassett had plied his marital
chores as diligently as he applied himself to his chemicals, perhaps Margaret would not have been so bedazzled with the charming eastern gentleman and would
not have teased Burr into her bed. If Aaron Burr had
been as dedicated to his goal as to his pleasures, he
would have resisted the charms of the young Irish-
woman. If Harman had not stung his eyes with acid
fumes, so that he had to quit his work early one evening, he would not have scared all desire for Margaret's creamy flesh out of Aaron Burr by entering his
wife's bedroom by one door just as Aaron, clothing
gathered in his shaking arms, dashed out the other.
But Harman did spill acid, and the fumes did sting his

eyes even after he rinsed them repeatedly with cold water; and Harman did walk into the bedroom to find his wife flushed and flustered. After that near brush with disaster, Burr told his little Irish love that it would be best if they paid homage to honor and stoutly resisted the call of the flesh.

Unfortunately, Margaret could not have agreed less. The dashing easterner had brought excitement into her life. Her youthful body, which had flowered under the sporadic ministrations of her husband in the early years of their marriage, had been sadly neglected. She found glorious fruition in Burr's arms, for he—although he was no youth—had youthful élan.

She pouted. She flirted openly with Burr, causing him to pale with apprehension. Incredibly, Blennerhassett, lost in his scientific dabblings and the dreams of power and empire that he shared with the dazzling Burr, seemed not to notice. Doubly neglected, second in the affections of both her husband and her lover, Margaret looked around at the men who were gathering on the island. She saw not one that she would want to be within ten feet of her, much less in her bed.

But she promised herself that as soon as a man who met her specifications appeared on the island, she would bring him to her bed. He would need to be clean, of course, and not old. She closed her eyes and fantasized. Her dream lover materialized in her imagination. He was at the zenith of his manhood, blond, beautifully built, and quite polished. He spoke with an English accent and had sparkling blue eyes. He was, she decided, a sylvan Adonis. And he was all hers.

Chapter Seven

Captain Micah Davidson locked himself in his cabin with his grief as the *Orient* sailed northward with Horace Wellman in command. For a period of three days the first mate attempted to rouse the captain, and Cook tried to deliver food. But these gestures were acknowledged by a gruff order from behind the closed door to go away.

"It is natural for a man to love his daughter," Wellman said to Little Hawk at the beginning of the fourth day of the captain's self-imposed isolation. "But I'm beginning to wonder if he isn't allowing his grief to weigh on him too heavily."

Two things concerned Wellman. The most immediate was the weather. The ship was pounding along with her sails canted before a stiff, northwest wind that had been increasing since dawn. The thin and watery sun glowed through a thick haze reaching all the way to the eastern horizon. Wellman decided to send men aloft to take in canvas as the force of the wind threatened to build to a half gale. Fortunately, the *Orient* was still a tight ship, even though she had come thousands of miles and her time in tropical waters had allowed the growth of grass and barnacles on her hull. She liked to fly before a shouting wind, but the western sky was piled high with dark clouds that promised too much of a good thing. Wellman had never sailed the Pacific, but he'd seen the same kind of sky at the same northern latitudes in the Atlantic. He figured the storms of the northern Pacific would be just as severe as the winds that raged down from the Arctic in the northern Atlantic. He did not doubt his ability to handle the ship, but it was, after all, the captain's responsibility.

In Wellman's opinion Davidson was neglecting a second responsibility. He was allowing his black grief to blind him to the fact that the crew was more than a little disturbed by the continued presence of a dead body on board the ship. In spite of the carpenter's and Little Hawk's assurances that corpses had been transported before with no repercussions, sailors crossed themselves every time they had to pass the carpenter's shop where little Esther's body was preserved in a keg of rum. Some of the crew were being shamefully petty about that rum, saying that, by God and by gum, it was in their papers that the ship furnish them their dram of grog at specified times and how, by gor, was that to be done if they ran out of rum because of the captain's odd way of treating his dead?

The begrudging complaints about the cask of rum did not bother the first mate. What he didn't like was the sullen silence that greeted him when he walked among the men on the deck. True, they obeyed their orders smartly. They were all good men. Those who had been a bit green at the beginning of the voyage had by now been thoroughly trained in the ways of the sea during the long reach down the eastern coast of South America and hardened in the freezing, iron cold of the Southern Sea. But men of the sea are a

superstitious lot. They had submerged their dread of
having a woman on the ship, for some of the older
ones had sailed with Davidson when he had both his
wife and his daughter living aboard; but they could
not overcome their dread of keeping the dead girl
among them in a totally unnatural way.

It was bad luck . . . bad luck . . . bad luck. When
a person died at sea he or she was supposed to be
sewed into an old piece of sail and consigned to the
deep with due and proper ceremony followed by a
hymn or two.

" 'e damn well pickled 'er," said a former member of His Majesty's Royal Navy. "Oi never 'eard o'
such a thing."

By midday the *Orient* was hard put to keep to
her course. A gale that reminded the men of the ordeal they'd barely survived in the Drake Passage
shifted into the southeast and sent the ship scudding
forward with only a minute amount of canvas spread
for steerage.

The *Orient*'s destination on the western coast of
the continent was the mouth of the river that had been
named by Captain Robert Gray in 1792. Gray, a Boston man like the first mate of the *Orient,* called the
river the Columbia, after his ship. The charts that
Horace Wellman consulted had been compiled from
several sources, including Gray's own notations, but
were based on Spanish charts that were disturbingly
out-of-date. Wellman's last accurate position had put
the *Orient* above forty-five degrees north latitude, and
she'd been driving to the northeast, feeling her way
toward landfall for days before the storm. So Wellman
found himself on a ship being driven northeastward
toward an unknown shore by raging winds and mountainous, cold-water seas. He sent men aloft and ordered a change of course to the northward. The action
meant hard work and danger for the men, for now
the ship was no longer running before the wind with
a sea anchor in trail. Instead she was bucking the big,
white-topped rollers on the quarter. There was no

grumbling, though, for each man realized that the ship's safety and his own life depended upon the first mate's judgment and the crew's obedience to orders. Even if some sailors entertained mutinous thoughts, no man had ever taken time out in the middle of a howling storm to rise up against a ship's officer.

The storm ended with a startling suddenness. The winds fled past, leaving the *Orient* rolling in waves that were now smooth atop. Dawn brought a cheery, blazing sun and bonny skies. The temperature was cold, crisp. And to the east lay a densely forested coastline.

"So," Wellman said, allowing himself the luxury of a smile, "will they call that bad luck?"

A sighting told him that the storm had blown the ship past the latitude of the mouth of the Columbia. "Way I figure it," he said to Little Hawk, "that's Vancouver Island. If I'm right, we're north of Juan de Fuca Strait." He called out orders, and the men were streaming aloft, preparing to come about.

Captain Davidson came out on deck. His eyes were sunken in black circles. His face looked thin. In the crisp, fresh morning air there was a stench of neglect about him. "What land, Mr. Mate?" he asked.

"Vancouver Island, sir. I'm preparing to come about to set a course to the south."

"We will enter Juan de Fuca Strait, Mr. Mate," Davidson said, "and find a suitable mooring spot. Please give your orders accordingly."

"Aye, aye," Wellman said. He bellowed out the orders. A cheer went up from the men on hearing that they were soon to be walking on God's own solid earth. Wellman grinned and winked at Little Hawk.

"Does this mean that we will·be long delayed in reaching the mouth of the Columbia, sir?" Little Hawk asked.

"Not long, Hawk," Davidson said. "Not long."

The *Orient* dropped anchor below a magnificently wooded slope. Pines and firs reached toward the sky. The men pointed toward a small, rocky beach. A wa-

terfall showed whitely among the trees to indicate a
source of sweet, fresh water.

"I would guess, Mr. Wellman, that a man could
bag a deer or two without much effort," Little Hawk
said.

"Have at it, Mr. Hawk," Wellman encouraged.
"Fresh meat will be very welcome."

"If it's all right I'll take along a couple of men to
help me carry," Little Hawk said.

Wellman chuckled. "I do admire optimism. Of
course, take your choice."

Little Hawk picked two of the younger men. They
clambered into a longboat almost filled with water
casks and were rowed ashore. Each man carried a
rifle. Little Hawk led them to the stream that poured
down from the heights, and walking along the water's
margin, they entered the forest. He saw deer tracks
immediately, but the two sailors were making enough
noise to scare away every animal within five miles. He
seated them on rocks beside the stream and told them
to be absolutely quiet until they heard him fire. He
took two rifles, one in each hand, and picked his way
silently upstream.

In a fern-filled glade he saw four deer, two prong-
horn young stags and two does. He dropped one stag
with a neat shot to the heart, discarded the empty
rifle, then sighted the second weapon in time to drop
the other stag in midleap just as it was about to reach
safety among the trees. The Seneca sat down to wait
for the two sailors. While he waited he reloaded his
two rifles. He figured that he'd send the men back to
the ship with the deer and go get one more.

The snap of a twig behind him froze him. He
eased a rifle into position and turned slowly. Four
warriors dressed in skins and furs came into view. On
their heads were odd, pointed caps. Each had his bow
in hand, with an arrow notched and ready.

Slowly Little Hawk lifted his right hand, palm out
in the universal sign of peaceful greeting. He spoke
first in English. The broad, dark faces remained pas-

sive. He tried Spanish, saying, "I come as a friend. My companions and I are hungry for the sweet, red meat of the deer. I petition you for permission to hunt on your grounds."

"You hunted before you asked for permission," said the largest of the men in heavily accented Spanish.

"For which I beg your indulgence," Little Hawk apologized. "My chief aboard the big ship, where there are many rifles, will reward you in return for the meat."

One of the warriors lifted his bow and put tension into the bowstring. He spoke in a language that Little Hawk did not understand. Little Hawk prepared himself to leap aside and to kill the largest Indian with the rifle before drawing his tomahawk.

"I am Youbou," the war chief said. "You may have one opportunity to defend yourself."

Little Hawk started. He had seen the warrior's lips move, but the comprehensible words had not come from the Indian facing him, but had echoed from within his own head and in the spirit voice of his mother, Emily.

Davidson's reason for seeking the first available landing site was quickly made evident. He wanted to bury his daughter. He gathered a work party and had a boat lowered. Six strong men were needed to manhandle the heavy cask out of the carpenter's shop. A hoist was rigged to lower the burden carefully into the longboat.

Davidson chose a place on a little rise of land just beyond the rocky beach. The work party dug and chopped through a layer of roots and peat into gravel-rich soil. As the digging became more difficult, other members of the crew came ashore. The party that had been filling water casks joined the grouping.

" 'e ain't diggin' no grave for a little girl," said the man who had deserted the Royal Navy.

Davidson had laid out the hole to be square, measuring about four feet to a side.

"Reckon he's goin' to leave her in the barrel," said a grizzled old salt who, although he wouldn't have admitted it, sadly remembered the days when Mrs. Davidson was alive and Esther was only a toddler.

"It ain't Christian," another sailor grumbled. "It just ain't Christian."

"*You* want to see how she looks after being pickled?" the old man challenged.

The difficulty of the digging forced Davidson to abandon his plan to have at least four feet of good, solid earth atop the cask. Men attached ropes and lowered the cask into the hole. It rested in its upright position. Davidson crumbled a clod of soil in his hand and let it rain down onto the wooden top of the barrel. He nodded grimly, and the men pushed dirt into the hole and packed it down. Davidson worked with them to cover the mound with stones. That done, he opened his Book of Common Prayer and read the solemn funeral service in a strong, clear voice, which reached across the water to the deck watch aboard the *Orient* . . . and up the slope into the trees where a half-dozen Indian warriors wearing odd, pointed caps watched in puzzlement to see the white men bury an entire barrel of *aguardiente de caña*, the strong spirit of the sweet cane.

Renno and Roy had been ferried to Blennerhassett Island in a dugout canoe by a Shawnee boy who handled the crude boat well in the strong currents. A few men in ragged homespun and faded buckskin were lounging around the dock. They looked with idle curiosity at the newcomers. Renno handed the boatman a piece of silver. The boy made no effort to express thanks, nor did his expression change. He simply pushed his canoe away from the dock and was gone.

"Howdy, boys," Roy Johnson said, sweeping the coonskin hat off his head and making a mock bow.

One or two of the men mumbled a return greeting.

"I take it," Roy said, "that none of you is Mr. Aaron Burr or Mr. Blennerhassett."

"You taken it right," a bearded bear of a man said, showing his teeth in a grin. "You're a right smart feller."

"Just where might I find one of the aforementioned gentlemen?" Roy asked.

"Wall," the big, bearded man said, rising to stand at a height of well over six feet, "that depends on who wants to know."

"I'm not sure the question is important," Roy said, standing up to the challenge. "That is, if you object to my asking."

"That way," Renno said, pointing to a well-beaten path leading toward the interior of the island.

Roy took a couple of steps, only to find his way blocked by the big man.

"Where yawl think you goin'?" the bear asked.

"Well, we thought we'd go find Mr. Burr or Mr. Blennerhassett for our own selves," Roy said, "since you don't seem to be inclined to help us out."

The big man weighed in, Renno estimated, at about two hundred and seventy-five pounds. His thighs bulged against his buckskin trousers. His fists were the size of small melons.

"You wanta talk, you talk to Hoss Beaver," the man said.

"That be a man or a varmint?" Roy asked, for by now he was feeling a trifle put out by the bearded bear.

As the giant drew back to strike Roy, his clublike hand moved in what seemed to Renno to be slow motion. The sachem reached for his tomahawk and was reaching to pull Roy aside with his other hand. But before Renno could do so, Roy brought the butt of his musket up from his knee and buried it into Hoss Beaver's crotch. The big man screamed like a wounded panther, went down on his knees, and held his throbbing masculine valuables in both hands.

"If I were you," Roy said, "I'd either work on being a mite quicker, or I'd act more polite to strangers."

Renno showed his blade, brightly polished, the edge razor sharp, to two men who immediately lost any inclination they had of getting in on the action. Hoss Beaver rolled onto his side, knees up.

"You'll be all right in a few minutes," Roy drawled, stepping around him. "I didn't hit you hard enough to bust 'em."

"You're getting right mean in your old age," Renno said as they walked up the pathway.

"Well, now and then I just get tired of living in a world with no manners," Roy said.

Renno chuckled. "I'll remember that."

Ahead the underbrush opened up into a wide, green area beyond which were a low stone wall, a formal garden, and a house that rose three stories high and spread out over what looked to be about half an acre.

"My God," Roy breathed, "it's bigger than Huntington Castle."

Renno, too, was impressed, for he had not expected a stone-built English manor house on an island in the Ohio River. The formal garden was well tended. There was a large brass knocker on the thick, front door. A servant in livery looked out at them as the door opened.

"You men are not to come to the house," the servant said.

"What would you suggest, then," Roy asked, "when we want to see the big cheese around here?"

"If you mean Mr. Blennerhassett," the servant said firmly, "he will see you in the quarters when he has finished with his day's work."

The man started to close the door. Roy put out his hand. The servant strained. Roy seemed to be quite relaxed, but the door stayed open.

"Sonny," Roy said, "we have come a long way. Now you lower your nose and go get the mister, or I'm going to see about rearranging your face."

"What is it, Sean?" a female voice asked.

"Some of Mr. Burr's hooligans, ma'am," the servant sniffed.

A beautiful woman had pulled the servant aside and stood in the door. She was wearing a simple white gown without petticoats to expand its skirts. A sash was cinched tightly to emphasize her small waist. A lace yoke was rounded outward by her generous breasts.

Roy removed his cap. Her eyes swept over him quickly, dismissively, but lingered and widened on the bronzed face of the man standing at his side. "And you are?" she asked.

"I am Colonel Roy Johnson of Tennessee. This is my son, Renno."

"Renno?" She cocked her head and examined Renno from his moccasined feet to his tousled blond hair. "Renno Johnson, is it?"

Renno nodded. He didn't want to waste time explaining his relationship to Roy.

"We'd like to see Mr. Burr," Roy said.

"Mr. Burr is away," the young woman said. "Are you here to join Mr. Burr's army?"

"That's the idea, ma'am," Roy said.

"Please come in," she said, surprising her servant. It was obvious from Sean's expression that Mr. Burr's hooligans were *never* allowed in the house. "I am Margaret Blennerhassett."

"Pleased to meet you, ma'am," Roy said, while Renno inclined his head but said nothing.

"I'm sure you're thirsty," Margaret said, her eyes on Renno.

"A swig or two of something with a little fire in it wouldn't be bad," Roy allowed.

Margaret, laughing, led them into a formal parlor and indicated chairs. "Now tell me why you came all the way from Tennessee to join us."

"Well, we heard that Mr. Burr was actually going to accomplish something, where others have just been talking about it for years," Roy said.

"I believe that Mr. Burr has promised that all of those who fight with him will be given grants of land," Margaret said.

"That's what we heard," Roy confirmed.

She went to a table, poured two glasses half full of brandy, swayed to extend them. Roy took his eagerly.

"Thank you, no," Renno said.

"You're English?"

"I am Seneca," Renno said.

"You speak English beautifully."

"Thank you."

"You don't care for brandy?"

"No, thank you." The woman made him uneasy, and under such circumstances he tended to become very Indian, stiff, formal, speaking in as few words as possible.

"Well," she said. She extended her glass. Roy tapped his glass against it. "Cheers."

"When do you expect Mr. Burr?" Renno asked.

Margaret smiled. "You've only just arrived. Are you so eager to leave our island?"

"*I* could get to like it here," Roy said after sipping the good, French brandy.

"I imagine that Mr. Burr will return within the week," Margaret said. "In the meantime, Mister, ah—?"

"My name is Renno."

"In the meantime, Mr. Renno, I want to hear all about you." She glanced at Roy. "And your father, of course."

"Renno, here, is a war chief of the Seneca," Roy said enthusiastically. He was obviously aware of and amused by Renno's discomfort.

"How very interesting," she said. "But—"

"Yep, he's mostly white," Roy said.

"But aren't the Seneca northern Indians?" Margaret asked.

"It's a long story," Renno said.

Margaret seemed to accept that. "I do believe that Cook has prepared chicken and pastry for the evening meal. You can tell me your long story then. Six o'clock sharp, please."

The men had walked away from the impressive manor house toward a conglomeration of sheds, lean-tos, and tents on the southern tip of the island. "I believe the little gal took a shine to you, Son," Roy said. "If I were you, I'd remember that she has a husband."

Renno pretended not to hear. Roy was still chuckling as they walked out of a clump of underbrush and into a cleared area around the makeshift quarters of Aaron Burr's army.

"Pretty sorry accommodations," Roy said, looking around. "I'd prefer to make camp in the woods."

"Isn't that a friend of yours?" Renno asked as Hoss Beaver, looking big enough to be two bears in one hide, stepped out from behind a shack.

"Old man," Beaver said, his voice rumbling deep in his chest, "you almost ruined me."

"Well, don't press your luck," Roy warned.

"What I want you to do," Beaver said, "is put down that rifle of yours, and then you and me is goin' to have a little talk."

"Take it up with my bodyguard," Roy said, jerking a thumb at Renno. "He handles my small chores."

"Huh?" Beaver looked puzzled.

"Renno, here, says he can handle you with one hand tied behind his back," Roy said.

"My business ain't with him," Beaver said.

"I told you," Roy said patiently, "that Renno handles the small stuff for me. Now don't bother me anymore, Hoss."

"His business isn't with me," Renno said, paying Roy back for his behavior at the Blennerhassett home.

"You ain't gonna fight me, old man?"

"You don't catch on too quick, do you?" Roy asked. He winked at Renno. "Son, if we're gonna get any rest at all before we join that pretty little gal for supper, I reckon you're going to have to talk to Mr. Beaver."

Hoss Beaver had attracted an audience. About two dozen men were gathered behind the big man.

Renno sighed and stepped forward. "I would guess, Mr. Beaver, that you're the head knocker around here."

" 'at's right, boy," Beaver said, smirking.

"If I ask you kindly to step aside, to let my feeble old father and me pass so that we can find quarters and rest a bit, would you agree?"

Renno's soft voice and clearly enunciated words puzzled the big man. "Huh?"

"I'm asking you, Mr. Beaver, to forget the little disagreement you had with my father."

"Oh," Beaver said, touching his crotch gingerly. His face darkened as understanding dawned. "Reckon I can't do that."

"Too bad," Renno said. He turned to hand his rifle, bow, and quiver to Roy.

"You aim to use that there tomahawk?" Beaver asked.

"No, I won't need it," Renno said, handing that weapon, too, to Roy. "Are you sure, Mr. Beaver, that you wouldn't like to shake hands and be friends?"

"You can be my friend after I tromp on you," Beaver said, winding up for a haymaker with such obvious crouchings and tensing and movements of his big arms that Renno had all the time in the world to dance in and lance two blows to Beaver's chin that would have felled most men. Beaver's huge fist whizzed past Renno's nose. The sachem knew that he would be in big trouble if Hoss managed to land a blow from that fist. Renno laced a right and left into the big man's middle and was rewarded by a pained and surprised grunt.

"You've let yourself get soft, Mr. Beaver," Renno said. "After you finish tromping on me, I'll be glad to show you how to get rid of that soft belly, if you care to."

"Huh?"

"But in the meantime—" Renno stepped past a ponderous swing of Beaver's arm to pound the belly, then, before dancing away, he landed a painful blow to Beaver's left kidney.

Beaver gasped. "Stand still, dang you!"

"We can quit right now, as far as I'm concerned," Renno said.

"Huh?"

Renno tried the big man's chin again, but to no effect. It was like throwing his fists against a stone. He feared that he had smashed at least two knuckles. He went back to the midsection, and after a while Beaver was gasping and bent over as he tried to catch the more agile man with one of his sledgehammer fists.

"Hoss," Roy called out, "I'm getting a little worried about you. If you don't tell my boy you've had enough, I'm afraid he's gonna do some permanent damage to your innards. Now, we don't want that to happen, so why don't you and Renno just shake hands and call it quits?"

"Huh?"

"Oh, hell," Roy said, stepping forward. "Don't hit him anymore, Renno."

The sachem backed away.

"Good," Beaver said. "Now I *will* tromp on you a little."

"Oh, well," Roy said, resigned, then kicked the big man in the groin and also stepped back as Beaver toppled.

"You did it again," Beaver moaned, holding himself.

"Better you be a little sore in the privates than have your guts busted," Roy said. "You'll thank me, once you've thought it over."

Roy stepped over Beaver's legs and turned. "Coming, Son?" And as they walked through the crowd toward what seemed to be an unoccupied lean-to, Roy put his hand on Renno's shoulder. "You done good, boy."

Renno laughed. "We didn't make any friends back there."

"Oh, I don't know. . . . What is friendship? It's based on respect, and I'd guess that those who saw you in action have got a lot of respect for you now."

Margaret Blennerhassett had changed for dinner. Her raven black hair was piled atop her head. She still wore white, but the gown was elaborately decorated with Irish lace, and the skirts belled out with rustling petticoats. The cut of the bodice was designed to make an enticing, creamy display of the swelling curves of her breasts, with a large area of her smooth chest and the beginnings of softness exposed to the lamplight.

"My husband has decided to join us, gentlemen," Margaret said as Sean, the butler, escorted them into a huge, formal dining room.

Harman Blennerhassett wore a wrinkled brown suit. His linen was white but wilted. He rose from a chair at the head of a long table. Margaret did the introductions. Blennerhassett made no move to extend his hand. Renno nodded his head stiffly.

"Howdy, Mr. Blennerhassett," Roy said. "Good to see you. Maybe in the absence of Mr. Burr, we can talk some turkey with you."

"Sit, please," Blennerhassett said.

A servingmaid ladled soup into bowls. Roy picked up his bowl and began to drink from it, deliberately acting the part of the frontier bumpkin. Renno suppressed a smile. Roy knew perfectly well how to use the cream-soup spoon that was arrayed with other pieces of gleaming silver beside his place.

"You told my wife you were *Colonel* Roy Johnson," Blennerhassett said. "Just how did you acquire that title?"

" 'quired it serving with the Tennessee Militia," Roy said before slurping his soup again.

"I imagine then, that you know General Jackson."

"That I do," Roy said. "It was Andy what told

me about Mr. Burr's plan to go slice off a little bit of New Spain."

"Indeed," Blennerhassett said sarcastically.

"You ain't callin' me a liar, are you, Mr. Blenner-hassett?" Roy asked, putting down his empty soup bowl with a thump.

Blennerhassett shrugged. "I don't know you well enough to call you a liar, Mr. Johnson."

Roy grinned conciliatorily. "Look, I didn't ask your wife to have us to supper. We just came up here to see if Mr. Burr could use a couple of fellers who know how to handle a rifle, that's all. Now if you don't want to hear what I have to say, don't ask questions."

Blennerhassett nodded, his lips curled in a tight smile. "I find it interesting," he said, "that you yourself are very much as Mr. Burr has described Andrew Jackson to me."

"Well, we weren't exactly cut from the same cloth," Roy said, "but we're alike in a lot of ways, me and Andy."

Sean was serving steaming chicken and pastry. Roy took a bite almost as soon as it hit his plate and said, "This is mighty fittin', Miz Blennerhassett."

"And you, sir," Blennerhassett said to Renno, "are you a colonel, too?"

"No," Renno said.

Blennerhassett waited expectantly. Renno's eyes were ice and fire. The Irishman dropped his own eyes and began to eat. "Well, Burr will be back in a couple of days. I'm sure he'll find a use for your, uh, talents."

Blennerhassett ate as if he hadn't seen food in weeks. He bent over his plate with his elbows on the table and forked large chunks of chicken into his mouth and stuffed pastry in behind them. Barely chewing, he washed the food down his throat with copious draughts of water. Renno watched in amazed revulsion, waiting for the man to choke. But Blenner-hassett, unscathed, cleaned his plate and stood up.

"Please continue without me," he said. "I must return to my work." He vanished through the doorway.

"Do I get the impression, Miz Blennerhassett," Roy asked, "that your husband doesn't approve of us?"

"I don't ever invite Mr. Burr's recruits into my home," Margaret said.

"I was wondering about that," Roy admitted.

"But I invited you because I wanted to hear Renno's story as to how he happens to be a Seneca war chief in Tennessee."

"Well, it's a long tale," Roy said. He rose and scratched his stomach. "And I've heard it. So if you'll excuse me I'll leave him to tell it to you."

Margaret nodded graciously and rang for Sean to show Roy out. Renno raised one eyebrow at Roy, who winked at him.

"Mighty fine vittles, ma'am," Roy said. "I thank you for 'em." Then he left with the butler.

Renno continued to eat. Margaret picked at her food, taking little dainty bites. "Well?" she asked at last.

"My father led a group of the Seneca to the south to live in the lands of the Cherokee," Renno said.

She waited, then finally asked in exasperation, "Is that all? That's the long story?"

"There's more."

"Come, then," she said, rising, placing her napkin on the table. "You can tell me over brandy and a cigar." She smiled as she came to take his arm. "But then you don't drink, do you?"

She led him into an intimate little room decorated in rosewoods and pink. He accepted a cigar. She sat facing him, her dark eyes searching his. He told her, briefly, why his father had decided to leave the Seneca homeland after the great white man's war.

"You are no mere Indian," she said.

"I would like to think that I am not a 'mere' anything."

"You're an educated man."

He was silent.

"You speak English as if you were to the manor born."

"My wife was, as a matter of fact," Renno said.

"I see," she said quietly.

"And I have traveled in England."

"Your wife?"

"Her father was and her brother is Lord Beaumont."

"I *am* impressed." She rose, paced in front of him for a moment or two, then sat beside him, her hands on his arm. "You are, all in all, a very impressive man."

"So," Renno said, and puffed on the cigar.

"We are, I assure you, quite alone," she said, smiling into his face, her black eyes sparkling. "It was perceptive of you to arrange for your father to leave us," she said.

"I had nothing to do with that."

"Then it was perceptive of him," she said. "It is so pleasant to have someone with whom to talk. Someone who knows the world, as you do."

"Only small portions of it."

"My husband will be at his work well into the night," she whispered. She leaned against him, putting her slight weight behind one soft, rounded breast pressed tightly to his shoulder.

"It is not my wish to compromise you," Renno said. "You have been very gracious to me and my father-by-marriage."

"That's your father-in-law?"

"Yes."

She laughed appreciatively. "A *very* understanding man." She stood and pushed her knees between his legs. Her hair had started to fall out of its knot.

"You have the sun in your face," she whispered, kneeling before him, her body between his knees. "And the sky in your eyes."

Chapter Eight

Winter had not yet gained the strength to bind the Pacific coast in snow and ice. On the day that Little Hawk made his hunt and quickly dropped two yearling deer, the air was cold and crisp, the sky free of mist or haze. It was, he felt, altogether too beautiful a day to die. As he faced four grim-faced warriors who were armed with bows and stone axes, he knew that he was dangerously close to death. Not even the Little Hawk of the Seneca, son of the white Indian, could hope to be fast enough to kill all four of the warriors before at least one of them got off an arrow.

He moved his rifle so that the muzzle was aimed at the chest of the largest warrior, obviously the leader of the group. "Brother," he said in Spanish, "I have no desire to shed the blood of one with whom I share common ancestors."

"I hear your words," the warrior said in the same language, "but I do not see the face of a Spaniard."

"You see one who comes from the land where the sun rises, from the United States. You see the face of a Seneca, a man of Indian blood." He lowered his rifle and took a step forward. "I speak the language of the Turtle Warriors only because it is a tongue that we share." He used the Choctaw term for a Spanish soldier, so called because the first Spaniards to invade the southeastern portions of the North American continent wore metal armor like a turtle's shell.

"You come with many men armed with rifles."

"But we come in friendship," Little Hawk said. "My chief, the captain of the ship with the tall, white sails, would trade with you. In exchange for your furs we have the wonderful things made by the white man." He slowly drew his knife and extended it, haft first, toward the large warrior, who took it and tested its sharp edge. He seemed satisfied.

"Knives and other tools of steel," Little Hawk said. "Cooking vessels for your women. Colorful cloth and wampum beads for decoration."

The big warrior tried to return Little Hawk's knife.

"No, it is yours," Little Hawk said.

"What is this Seneca of which you speak?"

"That is the name of my tribe," Little Hawk said. "And yours?"

"We are Heceta. I am Youbou, war chief of the Heceta."

"We are well met, Youbou," Little Hawk said, putting his rifle aside and stepping forward to give the Heceta the warrior's clasp. He found that the Heceta version of the clasp was not much different from his own.

Youbou spoke to his warriors in his own language. The three lowered their bows, put the arrows back in their quivers. There was another moment of tenseness when the two sailors came crashing into the glade, but Little Hawk spoke quickly, telling them that the Indians were friends. The sailors were sent

back to the ship with the carcasses of the deer, then
Little Hawk accompanied Youbou and the others to
what was obviously a temporary encampment in a
pleasant little glade beside the creek.

Youbou explained that the lands of the Heceta
were farther to the south and that the tribe had
trekked north toward the end of summer for the fishing and hunting on the big island.

Little Hawk led Youbou and a select delegation
of Heceta to the shore, where they met with Captain
Davidson. Davidson had overcome or, at worst, had
submerged his grief over Esther's death. His Spanish
was worse than Youbou's, so Little Hawk acted as an
interpreter. That he was successful was illustrated by
the fact that within the hour sailors were carrying
trade goods from the hold of the *Orient* to be dis-
played before the Indians. The Heceta returned to
their encampment and returned with cured pelts: fox,
seal, otter, bear, and beaver. The pelts were of supe-
rior quality. The Indians were very skilled at the craft
of tanning.

The haggling was spirited and friendly. Amused
sailors gathered around with great interest to watch
the goings-on. Because of the duration of the voyage
of the *Orient*, this was a profit-sharing venture. If the
negotiations went well, these sailors would feel more
than adequately compensated for the hardships they
had endured. A favorable trade meant even more
money in the pockets of each member of the crew
when the furs were sold in China.

"Hold his feet to the fire, Cap'n," a sailor yelled
out as Davidson haggled with a sturdy young warrior
who had brought a pile of fine seal pelts.

The bartering was successful. Everyone felt satisfied. At the end of the day the Heceta were camped
on the shore and admiring their new belongings. Fires
sparked cheerfully. The aroma of cooking meat and
fish wafted out to the *Orient*.

Unfortunately, although the trading was good,
the Heceta were few in numbers. It soon became evi-

dent that dealing with this small tribe alone would not
fill the *Orient*'s hold. But in talking with Youbou and
others who spoke a smattering of Spanish, Little
Hawk gained the impression that there were no great
Indian nations along the Pacific coast—nothing to
compare, for example, with the far-flung dominion of
the League of the Ho-de-no-sau-nee in its time of
glory. No group even matched the much smaller Cherokee or Chickasaw or Creek nations.

Between the strait and the mouth of the great
river were the Makah, the Quinault, the Chehalis, and
the Chinook, in addition to the home villages of the
Heceta. Little Hawk told Davidson what he had
learned.

"It seems, Hawk," the captain replied, "that we
will have to work our way southward, trading with the
various tribes as we go. What impression have you
formed about the Indians that were mentioned to you?
Are they warlike?"

"Although there is no permanent Spanish presence among them, they've all come into contact with
Spain's warriors and priests."

"And I assume that's not good."

The young marine shook his head grimly. "No
tribe that has felt the heavy hand of the Spaniard re-
gards a white face with favor. The 'men in women's
dresses,' the priests, speak of brotherhood and salva-
tion, while the men in armor who come with them
take slaves and women." He thought for a moment.
"Youbou and his people may be able to help us. We'll
have to impress upon all of the tribes that we are not
men of Spain. As Youbou leads his people back to
his permanent villages, he'll travel through the lands
of some of the other tribes. If we continue to treat
the Heceta with respect, I'm sure that Youbou will
spread the word that the white men from the land
where the sun rises are different."

Davidson nodded.

"If I may make another suggestion, sir?"

"You may."

"The Heceta women are sleek and juicy. Our men have been a long time at sea. . . . Nothing would be more harmful to our purpose of showing that we are not like the Spaniards than for our men to consort with the Heceta women—whether or not the women show willingness."

"I understand," Davidson said. "I will speak to the men immediately."

The captain called the crew together. Many of them had been busy stowing the pelts in the hold, and this work had put them in a cheerful mood—the furs were beautiful and thick, and each man of the crew could imagine having a sizable amount of gold as his share of the profits.

"I have called you together," Davidson announced, "to congratulate you on your excellent behavior in regard to the Heceta."

The men cheered. "Long as they have them good hides, Cap'n, we'll treat 'em right," someone called out.

"Hear, hear!"

Davidson waited until the high-spirited shouts and applause subsided. "Aside from common humanity, our trading is a good reason to remember that we are guests here. But the Heceta are only the first of several tribes with whom we will barter. We must always remember that we are the intruders. We have no right to try to inflict our beliefs or our ways upon these people. Mr. Hawk, who, as some of you know, is aboard the *Orient* as a personal representative of President Thomas Jefferson, will now give you some guidelines in dealing with not only the Heceta but the other tribes we will meet as we work our way down the coast."

Surprised, Little Hawk stood silent.

"I think it will be best if you talk to them," Davidson said in a low voice.

Little Hawk stepped forward. "You have seen the gifts of fresh meat and fish that the Heceta brought to us."

"Mighty fittin' vittles, Hawk!" a man yelled.

"Let me be brief," Little Hawk said. "When the first white man stepped ashore on the North American continent, he was greeted with friendship and goodwill by the coastal Indians, just as we have been treated with respect and courtesy by the Heceta. Then problems arose with regard to property. The Indian, you see, does not recognize the ownership of individual parcels of land by one specific person."

"Hell, Hawk, we ain't here fer land."

Little Hawk held up his hands for quiet. "The white man began to claim *two* things as his own—land and women. The Indian, in many cases, was willing to share both."

"Now you're talkin'."

"But then the Indian learned that the white man's avarice did not lend itself to sharing, to reciprocating. The Heceta have already learned from the Spanish that it is not good to share land or women. Since, as someone said, we are not here for land, we must also remember that we are not here to take the Heceta's women."

"Well, we wouldn't want to *keep* 'em," a voice called out, and the remark earned raucous laughter.

"And that's the difference between the white man and the Heceta," Little Hawk explained. "If a white man proved himself worthy, he might be allowed to take a Heceta woman as a wife. But that would be a permanent arrangement. The Indian doesn't ordinarily believe in a short-term lease of a woman."

"I think, fellers," one of the older seamen said, "that Hawk is telling us to keep our peckers in our pants."

"Well, that puts it just about as clearly as possible," Little Hawk said. "One man could spoil this entire endeavor. One man acting on his own selfish impulse could turn the Heceta against us. Word would spread that we are no better than the Spaniards. There would be no more good trading such as that which we have enjoyed today."

"Then we'll have to watch ole Sandy," a voice yelled out. "He's a randy rascal."

There was general laughter. One of the older men, a veteran salt called Faust, stepped forward and turned to face the crew. "You swabs laugh, but by God you'd better heed what Hawk and the cap'n said. I got big plans for my share of this here voyage. I been working all my life for a chance like this. I catch one of you even looking at a squaw, and I'll personally cut your tallywhacker right off."

"Ooooooooh," several men moaned in unison, and there was more laughter.

The trading began again shortly after sunrise. Youbou was among the last to bring his pelts, and they were prime. His demands, however, were different. The other warriors had been pleased with colorful cloth, steel knives and axes, pots and pans, rouge, and beads.

"I will have a rifle," Youbou said, "and that which makes it spit the fire of death."

Davidson was hard put to explain that he had no extra rifles available for trade. Moreover, Youbou did not comprehend that the rifle would be useless once the Indian had expended his supply of shot and powder. In the end a sullen Youbou accepted knives and axes and cloth for his pelts.

Another crisis arose when a small group of younger Heceta warriors demanded rum, the spirit of the sweet cane. Davidson said that there was no rum for trade. That answer was not acceptable to the young Heceta men. Strong antagonism emanated from the young warriors, especially after Youbou backed their demands. Little Hawk talked soothingly to them, explaining that rum was nothing more than a fleeting pleasure. Men who had worked so hard at the hunt and women who had cured and tanned the fine pelts deserved something more lasting, he said, than rum, which, once consumed, was no more.

In the end, with the trading all done and the Hec-

eta celebrating around their fires, goodwill seemed to
have been reestablished.

"Hawk, would it be a good idea for you to talk
with Youbou and arrange for one of his people to sail
with us?" Davidson asked. "Since the Heceta trekked
from their village to the strait without problems, I'm
assuming they're at peace with the other tribes. Maybe
having one of them with us to tell the others that
we're good fellows might be worthwhile."

"I will speak with Youbou," Little Hawk agreed.
He went ashore in a longboat to find the Heceta
chief at his meal. The marine was offered smoked
fish, which he accepted and ate with pleasure, for the
boneless flesh of the large fish was tangy and chewy.
The atmosphere was friendly. Men and women danced
and sang all around Youbou's fire. Thus it was a surprise to Little Hawk when the war chief reacted angrily to the suggestion that one of the Heceta sail with
the *Orient* to be dropped off at the permanent Heceta
village down the coast.

"So it comes to this after all," Youbou muttered.
"When they leave, all white men want to carry away
our young people."

Little Hawk's attempted explanation was brushed
aside with a sweep of Youbou's hand. "There will be
no Heceta on the great ship! There will be no more
Heceta slaves taken to the land of the white faces!"

"Great chief," Little Hawk said, realizing that on
that subject Youbou was incapable of listening to reason, "forgive me for suggesting it. My request was
made in friendship and good faith. We will forget that
I mentioned it, and we will continue in peace and
friendship."

"So be it," Youbou said with finality.

There was a silver coin of a moon, huge and brilliant in the pure-aired sky. By its light the young warrior Pomo, son of Youbou, led a small band of the
tribe's older boys in new warrior headdresses to a
knoll near the shore. In this place he found what he

was looking for: a mound of stones over freshly dug earth. Pomo had seen the white faces bury an entire barrel of the spirit of the sweet cane, and tonight the warriors would unearth it.

There was some grumbling, for such work as moving stones was for women. But Pomo urged his friends on by reminding them of the one time that the Heceta had tasted the fiery liquid of the Spaniards. Not one of those who removed the stones from the mound and began to dig into the loose earth had tasted rum; they had been too young at the time. But they remembered how the older warriors—their fathers and uncles—had danced and how they had sung so happily and how they had fallen down laughing. Chief Youbou's determined attempt to obtain rum by trade had convinced Pomo and his young friends that the liquid was a very desirable thing.

"The white faces lied to us," Pomo said. "They said they had no rum. In fact, they hid the rum in the earth so that they would not be forced to share it."

It was good coup to foil the selfishness of the white faces. An entire barrel of rum would make all the warriors happy. Pomo, who had seen the perfidy of the white faces and who had organized the recovery of the hidden treasure, would be sung in Heceta legend by future generations.

"It is here," a young warrior said as his stone digging tool, borrowed from his mother without her knowledge, scraped the top of the barrel. Soon the cask was exposed down to its midpoint, and the young men struggled to lift it from the hole. That proved impossible. It took another hour to dig around the barrel so that four boys could stand in the hole and lift the heavy burden to ground level.

Pomo could not discover how to open the top. Finally he smashed the wood with the new steel-bladed ax that he had gotten in exchange for his pelts. A strong and delicious scent emanated from the broken top.

"There! You see? It is rum," Pomo said happily.

"Yes," confirmed another. "I remember the scent. It lingered on my father throughout the night and into the next morning, even after he was sick and vomited."

Pomo pulled away the broken pieces of the top, and in the bright moonlight the dark rum swirled and splashed down the sides of the barrel. He cupped his hands and dipped them, only to feel a solidity just under the surface. He closed his fingers on something that felt like grass and pulled. The staring face of a dead girl, bleached grub white by the alcohol, swam upward to gleam palely and wetly in the moonlight.

"Woooooooohaaaa," Pomo wailed. He leaped backward and screamed like a woman as he tripped and fell. In his haste to escape the spirit face that had emerged from the rum, he scuttled a few feet farther on his hands and knees. One of the other boys looked and saw the dead face and began to chant a prayer to the good spirits. Pomo halted, feeling foolish, for nothing was chasing him. Eager to reassert his manhood, he walked back and seized the wet hair of the dead girl and lifted her, spilling rum over the sides of the barrel.

"We must go. The spirit of the dead is in the rum," quavered one of the boys.

"It is nothing more than a white man's trick," Pomo scoffed. "Why would he ruin good rum?"

"For me, at least, it is ruined," said the youngest of the warriors, who, unlike the others, was not yet on the verge of manhood.

"Help me," Pomo grunted, tugging on the body. Two additional pairs of hands helped him lift the small, thin body from the barrel. With a shudder of disgust Pomo directed them to throw the body down the slope. It fell with a wet sound and rolled, arms and legs flopping, to come to a halt on the pebbles of the beach.

The barrel was almost half full of liquid. It smelled like rum. It had to be rum. "Try it," Pomo urged. No one was interested. "So be it," he said.

"You, young one, go to the camp and bring a vessel of clay."

The youngest, pleased to leave the place where the dead was immersed in rum, ran away, to reappear in a few minutes with a ceramic pitcher. Pomo dipped the pitcher full and led the way back to the shore, where the celebration was coming to an end. Most of the tribe, ready to sleep, had gone back to the temporary camp beside the stream. The two women that Pomo sought were still present, sitting together by a small fire and wistfully watching the few remaining dancers.

"You there," Pomo called as he approached.

The two women, one of them quite young, the other having seen her twenty-fifth summer, were the tribe's unfortunates. They had been widowed by the same boating accident. They had no relatives. Without a man to provide for them, they lived on the charity of the tribe, obtaining their meat mostly from young fellows of Pomo's age who exchanged food for a certain commodity that only a woman can provide for a man.

"Have you killed a deer?" asked Qualmi, the younger widow.

"I have something better for you," Pomo said. He held the pitcher under Qualmi's nose.

"It is a vile smell," Qualmi said, grimacing.

The older woman, Kima, stepped to Qualmi's side and sniffed. "Ah," she said, "the strong spirit of the sweet cane." She seized the pitcher from Pomo's hand and drank. *"Yeee ha!"* she cried in a shrill, quavering voice as the fiery liquid rolled into her stomach.

"Good?" Pomo asked with a snicker.

"Like lava from the smoking mountain," Kima said, then drank again. "Join me, Qualmi, and we will make big laughter, you and I, since these *men* apparently have no stomach for the white man's liquid fire."

Qualmi took a tentative sip then, urged on by Kima and the others, drank deeply.

Pomo and the other young warriors squatted on their heels. They whispered to one another and snickered as the two widows drank the rum as if it were nothing more than water. The effect on the two women was almost immediate. Qualmi began to sing a song of her own composition, a song she sang to the tribe's men whenever she was hungry. She sang of her youthful charms, of her compact, small-waisted body. Kima joined her. The song was interrupted quite often as one woman or the other drank from the clay pitcher or when they dissolved into tipsy laughter.

One of the young warriors, new to lovemaking and inflamed by the nearness of the younger girl, aroused by Qualmi's intimate descriptions of her own feminine features, seized her by the arm and led her up the slope into the trees. Kima smiled invitingly to the others, but they merely hunkered there, watching her drink.

"How do you feel?" Pomo inquired.

Kima laughed, made suggestive motions with her hands, then reached for Pomo's loins. When he edged away, Kima told him, "Take your own hands, Pomo, and feel for yourself. Then you will not have to ask how I feel."

"You are not sick?"

"Do I look sick?"

"She is not sick," Pomo, rising, said to his friend.

"Where are you going?" someone asked.

"Come with me," Pomo said.

Kima accompanied the boys.

Pomo dipped the clay pitcher into the barrel of rum. He swallowed deeply, breathed hard, and then drank. He felt the heat in his mouth, down his throat, puddling in his belly. He passed the pitcher, and all but the youngest drank. Qualmi and her latest lover came down from the thicket of trees. The girl was singing and laughing. One by one the young men took the widows into the trees and came back later, looking smug. While they waited their turn, the warriors drank. One by one they began to stagger. The young-

est warrior, feeling left out, sat by himself on a fallen
log and observed his friends.

Pomo, setting an example as the leader and the
chief's son, drank more than did the rest. His thirst
was further whetted by watching the other young men
go off with Qualmi. He wanted a turn. Now. But then
he felt his gorge rise. He fell to his hands and knees
and vomited up acidy liquid. Soon he was drinking
again, but more slowly.

"Pomo," Qualmi said, pushing a bared breast
against his shoulder, "you have not loved me this
night."

"Another time," Pomo said, for his head was
spinning.

"It can be for the last fish you brought to me,"
Qualmi offered.

"You need feel no obligation," he said coldly.

"Then it will be only for love," Qualmi said.

"Your appetite is a shameful reflection on all
good women," Pomo said.

"I will remember that when next you come to me
with your breeches protruding in front."

"Take your lust to the white man," Pomo said in
disgust. He was feeling quite sick. He crawled away
from the fire and vomited again.

On the way to the camp Pomo staggered and fell
into the creek. The cold water cleared his head and
made him realize that he was alone. He went back to
the knoll to find his friends snoring drunkenly, lying
on the dew-dampened ground. He, at least, could
walk. He stepped over one sprawled, lax body and
snorted with disdain. The two women were nowhere
to be found. Too tired to go back to the camp, he lay
down and fell asleep.

Qualmi and Kima were still awake when the last
of the young warriors was snoring. Eventually the
youngest boy had been shamed by the others into
drinking rum. And he, like the others, had been overcome by overindulgence.

"Look at me," Kima said, trying to walk. "My legs have turned to water."

Qualmi giggled. "Our brave and stalwart men have deserted us just when I am feeling most joyful."

"Perhaps we should find our beds before we fall onto the ground beside our grand protectors," Kima said.

"I am not ready for sleep."

"Then you must sing alone," Kima said, sighing with exhaustion.

"Pomo told me to go to the white faces," Qualmi said.

"No!"

"By all of the spirits, I do swear it," Qualmi said. "And since he is the son of our chief, who am I to question his wisdom?"

"I have heard from an old one, a woman of the Chehalis who was taken forcefully by a Spaniard, that the white faces have barbs on their *miembros viriles* that rip and tear."

"Nonsense," said Qualmi, moving away. "If that were true there would not be so many white faces. I want to find out for myself."

"Qualmi, don't go," Kima begged. But the younger woman wobbled down the slope toward the beach. Kima shrugged. "Well, if you are determined, wait for me."

They almost overturned a canoe while getting into it, and they paddled in opposition to each other, going nowhere, giggling giddily and looking up at the whirling stars. Finally Qualmi convinced Kima to put her paddle aside and let Qualmi do the work. Slowly the canoe moved toward the *Orient,* where the night lanterns burned fore and aft.

As it happened, the ship's limey, the deserter from the Royal Navy, was on watch. He heard the canoe bump against the hull. Then came a sound that sent him scurrying to the rail—girlish giggles.

" 'ere, you 'eathen," he called down. "Get that canoe away from 'ere."

A woman called up in her own language, but the limey could not understand a word.

"Wot is it you want?" the limey demanded.

The younger woman put her hands under her generous breasts and lifted. Soft, smooth skin gleamed as her unlaced tunic separated. She made motions with her hands. First she indicated the act of eating, then another act that required two people.

The limey could not mistake her graphic sign language. When Qualmi found the rope ladder and began to climb unsteadily toward him, the sailor looked around guiltily. The deck was deserted. Officer country was dark and quiet. He helped the girl over the railing and onto the deck. She giggled and, clinging to him, did not object when his hands began to determine that Heceta Indian girls were constructed with the same basic materials and patterns that went into girls the world over. Guilt feelings returned. The captain's orders had been specific: no fraternizing with the heathen women. But, Lord, the sailor wondered, how strong could a man be when one of them came aboard smelling like a keg of rum—and God only knew where they got *that*—and practically dragged a man down onto the hard, wooden deck? His libido was shouting to him to seize the moment, but his common sense was quivering in fear.

The other woman managed to climb the ladder as well. She stood nearby and giggled nervously.

"Wait right 'ere," the limey told the two women. He ran on tiptoe to the hatch leading to the crew's quarters. He intended to wake his best friend for a strategy session. He didn't notice until he was down the ladder and into the quarters that the girls were right behind him, padding along silently in their moccasins. He put his hand on his friend's shoulder and squeezed.

"By Gawd!" Someone gasped as the older woman stumbled against his hammock and ended up in his arms.

Soon the whole crew was awake. The visitors

were giggling happily, having a good time opening
themselves for the sailors. The limey's friend stood
watch for a few minutes, but he muttered, "God,
Limey, the cap'n will have us shot."

"Wot he don't know won't 'urt 'im none, now
will it?" the limey asked.

Qualmi's head was hurting dreadfully. Although
she was happy to discover that the old Chehalis
woman had lied, the pain in the girl's head made it
impossible for her to take pleasure in the ministrations
of yet another of the *Orient*'s crew. "I am tired," she
said. "I want to go home now."

The crewman murmured something incomprehensible as he nuzzled her neck.

"Release me, now," Qualmi said angrily.

But the sailor only wrapped his arms around her
and put his weight on her as she tried to slip away.
She bit him on the ear and ripped away a good portion
of his lobe. He yelled in surprise and pain.

Qualmi screamed at the top of her voice, "I will
go home now!"

"Yes," Kima said, the word being forced out of
her in an explosive grunt. "We will go home now."

Someone whispered hoarsely and made shushing
noises.

Qualmi reeled from the impact as the sailor atop
her hit her in the face with his fist. His blood was
running down onto her. She used all of her strength
and pushed him off and away and began to crawl
toward the lighter area, where the hatch opened
upward.

The wounded sailor's moans brought the lookout
to the hatch. He made shushing sounds, too.

Qualmi crawled up the ladder. "Kima, come,"
she called back, and the older woman followed . . .
until a pair of strong hands grabbed her from behind.

Since his daughter's death Micah Davidson had
become a fitful sleeper. He awoke with a vague im-

pression of having heard an unusual sound. He lay quiet for a long time and listened intently. The ship's rigging was creaking to the gentle movement of a night breeze. Then a thumping sound came through the hull. He rose and, dressed only in his long underwear, opened the door to hear a woman's voice speaking Heceta. He grabbed a sea coat, pulled it on, and ran down the deck to see the limey struggling with a half-dressed Indian woman.

"What in the name of all that's holy—"

"Gor, Cap'n," the limey said. "Am I glad to see you, sir! This baggage sneaked aboard. Out to steal anything she can put 'er 'ands on, I'd say."

From the crew's quarters came a woman's screams.

Davidson ran to the hatch. A sailor was making the beast with two backs immediately below.

"Saints help us!" Davidson exploded. Then, in a roar, "You there! Release that woman immediately."

The sailor did so, and the woman, carrying her tunic, came scrambling up the ladder. Her large breasts gleamed in the moonlight.

" 'onest to God, Cap'n," the limey said, "they came aboard on their own."

"I pray that you haven't ruined this expedition," the captain fumed. In Spanish he said, "Women, you must leave this ship immediately."

Qualmi giggled. She understood just enough Spanish to tell the silly white face that that was exactly what she was trying very hard to do. She ran to the rope ladder and looked down. The canoe was gone. Suddenly the night had lost all of its magic. She held on to the rail to keep from falling and began to weep.

"My God," Davidson said. "She's drunk."

"Drunk as a lord, sir," the limey confirmed.

The ship's supply of rum was under lock and key. "Where did they get liquor?"

"I don't know, sir."

"And why is she crying?"

"I suppose because their boat is gone, sir," the limey said.

"Break out a longboat and put them ashore."

"Aye, aye."

But when a boat crew came swarming up the ladder from crew's quarters, first one woman and then the other dived overboard, hit the water with great splashes, and, revived by the cold, swam strongly for the shore.

"I will know, and now, who is responsible for this," Davidson seethed. "I want the name of every man who took advantage of those drunken Indian women, and I want to know where they got rum."

Old Bill, the senior member of the crew, stepped forward. "As for names of them that took the females—I ain't sayin' took *advantage,* mind you, for they came into crew's quarters on their own—just take a roster of the crew, sir, and then punish every man as you see fit."

"All?" Davidson asked incredulously. "How long, then, were they aboard?"

"From just after the beginning of the midwatch, sir," the limey said.

"You damned fools," Davidson fumed. "No, I won't try to punish all of you. The damage you have done to our good relations with the Indians will punish you where it will hurt you most, in your purse."

"I swear, Cap'n," old Bill said, "them females was *willin'.*"

"I will hear no more," Davidson said, disgusted.

He walked to the bow of the ship and watched the sun rise over the wooded ridges to the east. He was tired. He hadn't had enough sleep. He hadn't slept soundly for a long, long time. He was furious with his crew. They'd been such a solid, dependable lot until now. He sighed. Many a good man had been ruined by letting his brains sink below his waist. But where did the Indian women get liquor—rum, by the smell of them?

A cold chill ran through him as a possible explanation dawned. He walked rapidly amidships. "I want a boat immediately," he ordered.

"Aye, sir," the limey said.

The boat crew was turned out again. The long-boat was lowered. Davidson saw a writhing, flapping mass of dark birds long before the prow of the boat ground into the pebbles of the beach. He leaped into the cold water and waded ashore, yelling and beating his hands together. One by one the vultures lifted away, squawking alarm. Something long and stringy dangled from the beak of one of the dark birds.

A moan of soul-deep anguish issued from Davidson's lips. The worm-white little body had been ripped open. The lips, nose, and eyes were gone.

"Oh, my God," a seaman said, coming up short behind Davidson.

The captain looked up the slope to see the rum barrel sitting on the knoll. There were four or five dark shapes near it.

"Keep the birds away from her," he snapped at the seaman.

He ran up the slope, panting, feet slipping on the rocks. There was a strong smell of rum and acid. Five Indians lay in their own vomitus. Davidson bent and jerked a steel trade ax from the belt of one of the warriors. The ax made a dull thunk as it sliced through the skull of the drunken warrior. Consumed by madness, the captain moved swiftly from sleeping boy to sleeping boy. The ax rose and fell. He could hear himself cursing in a strained voice. And when it was done and blood flowed from the broken skulls of all five, he took the ax to the barrel's staves. The remaining rum gushed onto the ground and mingled with the thick, red blood of the dead.

When Renno was a boy he conducted the usual experiments with the opposite sex, taking all the liberties that were allowed a Seneca youth and going a bit further when the maiden was willing. As a boy he had been in love—or so he thought—with an Indian lass, and she with him. The consummation of that love was quite exciting and the physical memories lasted longer than the pain of the lost love.

As an adult, he had had three wives: the pale-haired Emily, mother of Little Hawk and Renna; the dark, lovely An-da, mother of Ta-na; and the flame-haired captor of his heart, Beth Huntington. He had reared a daughter and had seen her married, widowed, and remarried. And yet, based on his experience, he would not have described himself as a worldly man regarding male-female relationships. Most certainly he had never encountered a woman like Margaret Blennerhassett. Her open sexual aggression left him stunned.

She was a most attractive woman, small, pert, clean-smelling, and warm. There was in him that part of the man that responded to her obvious invitation. He was far from home, and he had been separated from Beth for long, long weeks. He was virile, active, healthy, and mature. A charming, sensuous woman pushed her legs between his, her head bent toward him. He was not prepared for such temptation. He was not a saint, just a man. His hands reached out, cupped her narrow waist, palms resting on the outflow of her lovely hips. As her soft lips came to rest on his mouth, for long, swelling moments, he was lost.

Then she spoke, and her words pierced and destroyed his haze of desire. For a reason that he would never understand she chose words that were almost identical to those spoken to him long ago in a place far away from the Ohio River by a young English girl with hair the color of autumn leaves. Perhaps it was a common heritage of the British Isles that led Margaret to say, as Beth Huntington had said years before in a leafy glade in the forests south of Quebec, "You have the sun in your face and the sky in your eyes."

He was Renno, Seneca, sachem, husband, father. He kept his hands at her waist as he stood, then used them to push her away as she tried to press against him.

"I believe, my lady," he said, "that you should reconsider your actions."

She smiled at him. "Am I being so coldly rejected?"

"Not coldly," he said ruefully. "With much regret. With, I might add, a rather painful sense of loss as I scold myself."

"I think it is I that you scold," she said with a frown.

"You are more valuable than this momentary whim to give yourself away," he said.

"For God's sake," she said angrily, "now the man is going to lecture me."

"No—no lecture. Just this: you are very beautiful. You're young. You would tempt any man, as you have tempted me. But is that what you really want?"

She turned away. "Is it because of the wife you mentioned?"

"I made my pledge to her."

She turned to face him, her full lips parted in a smile. "Do pledges have chains that reach so far?"

"If there are chains, they are here, around my heart, for my commitment to my wife is also a commitment to myself."

"Good God," she said. "A man of honor."

"I try to be," he said.

"And that is why Aaron Burr will destroy you," she hissed. "Burr devours men of honor for starters." She reached out and pushed him toward the door. "Go home, Renno of the Seneca. Go back to your wife."

"That I will do, in its time," he said. "And now, Mrs. Blennerhassett, if you will excuse me—"

Suddenly her mood changed. "Please don't go."

He smiled, bowed. "Good night."

Roy was lying in his makeshift bed, but he was not asleep. "You made the long story awfully short."

"Our hostess lost interest," Renno said.

"Learn anything you didn't know?" Roy asked.

"I'm not sure," Renno said, remembering the softness and the warmth of Margaret's hands on his arm.

"Did she mention anything about Burr?"

"No," Renno said.

"You're talking so much you're keeping me from my sleep," Roy said. "Why don't you hush?"

Aaron Burr returned to Blennerhassett Island on the third day after the arrival of Renno and Roy. While waiting for Burr, Roy made his peace with the big, bearded Hoss Beaver by telling the giant that when called upon to fight a bear of a man like Hoss, an old man such as himself had no choice but to use unfair tactics.

"Now, Hoss," Roy said, "both you know and I know that you could pick me up and break me with one hand. I consider myself to be fairly sensible. Would any fella with half a brain let a bear like you break him wide open when he could prevent it with a friendly little kick in the jewels?"

"Huh?" Hoss replied.

"Think about it," Roy urged.

Renno used the time to explore the island. It was unremarkable, except for the Blennerhassett establishment. There were the usual trees and heavy underbrush. Domestic hogs were allowed to roam freely, so tunnellike trails had been pushed through the bush. Once, he came upon Margaret strolling along the river. She smiled and nodded. He bowed.

Walking on, Renno discovered that the laboratory, in one wing of the house, had high windows that required the scaling of a handy tree. From that leafy vantage point Renno saw Blennerhassett bending over a workbench that was cluttered with odd glass vessels and blown-glass tubing. An acrid smell drifted from the window.

In the three days before Burr's return no new recruits arrived, and when the former vice president came, he brought with him only six men.

Roy introduced himself, and Burr's handsome face expanded in a wide smile. "Colonel Johnson, what a pleasure," he said. "General Jackson has mentioned you to me. Now, for the first time, I feel dead certain that our hopes will be realized. With men like you on our side, how can we fail?"

"Renno, here, is a pretty good hand, too," Roy said, for he was a bit embarrassed by Burr's enthusiasm.

Renno had been taking the opportunity to examine Burr closely. The thin face, the receding hairline, and the sophisticated cut of Burr's attire gave a first impression of genteel elegance. The smile seemed to be genuine, the voice vibrant and warm, full of implied goodwill.

But something about the man belied the first impression. Perhaps it was the quick shifting of Burr's eyes from Roy's face to Renno's. Perhaps it was nothing more than the way Burr seemed to lean backward as he took first Roy's hand and then Renno's. His handshake was firm and dry. Why, then, did he seem to be intent on putting as much distance as possible between his eyes and those of the man whose hand he was shaking by arching his back and throwing his head high?

Chapter Nine

Toshabe said nothing when her younger son failed to carry his newborn daughter to the icy creek for the ceremony of cleansing. She had found that two of the very few blessings of age were patience and an understanding that in spite of the efforts the individual might or might not make, the world goes on. In her sixty-plus summers she had seen the way of life and the mores of the Seneca go through consequential changes; thus, delaying the dedication of the new child to the Master of Life through immersion in pure waters did have some precedence. In fact, in the homelands it had been permissible to postpone the rite in times of blizzard or unusually severe cold. True, the mild night of little Ah-wen-ga's birth did not qualify as severe. Although she would not have admitted it, Toshabe was relieved when El-i-chi, as father and tribal shaman, announced that his daughter would be dedicated at a later time, when Ah-wa-o could be in attendance.

At last that time arrived. On a day that masqueraded as spring, the entire band of Seneca plus an equal number of Cherokee had gathered at the swimming creek. There would be more winter, but on that afternoon the breezes were from the south, the sun owned the sky, and people were quite comfortable going about without a coat or a wrap.

"Brother," Beth said to El-i-chi, "you could not have chosen a lovelier day."

Ah-wa-o, the Rose, carried her daughter proudly to the ceremoniously dressed shaman. Ah-wen-ga cooperated beautifully as she lay naked in her father's hand to be chanted over. Then she was adorned by her grandmother with just one vertical slash of red paint, the color of Indian pride, on her forehead. Ah-wen-ga squinted against the sun and made contented sounds.

The older ones among the Seneca, who had seen many such ceremonies, chuckled wryly when it became evident that El-i-chi was going to stretch the dedication to its seldom-seen fullest extension. Quite often in the homeland, winter had a fierce bite, and wind-generated tears froze on the cheeks of participants and spectators. The shaman, merciful and himself cold, would cut short the chants and prayers, touch the baby's bottom to the almost-frozen water exposed by cutting a hole in the ice, and then everyone would run for the comfort of the village longhouses. Thus it was satisfying now to the tradition minded to be pleasantly warm and to hear the old words sung in an atonal, rhythmic cadence by their shaman.

El-i-chi dipped Ah-wen-ga up to her chin into the creek. He cooed soothingly as she flapped her arms and opened her eyes wide in alarm. To his pride she did not cry. He lifted her high in both hands, water dripping from her tiny body onto his face.

"Master of Life, I offer this little one to you to

do your service for good as she becomes first a child, next a maiden, and then a woman and mother. Hear me, Master of Life: guard her well and bless her with goodness."

Ah-wa-o dried the infant with a towel provided by Beth, then wrapped her in a blanket. El-i-chi, eyes closed, head back, hands raised high, was calling to the Master of Life for a sign, an omen of good to guide the development of the newly dedicated.

During the long, comforting ceremony one insignificant cloud had drifted up from the southeast. It had not done much to mar the open blue of the sky, for it was only a small cloud, not even very dark. But as the shaman reached for the sky and chanted his prayer, the cloud edged across the sun, causing shadows to fall over the swimming creek. An old woman mumbled a nervous prayer.

El-i-chi opened his eyes. The dark shadow of the cloud fell on his soul as well as over the land, and he was concerned. He raised his voice, amplifying his prayer for the blessing of his daughter. His words were lost in a swift crash of lightning. A racking detonation of thunder caused cries of alarm as a pine tree was blasted not more than two hundred feet away. The swaying top of the tall pine, severed, started to lean outward even as another crack of doom burst fire from another tree, two hundred feet away in the opposite direction.

A woman screamed. El-i-chi, awed, fell silent. Twice more the tiny cloud lanced thunder and fire, and four trees smoked and shuddered. Four lightning strikes that formed a square now centered on the gathering at the creek. The severed tip of the tall pine crashed to the ground. Then, except for moans of terror from some of the women, all was silent.

"It is a terrible sign," someone said in awe.

"May the manitous protect her," Toshabe said, touching her new granddaughter.

El-i-chi chanted a prayer softly. The small cloud slid away from the sun and left brightness in its wake.

A bobwhite quail called for his mate, who had fled during the bombardment from the heavens.

And words formed in El-i-chi's mind, words that were not his own. The voice was that of the woman for whom his daughter was named, his grandmother Ah-wen-ga.

The fire from the sky did not strike the child, the manitou whispered.

At first, when the family gathered in Toshabe's longhouse, the cloud that had spoiled little Ah-wen-ga's moment seemed to have moved indoors. Toshabe tried to lighten the atmosphere by issuing orders to the younger ones, telling the boys to do their romping outdoors until they were called, then giving Ena, Naomi, and We-yo chores in preparation for the meal. Ah-wa-o took care of the infant.

"And you, Flame Hair," she said, "taste this and see if it needs more salt." She dipped a wooden spoon into a big pot of stew. Beth blew on the liquid to cool it, then tasted.

"It's just right," Beth said. "What can I do to help?"

"Summer Moon?" Toshabe asked, and Beth nodded.

She entertained Summer Moon with a happy little song that she had learned as a girl in England. El-i-chi and Rusog stopped their conversation to listen.

"There are too many women and not enough men in this house," Toshabe complained.

Beth, who needed no reminder that Renno was not among those who would eat Toshabe's meal, said, "I agree. When the wanderers return, I think that you and I should clip their wings once and for all."

Toshabe made a hissing sound of amused derision. "Not likely," she said. "It would be a fool's errand to try to coop up those two." She talked as she added cubed potatoes to the stew. "I had to listen to the smooth talk of that white-faced man. I was content living alone, with my children and my grandchildren about me. Then he spoke as smooth as oil, and I said, 'Yes, I will marry you, Roy Johnson.' And what does he do? He leaves to go to New Orleans and only the manitous know where else. He comes home, and I grow accustomed to having a man in the house once again. Then my son the sachem says, 'Come, Roy, we go,' and what does my husband do? He prepares his kit for travel."

"Thank the manitous, Toshabe," said stolid Rusog, "that you have such a dependable son-by-marriage, who stays at home to look after you."

"So," Toshabe said, smiling to show that she appreciated Rusog's rare attempt at levity. "My life is not a total loss, eh?"

El-i-chi cocked his head to catch a soft sound. Rusog, too, heard. A wind mourned in the overhanging roof members. Toshabe put down her spoon and walked to the door. A wall of blackness was standing in half the western sky. A fitful wind stirred dust in the commons. Even as she watched, the storm line came soaring upward.

Gao and Ta-na strolled onto the commons and, seeing their grandmother, waved. "It will rain, Grandmother," Ta-na called out.

Toshabe ushered the boys into the longhouse with a pat to two dark-haired heads. "Rain comes," Gao said.

"It is early for such a storm," Rusog said as the wind gusted to howl around the eaves.

The rain came in a rush. One second there was only the wind, and then the sky tipped and poured a roaring surge of huge drops that found their way through the smoke hole and, swirled by the wind, sizzled in the fire and dampened the faces of Ah-wa-o and Naomi. Thunder rumbled from a distance and moved closer in an almost continuous bombardment of sound. A sharper crack told of a lightning hit in the woods beyond the village.

"The food is ready," Toshabe announced.

It did not seem odd to any of the group who

found seats on the beds, on the floor, on the log
benches that the meal was served on fine bone china
from Prussia. Ta-na and Gao tended to forget the use
of a fork, finding their fingers to be more efficient,
but no one chided them. The heavy rain pounded on
the roof. One pod of thunder and lightning passed
over, then the rain ceased as suddenly as it had begun.
The silence was eerie. From the distance came a low
roar punctuated by the growl of approaching thunder.

Rusog dropped his fork with a clang, put his plate
aside, rose, and walked to the door, his expression all
concern. The distant roar was louder, a sound like the
bellowing of a thousand demons. As Rusog opened
the door a lightning bolt exploded not a hundred yards
away.

El-i-chi, too, was alarmed. He stood at Rusog's
shoulder. Rain came again to obscure vision as the
roar became oppressively loud—a thousand laden,
steel-wheeled wagons being pulled at a gallop over a
rough road.

Rusog's face showed something that El-i-chi had
never thought he would see there; but at that moment
Rusog faced something more terrible than any mortal
enemy. He had never felt fear in the days when he
fought at Renno's side against daunting odds. He
could have faced an enraged bear without letting that
look of alarm distort his face, but the thing that roared
toward the village could not be faced by mere man.
The sound of the rain was drowned by the roar. The
thunder merely augmented it. Lightning was continuous, allowed Rusog and El-i-chi to see the swirling,
hellishly black funnel of destruction bearing down on
them.

It came with the speed of a dove fleeing the
hawk. It roared and ate the forest, and branches and
shattered trunks spun off, flying outward from its
black sides.

El-i-chi, awed by the sheer power of the spinning
evil, muttered a prayer to the Master of Life. He had
never seen such a storm, but he had seen the results

of one's passage. Soon the dark funnel would slash
into the village, and the frail longhouses and log cabins would be smashed and scattered. This, on the day
of his daughter's dedication. This, in addition to the
evil omens during the ceremony. He lifted his hands
and cried out in protest. He was mortal man defying
the elements, reaching out in desperation to his God
as many men had done before him, only to be denied,
crushed, torn by fang and claw, drowned by raging
waters, buried by upheavals of the earth, or mangled
in the storm. Some white settlers dug holes into the
ground as a retreat from the spinning, roaring engines
of destruction that were the spring storms. The Indian
had never felt the need, being more stoic, feeling that
if the Master of Life deemed it time for him to go to
the Place across the River, no hole in the ground
would thwart the purpose of the most powerful one.
So for El-i-chi, his family, and all the members of his
village, there was no place to hide, nowhere to run.
There was only faith in goodness and a shaman who
stood in the driving rain, his face lit by the continuous
flashes, his voice lost in the crash of thunder and the
fearful bellow of the storm. He stood proudly, arms
raised, as rain slashed against his face. He felt the
advance force of the spinning cloud. Grit and dust
flew into his face, but he would not move.

"What is it?" Beth cried out as the sound became
all encompassing. Naomi stood beside her and put her
arms around Beth.

El-i-chi called on all the powers of good to turn
the roaring evil that came inexorably onward. At the
last moment the roar diminished. The funnel that had
scythed a path of destruction three hundred feet wide
through the woodlands adjacent to the village lifted,
skipped over the longhouses and the cabins, and lowered itself to slash and rip at the forest on the opposite
side.

"My brother is favored by the manitous," Rusog
said, looking with new respect at El-i-chi.

El-i-chi heard Rusog's voice, but he heard another voice as well. Once again his grandmother spoke to him. *The winds,* the spirit voice said in his head, *blew not for the child*.

"So," Toshabe said with a small, nervous laugh. "We will finish our meal."

In a night made stygian black by low, dripping clouds, Ho-ya, Gao, and Ta-na did warrior's duty by escorting Beth and Naomi to Huntington Castle. They stayed until Beth had stirred up the fire in the cozy sitting room and until Naomi had served them milk and cake. Then the rain and wind had started up again, and the escorts hurried home.

After they were alone in the room, with Naomi having a second piece of cake, Beth sighed and said, "This night seemed to last forever."

The hands of the clock over the mantel stood at ten o'clock. Beth had declined cake when Naomi served it to the boys. She was not overweight, but some of her favorite gowns were getting a bit tight in the waist. She took just one bite or so less at mealtime and felt guilty about such treats as the chocolate cake that she and Naomi had baked. But, ah, it did look good.

"I am a weak creature of no will," she said, rising. "Can I get you anything else?"

"I could eat another piece," Naomi said, "and get as fat as a pig."

"Today we have survived lightning and tornado," Beth said. "Let's be reckless."

"We deserve a treat," Naomi agreed. "But let me get it, Beth."

Beth ignored the offer. She returned from the kitchen with the remains of the cake on a plate and a pitcher of milk that had been kept cool in a window box exposed to the outside air.

Usually the women were abed before ten o'clock, but neither of them was sleepy. Together, they became quite intemperate and finished off the cake. Beth, rubbing her stomach, finally loosened her bodice and leaned back in her chair to watch the play of flames in the fireplace. Her thoughts were on Renno. She had no way of knowing where he was, whether or not he had reached the Ohio, or when he would be coming home; but not for a moment did she doubt that he would return to her.

Naomi, cozy, her stomach full of cake and milk, closed her eyes and dozed. The house groaned and cracked as the cold air that followed the storm front contracted its timbers.

The blood of the white Indian ran as strongly in the veins of El-i-chi as in his older brother, Renno. The urge to experience new things, to see new places, to discover what lies beyond the next ridge or the next tree line seemed to be a part of the heritage passed down by the first Renno.

El-i-chi looked back with some nostalgia on the time when, as exiles from their own people, he and his Rose lived in a secluded bower in the virgin forests north of the Ohio, just the two of them swimming in a lake with water so pure that they could see fish swimming far down in the crystalline depths, roving among the forest giants to gather the fruits of the summer, and traveling unhindered when the need arose to change one place for another.

El-i-chi had seen almost as much of the world as had Renno. But it seemed to the shaman that Renno was always dashing off somewhere to do his duty to the nation he supported, the United States, leaving El-i-chi at home to mind the fires. In bed in a cozy cabin with his Ah-wa-o's petitely lush body spooned warmly against his, her breathing deep and even as she slept secure in his arms, his contentment outweighed his wish that he was with Renno and Roy— but only by the narrowest of margins.

There was an uneasiness in him that banished sleep. He couldn't quite put a name to the feeling of dread that weighed heavy on his peace of mind. El-i-chi did not concern himself too much about the safety

of Renno and Roy; he knew his brother and had the
utmost confidence in Renno's ability to take care of
himself. Roy, too, although he was getting grizzled
around the muzzle like an old boar bear, was a handy
man to have around in a fight. No, his dread was
more than wondering how Renno and Roy were far-
ing—they had had ample time to reach the Ohio and
to travel along the river in search of the mustering
place for Aaron Burr's army.

El-i-chi shifted his legs restlessly and moved his
arm so that his hand lay over Ah-wa-o's heart, as if
by feeling her life beating, *chug-chug, chug-chug,
chug-chug,* he could reassure himself that all was well.

Beside their bed little Ah-wen-ga slept, covered
by a fine, pink woolen blanket given to her by Beth.
Gao and Ta-na were behind a partition they themselves had built of canes from the creek, interlocked
then draped with hides. One of them was making a
little buzzing sound like a lazy bee.

He and his were snug, safe. The voice of the manitou had told him that the signs of that eventful day
had not been intended to predict the future of his
infant daughter.

The fire from the sky did not strike the child, the
spirit voice had said. *The winds blew not for the child.*

Why, then? If the dire omens were not meant for
Ah-wen-ga, then who?

He moved his lips silently in an ancient prayer
for life and happiness, protection for those closest
to him and for his extended family. And then, as
sleep came near, he prayed for wisdom, for the ability
to see as he had once been able to see, to be able to
discern at a distance and into the future in order to
know for whom the winds blew, and to know in detail
the warnings of the four lightning strikes at the time
of his daughter's dedication.

He slept fitfully. Once he awoke with a cry, for
he had dreamed that the evil shaman Hodano had
returned to threaten—who? Once again the question
was unanswered.

*   *   *

Naomi was sleeping in her chair. Beth was far away in spirit, remembering events from her childhood, wondering if she could convince Renno to accompany her to England when summer came again to see William and Estrela. Perhaps the two old warhorses of Europe, England and France, might settle their differences or declare a temporary truce. Either condition would allow Renno and her to go to Paris to see Renna and Beau and their first grandchild. Beth was closer in a mother-child way to Renna than to Little Hawk, because Renna had been younger when Beth became her mother-by-marriage. Although Renna's daughter, Emily Beth, did not carry Huntington blood, Beth considered the child to be every bit as much her grandchild as Renno's. Beth had felt very much honored when Renna's letter informed her that the baby had been named for Renna's two mothers.

It would be so wonderful, Beth was thinking, to see Renna and to hold little Emily Beth. Her thirty-ninth birthday had just passed, and she didn't feel old or, in fact, look old enough to be a grandmother. Aside from the occasional tightness of her gowns in the waist, she had the figure of a younger woman. No gray had crept into her flame-colored hair, and aside from the smile and sun crinkles at the corners of lips and eyes, her classic English complexion, although bronzed slightly by the sun, was intact.

"Damme," Renno had teased after he'd finished a whooping dance of celebration upon reading that Renna had given birth, "I am now reduced to sleeping with a grandmother."

She was quite ready for Renno to come home so that she could sleep with a grandfather, but the menacing apparition that appeared silently to stand and drip rainwater on a fine, Persian carpet was not Renno. She had heard nothing except the wind and the rain.

"Who are you, and what in the devil do you mean

coming uninvited into my home?" she demanded, leaping from her chair.

Beth's voice awakened Naomi. Her eyes turned to Beth's face, for there was a core of uneasiness in her words. Then her head jerked to see the two men, wet, dripping, smirking. At first Naomi thought she was still dreaming. The nightmares had gradually faded with the passing weeks, but a day never went by without something to remind her of the dreadful year she had endured as a captive of the three Morgan men.

"Wal, iffen it ain't my lovin' little wife," said Bearclaw Morgan. "Tommy, say how-do to your stepma."

Naomi made a sound like a squashed frog—half croak, half an exhalation of air. Tommy Morgan's mouth was hanging open in an idiotic grin. He took a step forward, and all of the old horror and helplessness came back to Naomi. She might as well have been alone in the room with the two men. She could only watch helplessly as Tommy advanced. She could do nothing more than moan weakly as he put his hand on her leg and said, "How-do, Stepma."

Beth was trying to watch both men at the same time. She sensed that the younger one was a threat, that his damaged brain would make his actions unpredictable. But she recognized that the greater danger came from the huge, shaggy man with the sand-colored eyes and the bushy black beard. She knew that it would be useless to try to reason with them. The worst had happened. Bearclaw Morgan and his son were there.

The big man stood dripping water on the carpet. As Beth looked at him he lifted his feet one by one and, in petty defiance, wiped mud on the carpet. Naomi's fears were coming true in spite of Renno's reassurances that the Morgans would never be able to threaten Naomi in Beth's house with El-i-chi and dozens of Seneca and Cherokee warriors so close at hand.

"No, no," Naomi was whispering as Tommy leaned over her, mouth agape, his pale eyes not participating in the big, wide-lipped grin that was on his face.

"You done missed me, ain't you?" he asked.

With a swift movement he ran his hand up her dress. His attempt to seize soft flesh was foiled by her pantalettes. He laughed. "By doggies, Pa!" he shouted. "She's done found herself some underwears."

He pinched her through the flannel knickers. Naomi yelped and flailed her hands wildly. He ducked under her blows, laughed as he pulled in his head like a turtle. Her right hand contacted the knitting basket sitting on the table beside her chair.

"Stop it!" Beth ordered, moving toward the struggling couple.

"Leave them alone," Bearclaw Morgan ordered Beth. His hand grasped the handle of a tomahawk at his belt. "You don't need to git eager, gal. Tommy'll git to you next."

Naomi's hand fumbled in the knitting basket and closed over a bone crochet hook. Tommy's searching fingers had found her labia, and he was pinching her painfully. He threw back his head, and a demented laugh came from his mouth. She drove the crochet hook deep into his eye. He screamed and staggered backward. The bone stem wagged up and down as he pawed at it, his voice thin like that of a frightened child.

"Damn you!" Bearclaw Morgan yelled, leaping toward his son.

Tommy's hand closed over the stem and yanked. He screamed again as the hook at the end ruined his right eye, leaving him half blind, driving him wild with the pain as a portion of his eyeball was ripped away.

Beth took advantage of the momentary chaos. She knew that she would be helpless against the strength of Bearclaw Morgan. She would need a weapon. Her longbow and quiver were hanging over the mantel, but both the screaming boy and the big man were between her and the fireplace. She was fleeing the room when Bearclaw saw her. He roared and gave chase. She ran down the hallway and into the kitchen, leaving the swinging door pounding back and forth behind her. She slammed open a drawer, seized a heavy carving knife, and turned to face the intruder.

Bearclaw came through the door and halted. The way she was holding the knife, straight and low, gave him pause. They both knew that he could kill her either with his pistol or his tomahawk, but he had other plans for her.

"Look, little lady," he soothed, "we'uns ain't come here to hurt you. I jest come to git my propitty back."

A frantic scream came from the sitting room.

"Now he ain't gonna do her no permanent damage, even though she did put outen his eye," Bearclaw said, edging toward Beth.

Beth was remembering the things that Naomi had told her about the Morgan men, the idiot especially. It was Tommy, she remembered, who did the honors at hog-killing time by slitting open the bellies of the animals first, cutting their throats only after their agonized squeals ceased. Now he himself was hurt, and Naomi's scream, which came again, belied Bearclaw's words.

"I done tole you I ain't gonna hurt you none," Bearclaw said, still moving toward her.

She snapped back her arm and put all of her strength behind the throw, just as Renno had taught her. The heavy knife flew true and buried itself in Bearclaw's stomach. Her hand fumbled in the drawer for another knife, for the big man merely grunted, glanced down once at the hilt of the knife, and came on. He knocked the second knife from her hand and even as she tried to sidestep the blow, landed a fist to her temple that brought swift blackness.

A raw, throat-straining scream wakened her. Something heavy lay across her legs. She sat up, and her hand flew to her head, for needles of pain made her see white and caused her to be dizzy. When she could focus, she saw that Bearclaw Morgan lay across her lower body. She edged backward, reluctant to touch the wet, black, matted hair with her hands. His wet clothing gave off a stench unlike anything she had known. She freed one leg and kicked at his shoulders until she could withdraw the other. Naomi screamed again.

Beth ran down the hall not toward the sitting room but to Renno's special retreat, where an assortment of weapons hung on the wall. The musket that had once been carried by Renno's father was there, along with newer pieces. There were a brace of dueling pistols and several swords, including a scimitar that Little Hawk had brought home from North Africa as a gift for his father. Breathing hard with fear and exertion, her heart pounding, she jerked down Ghonkaba's musket, for it was the nearest. Renno kept it in perfect condition. She loaded it frantically, clumsily, with shaking hands. Naomi's screams rang in her ears as Beth tamped the musket down and cocked it. She hurried down the hallway.

When she reached the doorway to the sitting room, she saw that Tommy Morgan's eye was bleeding, sending an oozing stream of blood down his cheek and onto his wet clothing and the carpet. He had tied Naomi to a chair with her own underclothing. Her dress was pushed up around her waist. Tommy stood before her. In his hands were the fireplace tongs, and in the tongs was a glowing ember. As the girl turned her head, an awful raw burn on Naomi's cheek told Beth the reason for the girl's agonized screams.

Now Tommy was pushing the smoking, glowing ember toward Naomi's middle. Beth did not hesitate. Ghonkaba's musket roared, filling the small room with sound, smoke, and the acrid scent of burned powder. Tommy was knocked backward as the ball took him directly in the chest. The ember fell between Naomi's thighs and began to burn the upholstery of the chair. Beth leaped forward and swept it onto the floor, then kicked it at the stone hearth.

One look at Naomi's face made Beth fear for the girl's sanity. Her mouth was taut, her eyes were wide and staring unblinkingly. Beth whispered soothingly as she rapidly untied Naomi's hands and feet.

"It's over," Beth whispered. "It's over. They're both dead."

Naomi seemed not to hear.

Beth stroked her hair and said, "We must do something for that burn."

Naomi's eyes had not yet blinked. With a sudden howl that was half-animal Naomi pushed Beth aside. Tommy Morgan had lifted himself to one elbow and had drawn back his right arm to throw a knife at Beth's back. The knife flew past Beth's head to thunk into the far wall. Naomi kicked Tommy in the mouth with the side of her foot. He fell back. A tooth skipped across the carpet. Blood from his chest wound was reddening his coat. Naomi kicked him in the belly. He moaned and tried to roll away, but she seized the heavy poker from the fireplace and began to beat him in the face. After a few blows the idiot's feeble struggles ceased.

Beth's impulse was to stop Naomi as she continued to beat Tommy's head with the poker, grunting with each blow.

"He's dead," Beth said. "You can stop now. He's dead."

Naomi screamed something incomprehensible and shifted the target area for her blows to Tommy's lower regions. Beth was feeling nauseated, but she reasoned that Naomi's violence might just be what was needed to stop her nightmares once and forever. So Beth turned away and waited. Naomi stopped belaboring Tommy's body and stood, bent nearly double, panting with her efforts.

"Bearclaw?" she asked, gasping.

"Dead."

Naomi threw the poker onto the ruined carpet and seized Tommy's body by the shoulders. Quickly she dragged him to the fireplace, and before Beth, who was feeling quite weak, could stop her, she lifted Tommy by the shoulder and thrust his head toward the flames. The stench of burning hair and flesh filled the room. Beth started toward the fireplace to put a stop to it, but she jerked to a horrified stop when the body began to spasm and the most terrible sound she had ever heard came from the fire. Naomi's screams mingled with the agonized sounds that came from Tommy's burning flesh and hair as he struggled to his feet and, hands held out as if to guide him in his blindness, moved toward the two women.

Naomi was still screaming when she seized Ghonkaba's musket and swung the butt with all of her might. The blow took Tommy directly on the bridge of the nose to shatter bone and send fragments into the brain. He fell, this time forever.

Beth sank down weakly, fearing that she was going to faint. The side of her face ached dreadfully. A tentative touch told her that she would have a sunburst of a black eye where Bearclaw had punched her. Naomi fell to her hands and knees and crouched there, gasping for air, her chest heaving.

"You're hurt," Naomi said at last, rising to come to examine Beth's face.

"Not nearly as badly as you," Beth said.

"You're sure Bearclaw is dead?"

"Yes. In the kitchen."

Naomi ran from the room to satisfy herself. Beth went with her. Bearclaw's sand-colored eyes were open in death. They went back to the sitting room and sank into chairs.

"They're both dead," Naomi said.

"Yes."

"Then it *is* over." The girl leaned her head back, closed her eyes, and shuddered.

"We must get them out of here," Beth said. "I will not have them in my house."

"Yes, all right."

The small Persian carpet at the entrance to the room was ruined, soiled by mud and blood. Beth and Naomi rolled Tommy Morgan's body onto the rug and, working together, hauled him to the kitchen entrance of the house. The rain had settled in to be an all nighter, falling not too heavily but steadily. They pulled Tommy's body to the edge of the back porch and rolled it off, into the puddle of rainwater that had accumulated there.

"In the morning I'll take him to the hog pen," Naomi vowed. "Just like he did to my father and mother."

Beth was feeling giddy. "Then would you want to eat ham and bacon?"

Naomi's eyes lost the maniacal gleam that had been in them since she leaped from the chair to kick Tommy Morgan in the mouth. Some madness seemed to drain from her. "No. You're right, of course."

The task of removing Bearclaw Morgan was less difficult because he was already near the kitchen door. His body thudded down atop his son's. Rainwater poured onto the two bodies, diluting the blood that still oozed from them.

"I will never be able to enjoy this room again," Beth said as she rolled the bloodstained carpet so that they could carry it out the back door, to be tossed onto the corpses.

"Then they will have won," Naomi pointed out. "It was their living presence, not their death, that soiled your home."

It was morning before they had finished scrubbing away the blood and mud from the sitting room, the hallways, and the kitchen. With dawn the rain ceased, and as if by miracle the sun rose cleanly and brightly. Neither woman wanted to stay alone in the house, so they both walked to the village to find El-i-chi. He and Ah-wa-o were at their morning meal.

"We will need your help, Brother," Beth said.

El-i-chi nodded. "Is there time for me to finish my meal?"

"Of course," Beth said. "There are two men that I want you to see, but they're not going anywhere."

"You're sure?"

"I'm sure."

"Will you have some food?" Ah-wa-o offered.

Beth wasn't hungry.

"Yes, please," Naomi said, taking a seat.

"White man's food," El-i-chi said, winking at Beth as Ah-wa-o spooned porridge into a bowl for Naomi.

The girl ate hungrily. Beth watched her, incredulous. After breakfast Beth led El-i-chi to the back porch of her house. Naomi stood to one side.

"If you can remove them, I would be very grateful," she said.

El-i-chi leaped off the porch and lifted the rug that covered the bodies. Startled, he looked up at Beth.

"The Morgans," Beth said simply.

El-i-chi nodded. Renno had mentioned the men by way of putting him on alert. The shaman pulled the knife from Bearclaw's stomach, for it was a good tool, to be cleaned and used again. He pursed his lips and shook his head as he examined Tommy's burned and battered head.

"Beth," he said, "this is a story that I must hear."

"Of course," she said.

"But first, as you have requested, I will remove them."

"We will be ever so grateful," Beth said.

"I'll go find some help," El-i-chi told her.

Beth and Naomi went into the house. Recognizing El-i-chi's practicality, Beth soaped the good carving knife, washed it, dried it, and put it back into the drawer. She walked into the sitting room, which was not only her favorite cozy place but Renno's.

"I think I'll use the carpet from the west-wing guest room in here until I can order another," she decided, for there were no ghosts in the room. The room had known love, goodness, and comfort. She would not let animals spoil that for her.

Chapter Ten

Realizing that something was terribly wrong, the two seamen who had rowed Captain Micah Davidson ashore had started running up the hill behind him. They did not reach the gravesite until after Davidson had done his bloody work among the sleeping Heceta.

"We're in trouble now," said one of the men as he looked around.

"Go to the ship and tell Mr. Wellman to arm the crew and put them ashore," Davidson ordered.

There was a look in the captain's eyes that made the idea of leaving him on shore seem very intelligent. The two sailors hurried down the slope and jumped into the boat.

Seeing the world through a red haze of anger, Davidson followed the men down to the rocky beach. He removed his sea coat and wrapped it around the remains of his daughter. He carefully picked up the

limp mass and carried it up the slope to the disturbed
grave. Stone digging tools were lying beside the broken barrel. He put his burden down, took a tool, lowered himself into the grave, and began to dig out the
disturbed, rocky soil. He was oblivious to the newly
dead. The vultures who had been interrupted during
their morning meal by his discovery of Esther's body
grew more bold as the captain, muttering to himself,
worked to deepen the grave. Soon several of the
braver, or hungrier, birds were plucking at the eyes
and soft spots of two of the young Heceta warriors.

Horace Wellman was in the process of launching
another longboat so that he could go ashore to find
out what the captain was doing. Little Hawk, roused
by the activity aboard ship, had armed himself with
rifle and tomahawk. The boat was in the water when
someone spotted the captain's longboat pulling away
from shore. The men were rowing fast. The two sailors clambered aboard when the longboat reached the
Orient.

"Mr. Wellman," one of them said, gasping,
winded by his exertion, "Cap'n says to arm the men
and get 'em ashore."

Little Hawk let his eyes sweep the shoreline.
"What happened?"

"Cap'n, he done kilt half a dozen of them Heceta.
They done dug up the little girl. I never seen nothin'
like it, the way he was carrying on. Buzzards been at
the little girl's body—"

"Mr. Wellman, if I may make a suggestion?" Little Hawk said.

"You're our Indian expert, Hawk," Wellman
said.

"No armed parties on shore. Alert all the men
and issue arms, but keep them aboard ship. I'll take
these two men—"

"Mr. Hawk," said one of the rowers, "I'm all
tuckered out."

"Two men," Little Hawk said, "and bring the

captain aboard. Then I'll find Youbou and talk with him. There's a slight chance we won't have to fight. Most tribes have strict taboos about disturbing the dead. If some of Youbou's people dug into Esther's grave, Youbou might forgive the captain's actions."

"All right, Hawk," Wellman said. "If that's what you think is best."

Little Hawk could hear Wellman calling out orders as the longboat, with two fresh men to row it, left the *Orient*. When the boat was within a couple of hundred feet of the shore, he could see the captain's head protruding from the grave. But Little Hawk also noticed Youbou and a dozen Heceta men emerging from the trees above the grave. Little Hawk stood up in the boat and cried out, "Great Chief, I would speak with you!"

A dozen bowstrings were pulled. A dozen arrows flew. Micah Davidson was pierced in at least ten places from the waist up. One arrow sank its stone barbs into the hollow of his throat.

"By God, they've kilt him," said one of the rowers.

Half of the Heceta attackers ran down the slope. Little Hawk told the rowers to hold their distance. With the wind blowing into shore, he estimated that the longboat was just out of range of the Heceta arrows. On the knoll Youbou knelt beside a body, and a wailing, quavering sound of mourning came from his throat. The Seneca recognized the name Pomo and knew that the captain had killed the chief's young son.

Arrows from the Heceta who had reached the beach fell just short of the boat. "We'd better get back to the ship, Mr. Hawk," one of the rowers said nervously.

"We should have done what the captain said," the other man muttered. "Get out the weapons and kill all of the savages."

"Hold where you are," Little Hawk said.

Youbou arose and walked slowly, woodenly,

down the slope to stand on the beach. His arms were crossed; his head was held high.

"Youbou," Little Hawk called out, "you saw. You saw that the spirit of the dead daughter of Captain Davidson was insulted. Was it not his right to punish those who had disturbed the sleep of the dead?"

"No!" he shouted. "It is the duty of the chief, of Youbou, to punish any transgressions by his people."

"And so you have punished Captain Davidson. Blood has been shed by both sides. Captain Davidson avenged himself against those who disturbed the grave of his daughter. You and your warriors have avenged their death. We have been brothers, friends. Let us put this trouble behind us and continue to be friends."

Little Hawk could not hear what the warriors said to Youbou, and if he had heard he would not have understood the Heceta language. The chief listened, then shook his head violently.

"They must be telling him to kill all of us," one of the men ventured.

"Wait," Little Hawk whispered, for Youbou was speaking to his men, gesturing expressively.

Finished, Youbou turned to face Little Hawk. "The warrior from the land of the rising sun speaks wisdom. We will let blood atone for blood. We will be friends."

"I will come ashore with men to bury the captain and his daughter," Little Hawk said.

"Come in peace."

The longboat went back to the ship for men and tools. "Can we trust him?" Wellman asked after Little Hawk told him what the chief had said.

"What choice do we have?" Little Hawk asked. "We can, of course, haul anchor and leave now."

Wellman looked as if he was sorely tempted. But he shook his head. "We can't leave them up there for the buzzards, Hawk."

"No," Little Hawk agreed. "I expect we can't. I'll tell the carpenter to make up a couple of coffins."

On the shore, members of the crew used shovels and pickaxes to enlarge the original grave. Little Hawk and Wellman, along with junior officers and a few select members of the crew armed with rifles, stood watch. No Heceta was seen. Micah Davidson and his daughter were buried side by side. Wellman, now captain of the *Orient*, crumbled a clod of earth onto the coffins, read from the Book of Common Prayer, and the men shoveled earth and gravel hurriedly.

While on land, Wellman decided to top off the freshwater supply. Little Hawk and his chosen men acted as an armed guard while the longboats, laden with the water casks, plied to and from the ship. Still no Heceta was seen. By the time the water containers were aboard and secured, the men were physically and emotionally exhausted.

"We'll get a good night's rest," Wellman said, glancing at the setting sun, "and bring the anchor up with tomorrow's dawn."

Little Hawk looked at the empty beach, his eyes lingering on the tree line. He felt uneasy and said so, but Wellman was the captain, and the decision had been made.

Darkness had not yet fallen when movement was seen on the shore. Two Heceta canoes were launched. Captain Wellman was called. Little Hawk came on deck with him.

"*Hola! Halcón Poco,*" Youbou called from the leading canoe.

"*Salud, Jefe,*" Little Hawk called back.

"Why do you make preparations to leave when there is more trading to be done?" Youbou asked as the canoe drew near.

"I don't see how they can have any more pelts," Wellman murmured. "Ask him what he has to trade."

"That which the white faces who wear metal value most," Youbou answered.

The conversation went slowly because Wellman didn't speak Spanish. Youbou explained, and Little Hawk translated, that the Heceta had traded with Indians to the north for walrus ivory and ambergris. The chief had spoken two magic words. Ivory was prized by all men of the sea as the basic raw material for scrimshaw carvings, which could be sold at excellent prices. Ambergris, that odorous waxy substance from the intestinal tract of the sperm whale, would bring a fortune in China, where it was highly valued as a spice for food and wine.

"You come, *Halcón Poco*," Youbou said. "Come and bring your chief to see, and we will talk trade."

"What do you think, Hawk?" Wellman asked.

"I think, sir, that Youbou has at least forty warriors."

"But he sounds reasonable enough," Wellman said. "And ambergris and ivory may be worth more than all the pelts we have in the hold." He scratched his chin. "What if we take, say, five or six men with rifles? If old Youbou has anything up his sleeve, seven or eight rifles should make him think twice."

"The decision is yours, Captain."

"Tell the chief that we are very interested," Wellman said.

Two longboats carrying four men each left the *Orient*. The shore was deserted. Little Hawk led the way upstream to the Heceta camp. Fires burned brightly. Youbou came to meet them, his right hand held up in the sign of peace.

"Mr. Wellman," Little Hawk said, "do you notice anything unusual?"

Wellman looked around nervously. "Can't say that I do."

"Where are the women?"

"Ah," Wellman said. He turned to the men and whispered, "Stay alert."

Youbou led Wellman and Little Hawk to his fire

and offered smoked fish. It would have been impolite
to refuse. The smoked salmon was quite good. Youbou ate slowly and in silence. A half hour passed before Little Hawk thought that it was timely to ask to
see the trade items. Youbou gave orders. Two men
came from a hide tent with a large chunk of light gray
material. Judging from the way the men strained to
carry the object, it was heavy.

"Glory," Wellman breathed, "there must be
more than a hundred pounds of ambergris."

Others came with walrus tusks, nearly two dozen
of them, and spread them on the ground in the flickering light of the fire.

"For this, which the white face prizes," Youbou
said, "we will have rifles and rum."

"We have no rifles or rum for trade," Wellman
said. "You have seen what rum does to your young
men and your young women. Many are dead, including our captain, because of rum."

"The white face poisoned our people by putting
a dead body in the rum," Youbou said.

Little Hawk tried to explain about Esther. He
played on the Indian's reverence for the spirits of the
dead, telling Youbou that there had been only one
way for Davidson to bring his daughter to land to be
buried in the good earth according to her wish, that
there had been no intention of doing harm to any
Heceta.

Youbou waved his hand impatiently. "Here are
great riches," he said, indicating the ambergris and
the ivory. "If the white-face chief does not want them,
the Spanish will when next they come to trade for our
furs."

"Tell him we will give him many blankets," Wellman said.

Youbou spat at the offer. "Does the white-face
chief refuse, then, to give us guns and rum?"

Little Hawk tried to explain. As he leaned forward to place emphasis on his words, an arrow made

a *zizz*ing sound past his ear to bury itself in Horace Wellman's throat.

Old Bill and the limey were on watch aboard the *Orient*. Other members of the crew were on deck, their rifles and blades close at hand. An hour had passed since Little Hawk and the captain left the ship. Without any dire events the men had relaxed. It was old Bill who heard the sound of paddles in the water.

"Lord," he said as he heard feminine laughter, "here they come again. And it looks like they brought some friends."

The third mate of the *Orient,* a lad of just eighteen, became angry when he heard the sound of giggling. After four canoes banged into the side of the ship and female voices called up to the sailors who were now lining the rail, he hurried to the spot.

"There's the two 'oo was aboard last night," said the limey, pointing.

"You there," the young officer shouted as the women began climbing the rope ladder. "Let go of the rope! Go away."

"Go away," minced a sailor standing behind the third mate. "Now *you* go away, please."

"This is no time for impudence," the mate argued. "Bill, don't let those women aboard."

Several more women, led by the two beauties from the night before, were climbing over the rail.

"Wot's the 'arm?" the limey coaxed. "Think about it, mate. Wot's the 'arm?"

"Well, friend," old Bill said, "I am under orders never to touch another Indian squaw. On the other hand . . ."

"Are you disobeying my order?" the mate challenged.

"I reckon I am," said Bill.

The women were dragging two grinning sailors toward the hatchway that led to the crew's quarters.

"I will have you all hanged as mutineers," the young mate threatened, his voice rising.

"Now, mate," old Bill soothed, "there ain't no call for that. We sail tomorrow. As the limey says, what's the harm in the boys having a little fun? It ain't as if we're forcing these gals. We didn't go ashore and carry them off to the ship."

"It will be on your head," the young mate said weakly. "On your head, do you understand?"

"I understand, sir, and thankee," Bill said, fondling a giggling Heceta girl.

Soon the deck was deserted. The third mate, sulking because the men had defied him, died in his cabin after the full force of Heceta warriors, having approached the *Orient* in the ship's own longboats, stolen from the shore, climbed over the rail and fanned out quietly through the ship to put an end forever to the lust and greed of the white faces.

Little Hawk rolled to one side, came to his feet with his rifle in his hands, and leaped directly across the fire. He heard a scream of mortal agony as one of the sailors died. Rifles discharged—one, two, three times—and then there was silence as he ran, bent low, toward the creek. Arrows whizzed past him. One of them tugged at the fringe of his buckskin sleeve. He hurtled into the middle of the creek, lost his footing, then managed to scramble up the far bank while holding his rifle high.

He glanced back. The last of the six men who had acted as an armed guard was going down under an onslaught of blade-wielding Heceta. A whoop came from a warrior who was splashing through the creek, hot on Little Hawk's trail. Little Hawk fired from the hip, and the Heceta went over backward with a splash. But others were directly behind him.

The dark woods swallowed Little Hawk. He moved as swiftly as possible. As his eyes gradually adjusted to the pale glow of moonlight filtering down through the treetops, he increased his speed. He burst out of the trees and onto the beach. His heart lurched when he saw that the longboats were gone. From the ship came Heceta war cries, a scream of fear or agony, and a gunshot.

He ran up the beach and was grateful to find a canoe. Little Hawk paddled toward the ship. A large number of canoes and the two longboats were drifting near the *Orient*. The sounds of battle from the ship were not encouraging, for there were no more shots— only the whooping of the Heceta, a forlorn dying scream. Little Hawk eased the canoe alongside, then took time to reload his rifle and check to be sure that his tomahawk was still on his belt. Then he seized a rope ladder. When he peered over the rail, he saw dead sailors strewn across the deck. From the crew's quarters came the sound of struggle, then a whoop and momentary silence before a Heceta warrior broke into a song of triumph. Others joined in. The victorious Heceta spread out over the ship, smashing and looting. A warrior laden down with bedclothes, blankets, and sheets came from the captain's cabin.

So far as Little Hawk could tell, every man in the crew was dead. Indian women began the grim, bloody job of looting the fallen. They worked well into the night by torchlight. The flames of the torches danced with those who held them.

Little Hawk pulled himself along the rail to the bow of the ship and climbed aboard, concealing himself behind the anchor capstan. He felt very much alone. More canoes bumped against the ship, and Youbou came aboard. As he looked at the man, Little Hawk realized that his anger about what had happened was directed more toward Captain Davidson, whose insanity had driven him to mad violence, and the greedy captain Wellman than toward the Indian chief.

The rest of the women of the tribe came in twos and threes, towing their young behind them, carrying babes in arms. The *Orient* was crawling with the entire Heceta tribe—perhaps fifty warriors and as many

women, with children of all ages. The women found
the larder and began to bring out food. What they
couldn't eat, they lowered into the canoes—except the
flour, which was poured onto the galley deck. Unat-
tended, the children rolled in it, then ran around,
shouting and laughing and trying to frighten one another. The women, meanwhile, quarreled and fought
over blankets and clothing. At last all the cabins and
the quarters were looted.

And then someone found the rum. A cask was
manhandled up onto the deck, where a warrior
smashed the head of the cask with his ax. Pewter cups
from the crew's quarters were dipped into the dark,
potent liquid.

Little Hawk had been weighing his options. He
was the sole survivor of the *Orient* expedition, and he
was thousands of miles from home by land, on the far
side of an unexplored continent. Even if the Heceta
abandoned the ship, there was no way one lone man
could sail her over the long, watery distances down
the western coast, past Central America, and southward along the South American coast to the cold hell
of the Southern Sea. There seemed to be only one
course of action open to him—somewhere to the south
the great Columbia River entered the sea. The mouth
of the Columbia had been the target for the Lewis
and Clark expedition. Little Hawk decided to make
his way southward to the river, and if the manitous
were kind, there he would find white men. If not . . .
well, he had legs and he had feet.

Before taking action, though, he needed provisions—powder and shot and warm clothing. He watched
and waited as the rum began to affect the celebrants.
Within an hour both men and women were passing
out from the strong drink. A warrior stumbled toward
the bow, and Little Hawk, thinking he had been spotted, prepared to fight. But the Heceta vomited, col-
lapsed, and was still. Little Hawk quietly stole the
warrior's bow and a quiver of arrows.

A shrill cry of triumph brought his attention back

amidships, where there was much singing and dancing. Inebriated warriors rushed upward from the hold. They apparently had found the magazine and smashed their way into the ship's arsenal of weapons. The men wrestled good-naturedly with one another for possession of the rifles, along with barrels of black powder and bars of lead for casting shot. The keg of powder was quickly opened with an ax. A warrior used his hand to pour powder down the barrel of a rifle, lifted the weapon and pulled the trigger. "Pow!" he yelled, trying to make the sound of a shot as he pulled the trigger again and again.

Then Youbou pointed a rifle at the dark sky and pulled the trigger. When nothing happened he pulled the trigger again and again, then, in drunken disgust, hurled the rifle overboard.

Little Hawk decided that it was high time to go. On his belly and beyond the light cast by the torches, he slipped past the mob of Indians and entered what had been his cabin. It was in ruin, but his bearskin robe had been thrown into one corner and his spare powder and shot were still stored under his bunk. He figured he'd better settle for what he had.

He crawled to the rail. With just his head showing, he looked back to see that the powder keg had been overturned. Black powder was pouring down the hatch and into the hold where, in the magazine, there were another half-dozen kegs of powder.

His breath caught in his throat as a drunken woman carrying a burning torch stumbled and fell. The flames of the torch ignited the trail of black powder with a *whoosh* of sound and a puff of smoke.

Little Hawk knew that he had only seconds to try to get away from the ship. He leaped down into one of the longboats. Fortunately the Heceta had left the oars in place. He turned his back to the bow and pulled strongly on the oars. His life depended upon putting distance between the longboat and the ship. His heart pounded with his urgent efforts, and his back began to ache with the power of his pulls.

Slowly, so slowly, a gap opened. He prayed to the manitous that it would be enough. The towering, shadowy hull of the ship was no longer directly overhead, and then he was far enough away to see the ship's length.

"A minute more," he told his back and palms and heart. "Only a minute more."

Suddenly a tower of fire climbed the night sky, and a hot wind blasted past him. The *Orient* lifted herself from the water, and then her sides expanded. The ship became a ball of flames filled with dark, flying things that soared toward Little Hawk on the wings of death. The roar of the explosion deadened his hearing. His head seemed to swell to bursting. He threw himself flat in the bottom of the longboat. Debris smashed at the stern and splashed in the water. Something burning spiraled down through the sky and glanced off the covered bow of the longboat to sizzle in the water. A cinder landed on Little Hawk's neck and burned him painfully.

When things stopped falling he sat up and took the oars. Where *Orient* had lain there was a glowing, smoking hulk that, as Little Hawk rowed away, sank slowly into the water.

He stopped rowing and let the boat drift as he chanted a song for the dead—for the crew of the *Orient* and for a whole tribe of Indians, the Heceta men, women, and children. As a man of honor he was willing to accept his share of the blame for the death of so many people, for he should have been more insistent against Wellman's going to the Heceta camp; but the Seneca in him told him that the fault was not his. The blame lay in the white man's avarice, for Wellman had been intent on obtaining the ivory and the ambergris. Futhermore, nothing Little Hawk could have done aboard the *Orient* would have prevented the explosion of the powder magazine, for he had had scant seconds. A warning to the Heceta would have resulted in his own death and would have come too late to save them. What had happened, he reasoned as he took up his oars and rowed to shore a mile or so away from the scene of the explosion, was the will of the manitous.

With the morning Little Hawk made his way carefully to the camp of the Heceta. One old woman greeted him. She was leaning against a rock, her hands hidden in her lap, a deerskin across them. She had lost most of her teeth. He could not understand her words. She tore at her hair and wailed. She pointed toward the strait and wept. She knew.

"Yes, old one," he said in Spanish, "you and I are alone."

"The hounds of all evil will punish you, white face," she said.

"So," Little Hawk said.

He made himself a travel kit with material taken from the Heceta camp. By the time he was ready to leave, he had packed smoked fish and venison jerky, spare moccasins, two blankets, and a good supply of stone-tipped arrows for his Heceta bow.

"Old woman," he said, "I travel south by boat. Come, and I will take you to your home."

"There is no one there," she said.

"You will die here," he warned.

"You speak true." She pushed aside the deerskin. She had slashed her wrists, and her doeskin skirt was awash with her blood—so much blood that Little Hawk merely nodded in sadness. "May your way to the Place across the River be swift and peaceful, Grandmother."

He stayed beside her, then took the time to bury her.

Later, when he came out of the strait, the sun was just past the zenith. A long, low swell lifted and tossed the longboat as he turned the prow to the south. The manitous were with him all that day and far into the night. Weariness forced him to shore, to cover himself with his bearskin and the blankets and sleep sodden and chill, to rest the dreamless sleep of the bone weary.

He rowed slowly to the south for several days. One night he fell asleep in the boat and awakened the next morning to an odd world of glassy water and a fog so dense that he could barely see the bow. He was shivering with cold, for the dense fog had soaked his blankets. He drew the bearskin robe around himself tightly, chewed on jerky, and waited for the fog to lift, but it persisted. An ever-so-gentle swell lifted the glassy water under the boat.

Little Hawk slept again. This time a different motion woke him. The swells had grown, but the water was still smooth on the top. Gradually he became aware of a chilling sound—the soft, repeated roar of waves breaking on a rocky shore. He did not want his boat to be thrown onto those rocks. He gripped the oars and turned the boat's bow into the swells and began to row. Slowly, gradually, the sound of the surf faded behind him. For another night and well into the next day he fought the pull of the unseen shore by rowing against the swells. Finally the sound was far away, but whenever he rested, he heard the roar increasing in volume. And during that time the smooth swells began to lift themselves, to rear up their heaving backs until the longboat was riding up and over and swooping down, down into the smooth troughs.

When the fog lifted late in the day he saw an intimidating shoreline of high cliffs. In front of the cliffs, isolated spires of stone rose from the waters. The huge swells humped themselves up as they neared the shore, decorated themselves with a white, frothing top, and, barely parted by the offshore spires, smashed themselves against the sheer cliffs with a power that sent salt spray fifty feet upward. Thoroughly spooked by the prospect of having the boat splintered against the rocks, he rowed. And rowed. And rowed. Blisters formed and broke. The sea was angered by his stubbornness, by his determined fight to avoid death

among the rocks. The sea rose up and smote him fore
and aft with windblown breakers that threatened to
swamp the longboat. The wind and the waves bore
him steadily toward the cliffs.

Night was coming. Dark clouds had replaced the
fog. The wind was howling toward the shore. He knew
that he would not be able to hold the boat through
another night against the titanic force of wind and sea.
He held on to a line attached to a cleat on the bow
and stood up, balancing himself with the rope against
the throw of the sea. Amid the towering cliffs and the
shattered spires he saw an opening, a hint of sand. He
chose bearings to guide him, sat down, turned the bow
of the boat toward the shore, and put his back into
the pull. A towering wave lifted him and carried him
like a leaf along its front. At a hiss of speed and
movement, he turned to see the cliffs approaching
with dismaying swiftness. The boat fell off the back
of the wave, and Little Hawk struggled to keep the
bow pointed toward the break in the rocks.

Another wave, this one with long, white teeth
atop, smashed into him, and the longboat lurched
heavily under a weight of water. The breakers towered
over Little Hawk, engulfing the boat time and again
as he fought and pulled on the oars. The little beach
looked as if it were far, far below him. The boat rolled
in the grip of a huge, snarling breaker and skidded
against the rocky bottom. He felt a jar and was thrown
free, then dragged by an irresistible force along the
bottom. Rocks slashed and bruised him. He fought
his way to the surface, filled his spasming lungs with
moisture-laden air, then was rolled again by the
smashing seas. His strength failed. He saw a flash of
white light as he was tumbled against small stones,
and then he knew no more.

Harman Blennerhassett was almost as bedazzled
as was his wife by Aaron Burr's charm, although not,
since he wasn't built the same as Margaret, with the
same results. On the first night of Burr's return, Har-

man ordered a very special feast—frog's legs and freshwater mussels. Burr had dressed formally for dinner, as had the host and hostess. A chandelier gave warm, orange candlelight as the niceties of civilization were observed on an island on the far western frontier.

"My compliments to your cook, Harman," Burr said.

"He prepares frog legs in the French manner," Harman said.

"I noticed," Burr replied. "And quite delicious they were."

Harman pushed back his chair.

"Now, Harman," Margaret said, "I will not have you dragging Mr. Burr off to have a cigar. If you want to smoke and enjoy a brandy, do it at table. I do not intend to be left alone."

"Yes, my dear," Harman said.

Both men lit up. Margaret accepted a snifter of brandy.

"Things are going well," Burr reported. "I am pleased with developments."

"And yet only two men have joined our force in recent days," Blennerhassett said.

Burr chuckled. "Actually, my dear Harman, those two men have *not* joined us. To put it more accurately, they have infiltrated us."

Blennerhassett looked alarmed.

"Not to worry," Burr said. "I knew the minute I laid eyes on them that they were not what they seemed to be. The younger one—" he looked at Margaret with a smile "—the rather handsome one is Renno of the Seneca. He and his father fought at the side of George Washington during the war, and he is an agent of my old *friend* Thomas Jefferson."

"Dear God," Blennerhassett said. "We must do something, and quickly."

"There is nothing to fear," Burr drawled. "For the present we can learn more from them than they can learn from us. Before we brush two pesky flies

out of our hair I want to know how they knew to
come here. I want to know if they were sent by Jefferson. After I learn those things, I will simply tell Hoss
Beaver to visit them as they sleep."

"It distresses me to hear you talk of cold-blooded
murder," Margaret said.

"Not murder at all," Burr said easily. "Merely a
condition of war. They are spies among us, and the
punishment for that is well-known, even if my former
commander before Quebec, General Benedict Arnold, did escape the gallows."

"It worries me to have them running loose on the
island," Blennerhassett said.

"Leave them to me," Burr said impatiently.

"As you say." He stubbed out his cigar. "If you'll
excuse me, I have work to do."

Burr waited until Blennerhassett had closed the
door behind him, then the visitor turned to Margaret.
"I am pleased, my dear, that his work is as important
to him as my pleasure at having you to myself is to
me." He arose, took her hand, and bowed to kiss it.

She pulled her hand away. He bent and tried to
kiss her lips, but she turned her head.

"What's this?" he asked.

"I don't feel well," she told him.

He took her hand. "A little back rub will make
you feel better."

"No." She didn't know why she had suddenly decided to rebuff his advance. It had been expected as
soon as Harman had gone off to his precious laboratory. Perhaps it was because she remembered what
Renno had said: "You are more valuable than this
momentary whim to give yourself away."

Burr's smile was more sneer than anything else.
He was not accustomed to being spurned by the likes
of Margaret Blennerhassett—a country girl, an Irish
peasant who had happened to marry a rich man. "As
you please," he said coldly. "Since you do not desire
my company, I bid you good night."

Alone, she finished her brandy. The servants

cleared the table, and for a few minutes she heard
sounds from the kitchen area. Then the big house was
quiet. She took a lamp and walked to the door of
Harman's laboratory. When she knocked, he called
out, "Who is it?"

"It is I."

"Margaret, please," he said irritably. "I have
asked you not to interrupt my work."

She went to her room, wrapped a dark shawl
about her shoulders, opened the French windows, and
went out into and beyond the garden. The camp of
Burr's army was quiet. The fires had burned down
into glowing piles. The men lowered their eyes as she
walked past. Those who gave her directions treated
her respectfully. Loud snores came from several tents
as she made her way toward the lean-to occupied by
Renno and Roy.

Renno, only half-asleep, heard her coming. He
put his hand on Roy's shoulder. Roy came awake instantly, silently, his hand on his rifle. He peered into
the darkness. "It's just Miz Blennerhassett," he said
as Margaret drew very near.

"We are here," Renno called softly.

She bent, came under the roof of the lean-to, and
knelt on the end of Renno's blanket. "Aaron Burr
recognized who you are and knows why you are
here," she said. "He knows you fought with Washington and that you are President Jefferson's man."

"So," Renno said.

"He wants information from you, and then he's
going to have you killed," Margaret said.

"We are in your debt," Renno told her.

"I think it would be best if you leave tonight,"
she said.

"Sounds like a good idea to me," Roy seconded.

"Do you know when Burr intends to start south?"
Renno asked.

"No," Margaret said. "He remarked over dinner
that he was pleased by the way things are going,
though."

"You'd better get back to the house, Miz Blennerhassett," Roy said, " 'fore someone sees you out here."

"Yes." She rose. "May God go with you."

"And you," Renno said.

She backed out from under the lean-to, straightened, and turned toward the house. She gasped and turned to flee, but one of the six men with Aaron Burr seized her.

"Gentlemen," Burr said smoothly, "if you will please join us, we have some urgent business to undertake."

"Go," Renno whispered to Roy, pushing him toward the opening. Then he himself rolled to his stomach and slithered under the back wall of the lean-to. He came to his feet quickly, tomahawk in hand.

When a Seneca is fighting for his life and for the life of a friend, there are no rules. Two men died with a back-and-forth slash of Renno's blade before the others realized that terror had attacked from behind. Roy gave a whoop and jerked the butt of his rifle upward, to smash into a chin and send a man tumbling. Aaron Burr stepped backward, reaching for his pistol. Renno's rifle spoke, and Burr felt the breeze of death whistle past his temple. Another man went down under Renno's tomahawk. Roy's blade flashed. The surviving man, Hoss Beaver, stood uncertainly as Renno faced him.

"It's just old Hoss," Roy said. "Let's get out of here."

"Burr!" Renno called out, for that man had taken Margaret's arm and was running with her toward the manor house.

"Come on, Renno," Roy urged. "This whole ant heap is gonna come crawling out before you know it."

Renno did not respond. He handed Roy his discharged musket and ran after Burr and the woman. Shots rang out, but in the confusion men were shooting at shadows. Burr turned and fired his pistol. Lead flew through the air near Renno's ear. More shots came from behind, and the white Indian realized that men were shooting at him from the camp. Ahead, Burr and Margaret faltered and fell. This gave Renno the break he needed. Burr was back on his feet and running in seconds, but Margaret was a white, limp heap as Renno reached her. He fell to his knees beside her. She was warm, but when Renno put his finger on her neck to search for a pulse, he felt wetness. His questing hand encountered lacerated flesh. A heavy caliber musket ball had struck the side of her neck, smashing through an artery and into her throat.

Margaret's chest was heaving as she tried to draw breath. The larynx's shattered tissue and cartilage foiled her efforts. The woman's hand closed on Renno's wrist softly—a small touch, a butterfly's kiss. In the moonlight he could see that her eyes were open. Her chest heaved once more, and then she was still.

Roy's voice penetrated Renno's rage. "They headed for the river, boys!" Roy yelled. "A whole passel of 'em! Injuns!"

Burr's valiant men rushed toward the river. Muskets thundered as they fired at shadows. Roy ran to where Renno held Margaret's head in his hands.

"That's a lot of blood, Son," Roy said.

"She is dead."

"Then we can't help her. We've got to save ourselves before Burr gets up enough nerve to come back and tell these yahoos that he doesn't like us anymore."

Renno did not run from a fight, but he had no quarrel with the deluded men who had been lured to the island by Aaron Burr. Not one of them would have deliberately killed Margaret Blennerhassett. Her death was an act of fate, a thing willed by the manitous for some reason beyond Renno's knowledge.

"They'll take care of her once they find her," Roy said.

"So," Renno said, and he and Roy retrieved their belongings and melted into the night.

They took a boat from the southern tip of the island and rowed to the western shore. In the shadows of the waterside trees, they took the boat miles to the south before sinking it and striking out into the woods. Dawn was just beginning to lighten the shadows. They trekked west, into the Indiana Territory and toward Vincennes, where they would find William Henry Harrison so that he, like Andy Jackson, could be warned against giving his support to Aaron Burr.

Renno and Roy paused in the early afternoon, ate of a fresh kill, and drank deeply from a rushing forest rill. The older man fell asleep immediately. After Roy was breathing deeply and evenly, Renno left the camp to find a secluded clearing a mile upstream. He sat down, crossing his legs, put his hands in his lap, and allowed himself to mourn for the dark-haired Irish girl who had died because she cared enough about two men she scarcely knew to warn them of danger. He chanted a song for the dead and waited in silence for a message from the manitous. When the moon was high and he had heard no spirit voice, he went back to camp, built up the fire, and fell asleep.

Chapter Eleven

To cover thirty miles a day when the trails were good was no strain on Renno, but Roy was, as he told Renno after three days of travel west from Blennerhassett's compound, "not the hoss I once was."

It rained. It started raining soon after they left the banks of the Ohio, and the showers continued off and on, day and night, for three days. Roy's joints ached. When he sat down to rest, getting up was a slow, groaning process.

On the fourth day Renno turned to the south, back toward the Ohio River. If he had been alone, he could have reached his destination quicker by taking the most direct route across an impressive width of the Indiana Territory, but he himself was not displeased to have a dry place to sleep, aboard a flatboat that welcomed two paying passengers. So it was that they floated down the winding Ohio to within a few miles

of the junction with the Wabash, where they were put
ashore at the top of a northward loop of the river.
Well-rested, they made the fifty-mile trek to Vincennes in three easy days.

Vincennes was an old town by frontier standards.
By the almost forgotten Indian standards, it was an
ancient site. An Indian village had existed there from
the time of the beginning. The location was so admira-
ble that French traders began the conversion from Indian village to European-type town in 1702. As Roy
and Renno approached, they found signs of all three
stages of the city's development. Indian lodges, poorly
kept and filthy, were on the outskirts of a raw frontier
settlement, which, at its center, showed some remaining French influences.

As capital of the Northwest Territory the town
had taken on an importance that it had never attained
under either Indian or French domination. From his
Vincennes headquarters Governor William Henry Harrison was responsible for a vast extent of land that
stretched from Cincinnati in the east to the Mississippi
in the west, and from the Great Lakes in the north
to the Ohio in the south. Politicians envisioned the
formation of at least four states from the territory
once it had been tamed and peopled with settlers.

The young lieutenant who had been Anthony
Wayne's aide-de-camp at Fallen Timbers had matured
into a tall, long-faced gentleman in his midthirties. His
clerk-secretary was a young sergeant who looked with
some scorn at the trail-worn pair asking to see the
governor. He was demanding loudly that they state
their business when Harrison, not always known for
his formality, yelled out, "What in Hades is going on
out there?"

"Lieutenant Harrison," Roy bellowed, "get your
carcass out here! Front and center."

The young sergeant went pale. Informal or not,
Harrison was the boss, the commander, and he ran a
tight military organization.

"Who's that yelping like a wild Indian?" Harrison

shouted, coming to the doorway. "Well, I'll be dogged," he said. He stepped forward eagerly, took first Roy's hand, and then grasped Renno's. "If you two ain't a sight for sore eyes." He turned to his clerk and said, "Sergeant, go see if you can rustle us up a pot of hot coffee."

He escorted the two visitors into his office. There were three chairs of frontier construction with fur cushions. "Take a load off," Harrison invited, "and tell me what brings you so far north."

"Well, Lieutenant," Roy began, then slapped his knee and grinned. "Well, that's me—just an old fool living in the past. Forgive me, Governor."

Harrison chuckled and waved off Roy's apology.

"We've been over Marietta way," Roy said.

"Any particular reason, or were you just reliving old times?" Harrison asked.

Roy scratched his chin. He'd shaved last aboard the flatboat, and the three-day-old beard was itching him. "We had some times, didn't we?" he asked, reminiscing. "Good and bad. Can't say I'd want to do it again, but looking back, it seemed like a good idea at the time."

Roy took his time getting to the point. Harrison wouldn't rush him. The governor had grown to maturity among folks like Roy, and he wasn't about to be rude. Roy knew that men like himself and his son-in-law, who sat quietly, his piercing blue eyes looking steadily at Harrison, were the kind of people who had made it possible for the United States to fight its way past the first mountain barriers and extend tentacles of civilization into the great western land areas.

"Life with General Wayne wasn't dull," Harrison said.

"Not dull a'tall," Roy said.

"Which way did you come?" Harrison asked.

"Down the Ohio, then straight north," Renno answered.

"I reckon, then, that you didn't encounter too many Indians."

"Only a few," Renno said.

"Tame ones," Roy added. "Is Tecumseh still try-ing to make trouble?"

Harrison shrugged. "Isn't there always some kind of trouble out here? But to answer your question, I think that Tecumseh and his younger brother are find-ing out that it's not all that easy to unite the Indians."

"Well, that's good," Roy said. "We didn't come out here to get involved in another Indian war."

"Let's pray that there will never be another," Harrison said with feeling. "As you may know, I've been instrumental in negotiating several treaties that have opened up large areas to white settlement. I firmly believe that most of the Indians are satisfied with the terms of the treaties and with the remunera-tion we've given them for their lands."

"But not Tecumseh and Tenskwatawa," Renno said.

"No."

"As I said, Governor, we didn't come out here to fight Tecumseh or anyone else. . . ."

Harrison grinned. "You're going to get around to it now?"

"We just spent some time with a fellow I under-stand might be a friend of yours—Aaron Burr?"

Harrison raised his eyebrows in surprise. "I have corresponded with Mr. Burr. Are you with him, then?"

"Nope," Roy said quickly. "We don't like the company he keeps."

"He has assured me that Andy Jackson and John Sevier will be at his side," Harrison said, "and that the force will be made up largely of Kentucky and Tennessee men."

"Governor," Renno said, "Mr. Burr's army con-sists of perhaps fifty men."

"Bums and waterfront loafers," Roy said. "They, uh, enlisted because the food is pretty good. As far as Andy Jackson is concerned, well, Renno and I had a talk with him before we left Tennessee. He's changed his mind about throwing in with Burr. If you were considering it, then you must not know who Burr is working with."

"Aside from those whom I mentioned—"

"Well, the man who first dreamed up this latest scheme, the man who is Burr's prime partner, is James Wilkinson."

"The devil you say!" Harrison rose from his chair and paced the floor. He was obviously angry. "How that man continues to hold high position, I will never know. I myself sent in reports of his treachery and overt attempts to sabotage General Wayne's campaign against the Ohio Indians. And now Wilkinson is governor of the Louisiana Territory. My God!"

"Need we say more?" Roy asked.

Harrison shook his head emphatically. "This Burr," he said. "What sort of man is he?"

"As smooth as snake oil," Roy said.

"And if he moves south, will he pick up more men as he goes?" Harrison asked.

"Governor, I would think no more than a few," Roy said. "If this thing had happened a few years back, when the Spaniards had us blocked in down at the mouth of the Mississippi, I reckon a good man like Jackson or John Sevier could have raised a fair-sized army, enough men to give the Spaniards fits. But now? Well, we're not on the fighting edge down there in Kentucky and Tennessee the way we once were. Mr. Jefferson's buying the Louisiana Territory has made a difference, too. Those who would have been restless enough to sign on with an army trying to take land from the Spanish now have half a continent to claim."

"I think, sir," Renno said, "that any man who is associated with Aaron Burr will find himself in deep trouble in the future."

"I appreciate your information." Harrison pondered for a moment, and then understanding dawned. "You came several hundred miles just to warn me against Aaron Burr?"

"I reckon we did," Roy said.

"Gentlemen, I am touched by your concern for me!"

"Well," Roy said, grinning, "you were a pretty good lieutenant. I saw some hope for you even then."

The governor laughed. "Please stay for a while," he urged. "We'll roast a pig and break out the hard cider—"

"Now you're talking," Roy said.

"Perhaps I might even talk you into staying longer," Harrison said. "I've got a big chunk of country in my charge, and I sure could use a couple of men like you to help me keep an eye on it."

"Thank you for the offer," Renno said, "but I will be going home to my family."

"How about you, Roy?" Harrison asked. "Old bear of a bachelor like you. Want a job?"

"Well, Governor, I'm afraid I've gone and got me a family, too."

"You never," Harrison scoffed. He winked at Renno. "Has this old boar gone and found himself a pretty young wife?"

"I think she is rather pretty," Renno said, grinning. "But young? No. Somehow he talked my mother into marrying him."

"I'll be dogged," Harrison said, obviously enjoying himself.

Soldiers isolated in a far western post needed little excuse to throw a party, and since Harrison was, at heart, a soldier, he seized the opportunity offered by a visit from old friends to "put on the dog." There were spirited fiddling and a lot of stump juice and hard cider. The gathering was mostly army, but there were a few civilians—traders and trappers who made the capital of the territory their headquarters. A few of the officers had managed to bring their families west with them. Even with the wives and daughters of the civilians, there was a minority of one woman to every five men. The ladies who were of a mind to

dance had enough of that activity to last them for a
spell. There was not one roasted pig but five, and by
the time the drinkin' likker began to run out, there
was nothing left of the feast but pig bones.

Well-fed and feeling spry from Harrison's hard
cider, Roy kicked up his heels with the ladies.

"Is this the old man who couldn't keep up with
me in the woods?" Renno inquired when Roy swag-
gered back to the table where Renno sat with Harrison and his top-ranking military aide.

"Now, Renno, don't start on me;" Roy warned,
lifting his cup. "So few of these northwestern fellers
know how to treat a lady. A Tennessee gentleman like
me has to educate 'em and teach 'em how to dance
properly. I'm just doing my duty."

The next morning Governor Harrison repeated
an offer to provide a military escort down the Wabash.
Renno said that wasn't necessary, that Roy and he
would be moving fast. They said their good-byes and
set off in a finely constructed canoe laden with provisions, blankets, spare clothing, and extra weapons
that Harrison had insisted upon giving them.

The weather held fair and mild. The river did
most of the work. Renno sat at the stern and guided
the drift of the boat, taking a lazy stroke now and
then with his paddle. Roy leaned back, smoked his
pipe, and reminisced about Anthony Wayne's Ohio
campaign.

"It's kind of sad in a way," he remarked.

"Sometimes thinking of the past is a melancholy
pastime," Renno agreed.

"No, I mean it's sad that you and I probably
never will be a part of anything like that again. You
can tell your grandchildren that you were with old
Mad Anthony Wayne when he fought the battle that
gave this country room to expand. It was grand,
wasn't it? And we were a part of it! But we'll probably
never do anything half that grand again."

"So," Renno said. He did not say that every time

he thought of the campaign and its climactic slaughter at the Fallen Timbers, he could not help but wonder if he had been fighting the wrong enemy.

"What's on your mind, Son?" Roy asked.

Renno shrugged.

"Something's eatin' at your gizzard. I know you well enough to know that."

"I was thinking of Tecumseh."

"Ah, and you were thinking that if push came to shove you might have to fight him, and there you'd be again, fighting against people of your own blood."

"You do know me well," Renno admitted.

"Yep, I reckon I do." He mused for a long time.

Renno, too, remained silent. A great eagle swooped down not a hundred feet in front of the slowly drifting canoe, dipped its sharp talons into the river, then struggled upward, wings pounding the air. A wriggling water moccasin dangled from the eagle's claws. On a log sticking out from the bank a file of turtles stretched their leathery necks into the sun.

"If I get too close to the quick, Renno," Roy said, "just tell me to hush. I feel I've got the right to say just about any fool thing that comes into my mind because I was your father-in-law and now am your stepdad. But beyond that, I think of you as my best friend, and I hope you feel the same way."

"So," Renno said, his face going stony in his reluctance to voice such a strong emotion as the deep affection he felt for Roy.

"I tease Toshabe about being white by injection," Roy said.

Renno's face became even more expressionless. Roy's joke came as a shock, for he had never conceptualized his mother as being some man's woman—not as his father's love object, not as the lover of the Pine Tree warrior Ha-ace the Panther. It made him feel peculiar to hear Roy speak of her that way.

"When, in fact," Roy continued, "I'm more Indian than she'll ever be white. Maybe when that scamp—I'm talking about Little Hawk, when he was a boy—maybe when he almost cut my finger off so he and I could mingle our blood and become brothers, it really took. Maybe now I'm more Seneca than I am white. I know how you felt when Harrison was trying to get us to stay and work for him. You were thinking that if you stayed you'd have to fight the wrong enemy again sooner or later, weren't you?"

"That was on my mind," Renno confessed. "I have prayed to the manitous that I never have to spill a brother's blood again."

"I wonder if you and I haven't had enough fighting altogether," Roy suggested. "I wonder if it isn't time for us to go home and stay there. That mother of yours is one fine cook, and she's a better woman than an old timber wolf like me deserves. Makes me wonder if I have any sense at all, being out here, farther from my warm bed than I care to think about."

Renno grinned. "If all that fancy talk meant that you're ready to go home, then grab that paddle and let's go."

Soon it became desirable to hunt for fresh meat. They made camp on the west bank of the Wabash, where the land was wild, virgin. There were white settlements to the north, but around Renno and Roy's campsite, the forests stretched away in regal silence. The deer were tame and unhunted; although there were Indians in the territory, their numbers were few.

The men hunted together. Renno let Roy drop a yearling buck with his rifle. Roy strung the deer by its rear legs, slit its throat, and let the hot blood dampen the undisturbed accumulation of fallen leaves and detritus on the forest floor.

While the white Indian was waiting for the blood to drain, he sat with his back against a tree and gazed around appreciatively. Small birds were fussing at them from the trees. A wind blew aloft, sighing through the higher branches.

"Look at all this," he whispered.

"Peaceful," Roy murmured appreciatively.

"There are rationales on both sides," Renno said.

"For the Indian, it has always been thus. A man could travel for days in any direction before he crossed into another tribe's hunting grounds. One hunter had the use of hundreds, thousands, of acres, and those great expanses of emptiness were necessary to provide the game required by the families. Now the white man is here in his millions, and he can support a family on a few acres of land with his horse-drawn plow. Tecumseh—or any Indian who dreams of keeping such rich lands for the use of a few hunters—is living in the past."

"Hard to swallow, though, isn't it?"

"If I had my way, and if it was only me—" He paused.

"Not encumbered with a rich, beautiful lady of the British nobility?"

"—I would have such a place as this for myself. Here I would build my longhouse, and here I would stay. I'd plant a garden for the fruits of summer. There'd be pelts curing on the wall, and—"

Roy snorted.

"That's not for you, Renno. Never was, really. You might be happy living in the old way for a few months, maybe even a few years. Then you'd begin to wonder what was over that ridge to the west, or east, or north, or south."

Renno laughed. "As I have said, you know me all too well." He stood and began to carve out the choice cuts of venison. Under the circumstances there would be waste, but he had chanted silently to the spirit of the deer while Roy was sighting in on it. The soul of the deer was at peace. To feed the small scavengers of the forest was as honorable for the deer as putting meat into the bellies of two men.

The pair's travel plans were to take the Ohio to the Father of Waters and then down the big river to Chickasaw Bluffs, the starting point for the trek across country toward home. Their canoe hugged the shoreline as the Wabash joined the Ohio, then turned so that the afternoon sun was in their eyes.

*   *   *

A flatboat carrying twenty-two armed men left St. Louis and, days later, tied up on the northern bank of the Ohio at its conjunction with the Mississippi. The men were a varied lot. A few spoke English with a French accent. Most of them were young, on the verge of manhood, looking for a way on the frontier to make a name, find fortune, or just have something to do. Each man had been recruited by, of all people, a woman. This fact was so astounding to them that they rarely spoke of it. And none of them, for reasons of which they were not aware, compared notes about the beauty who had talked them into joining Aaron Burr's army. She was aboard the flatboat, this woman with her blond or red or black or brown hair, with her blue or brown or amber or green or black eyes. Now and then it seemed as if there were two women on the barge, for when one looked at the beautiful one out of the corner of his eye, he saw this other creature—aged, wrinkled, with thinning gray hair and clawlike fingernails. But she was chimerical and under a direct glance transformed into loveliness.

"Little love," each of the men had been told, "we will not show our affection for each other in the presence of all those others lest they feel deprived and jealous."

No matter how much a man thought about Melisande when he was alone, no matter how much he ached for her and didn't care if the other bastards were jealous or not, it was strange that when he got face-to-face with her, he remembered and honored her request not to attempt to assert his exclusive claim.

"When the job is done," the beautiful woman had promised, "after we have established our new empire, there will be land and the rich spoils of the Spanish for you. And then we will be together forever."

Only the woman with the thinning gray hair and the wrinkled face knew that far away, down the big river in Natchitoches, there was another man who awaited her. That man, James Wilkinson, had left Melisande in St. Louis at her own suggestion. She could be of much use to the cause, she had told him, by following him downriver with a large party of eager recruits for the Army of the Empire.

That aging woman had come to realize that her powers were not unlimited. She had seen her true little love die . . . the man she had taken in as a child when she was the Witch of the Pyrenean Woods . . . the man who for so long had taken sustenance from her fecund breasts. He had died at the hands of the white Indian, the man called Renno, the man whom she hated above all others on earth. And now she had only her dreams of becoming the power behind the man who ruled a vast land, a genuine empire. Emperor James Wilkinson would be controlled and guided by the true power, his empress Melisande.

And Burr? She shrugged mentally. He was useful. He would bring a vast army from the east. But when the time came, he would die. Or, perhaps, the emperor would be Aaron Burr, and she would be with *him*, looking into *his* eyes to say, "You will do exactly as I command." It didn't matter whether it was Burr or Wilkinson who had the title, so long as she was there to exercise her will and wield the true power.

At the moment she had the flatboat all to herself. She had sent all of her "little loves" to make camp on shore to wait for Burr's army coming down the Ohio. Melisande valued and needed her privacy. Exerting her will over so many. All her strength was sapped by trying to be everything to everyone—blond and frail to this man, buxom and brunette to another. She had made a room, using blankets as partitions. Inside, on her bed, she could relax and remember how her true love, Othon Hugues, would lie beside her, nuzzling her full, overflowing breasts. Just thinking so, she felt her breasts expand. With a curse and a feeling of great loss, she willed them to cease being fruitful. There was no little love to drink of their bounty. No man other than Othon had ever needed her in that way.

*   *   *

"Looks like a good day to stay in bed," Roy
Johnson grumbled as he chewed on warmed-over meat
and sipped coffee boiled over the open fire. "That is,
for a man who has enough sense to be at home where
he has a bed."

Clouds had moved in during the night, and with
them came a bone-aching chill. When the men were
under way in the large canoe, their provisions and
kits protected from moisture by a buffalo hide, Roy
crouched down on his seat and pulled his buffalo cloak
tightly around him. The clouds lowered damply to
hang just over the river. A fine mist dampened Roy's
developing beard and droplets rolled down his neck.

"I have to admit," he said, not being one who
was inclined to suffer in silence, "that I'm not likin'
this."

Drifting passively down a river in a boat was not
Renno's first preference for a method of travel. On
land his warrior's jog would have warmed him; but
even when he used the paddle to urge the boat to
move just a bit faster, he was still chilled by the fine,
cold mist. Up ahead ridges closed down on the river,
making for some impressive riverside bluffs. He guided
the canoe close to the shore, and when he saw a likely
shelter in a rocky overhang, he landed on a tiny, muddy
beach.

" 'Bout time," Roy muttered as he helped carry
the gear to the cavelike shelter.

Renno soon had a fire going. Roy huddled under
his buffalo hide and stared moodily at the flames.
Renno went off into the mist and came back with a
meal—a fat young turkey. The mist became a light,
cold rain. Roy tucked his chin down on his chest,
pulled his buffalo robe tighter, and had a little nap.
The fire cracked and popped. Rainwater dripped
down the rocks and accumulated into little pools. As
Renno turned the turkey on the spit and leaned back
against a rock, he thought that Roy was right. It was
a good day to be at home . . . a very good day for

bed—bed with a flame-haired woman who loved him.
Maybe Roy had a point in saying that it was time
for both of them to attend first and forever to home
duties.

He closed his eyes, then opened them, startled,
sensing a danger that would not define itself. He froze
and listened, but there were only the musical drip of
water and the cracklings and hissings of the fire. He
closed his eyes again, and again the alarm was instant.
He moved to the front of the rocky overhang and
looked up and down the river. The empty waters disappeared in each direction into the mist.

Renno went back inside, crossed his legs under
him, and stared into the fire. "Manitous?" he whispered. "Manitous . . ."

He was answered by a flare of warning, of danger. It was unseen and unexplained, but now he knew
it did exist. The flames had merged into a whiteness,
and the knowledge came silently from something unseen in the glare: the danger was not immediate, not
in the shelter of the rocky ledge with the smell of
roasting meat and the soft sound of Roy's deep
breathing.

"Tell me, manitous, is the danger for me or for
those I love?"

A fiery tendril pierced him as if to say, *It is for
you. The danger is for you.*

He chanted silently, closed his eyes, and tried to
sense the danger. But he felt only that vague, wordless
warning. A face tried but failed to materialize in the
fire, and a spirit voice formed sounds but not words.
The moaning, grieving sound caused the hairs to
prickle on his arms and the back of his neck. Then,
just as he was despairing of learning the meaning of
the spirit warning, pale-haired Emily smiled out at
him.

"Speak to me. Advise me," Renno said, holding
out his hands.

"When the tree branch of evil is in your hands,
snap it," the manitou said, then was gone.

Roy snorted and smacked his lips, then came fully awake to mumble, "Fire the cook, Renno. The food should be ready by now."

Renno shook his head to dispel a feeling of impending dread. He and Roy chewed silently on two big drumsticks as the drizzle continued. By the time darkness fell most of the turkey was gone, and with bellies filled, the men slept.

The rain became mist again toward morning and then lifted, leaving a lowering, glowering sky and a fitful, cold wind from the north. The fire had burned down so that the cave was cold and damp when Renno awoke. There was enough dry wood left to warm Roy's old bones before the pair packed their kits into the canoe and set off. As they approached the confluence of the Ohio and the Mississippi they saw the smoke of several campfires on the north side of the river.

"Indians?" Roy guessed.

"No." Renno knew that the fires were too big, too wasteful to be the cooking fires of Indians.

"Reckon we'd better have a look?" Roy asked.

"So," Renno said, turning the bow of the canoe toward the shore.

As the men on shore caught sight of the canoe, they began to gather by the river's edge.

"A passel of 'em," Roy remarked. "Each one of 'em has a rifle."

"Hooooeee, there," came a call from land. "Are you'uns from Burr?"

"Well, well, well," Roy said. "You don't reckon they're from the island?"

"No, I don't recognize any of them," Renno answered.

"Are you from Burr?" another voice asked.

"Give us time," Roy yelled back. When the canoe neared the bank he explained, "I didn't want to strain my goozle yelling."

"What word do you have?" a buckskin-clad frontiersman asked.

"Hold your horses," Roy said. "Who's in charge here?"

Renno noticed that several pairs of eyes shifted toward the flatboat tied securely to two trees on the bank.

"Ain't rightly no one in charge. We'uns come down the river from St. Louie to wait fer Burr and his army."

"Well," Roy said, "you've got a bit longer to wait."

"I fer one ain't gonna stay here all winter lessen I see the color of gold," a young man in homespun said in disgust.

"When does Burr plan to come downriver?" the man in buckskins asked.

Roy looked at Renno. A message in the sachem's stance—an alertness, tension, something unusual—told Roy to fall silent and wait for Renno to answer.

"He's no more than four days behind us," Renno said. "How many men are here?"

"They's twenty-two of us rarin' fer a fight," the young man said.

Renno nodded.

"Be plenty of that, comes the time," Roy said. "Is there a cook with this outfit?"

"Not so's you can tell it."

The men on the shore laughed.

"I was afraid of that," Roy grumbled.

"Want some help getting your things on land?" the young man in homespun asked.

"No," Renno said, "we'll be going on down the river."

"Afore night?"

"There are other groups waiting down below," Renno lied. His alert systems were charged and tingling out their little songs of danger, although the risk did not come from the camp of the men from St. Louis. Clearly they were just trappers and hunters and wanderers who had stumbled onto what they thought was a good opportunity. "What we'd like, my friends, is some coffee and maybe a little sugar if you've got it to spare."

"We come loaded for bear. I reckon we can spare you what you need," the self-appointed spokesman said. He turned to the young man. "Luke, you wanta get these gentlemen some coffee and sugar?"

"I reckon," Luke said.

"Yawl come on over to my shack and have a sit down," the man in buckskins said.

Renno secured the canoe, handed Roy his rifle to bring along, then took up his own. In the wilderness a man wasn't whole without his weapon. None of the St. Louis men saw anything untoward in the visitors carrying their rifles.

Renno's little songs of warnings were tinkling in his ears, causing spurts of alarm to shoot into his stomach. He looked around carefully. A movement on the flatboat caught his eyes, but when he snapped his head around to look, nothing was there.

Melisande had seen the white Indian coming for quite some time. She had seen him through the cold mist . . . had watched him at his fire . . . had willed him to come to her through a long night. Then she had seen him with her eyes when he landed at the camp. Her hatred was almost tangible as it struggled to reach out to him; but she knew from past experience that the forces of good were at the call of the bronzed, blond-haired warrior. Time and again she had met him in battle only to be routed. This time she would not be so foolish as to face him squarely, for not even the imps and demons of the evil ones could prevail against the full powers of what the Indians called the Master of Life. This time she would approach him through his weakness. This time she would use her wiles and rely less on the aid of the powers of evil.

She could hear what was being said. She could feel that Renno was wary, nervous. His manitous, however, powerful as they were, had not made it clear to him exactly where danger lay and in what form. If she could keep him in ignorance of her presence, she would win—but she would have to move swiftly. She could not afford to wait.

Even as her enemy and his friend walked toward a lean-to where a pot of coffee boiled aromatically over a fire, Melisande lifted her arms and, calling upon all of the evil powers, sent a wave of lethargy spreading over the camp. Already she had influenced each of the men at the time of recruitment, so all of them were receptive. One by one they found a place to sit or lie. One by one they closed their eyes.

The man in buckskins who was acting as host poured coffee into tin cups for Renno and Roy.

"Thankee," Roy said, sipping the scalding liquid. He smacked his lips. "Whooee! Boiled that stuff twice, didn't you?"

The man in buckskins didn't answer. He had seated himself. His head was hanging loosely to one side.

"I'll be daggummed," Roy said.

Renno's scalp tingled. He looked around. The other men were sleeping beside their fires. Some of them were sprawled full length; others sat, leaning.

"What do you make of it, Renno?" Roy asked, hiding a great yawn behind his fist. He shook his head to clear it, then sat down slowly. "By gum, whatever it is—" He did not finish the sentence. Although his eyes were still open, his chin sank to his chest and the tin cup rolled from his limp fingers.

Renno felt the tide of a force being directed at him. He turned to locate its source.

The witch stood on the flatboat, her arms extended toward him. Her eyes caught his, and he was nearly staggered by her beauty, her youth, her sensuous shapeliness. She wore nothing more than a white chemise, which showed her beautifully formed legs from above the knees.

"I am waiting," she intoned.

Renno nodded silently.

"Leave your rifle," she whispered.

Although a hundred feet separated them, he heard. He put his rifle down beside Roy.

"Come," she coaxed.

He walked slowly toward the flatboat.

"You won't need your tomahawk or your knife."

He discarded his weapons. Melisande frowned when he took the time to remove the sheath of his Spanish stiletto from his belt instead of merely throwing the knife onto the ground. Moreover, he bent to place the weapons carefully in a relatively dry spot.

"Come," she whispered.

He walked up the gangplank to the flatboat. The board bent and bounced under his tread, for he did not slow. He stopped upon order directly in front of the witch, who had taken the form of Emily, pale-haired and slender—Emily as a girl . . . Emily as she looked when she became Renno's wife.

He ached for her. His heart swelled for her. His hands itched to touch her. His eyes told him that his first love stood before him. His heart told him to reach out.

"Yes, yes," the witch urged. "Closer. Come just a bit closer, my little love."

One step, then two. He had the scent of her now, for the witch looked into him and stole his memories and put them into use against him.

Emily . . . beautiful, pale-haired Emily . . .

And in her hand was a knife, a long, thick-bladed killing tool honed to razor sharpness. She looked triumphant, as if she had won a great prize. Slowly she raised the knife and positioned it. Her eyes wore a look of satisfaction, of having a helpless man in her absolute power. She wanted to make it last. By the knife's positioning, he knew she would thrust the blade upward into the vee of his rib cage, then drive it through the diaphragm and into his heart. Why would Emily wish him harm? He could not believe she would

bring the blade up, for his eyes told him that this was
his pale-haired first love.

Her lips curled as she thrust.

Immediately Renno closed his fist over Emily's
fair, shapely wrist to feel the bony thinness.

His eyes still told him that it was Emily. He had
not fought against the illusion because he wanted to
give the witch confidence. He had to get near her
before she fled, before she flew, before she dissolved
herself into nothingness, as she had done the last time
they met.

She cried out as his strength frustrated the killing
blow. "You love me," she whispered desperately. "I
am your wife."

Renno twisted the bony wrist, and the knife clat-
tered onto the deck with a metallic clang. Her claws
searched for his eyes.

"Let me go, beloved!" she screamed. "Please,
darling, let me go!"

He seized her other arm. He had never killed a
woman. Worse, his eyes continued to tell him that this
woman was Emily. He was indecisive even as imps of
evil materialized and began to tear at the flesh of his
legs and thighs. He had given her time to muster her
strength.

Emily's voice came to him: *When the tree branch
of evil is in your hands, snap it.*

He released one of the witch's hands and jerked
her toward him with the other. She screamed and
called down the demons of evil to caper and tear at
Renno. He suspected that she could not use her powers to evaporate as long as he had his hands on her.
Now he had his arms tightly around her, immobilizing
her. She tried to slip away; but his grip was iron,
and the strong force flowing from him neutralized her
powers.

Snap it, the voice of the manitou urged.

He hesitated once more, and the witch's strength
grew. The imps of evil drew real blood, for he let his

guard fall for a moment. The pain served to alert him to his very real danger. If he allowed himself to believe that the misshapen horrors that gibbered at his legs were real, they would bleed him into helplessness. His faith and his alliance with the powers of good were his only weapons against the spirit allies of the witch.

Snap it! the spirit voice repeated.

He lifted her, and in his hands her thin, frail body felt like a dry branch. He snapped the branch across his upraised thigh as if he were preparing firewood.

The witch screamed in agony and despair as her back snapped, and she fell helpless to the deck. The imps and demons vanished.

Renno watched as she lifted her arm and reached for the fallen knife.

It is not over, the voice of the manitou warned.

He took the knife from her weak fingers and knelt beside her.

"You love me, dearest," Emily said, looking up into his face with a wan smile. "You would never harm me, my beloved."

He flicked the sharp blade of the knife across the pale, slim, beautiful throat. There was a gurgling sound. Behind him men began to awaken. Before his eyes Emily became the wizened, graying, black-toothed Witch of the Woods who, as he watched, spasmed and died.

Chapter Twelve

That year, the young pecan trees that lined the lane
leading up to Huntington Castle bore a harvest-
able crop of fruit for the first time. Throughout the
summer the green nuts swelled with growth among the
feathery leaves. The frosts of autumn browned the hulls
and split them open. In preparation for the fall of the
pecan nuts, Beth had hired two of Se-quo-i's nephews
to scythe down the grass under the trees. Now, on a
day that God had made—a glory of a day, a day that
was as invigorating as happy news, a day that was
warm but with a delightful hint of fall—Ta-na, Gao,
half a dozen other young scamps, and quite a few
adults had gathered by the trees. The boys were climbing about in the branches, shaking limbs to dislodge
the reluctant nuts from their husks. As Beth watched,
the boys reminded her of squirrels.

"Don't you dare break any limbs," she called up

to them in Seneca. "Ta-na, don't put so much weight
on such a small—"

Craaaaack!

Ta-na barely recovered as a limb broke underneath him. He was left swinging by his hands ten feet
above the ground.

"Ohhhh," Beth moaned.

Ta-na threw his legs up and over the limb, then
slithered back to the main trunk of the tree. "I'm
sorry, Beth."

"Do be careful," she said in English. "It has
taken so long to nurse these trees to bearing."

"It will not happen again." Ta-na grinned down
at her. "I'll be especially careful if you'll promise to
bake pecan pies."

"I'll bake if you'll shell the nuts," Beth offered.

All of the women of the white Indian's clan—
Beth, Toshabe, Ena, Ah-wa-o, We-yo—were under
the trees. Little Summer Moon was picking up pecans
and showing them to the baby Ah-wen-ga, who looked
as if she wanted to try to eat them, hull and all. Two
of Se-quo-i's nieces were helping, to assure that Se-
quo-i got his share of the nuts. Toshabe and Ena
would distribute the surplus to other families in the
two villages, for the crop was a bountiful one.

Gao came down from a tree. He had denuded it
of nuts to the best of his ability. He cracked two large
pecans in his hand and offered his grandmother an
unbroken half of a kernel. She leaned forward and
took it from his fingers.

"Good?" Gao asked as she chewed.

"Good," Toshabe said, "but without the tang of
the black walnuts and hickory nuts of the forests."

"So much easier to shell," Ah-wa-o pointed out.

"But not as suitable for making nut balls," Toshabe said.

"With my mother," Ena said ruefully, "the old
ways are always the best."

"There is nothing to equal the taste of a nut ball
made with black walnuts," Beth remarked, showing

that Toshabe's comments about the pecans were not taken seriously. Besides, she spoke the truth, and it did not hurt her in the slightest to please her mother-by-marriage by agreeing with her.

"My nephews have located a honey tree," Se-quo-i said. "When it is cold enough to keep the bees from being overly zealous in the protection of their treasure, I will bring you some honey, Beth."

"I think Uncle Se-quo-i is hinting for a piece of pecan pie, too," Ta-na said, laughing.

"You may put the proper appellation to it," Se-quo-i said. "I am *begging* for a piece—a very large piece—of Beth's miracle of the culinary art."

"Uncle Se-quo-i's been reading books with big words in them again," Gao said.

"Something that wouldn't hurt you at all, young man," Ena said, tweaking Gao's ear.

"I am going to be like my cousin Rusog Ho-ya," Gao boasted, "and forget my white blood and never speak English."

"That would not be too smart," Se-quo-i said.

Naomi, dressed in a very attractive Iroquois *a-kia-ta-wi* over deerskin leggings, was seated on the grass and playing with Summer Moon and Ah-wen-ga. Naomi and Beth had made the overdress of light wool cloth and decorated it with patterns of bead-work. Her taffy-colored hair glistened with highlights in the sun and was braided into twin pigtails.

"This one is such a tease," Naomi said to We-yo as Summer Moon first extended a pecan toward her and then jerked it back with a big smile and a liquid laugh.

Sitting side by side, We-yo and Naomi made a delightful contrast. The two girls were separated in age by only five years. Naomi was fair, her hair so light and fine, the tip of her nose decorated with two freckles. We-yo's beauty was dark and sultry, with lively black eyes and thick, Indian-straight hair.

Beth, glancing at them, felt a quick uplift of her mood. The appreciation of beauty tended to affect her that way—be it the splendor of a sunset, the tumble of agile young boys at play, or the natural grace of young women. Her thoughts meandered haphazard and undirected. The pleasure of looking at beauty brought to mind the most beautiful thing in her life, the love she shared with Renno. She was overcome with a quick pang of loneliness. Her mercurial change in mood transformed into concern for the two lovely girls, so different, but each of them alone. The man We-yo had loved was dead. The man that Naomi loved, although she had never mentioned it overtly, was far away.

It wasn't fair for a woman to be alone. It was not fair to herself, nor to the two younger ones. She would, Beth decided, have a few things to say to Sachem Renno when he returned. She would say, "Now you look here, Husband, I did not leave my home in England and I did not leave my shipping business in Wilmington to come to the western end of nowhere to spend my time alone. I came here to be with you, and, in the future, my dear, I am going to insist that you remember that."

But she smiled to herself and shook her head, for she remembered something that Toshabe had said more than once: "You might as well try to bottle a moonbeam as to try to keep that man out of the forests."

So there they were, women without men. We-yo, a widow; Naomi, still scarred by her ghastly experiences with the Morgans; she and Toshabe temporarily widowed by that disease that seemed to afflict their men more than most, the urge to be off and away.

In spite of the wave of loneliness for Renno, her life was good. Beth did not, in truth, regret the decisions she had made. The sun was kind and bright. The air was dry and perfect. She was comforted by the sound of young voices, the presence of good friends and relatives, and the gathering of long-awaited fat, sweet pecans in the various vessels. Behind the fence a spring foal ran stilt legged beside his dam. Overhead a vee of geese honked their way southward.

"I think," Toshabe said, straightening her back, "that we have picked up all of the nuts from this tree." She nodded at Naomi and We-yo, who were still playing with the young ones. "At least some of us have picked them up, while others have taken their ease."

"Let them enjoy the moment, Toshabe," Beth said quietly.

"Yes," Toshabe said, nodding, instantly understanding Beth's unspoken point. Whatever small happinesses came to one who had lost her husband and one who had lost her innocence were well deserved. After El-i-chi had disposed of the Morgans' corpses, he had told his mother about the invasion of Beth's house. This had led to an explanation of Naomi's history, and Toshabe's heart went out to the girl.

Now, the pleasant work continued in a leisurely fashion. Se-quo-i had instructed one of his nephews how to fashion a flail from a long, thin sapling taken from the grove along the creek. The last remaining nuts came down as the boys used the long flail to beat the tree branches.

Naomi's scream shattered the idyllic mood and setting. She leaped to her feet. Her cry was part terror, part negation.

Beth ran to her. Naomi's eyes were wide and dilated.

"Are you snake bit?" Ta-na asked.

"I'm so sorry," Naomi said, her hands on her chest. She was panting. "I don't know—I mean, I—" She fell silent, turned, and ran toward the house.

"Go to her, Flame Hair," Toshabe said.

Beth needed no urging.

Naomi had stopped in the entrance hall. "I'm so embarrassed," she said. She was shaking.

Beth gathered the girl into her arms. "Unwelcome thoughts?"

"No, not the old nightmares," Naomi quavered. "I hesitate to voice it, Beth, lest by putting it into words I make it real."

More than once Naomi had shown signs of having the sight that had once come to Renno and El-i-chi, the ability to see things at a distance and, often, into the future.

"Then I won't ask," Beth said.

"It was Little Hawk."

Beth felt a cold chill.

"I saw an angry, wild sea, and then his face. He was lying so still—"

Please, please, Beth was praying, *not Little Hawk*.

Naomi pushed herself away, determination in her face. "He cannot be dead! I will not believe it. I will not allow it."

She burst into tears, and as Beth took Naomi into her arms again, it was all the woman could do not to lose control of herself, too.

Winter enfolded the land in its chill embrace. The great bear in the sky dripped color onto the leaves, and so weighted, they fluttered to litter the ground and delighted children with the wonderful colors and the pleasing rustlings. The passage of time enabled Beth to put Naomi's vision aside, and Naomi seemed to have done the same.

Beth had spent more than one day baking pecan pies for her procession of male admirers, who ranged in age from thirteen, in the case of Ta-na, to maturity represented by Se-quo-i, Rusog, and El-i-chi. She was already making plans for Christmas, all the while hoping that she would not have to celebrate it without Renno.

Preparations were already under way for still another observance of the annual ceremony of the new beginning. Soon each Seneca would search his secret heart to discover new dreams to replace the old. Beth herself had new dreams. She mused on the possibility of convincing Renno to go to England. The travel party would include herself, Naomi—for the girl was, as far as Beth was concerned, family—and perhaps even El-i-chi and Ah-wa-o, the boys, and little Ah-wen-ga. They would travel across the mountains to North Carolina, to Wilmington and then on to England. She had another dream, too—of Renno's safe return and his promise not to leave her again.

Naomi Burns was not searching for new dreams. She had only one aspiration, and she feared that she wished in vain, for her only desire was that Little Hawk would love her. In spite of her vision of him, in which he was lying very still on a sandy beach with a wild sea raging in the background, Naomi had convinced herself that he would come back.

At times she felt as if she were two people. One was like a lost child, existing temporarily on the kindness of Beth Huntington. That Naomi was a soiled, forever-damaged thing that could not hope for normalcy or happiness. When that Naomi was in command, the young woman wanted only to go to her room, lie on the bed and stare at the ceiling, remember with noxious, damaging hatred the joy of revenge, and savor the remembered stench of Tommy Morgan's burning hair and his agonized, unhuman cries as he suffered terminal pain.

The other Naomi was full of wonder and a dreamer. She could not apply the events of that year with the Morgans to herself. She had rebuked the evil that had been visited upon her. She felt clean and whole. And she dreamed that Little Hawk would come back to her and that he would hold her as he had held her when she was just a girl, when her soft, warm lips had tasted his and in so doing had felt the kiss of a boy for the first time. That Naomi prepared the way for the fulfillment of her dreams by making a study of Seneca and Cherokee habits and customs. She spent time with Toshabe and listened to the articles of Seneca tradition. From Ena she heard stories of the trials and triumphs of Renno and his forebears. From stolid Rusog she heard bloody tales of Cherokee greatness, and from the urbane Se-quo-i came a wealth of information on just about every subject.

There had been times during her ordeal that she questioned not the existence of God but whether or not He cared, whether or not He involved Himself in the day-to-day affairs of man. Now although she did not abandon her faith, she came to wonder about and to see merit in the Seneca's reliance on the forces of good, epitomized by the Master of Life.

It interested her greatly when El-i-chi, in answer to direct but politely worded questions, told her that yes, both he and Renno—Renno to a greater extent—conversed with the manitous.

"I am not Seneca," she said, "so it cannot be Seneca manitous who show me things."

El-i-chi nodded, too polite to ask questions about her prophecies.

"Last winter," Naomi said, "when it was time for Toshabe to call out the names of the babies that had been born since the Festival of the Corn, I knew the names before she spoke them."

"Perhaps you had heard others speak of them?"

"Then why," she asked, "do I know that before the festival of the new beginning and the naming of the babies there will be two new ones born—one a girl called Winter Moon, the other a boy who will be named for Cornplanter, a great Seneca chief?"

El-i-chi made a mental note of the predictions. "I have never known of a white person having the sight," he said. Then he thought of the witch, Melisande, and said, "Unless she was a witch."

Naomi laughed uneasily. "I don't think I'm a witch. I don't want to be a witch. I'm not even sure I want to have the sight."

She told him about her vision involving Little Hawk. He frowned and muttered a quick prayer for his nephew's safety. He himself no longer had the sight. Perhaps, El-i-chi thought, it had come to him in a time of great peril and might come again if danger threatened him or his.

"So," he said. He grinned. "There are more things under heaven and earth, Horatio, than are dreamt of in your philosophy."

She laughed. "A Seneca shaman who quotes Shakespeare?" she said. "You all constantly amaze me."

He shrugged. "Well, you can't be around the flame-haired one without reading or being read to. That's just my way of saying that there are many things that I do not understand."

"In that," she said with feeling, "you are not alone."

At the exact moment when Naomi leaped to her feet and screamed on that beautiful autumn day in the Cherokee Nation, a younger maiden, just sixteen, was gathering shells on a stormy beach three thousand miles away.

Her name was Twana, and she was known by the members of her small tribe, the Chehalis, as the strange one. She had a pleasant, round face; full lips; alert, dark eyes. She was short and pleasantly plump, and her curves were ample—so much so that three times she had refused the offer of marriage from worthy young men whom only the strange one would have rebuffed.

Because Twana's father and his brothers were among the tribe's strongest men and best hunters, and because her father sat on the council of elders, her preference for solitude, for leaving the company of the other young women in order to wander alone the seashore, was tolerated.

Twana was an only child. Her mother had died in giving her life, and her father doted on her. He had held her on his knee when she was a child to tell her stories and legends, and one of the legends had had a strong influence on her. In it a Chehalis maiden became the beloved of a sky spirit, a man of surpassing beauty. From the time Twana was ten years old, first beginning to feel intimations of her sexuality,

she dreamed that one day she, too, would be loved
by some special someone, a man of surpassing beauty.
Perhaps he would not be a sky spirit, because spirits
were, after all, rather frightening, even when they
were good spirits. Twana knew that such fancies made
the other girls laugh at her and call her strange. She
didn't care.

And she did not care that no one else walked the
shore alone. She loved the sea when it was angry. She
never tired of watching the huge ocean rollers hump
up and tumble whitely onto the small, sandy beaches
or vent their fury in a frothing roar against the spires
of rocks and the cliffs. Storm waves delivered the most
beautiful shells, so she was often on the shore when
rain or windblown spray drenched her clothing and
pasted her dark hair to her head.

On a day in autumn she had made her way precariously down the cliffs to her favorite beach and was
walking idly, listening to the anger of the sea, and
watching the gulls conquer the wind to soar and glide
gracefully. She did not see the man lying facedown on
the sand with the last, dying ripples of the waves washing his feet until she was almost on him. She halted,
poised for flight.

The longtime Spanish presence in the area to the
south and the white man's hunger for furs, gold, and
land had assured that every tribe along the northwest
coast had knowledge of the men who wore shells like
the turtle. But this man lying so still on the wet sand
wore no armor. He was dressed like an Indian in deerskin, although his hair was fair. She crept closer. He
looked dead. His face was pale. A large bump on his
head oozed blood.

She squatted, pushing her doeskin skirt under her
knees with one hand. For long minutes the man did
not move, but she could see his chest lifting and lowering. So he was alive.

The tide was rising. The waves were beginning to
shift his feet with their motion. She stood, grasped his
wrists, and pulled him out of the reach of the dying

breakers. When she turned him over, the beauty of his face made her gasp. His skin was lighter than hers but bronzed by the sun. Perhaps he was only a Spaniard, and if so, her father and his brothers would kill him immediately.

As she knelt beside him, he opened his eyes. They were the blue of the sky—the most beautiful eyes she had ever seen. He moved his head. She drew back. His eyes found hers and widened. He spoke, and his voice, although it spoke a tongue she did not understand, a tongue that was not Spanish, was low and musical to her ears. He tried to sit up, then his eyes rolled up into his head and he fell back limply.

Afraid that he had died, she put her hand on his throat to feel his pulse. It was weak but regular. His skin was cold and clammy. She dragged him toward the cliffs, into one of her favorite retreats. There she had stored driftwood. There she kept water in a covered ceramic pot, and that day she had brought with her from the village smoked fish and cornmeal bread.

She dried the man's face and pushed back his wet hair. "You have been sent to me," she whispered. "You are of surpassing beauty."

The dream of the strange one had been fulfilled.

Not all of the twenty-two men who had been recruited in St. Louis by Melisande for Aaron Burr's army were in the camp. When the witch used the power she had established over each of them individually to make time stand still, a few had been out hunting. Others were scattered up and down the riverbank, fishing or walking. The men in camp were all sleeping, so not one of them had seen Renno walk onto the barge at the witch's call.

Roy Johnson had been looking directly at Melisande when she cast her spell. But her power over him was only partially effective because she had not had an opportunity to lay the groundwork for her mesmerism. Roy, in a state of near paralysis, watched Renno put down his weapons and walk to the flatboat.

He tried to call out a warning, but it was impossible
to act on his intention. He felt as if he were stuck in
thick molasses. He saw Renno lift the woman's frail
body and snap her spine across his knee, and Roy's
long, incomprehensible words began to come out of
his mouth when the blade of a knife slashed across
the witch's throat.

"Watch out for that woman!" Roy shouted after
it was all over.

But Renno was already in motion. He leaped
from the flatboat to the bank, then ran to gather up
his weapons. Roy seized his rifle and moved as fast
as he could to join Renno. Behind him he heard yells
and curses as the men recovered from the witch's spell
and saw their beloved lying on the deck of the flatboat
with her lifeblood staining the planking.

"Hear me!" Renno shouted. He had his rifle lev-
eled toward the nearest group of men. "I have no
fight with you."

"You kilt her," a young man cried out, his voice
made hoarse by his sudden tears. "Let's get that sumbitch, fellers. He done kilt Melisande."

"Like he says, fellas," Roy shouted, "we got no
quarrel with you. Once you take a look at her, I think
you'll understand that Melisande got nothing more
than she deserved."

"What are you all waiting for?" the young man
screamed. He grabbed his musket and brought it
around to aim at Roy's head.

With sadness, Roy dropped the boy before he
could fire his musket. Renno was ready to shoot the
next man who moved. Roy reloaded in record time,
and once again there were two muskets facing the
many men.

"The others will be coming on the run," Roy
said.

"Put your back to mine," Renno said. "We will
move slowly toward the canoe." To the tense, angry
men he called, "We want no more bloodshed. Before
you try to kill us, go look at the body on the flatboat."

A man rose without his weapon and walked toward the barge. Renno, still moving backward, his back to Roy's, was inching slowly toward the riverbank and the canoe.

The man who boarded the flatboat fell to his knees beside the fallen woman, turned her head toward him, then cried out and leaped to his feet. "This ain't Melisande!" he shouted. "This is some old hag."

Others left their weapons behind and quickly joined the man on the deck. As Renno and Roy gained the riverbank, two men who had not been in the camp came running.

"What's all the ruckus?" one of them asked.

From the flatboat a young man cried out, "Melisande! Melisande, where are you?"

"Something happened to Melisande?" one of the hunters asked.

"You wouldn't believe it," Roy told him.

The two hunters rushed past. Renno held the canoe steady while Roy got in, and soon they were moving out into the flow of the river. They were no more than fifty yards downstream from the camp when men ran to the bank and took aim at the canoe. A rifle ball splashed the water just behind Renno. Roy, sitting in front, threw up his rifle and fired, and a man went down. A smattering of balls sang past. One chipped wood from the gunwale of the canoe. Roy took Renno's rifle, aimed, and fired, and another man on the bank fell even while Renno put more and more distance between the canoe and the men on shore.

"If they all shoot like that," Roy said as the canoe moved out of range, "the Spaniards will have Burr's army for breakfast."

All that day Renno paddled slowly but steadily to add more momentum to the boat as it was carried down the broad, muddy Mississippi. Because there was very little wind he eased the boat across the wide waters to the western bank. Melisande's bereaved lovers had only their flatboat, so he didn't expect pursuit; but he saw no reason to take chances. It was not that he was running from a fight; but to have killed men bewitched by the evil woman would have been an odious misuse of his skills, an exercise in blood without any hint of reason. It would have been fighting just for the sake of fighting. He had spoken true when he had told the men that he had no quarrel with them.

During the days that followed, while the canoe drifted lazily southward and each watery mile brought them closer to home, Renno talked about the places he had seen in his travels. Roy listened, for he was enough like the Indian never to tire of hearing a rousing story. He very quickly got the point that Renno was making.

"I have fought in Canada," Renno said. "I have fought on the sea and on islands in the Caribbean. I have fought in the deserts of the Southwest and in Spanish Mexico and in the jungles of Africa. Wherever I have been, with few exceptions, I have fought and killed."

"Usually, I expect, to keep from being killed," Roy said.

"But what have I gained?" Renno asked. "Coup? Honor? Where are the souls of the men I have killed?" He was silent for a long time.

"Some of 'em needed killing," Roy pointed out. "Hodano and Othon Hugues, to name just two."

"Yes, that is true. But why was *I* the one chosen by the Master of Life to do the killing?"

"Son," Roy said, "I know what you're saying. I didn't exactly do a song and dance and get all thrilled up to my eyeballs when I had to shoot men back there at Melisande's camp. I shot 'em because they were trying to shoot us. I don't think God picked me to send those fellows to heaven or hell, whichever. I think you and I just happened to be there, and you did a duty that needed doing. You went to Jamaica to rescue a friend, and to do it you had to kill a few men. Same holds true for Africa. If I had to guess,

I'd say that such things happen because that's the kind of world we live in. You and I, we could go back east and get a little house in, say, Philadelphia or New York, and then we might go the rest of our lives without having to kill another man. On the other hand, the first day we were there some footpad might try to rob one of us and not care whether or not he killed us in doing so. In that case we might have to kill him right there on a civilized street. One thing for sure, as long as we go traipsing around out here on the front side of everything, we're going to find a fight now and then."

"Roy," Renno said, "I'm tired."

"Well, my back's feeling pretty good. Let me paddle awhile."

"It is not my arms that are tired. Not my body."

"Hummm," Roy said. "Well, I reckon that in a couple of weeks a certain redheaded gal will do away with that kind of tiredness pretty quick."

In the principal Chickasaw town on the bluffs overlooking the Mississippi from the eastern bank, Renno traded the extra weapons and blankets that had been supplied by William Henry Harrison for new moccasins and buckskins for himself and Roy. As they set off toward the east Roy was moving like a young man; Renno was not the only one eager to get home.

In the virgin wilderness Renno was feeling like himself once again. He voiced no more doubts, mused no more about the past. He moved with a skill that fooled the wary deer, that surprised the squirrels feeding on the forest floor. His eyes missed nothing, and his ears heard even the rustlings of a mouse in its small patch of grass.

The days passed. Winter had followed them southward, and there were times when the cold wind sent icy fingers through the openings of their clothing. Roy nearly died on a day when a dull, slate sky spit isolated sleet showers. The storm hissed and crackled through the trees and fallen leaves, masking the

sounds made by a war party of four young Chickasaw
warriors. Two things saved Roy's life—the low-
hanging limbs of a tree and Renno's superb reaction
time.

Roy and Renno had made camp under the protec-
tive overhang of a dense cedar tree. In order to attack
the two seated men from the rear, it was necessary
for the leader of the Chickasaw war party to bend
down and walk, crouching, under the tree. When the
warrior struck, his tomahawk snagged momentarily on
a small limb and dislodged a shower of sleet. Even
before the sleet fell on Renno, the white Indian was
moving. He swung his tomahawk so close to Roy's
head that the older man felt the wind of its passage.
The blade parried the Chickasaw's blow, which had
been aimed at the nape of Roy's neck, and crashed
past to sink home in the Indian's middle.

In tearing the blade free to be used again, Renno
had to expend great strength. The Chickasaw warrior's
entrails were pulled from his living stomach. He fell
with a muffled cry.

Renno dodged the blade of a second warrior, fell,
and rolled away from the low, overhanging branches.
He grunted with satisfaction as, out of the corner of
his eye, he saw Roy's rifle lifting. The roar of the
piece was loud, even in the muffling chatter of falling
sleet. A cry followed the shot.

Renno was suddenly very busy with two Chickasaw warriors just past boyhood. Lithe and well-
formed, they were dressed for war in warm skins and
furs. Their face paint spoke of their intent. Renno fell
back, crashing steel on steel as he parried a blow. His
counterstrike left a great gash across the forearm of
one boy-man. The two Chickasaw fell back. Renno
saw past them, to where Roy was reaching for Renno's loaded rifle.

"Hold your fire, Roy," Renno said.

One of the young warriors made a feint. Renno
did not move. "Brothers," he said in Chickasaw, "we
are of one blood."

One of the Chickasaw grunted in surprise. "The white face speaks our tongue."

"I am Seneca," Renno said, "brother to the Cherokee chief Rusog. We have a solemn peace with the Chickasaw."

The man with the cut was trying to stanch the flow of blood by lifting his arm.

"Your wound needs care," Renno said.

"Seneca or not," the other Chickasaw seethed, "you have shed our blood." He leaped to the attack, only to be thrust forward violently as Roy shot him in the spine. Renno moved aside to avoid the hacking, dying blow of the dead man's tomahawk.

The man with the gash in his arm began to sing in a high voice.

"Fool," Renno said. "You do not have to sing your death song."

But the boy-man came in a rush, his eyes wild, his mouth open in a whoop of despair and terror. The death he sought came swiftly with a merciful, crunching smash to the temple from Renno's tomahawk.

Renno stood with his bloody weapon dangling, his head down, his heart slowing from the heat of battle.

"Stupid boys," Roy growled.

Renno turned his face to the gray, spitting sky. His voice was an agonized, penetrating call that rang and echoed among the trees. "Manitous," he cried, "must we always fight among ourselves? Must we always fight against those who should not be our enemies?"

They moved camp. The dead were left where they fell. The Chickasaw had chosen the way of war. The loser who fought far from home would be food for the small scavengers, winged and otherwise; that was the way of it. But another tradition was not kept. No scalps were taken, for neither Renno nor Roy felt that it had been a victory to slay four Chickasaw boys who had been intent on proving their manhood.

The second campsite was not as cozy as the first.

The men built a hasty lean-to against a deadfall, and when Renno awoke with the gray, chill dawn, sleet that had accumulated on his blanket melted with his body heat, then refroze into a sheet of ice that crackled and tinkled to the ground when he got up. Roy was stiff in the joints. They were traveling light and had no coffeepot. Breakfast was jerky and corn. The men ate it on the march.

By the time they had to swim the frigid waters of the Tombigbee in order to travel on the south bank of the Tennessee, the weather had moderated. But it took Roy a long, long time to stop shivering as he dried himself beside a roaring fire.

"Renno, this traveling doesn't seem like such a good idea anymore," he said.

Now they used the well-marked tracks that connected Cherokee settlements. Renno, brother to the principal chief, Rusog, was welcomed whenever he and Roy chose to enter one of the Cherokee villages. The last days of their journey they were passed from one town to the next with well wishes and full bellies. Sleeping in a warm Cherokee lodge made life easier for Roy. He began to feel much better, and his step quickened when the ridge lines began to look familiar. Both men knew just when and where the trail they followed would bend toward the south and home. Individual landmarks were recognized and celebrated.

"Just over there," Renno said, "Little Hawk killed his first deer with the bow."

"Up ahead is the road to Tellico Bloc House," Roy said.

"That's where Little Hawk met Louis Philippe and Renna's Beau."

"Wonder how her little girl is doing."

The journey was behind them. Home was an easy two hours' walk. Small talk, old friends, comfortable with each other, men made lean and honed sharp by the wilderness, father and son. . . .

They paused to drink from a trickling rill. Roy

rose first and walked ahead up the slope, topped it with Renno several feet behind him.

"My Lord," Roy said in an awed voice. He was looking down into a little valley that had been denuded so violently that no tree stood erect. And up the far slope, leading directly toward the Seneca village, was the deadly track of a huge, spinning storm.

Renno, galvanized by the tone of Roy's voice, ran up the slope and jerked to a halt. They had seen just such an example of nature's fury once before, at the spot where Little Turtle chose to mount his last stand against Anthony Wayne's American Legion, causing the fallen timbers from which the battle took its name.

The tornado track was not new. Second-growth brush was green among the twisted, shattered, fallen trees. But it was wide—a huge gash of death cut into the emerald heart of the forest.

"I must go ahead," Renno said, fear a terrible weight on his heart. If the storm had continued in a straight line past the top of the ridge and down the other side, then his village, and Beth's house, would be as twisted and as dead as the shattered swath of forest.

"I'll come as fast as I can," Roy said.

Renno surged up the slope, running all-out, without warming up properly, so that his heart began to pound and his lungs spasm. He dodged among the trees, legs flashing, feet pounding without regard for the noise he was making. And as he ran he chanted his prayers to the Master of Life. He was human, and he did the human thing: he tried to strike a bargain with the powers.

"Let them be safe," he prayed, "and I will leave them no more."

He topped the ridge and halted, his eyes filling with tears of thanksgiving. The tornado track stopped short of the village, then continued again on the other side, having left a fringe of trees standing on either edge. He turned and called back down the slope to Roy, who was struggling upward, "It's all right! They're all right."

Roy was breathing hard when he gained the top of the ridge. He could see smoke coming from the longhouse he shared with Toshabe. "I'll have to admit," he said, "that when I saw that mess, it scared me quite a bit."

Renno was still chanting his thanks silently.

"Reckon none of us will be short of firewood for one helluva long time," Roy said, then laughed.

"So." Renno laughed, too, and the men's tension drained away.

"Well, you gonna stand here all day, or are we gonna go on home?"

Renno let Roy lead the way. If Roy's joints ached he didn't show it as he bounded down the slope toward the village.

Chapter Thirteen

Little Hawk saw a blurred image of a pretty, round face, dark and unsmiling. His head hurt. His body ached. He blinked his eyes, and his vision improved slightly. He focused on a pair of full lips that spoke in a language he did not understand. The throbbing of his head increased, and he closed his eyes. A vessel of water was put against his lips, and he drank. He slept and awoke to find that, although his head still hurt, he could see more clearly the woman—or girl— who sat by his side, concern on her face.

"More water?" he whispered.

She raised her dark, full eyebrows in question.

"Agua?" he asked, making a drinking gesture.

"Ah," she said, reaching for a clay bowl.

"Habla usted español?"

She indicated yes, but just a bit.

He tried English. Again she shook her head, with a shy, small smile of apology. He tried the few words

of the Heceta dialect that he had learned, but they,
too, were incomprehensible to her.

He reverted to a wordless language of gestures,
which had been used in various forms since time began
and men of different cultures tried to communicate.
He indicated the use of a bow, pulling an imaginary
string and making a "zing" to indicate the release of
an arrow. He pointed an imaginary rifle and said,
"Boom." Swung a tomahawk. He said, "Where?
Where?" spreading his arms, shrugging, and looking
puzzled.

Her expression brightened, then she left the cave
and came back with the bundle that contained his
weapons. As he had hoped, it had floated ashore
when the boat overturned. He unwrapped it and laid
out the weapons to dry. The rifle was beginning to
rust. He began to rub it with his sleeve. She took it
from his hand with a severe look and words that were
obviously a reprimand. She pushed him back and
made him lie down, then used a piece of doeskin to
clean the rust away as best she could.

Little Hawk tried to tell her that the job needed
oil, but he could not make her understand. He tried
to indicate animal fat by pointing to his mouth, chewing, and making other signs. She beamed, brought out
smoked fish and cornmeal bread. He decided that
eating was, at least for the moment, more important
than cleaning his rifle.

She knew only a few words of Spanish. When he
made the sign for large and said, "River, *río, río
grande,*" she understood and pointed toward the
south.

"Far?" He made motions of walking with his fingers and questioned her with his eyebrows.

She looked upward, made a round circle with her
finger, flashed the fingers of one hand. He held up
four fingers. "Four moons?" He indicated moon, then
held up his fingers. She shrugged, showed him one
finger, two fingers, and shrugged again. It was clear
to him that although she knew that the big river lay

to the south, she did not know exactly how far. He made motions with his fingers, pointed to himself, and said, "I go *río grande*."

She put her hand on his shoulder, pointed toward the light coming in the mouth of the cave, and hid her eyes. He got the idea, finally, that she did not want him to move until dark, when he could not be seen. He questioned her. She answered with silent war cries and, after patting her mouth with the fingers of her hand, shot imaginary arrows and stood to strut with her chest thrust out.

"The warriors of your tribe would kill me?" he asked, making appropriate signs. "Why?"

She touched his face with the tip of her fingers. *"Blanco."*

"Because I have white skin?"

"El diablo español," she said, frowning.

"No, *no español*," he said.

She shrugged and stabbed him in the chest with an imaginary dagger.

"They'd kill me anyway," he said grimly.

"Español," she said.

"All white men are Spanish," he said. Knowing the history of Spain's conquests in America, he understood. The cruelty and avarice of the Spaniards had alienated every tribe with whom they had contact, if those tribes had managed to survive the encounter.

They see, they kill, she signed.

When they no see, I go, he gestured.

She nodded. She pointed to herself, made walking motions with her fingers, then pointed to herself and to him. *I will go with you.*

At the moment he was too tired and too weak to protest. The girl left him, giving him signs to assure him that she would be back. Making good on her promise, she returned with food and sealskin cloaks. The wraps must have been taken from a discard pile so they wouldn't be missed; they were old and had tears in several places. Nonetheless, he was grateful for the warmth the cloak provided and the girl's cau-

tion. Although his clothing was dry, he had been cold
in the cave, and the heavy cloak felt good. He drew
it about his shoulders, chewed on smoked fish and
bread, and smiled at her. She took a small flower from
her dark hair and held it out. She pointed to the
flower, then to him.

"For me?" He smiled. "Thank you."

She smiled, pointed to the flower, then to him,
saying words in a soft, liquid voice. Only she knew
exactly what she was saying, but Little Hawk was un-
comfortably aware from her tone and expression that
her words held love.

He touched the flower and said its name in
Seneca.

She aped the sound.

He pointed to himself and said, "Little Hawk."
His Seneca name, he felt, was much too long and
complicated for her. He pointed to her and raised his
eyebrows.

"Twana."

"Twana," he said. He pointed to himself. "Little
Hawk."

"Lickel Haw," she said.

He laughed. "Close enough."

He slept. When he awoke, it was dark. Twana
had kindled a small fire that lit the cave with flickering
light. She made walking motions and pointed at him,
raising her eyebrows.

He stood and took a few tentative steps. He
hurt, but nothing was broken. His aches would, he
knew, loosen with movement. The bruises would fade
in time. He gathered his weapons, then put his hands
on her arms.

"Twana stay," he said, indicating that she should
sit, remain.

She shook her head violently.

"I go south," he said, pointing.

She shook her head. There were many men to
the south. He should go east instead.

Although he was not a womanizer by any means—

he had, unlike some of the other marines in North
Africa, passed up all opportunities to get to know the
Arab girls better—he was not inexperienced. He had
been given a secondary-school diploma in the art of
sexuality by the Witch of the Pyrenean Woods and an
advanced degree by the lubricious Mary Ann Lillie.
During his brief stays at home he had been aware that
several Seneca and Cherokee maidens looked upon
him with favor. He knew that the way Twana's eyes
caressed his face indicated more than mere curiosity
on her part.

He had no way of explaining to her that he did
not want the responsibility of her, that he would not
allow her to help him, that her obvious infatuation for
him was the emotion of a child and could never be
requited.

"Little girl," he said to her in Seneca, for the
words of his native language were more akin than either English or Spanish to the sounds of Twana's
tongue, "you trouble me."

She looked up at him seriously, a small smile on
her face to indicate that she was eager to please him.

"I come from so far away, and I will be going
back there, leaving you behind. I can't ask you to
leave your home and family to guide me to the big
river. I would have to leave you there."

She said soft things, smiled. She made the sign
for sleeping, putting her hands together and bending
her head to one side against them, blinked her eyes,
and pointed to her head to mean, he guessed, "When
I sleep I dream."

"Of you," she said, putting her finger on his
chest.

"No, no," he said, shaking his head. He pointed
at her. "You." To himself, "Me." He put the forefin-
gers of his right and left hand together and shook his
head. "Me, you." He separated his fingers. "Not one.
Not one."

Her face clouded, and she turned away, motioning him to follow. He had no choice but to do so.

Under the moonlight she led him past a village.
He heard dogs barking idly. She knew the trails well.
Sometimes it was so dark under the thick canopy of
the tall trees that he lost sight of her and followed her
by her soft footfall.

By first light they were well away from the coastal
cliffs. She made the sign for sleeping. He shook his
head and pointed southward. Again she shook her
head violently. He shrugged and gave in to her.
Twana made a bed of boughs under the limbs of a
deadfall. He started to cut boughs for his own bed,
but shivering to communicate that she was cold, she
took his arm and pulled him down onto the bed with
her. He made the sign for fire. She shook her head
and indicated that there were too many warriors for
them to risk a blaze.

She pulled the sealskins over them and pressed
herself against him. It had been a long night. He was
sore and tired. He slept.

They made good progress on the second night of
travel. Twana finally turned toward the south. Once
again they slept during the day. Twice hunting parties
came within hearing distance of their carefully chosen
hideaway.

There was very little talk as they traveled during
the night. Before sleeping and while eating, Little
Hawk learned that Twana was of the Chehalis tribe.
It was, he gathered, a fairly small group, not at all
like the nations of the eastern Indians in size or in the
extent of territory. To the south, she told him, were
the Chinook and the Cowlitz; to the east the Snu-
qualmi; to the north the Quinault and the Heceta.
Some of this information he had already learned from
Youbou.

Actually, many things could be learned through
a few common words in Spanish, the exchange of different words for a common object, and sign language.
Twana was sixteen years old, the only child of an
important Chehalis warrior. And she had known in

advance from her dreams that he, Lickel Haw, was coming into her life.

"You worry me, little one," he told her when he realized that she was looking upon him as the fulfillment of some sort of personal prophesy. He tried repeatedly to get her to go home. She adamantly refused. He resigned himself to her determination. Because the tribes of the area seemed to be on peaceful terms among themselves, he was hopeful that she would find a home with whatever tribe lived at the mouth of the Columbia. Or perhaps he could arrange for the warriors there to escort her back to her people.

"Little bird," he told her, "I have enough to concern me without worrying about what is going to happen to you. Fly away back to your father."

He had one hope for seeing his home again. If the circumstances of time and unknown distance favored him, he would find Americans at the mouth of the Columbia. But, ah, how small the odds were for that. No man on earth knew the extent of the western areas. The vast distances and hostile peoples could very well have swallowed Lewis and Clark and their companions. If indeed the expedition ever reached the west coast, it might have come and gone by the time Little Hawk reached the mouth of the Columbia. Or the group might have reached the Pacific by some route other than the Columbia.

When Little Hawk questioned Twana about the big river, her gestures indicated something huge, beyond her ability to explain. The way she signed it, the Columbia was deep within the earth, or, as Little Hawk took meaning, deep in a mighty canyon. He had seen stream-cut gorges in the Great Smoky Mountains. Some of them were so deep, so rugged, that it would take hours to descend to the bottom and climb up the other side. He imagined the Columbia in terms of his own experience—a river that had cut its way deeply into the hills, with trees growing on steep slopes on either side.

Remembering the gorges of the Smokies made him think of home. It would be winter there. Beth would be preparing for Christmas, and the men and boys of the tribe would be busily at work carving their false faces for the festival of the new beginning.

On the Pacific coast, winter proved to be a chill wetness that caught up with Little Hawk and Twana after their fourth night of travel. When it was daylight and time to sleep, they found shelter from a heavy fog that condensed on everything it touched. Twana woke Little Hawk in the middle of a dismal, gray afternoon. As they set out toward the south, their clothing was penetrated by a light drizzle that was given birth by the fog. Visibility was no more than a few yards, explaining why Twana decided that it was safe to travel by day.

The cold rain stayed with them, and because of the tears in their cloaks, the travelers were soaked to the skin; but even with the discomfort, the going was easier. They were moving now with an evenness of pace that put mile after mile behind them. Little Hawk's bow downed deer and small game. He did not use his rifle, for Twana continued to warn him that the area was thickly populated—although he saw no signs of that other than old moccasin tracks now and then on the game trails.

At dawn, when searching for shelter, sometimes they found a friendly cave; at other times they built leaking lean-tos beside deadfalls. The caves were, naturally, the more comfortable. Hidden from sight out of the persistent light rain, Little Hawk could safely build a large fire to dry their clothing and bedding. He would pull off his buckskin tunic and hang it up to dry while the evening meal roasted. Twana, too, would take off her shirt, but with a degree of modesty that made Little Hawk smile. She manipulated her sealskin cape to cover herself as she removed the garment, showing nothing more than movement under the concealment.

The weather had grown cool. It was an accepted

fact that they would share a bed, and often Little
Hawk would awaken in the night with Twana's solidly
built little body pressed tightly against his back. When
she was cold, he would roll over, put his arm around
her, and pull her into his embrace. They were, of
course, fully clothed, but even through her doeskin
shirt, skirt, and leggings he was aware that she had
rounded, feminine areas. When she pressed closely to
his back for warmth, he could not help but feel the
softness of her breasts. In short, he was becoming
more and more cognizant of the fact that she was a
woman.

That elemental condition of life came home to
him with shuddering surety on a night when the wind
howled off the sea to the west, driving before it a
cold, slashing rain that had soaked them thoroughly
before they found a cozy cave. They had dried their
clothing and eaten. The fire was being allowed to burn
down. Since it had been a trying twelve hours, traveling in the cold rain, Little Hawk fell asleep immediately, his arm around Twana. Her compact, very
feminine rump was pressed into the cup formed by his
body.

He awoke slowly to a sensuous awareness. He
thought at first that he was dreaming. Twana's hand
was between them, behind her back, and she was tugging surreptitiously on the flap of his trousers. She
had, in fact, loosed the ties and lowered the flap halfway. As it often happens with a young man at night,
he was aroused. Only half-awake, he moaned softly
as her hand touched him. A shudder of delight went
through him as he realized that she had removed her
leggings, that her skirt was lifted above her rounded
buttocks. She moved ever so slowly, ever so carefully,
positioning herself so that she took his manhood between her legs. He felt the heat of her, the moist
softness of her, and his loins thrust forward.

And into his mind flashed a face—a face that
smiled at him—two freckles on a dainty nose, taffy-
colored hair, and soft, full lips. He did not let Twana

know that he was awake. He grunted as if he were still asleep and pulled away from the heated temptation of her, turned his back, and quickly lifted the flap of his trousers into place.

He was confused. Every fiber of his being demanded that he turn back to Twana, that he seek out the damp, heated softness to which she had given him access. But the image of Naomi's face would not leave him. He cursed himself silently for being a fool. Thinking of Naomi always caused him to suffer mixed emotions. He could not separate the golden-headed young girl from the soiled-looking young woman he had rescued from the Morgans. It was a conflict he had not been able to resolve, so he had run far away, to escape Naomi and the ambivalent emotions she engendered in him. He told himself to get over it. But the geographical cure had not worked. He had brought his problems along on the journey. He had repeatedly reminded himself, "What you thought was soil on her legs, on her arms, on her neck, was not dirt but bruises."

Still, there was taint that was invisible, and three thousand miles away from Naomi, his youthful body trembling with the need that Twana's invitation had produced in him, he was still unable to sort out his true feelings for Naomi Burns. He knew only that man without a woman was incomplete, that the need for a woman was greater than hunger, stronger than fear, more persistent than the itch caused by red bugs in the summer.

For two days the weather improved. They walked by day, and Twana's spirits responded to the sunshine. She laughed at the antics of a squirrel trying to hide itself and at the same time investigate just what sort of creatures were coming toward its tree. She repeated the Chehalis names for everything: sky, tree, sun, hand, man, woman, the cardinal directions. She walked by Little Hawk's side and chattered away. As he picked up words in the Chehalis dialect, communica-

tion was becoming easier. But words were not needed
for him to understand when, in the middle of the
night, she communicated with him in the most basic
language that exists between man and woman.

They had found another cozy cave. Its good draft
pulled the smoke of the fire away from their sleeping
area. Although the day had been pleasant, the night
was cold. They slept pressed together under the sealskins. Feeling chilled, Little Hawk awoke to find that
the sealskins had been removed. The flap of his
breeches was open and folded down. His only covering was Twana. Even as he opened his eyes, she
lowered her body. He stiffened instinctively as heat
and moistness thrilled him. She cried out as she let
her full weight rest on him, and then she said in words
that she had very carefully taught him, "I am your
woman."

He was twenty-two years old, and he had the
powerful instincts that nature instills in the young.
There was no thought at that moment of Naomi
Burns. He knew only the heated delight of Twana as
he reached for her, pulled her down atop him to lie
impaled, and held her tightly in his arms. His lips
found hers, and she soon adjusted to kissing on the
mouth, that peculiar custom of the white man. That
night she became, truly, his woman. There was blood,
for she had been a virgin.

The next day as they walked south he learned the
words he wanted to say. He put them together that
night when, once again, she was his woman. She was
sore, so he was gentle. For a few moments, as he took
her, he felt guilty, for he knew that he would have to
leave her sooner or later. She was so young, so trust-
ing, so innocent. He had learned enough of her language and from her behavior to know that she thought
him the answer to her dreams. She was convinced that
he was the man of surpassing beauty that she had
imagined all of her young life. So, on that second
night, when she clung to him in surprised pleasure,
her eyes wide, her mouth open in wonder at what

was happening to her, he whispered, "Twana, you are beautiful, like the dove."

Although Little Hawk's desire to reach the mouth of the Columbia was still urgent, he rationalized that they had traveled long and hard and that it was out of consideration for Twana that he set a more leisurely pace, often stopping for the night with hours of daylight left in order to take advantage of a particularly pleasant camping site. They spent long, slow, mutually gratifying hours making love, using the words they possessed in common, and learning others. She spoke of the beauty of the seashells she gathered on the beaches and, laughingly, pointed to him as one very large, very *useful* discard of the sea.

Twana's effort at description and Little Hawk's imagination had not prepared him for the gorge of the Columbia. The sun was shining when the earth opened up under his feet, causing him to jerk back instinctively. Twana clung to his arm as they inched forward to stand on what seemed to be the edge of the world.

Hundreds of feet below them the wide river was smooth, slow moving, and placid. Across the chasm, almost obscured in mist, a waterfall trailed whitely down the face of a sheer precipice. The vast rent in the earth stretched away in a curve to the east, then beyond into distances in the west.

"I not go there," Twana said, pointing down into the gorge.

"No. Not yet, at least," Little Hawk said. "We go west, toward the sea."

They marched toward the setting sun. The river turned slowly toward the northwest as they followed the gorge through dim, misty, rolling forests. When, two hours before sunset, the mist thickened, cutting visibility, Little Hawk began to cast around for a good campsite. He found an open-sided shelter that was more overhang than cave. Twana began to gather firewood. Little Hawk had to admit that she was better than he at coaxing a fire into life. He was not accustomed to life in a climate of almost continual rain. He left her to her chore and set out to find their evening meal.

He passed up an adult doe not a quarter mile from camp. To kill a large deer for two people on the move was wasteful. He settled for two inquisitive squirrels and made his way back at the warrior's pace to the overhang. He identified himself as he came within hearing by cooing like a dove. There was no answer. Fully alert, he crept closer until he could see that Twana was not under the overhang. She had laid a fire, but it was not burning. Tomahawk in hand, he advanced, checking the ground carefully.

In the dry dirt under the overhang the story was told. Two men had seized her. Twana had struggled. Once, she had fallen or had been knocked to the ground. The two men had taken her northward, away from the gorge, along a deer track. It quickly became evident that she was leaving him an easy trail to follow. Twilight was falling, but he could still move at a run and not miss scuff marks or a freshly broken twig in the damp detritus. Almost before he could prepare himself for the encounter, he had overtaken them. The two men were dressed much like Heceta, but their headgear was different. They walked on either side of Twana, holding tightly to her arms. One of them turned his head and revealed four fresh parallel marks raked down his cheek. Twana had not submitted quietly.

As Little Hawk watched the three across a misty glade, an odd thing happened to him. Seeing Twana with the two men caused his stomach to lurch, and a feeling of sick dread slowed him for a moment. He assured himself that there had not been time for the two Indians to defile her. And in thinking thus, he experienced quick guilt, for in his mind the Chehalis girl had been—for a flashing moment—placed in the same category with Naomi Burns.

He waited until the two men disappeared into the trees, with Twana scuffling between them. Then the Seneca ran lightly across the glade and entered the dense forest. He did not use the game trail being followed by Twana's captors, although he stayed close enough to hear her struggles. After working his way ahead of the trio, he waited quietly beside the path, his tomahawk at the ready.

When they were a few feet away he stepped out into the trail. One of the men cried out in surprise. Twana, seeing Little Hawk, lifted her feet, putting all of her weight on the two Indians. They dropped her, and she fell to the ground, then rolled away even as Little Hawk leaped to the attack, his blade reflecting the fading light.

A quavering scream of pain came from one of the men as he slumped to the ground, blood gushing from the side of his neck. The other danced away and cried out an obvious threat as he reached for his war ax— a weapon of Spanish make, huge and deadly. Little Hawk caught only the word *español*. He was in no mood to be merciful. The nausea he had felt when he thought that Twana might have been defiled was still in him, festering into a desire to wipe his guilt away with the death of both captors. He leaped over the fallen man. The enemy parried his first blow with the flat side of his Spanish ax but fell back under Little Hawk's determined attack.

The young Seneca had been taught the art of battle extremely well. His repertoire of tricks had been learned from such masters as his father and his uncles, El-i-chi and Rusog. He soon learned that this coastal Indian, of the Chinook tribe, was not very adept at weapon skills. But even if he had known in advance that the men he faced in the fading light were not warlike, he would not have acted differently; they had taken something of value from him—that realization came to him in the midst of battle—and had caused him to suffer fear for Twana's safety. Worse, he burned with shame because, momentarily, he had rejected her for something over which she had had no control.

Death came for the Chinook with the large Spanish ax. He fell, moaning, dropping the weapon so that he could cup his spilled entrails. The Seneca delivered him from a long, lingering, agonized death with a crunching blow to the temple.

Twana was on her feet. She came to squeeze Little Hawk's arm, and he put his arms around her and kissed the top of her head. She smiled up at him, then moved away to spit into the faces of the dead men. Next she busied herself taking from them any article she felt might be useful. She walked proudly ahead of her savior on the way back to their camp. There she turned and put her hands on his arms. She had to tilt her head far back to look into his face.

"You are a man of surpassing beauty, and now I know that you are a great warrior." She giggled. "I am yours now," she said in words and signs.

"Yes," he agreed.

She shook her head and repeated herself. He finally got her meaning. He had saved her from being a slave of the Chinook. He had saved her life and her honor and, therefore, both were his. She was his forever.

"Little dove," he said, "what will I do with you?"

She had one heated suggestion. Ever practical, he felt that it was incumbent on him to refuse until they had built a fire and put the squirrels on spits to be roasted.

With the morning they traveled to the northwest, staying close to the rim of the gorge. When, now and again, Little Hawk approached the great chasm, he saw that the river was wider, and there were margins of land along its banks. The sea, he guessed, could not be very far away. The path they followed showed more signs of use. When he heard dogs bark, he left the trail and bypassed a village where great houses were formed of rough-hewn planks. Fat, healthy-looking children romped in the open spaces inside the town. A smell of cooking fish drifted to them.

"Chinook," Twana said. Because the men who had abducted her were also Chinook, Twana and Little Hawk put several miles between them and the village before moving back once more to look down into the gorge.

There, far away, almost hidden in the blue mists, was the sea. Below was the wide river. He searched eagerly for signs of Lewis and Clark's expedition but saw only water, the precipitous sides of the gorge, trees . . . empty wilderness.

"I think it's time," he told Twana, "that we go down."

She took a step backward, shaking her head, her eyes wide.

"We will find a place that won't be dangerous," he said.

"No go down," she said. "Run away." She made signs of running with her fingers.

"You'll do no such thing," he said. "Don't worry. I'll take care of you."

"No go down," she repeated.

As the gorge widened with the great river, the cliffs took on a less precipitous slope. It was midafternoon when Little Hawk found a place that appeared to offer access to the valley. He showed Twana his proposed route.

"First, we'll go along that broad ledge," he said.

The ledge slanted downward from the lip of the gorge.

"There, where the trees begin, it is steep, but we can go down slowly, holding on to the trees and the brush."

Twana was shaking her head doubtfully, but the prospect was not nearly as fearsome in this place as it had been when the sheer bluffs dropped off and away to the river hundreds of feet below.

He took her hand and lowered her onto the ledge, then joined her there. Directly below the beginnings of the ledge, the cliffs dropped away vertically to another rocky outcrop a hundred feet below. It was too steep in that particular spot for trees to take root, although there were sparse areas of runty brush here and there. He led her carefully down the ramp of the ledge.

The rock of the cliff was pocked with small caves. In a shaking voice Twana said, "Good camp, here."

"Camp down there," Little Hawk said.

"Ohhhh," she moaned, as she looked far, far down to the river.

"Get behind me," he told her. "Put your hands on my waist. We will walk very, very slowly."

She obeyed. He took short, careful steps, for the ledge was littered with loose pebbles, making the footing uncertain. He glanced to his right as he passed a small, dark cave. A feral smell filled his nostrils. He turned and whispered to Twana, "Come, hurry!"

They were ten feet past the low, dark entrance to the cave when he heard a sound that chilled his blood. Twana removed her hands from his waist and turned. He whirled just in time to see a blur of black motion burst from the cave. He was in the prime of his youth, and his reaction time was quicker than normal; but not even his superb reflexes matched those of the female grizzly who lashed out in protection of her den and her cubs and sent Twana tumbling outward and downward.

A hoarse cry came from Little Hawk's lips. His musket was up, pointing at the bear. With his peripheral vision he saw Twana spinning through the air. She struck the ledge a hundred feet below, bounced, and with a new looseness, arms and legs flapping, soared outward and away.

The female grizzly reared to her full height and roared her challenge. Little Hawk aimed at the heart, and his finger tightened on the trigger. Twana was dead, but he could not find anger—only wrenching sorrow. He had saved her from the Chinook, only to lose her to a force of nature. His finger moved away from the trigger. The bear knew only that men had invaded her territory, had come close to her den. He could see by her dugs that she had cubs.

"Hear me," he said softly, gently in Seneca. "I am Little Hawk of the Bear Clan of the Seneca. I wish you no harm."

The bear lowered herself to all fours, growled fiercely, and took a step toward him.

"Hear me, Mother. The totem of my clan is the bear. Do not make me strike out at my sacred totem."

The bear snuffled, lowered her head, and rocked back and forth on her feet. For long, long moments it was thus, the man with his rifle at the ready, the bear undecided, growls emanating from her like distant thunder.

"Go, Mother. Go back to your cubs," Little Hawk urged.

The bear reared once more, but this time she was silent. She pawed the air with her forefeet and opened her mouth to display an impressive array of teeth.

"To your cubs, Mother," he urged. "I forgive you, for you are not aware of what you have done."

The bear dropped to all four feet, and with one backward look she disappeared into her cave.

Darkness fell while Little Hawk was still descending through the trees and brush that clung to the steep slope. But he continued to lower himself down the wall of the gorge. He fell, rolled, and with a jolting impact was brought up short against a tree. Breath exploded from his body. Finally a winter moon rose and helped him during the last stages of his descent.

He found Twana's crumpled body lying on jagged rocks beside the river. He knelt at her side. Sharp pebbles cut into his knees, but the pain felt good somehow. She was bent into an unnatural position. Her arms and legs were at odd angles. He took her hand and moved her arm, thinking that he would arrange her in a more natural position. The arm bent limply, and there was a grating sound as broken bones moved.

Her moonlit face, miraculously, was undamaged and serene. He reached out and touched her cheek and keened a Seneca song for the dead. He didn't care if he was heard. He had told himself that he would not allow himself to love this Chehalis girl, but her face, looking so natural in the moonlight, had become dear to him. Her death, so sudden, so unexpected, as they neared the end of their journey, had left him feeling empty. Guilt gnawed at him because he had forced her to descend the cliff, something that she had feared greatly.

There was, of course, much blood. It was beyond belief that this broken, sodden thing had been the vibrantly alive Twana. He steeled himself and lifted the body, placed it on his sealskin cape, and covered it as best he could. For the remainder of the night he mourned her with chanting and song, surprising himself by remembering many of the ceremonial rites that, had the accident occurred at home, would have been performed by his uncle El-i-chi.

He spent the morning, also, saying farewell to the girl whose love for him had been so great that she had been willing to leave behind all that was dear and familiar to her. To her he had been the fulfillment of a dream. What, he wondered, had she been to him? A smiling, laughing companion for the long, arduous days of travel . . . a shared warmth in the night . . . a girl-woman of sweet and intoxicating appeal . . . fulfillment of that strongest of all urges save the desire to survive. But nothing more?

Using his tomahawk and his hands, he dug a grave in rich, silted soil and placed the shrunken, broken body into the pit. It was not deep, but when he pushed the displaced dirt atop her while singing a plaintive song for the dead, he knew that she would be protected from the soaring vultures that had been drawn by her death. Atop the packed earth he piled a cairn of rock. Her grave would be forever unmarked save for that pile of stone, but, he told himself, the location would be carved into his heart.

He sat on a boulder, looked at the new grave, and tried to define love. He had been sure, so very sure, that he was in love with Mary Ann Lillie. For a brief time it had been a pure love, admiration from afar. And then she had become the sexual aggressor, and their merged bodies, shared desire, and mutual satisfaction had made him believe that he would never love another. And yet when her father made it clear that a young man of one-quarter Indian blood was not fit to marry his daughter, Little Hawk had been more angry than bereft. When Mary Ann had so nonchalantly accepted the cataclysmic change in their lives, he had been more upset about losing his standing in the marines than forfeiting his sweetheart.

On the other hand, simply because he was crying from grief now, did that prove that what he had felt for Twana was love? Or was it sorrow or guilt? Was he stricken because he should have been strong enough to send the sixteen-year-old Chehalis girl back to her father? Because she had feared the descent into the gorge?

He would remember Twana always, and he would miss her sorely. He was sure he would awaken in the night and reach for her with his pulse pounding in need of her youthful ripeness. But why was he already becoming impatient to be away? Why were his eyes measuring the distances down the river toward the sea?

And above all, why, even as he chanted one final hymn to the dead, did a far different face intrude into his grief? Was Naomi encroaching into his mourning because, for one unguarded moment, Little Hawk had felt revulsion for the Chehalis girl, thinking that she had been raped by the two Chinooks?

"Leave me," he begged the taffy-haired image. "Leave me in peace."

He retrieved Twana's sealskin from the limbs of

a small tree where it had landed after falling the hundreds of feet from the ledge above. This night would be cold. As far as he could tell, he was alone at the bottom of the mighty gorge of the Columbia—there were no worn trails, no sign of man's presence. He set off downriver.

He had not gone a mile before he saw signs that man was indeed about. A relatively easy path showed a way to the top of the wall of the gorge, and he furiously berated himself for not being more patient. Twana could have reached the riverbank easily by using that path. At the foot of the trail a half-dozen excellently made canoes sat on the grassy bank. A drying rack was empty but still carried the odor of sun-dried fish.

He chose a canoe quickly and pushed it into the water. A hand-carved paddle fit his palms well. He eased away from the bank and into the slow-moving current, guiding the canoe with the paddle to keep it close to the shore.

The sun emerged from the haze and played a subdued light over the wide river. A hawk skimmed the surface, zoomed up and over Little Hawk, and gave a harsh cry.

"Hail, Brother," Little Hawk said, his heart soaring with the bird. He shook his head, for guilt came quickly. How could he take joy in the swift, sure flight of that other totem of his clan, the hawk, when Twana had died?

It was, he concluded in helpless confusion, a difficult world—and he was not referring to the fact that he might never see his home again, nor to the vast, unknown distances that separated him from his family. Instead he was wondering why it was difficult to think of Twana without his thoughts flying backward in time to a trembling kiss and to a bruised and frightened girl who clung to him and wept with gratitude.

Chapter Fourteen

Now the river changed. Little Hawk had emerged from the gorge of the Columbia. The mountains were behind him, but one snowcapped giant could be seen to the southwest. When he passed a tall, dark outcropping of rock that soared vertically into the sky on the northern side, he estimated the river to be two miles wide. He camped at night among fir and spruce trees and made his meals on the fatty, rich meat of a goose taken easily with bow and arrow along the riverbank.

He traveled the next day in a dense fog that seemed to close him inside a cocoon of silence. When the gray, wet mist was finally burned away by the sun in midafternoon, his heart leaped, for, after rounding a rocky crag on the left bank, the ocean opened up before him. Waves lifted and dropped his canoe, but because it was well constructed, he was not concerned. He dipped his finger in the water and tasted. It was

salty. As visibility improved, however, he saw he had
been mistaken in thinking that he was at the Pacific.
Land lay far away to the north. Soaked by the morning's fog, chilled, and miserable, he rowed to shore
and made camp.

With the morning he had several decisions to
make. For days he had numbed his mind with the
labor of paddling the canoe. Now, as he looked across
the great stretches of water in the Columbian estuary,
he began to feel the burden of loneliness. He had no
way of knowing how wide the river was at its mouth,
but the grandeur and the vastness of the waters intimidated him. He faced a formidable task, looking for a
few dozen men along such an extent of coastline. First
of all, assuming the expedition under Lewis and Clark
had managed to get this far and were still in the vicinity, he would have to guess which side of the broad
waters had been chosen as their campsite. Even that
assumption was based on conjectures so farfetched
that it strained any hope of favorable coincidence.

The Lewis and Clark expedition had not plunged
into a totally unknown land as they traveled up the
Missouri River. They had been given access to President Jefferson's archives of maps and data. They had
the Spaniard Antoine Soulard's maps of the Missouri,
plus the maps and accounts of John Evans and James
Mackay, who had been all the way up the river to the
land of the Mandan Indians. As for the area beyond
the Great Falls of the Missouri, the travelers had the
recollections of Mackay, who had heard Antoine La-
rocque tell of his exploration of the Yellowstone River
and its tributaries, the Big Horn and the Powder.

Still, there were the mountains, harsh and unexplored except by the Indians who made them their
home. There were the tyranny of distance, animals—
panther and bear—snow and violent storm, whitewa-
ter rapids, and potentially hostile natives. It had been
an act of faith for Thomas Jefferson to send Little
Hawk to seek Lewis and Clark at the mouth of the
Columbia or to find traces of them had they come and

gone. If the *Orient* had delivered Little Hawk to the Columbia his own destiny would not have depended on whether or not the expeditioners had found their way to the far Pacific. If they had not, or if they had come and gone, he would have sailed on to China with the *Orient* and thence, sooner or later, back to the United States.

Now, as he paddled against waves that grew rougher and wetter, he was a man alone. Perhaps one day he could make contact with another northwestern trading venture. Sooner or later another ship would come. The fur trade offered opportunity for riches, and where such potential wealth existed, there would come the men of the United States. He thought of what might have been. If Twana had not been killed, he could have settled in to a life with her to wait for a ship. But alone? . . . There were other choices. Since he spoke Spanish fluently, he could travel down the coast to settled areas and pass for Spanish. Then he might find a way to go by ship to South America or even to the Floridas.

The wind increased. Driftwood created dangerous obstacles as the waves built. Whole trees had been unearthed by some past flood. The half-submerged logs were easily capable of crushing the canoe. He ran the vessel ashore and built a shelter. He had great difficulty in starting a fire, and that made him think of Twana again. She had known from long experience where to find dry tinder in a wet land. He had constructed a roof of boughs and had a duck roasting over the fire when he heard a call that was obviously a hail. He reached for his rifle. Two tall, well-built young men emerged from the damp shadows of the huge trees, hands uplifted in greeting.

Little Hawk said in Spanish, "You are welcome."

"Español," said one of the Indians.

Little Hawk shook his head in negation and was surprised when the Indian smiled and said, "Ah, 'Mercan."

"American," Little Hawk said. "Yes. United States." He pointed east. "You know Americans?"

The Indian nodded. He pointed to his chest and then to his companion's and said, "Clatsop. Clatsop *amigos* 'Mer-cans."

"Adónde Americanos?" Little Hawk asked.

The Clatsop pointed toward the sea. He squatted, brushed aside fir needles, and drew a map on the ground. Little Hawk got the idea that he was to continue until he had rounded a little peninsula jutting out into the river, then go on until a large bay opened to the south, and finally cross that bay and enter a smaller stream.

" 'Mer-cans," the Clatsop said. He pointed to the cooking duck, then made the motions of eating.

Little Hawk had company for dinner. The two Clatsop did well by his duck, even though it was a large one, but he didn't mind. He was elated that Americans were near. Being a bit short on his evening meal was, in view of that news, not at all troublesome.

The storm blew for another day. The visiting Clatsop Indians went on their way, leaving Little Hawk to pace the shore and fret. The following morning the sun moved in and out among banks of gray cloud; but the waves were smaller, and the wind had calmed. He rowed with a will and rounded the peninsula described by the Clatsop. About five miles farther on he rowed around a sharp-nosed cape and could see land two to three miles on the other side of a bay. He found the mouth of a small river directly opposite the tip of the cape and rowed eagerly southward. When he saw log construction, he yelled out in joy. Obviously the work was that of white men. A log fort sat on a patch of high ground amid salt marshes and lowlands. Two long, log structures faced each other. The space between them was protected by palisaded walls.

"Hello, the fort!" he called at the top of his lungs.

There was only silence. He ran the canoe ashore and leaped out. On a tree near the shore he saw a carving and ran to read it: "William Clark, December 3rd, 1805. By Land from the U. States in 1804 and 1805."

He ran toward the log fort but halted in midstride when Indians dressed like the two Clatsop warriors he had met earlier stepped out of a gate. He lifted his right hand in greeting.

" 'Mer-can come back?" asked one of the Indians, a tall, handsome man in impressive furs.

"Where other Americans?" Little Hawk asked.

"Gone far," the Clatsop said, waving in the general direction of the rising sun.

Little Hawk grimaced. "How long?"

"You 'Mer-can?"

"Yes."

"You lose way, lose others?"

"Yes," he said, for that was the easiest explanation.

"You are?"

"Little Hawk."

"I Comowool, chief of Clatsop."

"I am honored," Little Hawk said with a small bow. "Great Chief, did the white chiefs take their party back up the river?"

Comowool nodded. "White chief give all this Comowool. It not yours."

"No, not mine," Little Hawk agreed quickly.

"You stay?"

"No, I go." He pointed toward the east.

After a brief discussion with Comowool, Little Hawk learned that the expedition had a month's start on him. That was not a problem. They were some forty men carrying supplies and food; he would be one man traveling alone. He would overtake them soon.

Early the next morning, with his canoe laden with dried fish and warm furs, gifts of the Clatsop chief, he paddled a few miles down the little river the Clatsop called the Netul and turned up the Columbia. The weather remained bad. When it wasn't foggy, the sky was overcast and spat out cold, nasty showers at frequent intervals. It was devilishly hard work to leave the tidal waters behind, for the springtime and the runoff from the distant mountains made for a strong current that had to be defeated by muscle power. At the junction of a river called Multnomah by the Clatsop, he found signs that the expedition had camped there. Encouraged, he paddled onward.

Nine days after turning his canoe up the Columbia, Little Hawk rowed toward the roar of tumbling white water. He worked hard against a strong current while hugging the rocky bank. What he saw made him wonder if he hadn't missed signs of the expedition leaving the river farther back, for the way ahead was impassable. Swollen by the melting snow of the distant mountains and by runoff from spring rains, the river formed a seething, roaring series of cascades.

Little Hawk felt only a little bit better when he found an abandoned campsite. A fire that had been extinguished before being allowed to burn down showed charred remains of what must have been a canoe. With the morning's light, he would scout around to see if the expedition had taken to land travel or if they had, with their considerable manpower, carried some of their boats upstream past the rapids.

He had no trouble falling asleep. His days were long and strenuous. He was sore and achy. Paddling against the river was the hardest work he'd ever done, worse than digging a six-by-six hole as a punishment meted out by his commander at West Point. He groaned in protest when something awoke him on a night illuminated by the lights in the sky; but he came to full alertness quickly, for when he reached out his hand, his rifle was gone.

Little Hawk leaped to his feet, tomahawk in hand. A scurrying sound told him the direction the intruder had taken. The Seneca launched himself with reckless abandon down the barren rocks toward the river, for to be without his rifle in the wilderness ahead was not his idea of having the situation under control. When he saw the dark outline of a man, he lifted his tomahawk. But a blast of fire erupted in front of him, and heavy lead from his own rifle plucked at the hair on the left side of his head. He gave vent to his anger and surprise at almost being killed with his own weapon. With a Seneca war cry he hurled himself at the thief.

One of his knees struck rock, and a bolt of pain shot through him as he bore the prowler to the ground. A whimper caused him to look down as he raised his tomahawk to finish the affair. A youthful face was lit by stars and moon. Little Hawk stayed his blow, then got to his feet, dragging the struggling intruder with him. It was a boy, a boy only shoulder high to him.

"Shall I kill you?" he asked in Spanish as the boy continued to fight him.

"Let me go!" the boy demanded in French.

"Not while you have my rifle," Little Hawk said in the same language.

"Take it then," the boy demanded.

"I do not like thieves," Little Hawk said, seizing the rifle.

"You are going to let me go?" The boy's voice was shaking with fear.

"Do you think I should? So that you can sneak into my camp on another night and, perhaps, succeed in stealing my weapons?"

"I will not come again. I needed the rifle."

"And so do I." Little Hawk grasped the boy's arm. "Come along."

He brought the young thief back to the campsite and there put dry driftwood on the fire. In the flickering light he saw that the boy was not dressed like the coastal Indians. He wore deerskin. He was well formed. His face was pleasant, with one surprising exception. He had a piece of ivory, or bone, thrust through a hole in the septum of his nose. It formed a sort of comical white mustache just above his upper lip.

"You will let me go?"

"Yes, but not now. Are you hungry?"

The boy shook his head, but his eyes slewed toward the half-eaten carcass of a waterfowl that was on the cooking spit over the fire.

"Eat," Little Hawk urged.

The boy's actions belied his statement. He ate ravenously, wiping his hands on his buckskins, then looked at Little Hawk warily.

"Why are you alone?" Little Hawk asked.

"I travel alone."

"So."

The boy was silent.

"Do you have a name?

"I am called Hohaptin."

"Why do you have something in your nose?"

The boy cocked his head. "Why do you *not* have something in your nose?"

"Because I have never been foolish enough to punch a hole in my nose."

The boy grunted. "But a man has this." He touched the ivory ornament. "For this we are known. The French call our tribe the Nez Percé."

"With good reason," Little Hawk remarked. "Where is your home?"

"Far," Hohaptin said, pointing toward the east.

"The other white men, did you see them pass?"

The boy nodded.

"Did they make portage around the *dalles*?"

"No. They burned their boats and bought horses from the Umatilla."

"Horses? Here?"

The boy nodded. "Not so many and not so fine as those among my people."

"Why did you not attach yourself to the white man's party if you are going east?"

The boy shrugged.

"Were you with them?"

He shrugged again.

"Tell me the truth, or I will pull your ears until they bleed."

"I was with them," the boy confessed.

"Let me guess," Little Hawk said. "You were caught stealing."

Another shrug.

"Speak," Little Hawk warned, catching an ear in a painful pinch between thumb and forefinger.

"I stole only a little tobacco."

"And did they make you leave their camp?"

"No. I chose to leave. A Nez Percé warrior does not serve those who insult him."

"Warrior?" Little Hawk laughed. "Someday, perhaps. Not now."

"If I had a rifle like yours—"

"You would *still* be a boy. A boy of, uh, twelve summers?"

"Thirteen," Hohaptin said quickly.

"Thirteen." Little Hawk mused. "Do you know the route that the white men will follow?"

"I know the trail to the land of my people."

"Good. I think, my little thief, that we will travel that trail together, if that is your wish as well as mine."

The boy shrugged. "It is difficult to hunt without weapons."

"I hunt, you eat," Little Hawk offered.

Hohaptin grinned widely. "If that is your wish."

Hohaptin proved quickly to be a good traveling companion. He did not indulge in small talk and stole two horses so smoothly that Little Hawk had to be profuse in his praise. The Nez Percé boy took a route away from the Columbia, across country, to the Clearwater River. Their way was through a grassy plain. Water was available, and Little Hawk killed a deer from a plentiful population. Hohaptin said that the region was the hunting grounds of the Walla Walla, but in the pair's transit, they saw no humans. It pleased Little Hawk, however, to find definite signs of a large number of white men having made camp beside a pleasant stream.

On the Snake River Hohaptin led Little Hawk into a Nez Percé village through a gauntlet of barking dogs and yelling urchins. Hohaptin rode directly to a centrally located habitation made of animal hides stretched over a wooden framework, the first such structure that Little Hawk had encountered. It looked as if it could be dismantled and moved easily.

Hohaptin was yelling as he neared the lodge, and when he pulled his horse to a stop and slid off, the skin flap over the door opened. A tall man with piercing black eyes glanced first at Little Hawk and then held out his arms to the boy.

"This is my father," Hohaptin said. "He is Chief Shortnose of the Nez Percé."

Little Hawk dismounted and held his right hand up in greeting.

"You have missed your party by some weeks," Chief Shortnose said, assuming that the visitor belonged with the larger group that had passed through the lands of the chiefs Twisted Hair and Cutnose on the way west, then again, eastward bound, at a time when winter was ending.

Little Hawk had already begun to gain a new appreciation of the travels of what the French called the "ragged men of the woods." Shortnose and several other Nez Percé spoke a variety of frontier French mixed with sign language that made communication simple. Their command of French, such as it was, proved that the European trappers and explorers had traveled far.

Through Shortnose Little Hawk learned that the Lewis and Clark expedition had spent some weeks with the Nez Percé while waiting for the snows to thaw in the high passes of the mountains that loomed whitely toward the sky to the east.

"And have the snows melted?"

"Perhaps, perhaps not," Shortnose said. "You go?"

"Yes."

"There are those who will guide you for a price," Shortnose said.

"Alas, I have nothing with which to pay a guide."

"But after you re-join your party? . . ."

It was a very tempting offer. Having the boy along had been a tremendous help and had saved Little Hawk many days of travel. But he had no money and had no right to contract the expedition to pay a guide.

"Great Chief," he said, "I wish that I could hire a guide. However, I will have to go alone."

"Perhaps the wolves will gnaw your bones," Shortnose warned.

"Perhaps," Little Hawk allowed.

As he set out toward what the Nez Percé called the Lolo Trail, he had dried meat in his kit and instructions from Chief Shortnose. Hohaptin had volunteered to go with him, but his father put a stop to that idea quickly, telling the boy that he had traveled enough for one year.

Within a surprisingly short time the Seneca was in the mountains. He found that not all of the snow had melted. The rocky trail was covered with ice in the mornings, and this ice cost him his horse. He had gotten an early start because the marks of passage of the large party of white men were still evident. The horse was picking her way upward on a narrow, rocky ledge alongside a swollen creek. Her front foot slipped on ice. She struggled for balance, and before Little Hawk could dismount, she tumbled into the rushing waters. Little Hawk, thinking first of saving his weapons and food, had just time to loose the pack and let it fall. Then he, too, was plunging toward the creek. He kicked free of the horse just before he hit the water. The horse screamed once and went rolling down the creek, banging with great force against rocks.

The current was very strong. Little Hawk fought to get his feet under him, but the water rolled him. The icy shock of it made breathing difficult as he thrust his face above the surface and gasped. He took water into his lungs and came up coughing, fighting for his life. Once more he was rolled by the cascade, and with his lungs bursting, he had one vivid thought: he would never see Naomi Burns again.

As his lungs convulsed for want of air and he fought to lift his head from the powerful force of the stream, he suffered a poignant sadness. The shock and pain of being slammed into a rock broke through his lethargy. His feet found purchase for a moment, and he gasped air past the restricting water in his throat. He felt pain in his thigh. He was a full hundred yards downstream before he managed to grab hold of a bush and pull himself out of the frigid water to lie coughing and vomiting water on wet stones.

His quick action in dropping his pack saved him from freezing to death. He had materials for making fire in the kit. He found a rocky overhang, gathered wood, built a roaring fire, then removed his wet clothing. His teeth were chattering with the cold, and his skin was blue. The cold had numbed the deep slash in his upper thigh and had, until he began to move around, largely prevented bleeding. Now blood oozed up from the cut, and he began to feel the pain. He rummaged in his belongings and found a large needle and, precisely for this purpose, a selection of hair from a horse's tail. His hands were shaking so violently that it was difficult to thread the hair through the needle. When he finally succeeded, he went to work immediately lest his determination fail him. He sewed up the jagged slash. That done, he felt more than a bit weak, so he chewed on dried meat while he put on his clothing, which was *almost* dry.

Sadly, the horse was dead. Little Hawk limped down the creek to find her lodged at the head of a rocky chute that poured water down a miniature cascade. Not wanting to repeat his involuntary bath he

walked out onto the rocks with great care and cut a
large portion of meat from the animal's exposed flank.
The meat was fresh, warm, and when it was half-
cooked, it was hot and juicy. It did much to restore
his strength.

Little Hawk found it difficult to judge the time
of year in the high mountains. The sun at its height
was almost directly overhead, but the temperatures
said that it was still winter. He had not seen a calendar
since he left the *Orient,* but he figured it must be at
least early June. As he made his way up the trail, he
looked now and again toward the snowcapped peaks.
He picked his way carefully until he was walking on
a hard crust over snow. Now and then his foot would
break through the crust, and he would sink into the
snow to above his knees. His injured thigh was very
sore. He was no longer capable of gaining on the expedition. He could do nothing more than plod ahead
during the daylight hours, climbing higher and higher.

He camped at a place where Indians had piled
stones in a cone six to eight feet high. Atop the cairn
was a pine pole reaching fifteen feet into the air. He
could not even guess the meaning or purpose of the
odd construction. He was too tired to speculate—too
cold, too fearful that he would be left behind to make
his way alone all the way back to civilization.

Little by little, however, his thigh grew less painful, and finally the trail began to lead downward. He
walked across a pleasant meadow and made good time
to a point on the north side of Lolo Creek, where a
hot spring filled the surrounding air with steam. He
bathed languorously in the spring. The warm water
soaked the horsehair stitches loose, and he pulled
them out one by one, whistling silently through his
teeth at the sharp pain.

Moving faster, well-fed on the meat of a young
deer, he came to a place where the tracks of the expedition separated—one party going south, the other
north. After some hesitation he took the northern
track. The debris at the campsite told him that the

expedition had rested there for more than one day.
He was drawing closer.

Day after day he marched on the trail of the
northern party. Slowly the landscape changed. The
mountain cold was left behind. Summer heat came to
him in the foothills, and the sun blasted him as the
countryside gradually opened into an awesomely wide
landscape of sparse vegetation and eroded gullies. He
had seen such wide vistas on the North African desert,
and although this land was not as arid as Africa's, it
was almost as empty. Once, he saw a file of horsemen,
definitely not white men, cross a ridge line a mile or
so away. He had heard tales from his father and his
uncle about the warlike proclivity of the Comanche
and the Apache, the Indians of the plains above New
Spain. He did not want to risk an encounter with warriors out to gain coup. Thereafter he avoided traveling
along the top of the ridges and kept himself always
alert. When he heard a sound coming from a dry water-
course off to his left, he froze. The sound was repeated.
His heart pounded, for he recognized the wet-slobbery
protest of a horse blowing through its lips in an attempt to spit out the bit. He crept forward.

He would never know what drama had been
played out in the dry creek bed. As he peered over
the brink, he saw a dead man—an Indian dressed in
a loincloth and little else. Judging from the unnatural
angle of his neck, it had been broken.

The horse was a handsome stallion. Its rope reins
were dangling, entangled in a dry bush. The stallion,
standing near the dead man, was spooked. Its eyes
were rolling whitely as the horse jerked on its rein
and caused the bush to move. The branches' whipping
back and forth further agitated a rattlesnake coiled up
within striking distance of the horse's forelegs.

Little Hawk positioned an arrow quickly, drew
the bow, let the arrow fly. The snake was pierced at
its middle, which was as thick as Little Hawk's arm.
It coiled and uncoiled, striking at the impaling bolt.
The wild movement of the snake caused the horse to

whinny in panic. Little Hawk leaped forward, soothing
the horse with his voice, and grabbed the rope. The
horse rolled his eyes and tried to rear up. Little Hawk
danced back, still holding on to the reins.

He managed to lead the frightened animal away
from the writhing snake. It took some time to calm
the stallion, but at last he was riding again.

Meriwether Lewis's determination to take back to
Thomas Jefferson as complete a picture of the great
west as possible allowed Little Hawk to catch up with
the expedition. Always just a few days behind, Little
Hawk read much of the story from sign—a dead Indian lying behind a rock with the sort of large hole in
his chest that is left by a heavy caliber rifle ball told
him that the passage down the great, sweeping, high
plain had not been without its dangers.

The party had split again. Little Hawk followed
horse tracks to an area of roaring cataracts, then
downriver to the mouth of an unknown stream flowing
from the north. He found a half-sunken canoe and,
with reluctance, turned his horse loose to take to the
water, for the stream flowed eastward.

Meriwether Lewis had not enjoyed the pleasures
of civilization for over two years, not since leaving St.
Louis before dawn on May 14, 1804. He had seen
more than his share of country and rivers, though.
Now, as he pushed his way through riverside brush
looking for a wounded elk, his long, patrician nose
was a little bit out of joint; he'd long since worn out
all of his decent woolens and was now dressed like a
French trapper or an Indian brave in buckskins. His
disgruntlement stemmed also from the fact that not
many days had passed since he had run for his life
from a Blackfoot war party and, indeed, had left a
Blackfoot warrior lying dead behind a rock. If that
were not bad enough, game had been scarce lately,
and for some reason William Clark had not waited for
him at the mouth of the Yellowstone as planned. All

Lewis found at Clark's abandoned campsite was a piece of paper fastened to a pole. The paper had nothing more than the name "Lewis" written on it. It seemed to Lewis that Clark could have managed to write one or two more words, could have written, perhaps, "Lewis: I've gone on downstream." Or, perhaps, "Lewis: Will meet you at such and such."

It was not that Lewis didn't know the way home. Home was a lot closer than it had been in over two years, for once they started the drift down the Missouri in earnest, they'd cover seventy to eighty miles a day.

It seemed, also, that his hunting companion of that day, Private Pierre Cruzatte, could have made a clean kill, of the cow elk. The animal had stopped, presented its side, and waited patiently to be dropped with a heart shot, but Cruzatte had shot it in the gut. Now the elk was hidden away somewhere in the infernal brush, among mosquitoes so big that they had probably eaten the cow elk and were now making mother elk sounds in the hope of attracting the cow's baby for dessert.

But maybe, Lewis thought, it was the mosquitoes that made Clark decide to abandon camp at the mouth of the Yellowstone before the northern party arrived there.

When he pushed aside a bush and saw movement ahead, Lewis poised himself for the shot that would put the wounded cow out of her misery; but before he could see her well enough to aim, he felt what could only be described as one great kick in the tail. Something big, powerful, and penetrating smashed through the top rear of his left thigh, leaving behind a canal of pure fire. The kick came to his right buttock as the rifle ball plowed a gash through the soft flesh there. Lewis was knocked from his feet to land heavily on his side. He held on to his rifle. He lay there trying to figure out what had happened. When he put his hand down to feel his buttock, his fingers came away warm and wet with blood.

To add insult to injury, the elk mustered enough reserve strength to go crashing off through the brush.

"Private Cruzatte," he called softly. "We are after four-legged game, Private Cruzatte, and not the two-legged variety."

There was no answer. He did some more exploratory feeling and found the hole in his buckskins, wet with blood, where the ball had entered his thigh. He couldn't tell how badly he was injured, but he knew that he was bleeding seriously enough to be concerned about it.

"Private Cruzatte!" he called again, louder this time.

Little Hawk was resting, enjoying a pleasant ride down the Missouri, when he heard the rifle shot from the brush along the bank. He knew that few of the Plains Indians had rifles, or even old muskets, so the odds were greatly in favor of that shot having been fired by a white man. The young Seneca picked up his paddle and guided the canoe to shore, secured the vessel, and made his way into the brush. Something came crashing toward him. He readied his rifle but lowered it when he saw that it was an elk. When he realized that the animal had been shot in the stomach, Little Hawk put aside his rifle and quickly sent an arrow of mercy to the elk's heart just as another shot blasted out from the brush.

He heard, "Private Cruzatte." Then, louder, "Private Cruzatte!"

Little Hawk slid soundlessly through the dense brush and found a white man lying in his own blood. There was no sign of his assailant.

"I need help," the fallen man called.

"I'm here," Little Hawk said, stepping out.

The man's head jerked around.

"Mr. Lewis?" Little Hawk asked, recognizing Lewis from his likenesses drawn in the newspapers.

"The same. Where in thunderation did you come from?"

Little Hawk had already loosened his sash and was binding Lewis's thigh. "Let's get this blood stopped, then we'll introduce ourselves," he said. "How many men are after you?"

"I think that there's just the one, and he's an army private who was supposed to be after a blasted elk."

"Mr. Lewis?" a third voice called.

"Yes," Lewis responded irritably. Then, to Little Hawk, "Blood stopped?"

"For the moment," Little Hawk answered. "How far to your camp?"

"Mile and a half or more."

"Too far," Little Hawk decided. "Would you please call in your man, sir?"

"Private Cruzatte," Lewis called. "I am here."

A young soldier in ragged buckskins burst through the brush, came to a halt, and lifted his rifle. He narrowly escaped having a tomahawk buried in his face. Little Hawk stopped his arm motion and hung on tightly just before loosing the blade as Lewis shouted angrily, "Put down the blasted gun, Cruzatte!"

"But you been shot," Cruzatte said, looking at Little Hawk in puzzlement, "and I thought he done the shooting."

"Private Cruzatte," Lewis said, "is your rifle loaded?"

Cruzatte blushed. "No, sir, I fired at that elk just a minute ago."

"I want you to go to your camp," Little Hawk told him. "Bring back at least four men strong enough to carry a litter."

"With a jug," Lewis added.

"Go," Little Hawk said.

Cruzatte crashed off through the brush.

"I'm going to carry you down to the riverbank," Little Hawk said.

He suited action to the words. Lewis was white lipped but silent. Little Hawk placed him on moss and went to the canoe. After retrieving his kit, Little

Hawk loosened the sash on Lewis's leg for a few seconds before tightening it again. Soon he had a fire going and a knife heating in it.

"Unfortunately," Lewis said distastefully, "you act as if you know what you're doing."

"Yes," Little Hawk said, readying his horsehair and needle, just in case they should be needed.

When the knife was white hot, Little Hawk asked, "Need any help getting your britches off?"

"Might," Lewis said. "It smarts quite a bit now that the initial thrill is wearing thin."

Little Hawk helped the explorer pull off his trousers and ragged long underwear, spread them on the moss, then helped him position himself there, facedown.

"Can't wait for the jug?" Lewis asked.

"Best not to. You're still bleeding."

"What did you say your name was?"

"I am Lieutenant Hawk Harper, U.S. Marine Corps."

"I'll be damned!"

"President Jefferson sent me to see if you were having trouble," Little Hawk said, grinning.

"You're joshing!"

"Not a bit."

"Well, I'll be damned." Although his face had become quite pale, he craned his neck around and answered Little Hawk's grin. "Well, friend, you couldn't have timed it better."

Little Hawk cut a green stick from a bush and offered it to Lewis to put into his mouth. "I won't tell if you yell, sir," he promised. He brought the knife close to the wound, then paused. "Do you know the day of the month, sir?"

"Eleventh," Lewis said.

"Of July?"

"August."

"Guess I got a little behind," Little Hawk said.

Lewis cried out as the white-hot steel cauterized the entry wound, and he screamed even more loudly when Little Hawk quickly applied it to the exit hole. Sizzling blood oozed, then clotted.

"Good," Little Hawk said.

"Harper," Lewis said weakly, "I think that other place is all right."

"Ummm," Little Hawk said, his fingers pulling open the gash in Lewis's rump.

"What I mean is, I don't think you'll have to— oh, hell . . ." He tensed in every muscle as the hot knife blade was laid flat on the wound.

The explorer had just recovered from his faint and Little Hawk was covering Lewis with his clothing when Cruzatte came back through the brush with four men. Lewis drank from the proffered jug and said, "Ahhhh," then fainted again.

"Put him on the litter while he's out," Little Hawk said, "and move as quick as possible. As long as he's unconscious he won't feel the pain of being moved."

"Who in the name of hades are you?" Private Cruzatte demanded.

"I think that Mr. Lewis might feel a little bit better about this if you would gut that elk over there before the taste gets strong," Little Hawk said. "I'll send someone back from camp to help you carry it—"

"You haven't said who you are," Cruzatte interrupted.

"I understand that the expedition had some advice on the way west, a guide," Little Hawk said.

"Well, I guess you could call it that. That Shoshoni gal Sacagawea—"

"Just as you had a guide on the way west," Little Hawk said, winking at Lewis, who had opened his eyes and was listening to the exchange, "so shall you have a guide on the way home."

"Hell, we don't need one now," said one of the litter bearers. "All we got to do is float down the old Mizzou to the Mississippi."

"Mr. Jefferson seemed to think differently," Lewis

said, winking back at Little Hawk. "You're the one he selected for West Point?"

"Yes, sir."

"And you're a marine?"

"Yes, sir."

"Well, you'll have plenty of time to explain. You want to hand me that jug again?"

Chapter Fifteen

The tattered members of the Lewis and Clark expedition continued to make excellent progress. He learned that on the Lolo Trail, which Little Hawk had found such slow going because of his wounded thigh and the snow, the expedition had covered twenty-six miles a day and had traversed the trail in only six days. Now the group watched the banks of the Missouri slide by at the rate of seventy to eighty miles a day. On the way west, in a time that seemed to many of them to have been a century past, each mile had been won with difficulty. No one, however, was complaining about the speed with which they floated toward the Mississippi.

Meriwether Lewis's wound was healed well enough for him to be walking again by the time the expedition reached the mouth of the Platte and began to meet trading parties moving upriver to do business with the Indians.

"Hawk," Lewis said proudly, "the lower Missouri has become a thoroughfare."

"So," Little Hawk said, not voicing his deep concern about what this influx of white traders would ultimately mean for the future of the Indians.

Expedition members traded hides and relics from the Indian nations of the Northwest for delicacies they had missed sorely. Tobacco, especially, was greeted with whoops of pleasure. Sugar, flour, chocolate, salt pork, all were welcome. The explorers traded their Indian leather tunics for linen shirts and bartered anything else the traders would accept for whiskey.

The appetite for news was almost as voracious as it was for civilized food. They heard for the first time that Aaron Burr had killed Alexander Hamilton in a duel; they shook their heads in bemusement over the strained relations with England and Spain. Meriwether Lewis was genuinely puzzled when he learned that General James Wilkinson was governor of the Louisiana Territory. Many of the men, although they were glad to be headed home, felt quick envy when they heard that Captain Zebulon M. Pike had left the Mississippi to explore the Red and Arkansas rivers.

"Yawl know that yawl air all dead, don't you?" asked a grinning St. Louis trader, one of the first whom the expedition met near the Platte.

"I don't feel dead," Lewis responded. "A little bit worn, perhaps, as if I'd been trampled by a herd of stampeding buffalo, but not dead."

"Yep," the trader continued, "you've either been et by wild animals, scalped by Injuns, or drowned in some white-water river. That is if you ain't out there on the west coast somewhere as slaves to the Spaniards."

"Well, sir," Lewis said with a wide smile, "those who had given us up for lost didn't know that President Jefferson sent a second expedition to give us a hand." He thumped Little Hawk on the back but did not explain to the trader.

The men saw their first non-Indian women in two

years when the boats put ashore at the village of La
Charette. Spirited dancing left many of the expedition
members tired and hung over for the 7:30 A.M. departure. A cannon salute greeted them downstream at
Cantonment Belle Fontaine, a military post established by General Wilkinson in the spring of 1805; and
on September 23, 1806, the boats reached St. Louis.
The expedition had traveled over seven thousand
miles.

In the excitement and pandemonium of the arrival Little Hawk had some difficulty in locating Meriwether Lewis. He finally caught up with him just
before Lewis was led off to be wined and dined by
local citizens.

"Sir," Little Hawk said, "I imagine that you will
be sending a messenger on to the president."

"As quickly as possible," Lewis confirmed.

"Would you be so kind, sir, as to include my
report to Mr. Jefferson in your packet?"

"Of course. You're not going to stay for the wel-
coming ceremonies?"

"No, sir, I think not. I've included a full report
of the fate of the *Orient* and her crew and of what I
saw of the Northwest before I caught up with you. I
don't think that Mr. Jefferson will mind if I detour by
my home on the way to Washington."

"I think that would be little enough reward,"
Lewis agreed. "As your temporary commanding officer, Lieutenant, you most certainly have my permission to take home leave."

"Thank you, sir."

"When are you leaving?"

"If I can have one of the canoes, I'll leave first
thing in the morning."

"God go with you," Lewis said.

"And with you, sir. May I ask your plans?"

"It'll take a while to settle accounts here," Lewis
said. "We'll pay off the enlisted men and discharge

them. Then, I imagine, we'll dispose of what's left of the expedition's assets, and I'll be going on to Washington.''

Thomas Jefferson hailed the word of the arrival of the Lewis and Clark expedition in St. Louis as the only piece of excellent news he had heard all year. Things were not going well at all for the president. For the first time, Jefferson had spent most of the summer in Washington, and he was personally unhappy. George Washington had chosen this particular site as a gesture to win Jefferson's approval of Alexander Hamilton's monetary policy. But the location had proven, in Jefferson's estimation, to be a terrible mistake. Washington City broiled in the summer sun, and biblical plagues of biting insects sought blood without any more regard for the president of the United States than for the poorest black slave.

In the Congress, a former friend and fellow Virginian, John Randolph of Roanoke, seemed determined to make trouble for the administration on several fronts. Added to the troublesome defection of Randolph and other former political allies were James Monroe's troubling communiques from London. He was hoping to secure England's promise to stop the illegal seizures of United States ships and the impressing of American sailors into the Royal Navy, but his efforts were at a stalemate. To make matters even more complicated, Jefferson knew that he had angered James Monroe by sending William Pinkney of Maryland to assist Monroe in the negotiations. Monroe apparently felt Pinkney might do to him what he himself had done in Paris: come into the negotiations at the last minute and take all of the credit for a success that Monroe's groundwork had assured. On Jefferson's part, the fear was that Monroe would be resentful enough to contest the presidency in the election of 1808 against James Madison, the man whom Jefferson wanted as his successor.

"James," Jefferson told his secretary of state, "I have enough on my plate without this."

He threw a neatly written letter in front of Madison and waited while Madison read it. "This bears out what we've been told by your Seneca friend," Madison said.

The letter was from Joseph Hamilton Daveiss, the U.S. District Attorney for Kentucky. As a staunch Federalist, Daveiss was, in the eyes of Thomas Jefferson, tarred by the same brush that had blackened the reputation of the Federalists in New England. In spite of that, Jefferson knew he could not ignore the accusations Daveiss made in the letter. The Kentuckian stated that General James Wilkinson "has been for years, and now is, a pensioner of Spain." He had, Daveiss wrote, as "a very exalted magistrate of this country, lately drawn on Spain for his pension."

Madison frowned as he continued to peruse the letter. "Well, Mr. Daveiss makes for interesting reading," he said at last.

"What do you think of the list of those men who he claims support Wilkinson and Burr?" Jefferson asked.

Madison read the names. "John Breckinridge, senators Adair and John Smith, Judge Sebastian of the Court of Appeals, Judge Harry Innes, Henry Clay, Governor William Henry Harrison." He shrugged. "If we are to believe Mr. Daveiss, the entire western portion of this nation is a hotbed of disunion, with every prominent Republican in the west involved in treason."

"I think, James," Jefferson said, "that I am more concerned about the possibility of a Spanish attack on New Orleans than I am about an attack by Mr. Burr on New Spain. I'm going to strengthen our border defenses."

"Under the command of General Wilkinson?"

The president nodded. "For the moment. In addition, I ask your support for a scheme that I am going to present to the Congress. I want to divide about two

million acres of land along our borders into plots of
one hundred sixty acres each. Those parcels will be
given to able-bodied colonists who are not currently
residents of the territory involved. The settlers will
have to agree to live on the land for a specified number of years and be willing to serve in the militia."

"Seems to me, Mr. President," Madison said with
a smile, "that you're going to try to raise a defensive
army on our borders with Spain without an outlay of
money."

"Exactly. I do believe that the plan has more
merit than attempting to establish a standing army,
which requires appropriations for pay, food, and
material."

"Would you by any chance have taken this idea
from the Roman military colonies on the borders of
the empire?" Madison asked innocently, although he
was still smiling.

"There are some positive lessons to be learned
from history, James," Jefferson said.

After Madison's departure, Jefferson sat at his
desk and penned a letter to his daughter in Virginia:

> "The lonesomeness of this place is more in-
> tolerable than I ever found it. My daily rides
> too are sickening for want of some interest
> in the scenes I pass over; and indeed I look
> over the two ensuing years as the most te-
> dious of my life. Absence from you becomes
> every day more and more insupportable. The
> day of retirement will be the happiest I have
> now to come."

At his headquarters in Natchitoches, General
James Wilkinson was in receipt of a letter in cipher
from Aaron Burr, in which Burr breathed the fire of
war. The message had been delivered by a young man
named Samuel Swartwout.

"Our mutual plans have matured," Burr wrote.
He was soon to depart westward accompanied by

his daughter, Theodosia, "never to return" to the East. He would rendezvous with one thousand men on the Ohio.

"The gods invite us to glory and fortune," Burr wrote. "It remains to be seen whether we deserve the boon."

Several things worried Wilkinson. First of all, he missed the woman who called him her little love, the all-wise woman who not only heated his blood with desire but gave him dependable advice. Melisande was long since overdue to have come to him from St. Louis. He felt uneasy without her. Moreover, Burr's grandiose boasts did not ring true in Wilkinson's ears. The former vice president assured him that the protection of the new nation to be established west of the Mississippi had been solemnly promised by England, but he had not given Wilkinson the name of any British official.

The governor of the Louisiana Territory faced New Spain across the Sabine, and he knew that should Spain decide to cross the river, the forces at his command would be hard put to defend the new lands of the United States. There had been several border incidents to testify to the fact that old Spain was not content with the new boundaries. Wilkinson was under orders by Secretary of War Henry Dearborn to repel any attack by the Spanish, but there were, even then, armed Spaniards on the American side of the Sabine. If he continued to be associated with Burr and if Burr actually did bring an army of a thousand or more men down the Mississippi, it could happen that he, Wilkinson, would be caught between two powerful forces, Spain in the south and the United States in the north.

Strange rumors had been floating with the traders down the Mississippi. These rumors said that it was not merely the purpose of the Burr expedition to seize Spanish lands in Mexico but to tear the western states and territories away from the United States, to be a part of the new nation. It was not that the rumor was new to Wilkinson, or that it was untrue; it was just that if every flatboater on the Mississippi knew Burr's plans, then Burr had been doing entirely too much talking.

Wilkinson was, above all, a cautious man. He decided that it was time to look after his own interests. First he sent a stiff note to the Spaniards ordering them to evacuate from United States territory at once or face the consequences. To his surprise the Spaniards obeyed the ultimatum and moved back across the Sabine. The threat of war with Spain was, thus, easily quieted. Wilkinson decided that he could, as the old saying went, have his cake and eat it too. It would be more profitable to him to continue in the pay of Spain and be sure that certain sums of money would accrue to him than to risk everything for an uncertain future with Aaron Burr. He began by arresting Burr's messenger, Samuel Swartwout, then sent off a series of letters denouncing Aaron Burr and revealing everything he knew about Burr's plan to Thomas Jefferson.

Several important events quickly followed Wilkinson's betrayal of Burr. First Wilkinson negotiated a treaty with the Spanish commandant, which, the captain general of Mexico said jubilantly, "ensures the integrity of the Spanish dominions along the whole of the great extension of frontier." Such a treaty was in direct opposition to Secretary of War Dearborn's intent, but it seemed to please Thomas Jefferson, who wrote his agreement that the Sabine be made a temporary line of separation between the troops of the two nations.

Jefferson's political opponents believed that the president's action regarding Wilkinson's treaty was prompted by growing concern about Aaron Burr's activities. Reports from the west became more and more alarming as citizens of Kentucky, egged on by their attorney general Daveiss, formed an informal militia and raided Blennnerhassett Island to punish the man who wanted to break up the union. To the disappointment of the lynch mob, Blennerhassett was not in residence. They contented themselves by sacking the

manor house and smashing the glass vials in Blennerhassett's laboratory. In Frankfort, Daveiss brought
formal complaints against Aaron Burr.

One friend of Thomas Jefferson's could have told
the president the true condition of Aaron Burr's endeavor. Little Hawk, traveling by canoe down the
Mississippi, caught up with Burr's flotilla just before
it was to leave the mouth of the Ohio. Curious about
the man who had killed Alexander Hamilton, he
hitched a ride on a raft. The men who welcomed him
aboard assumed that he had come to join Aaron
Burr's army, and Little Hawk did not disavow them
of that notion. He tied his canoe to the raft, found
himself a place to spread his blankets, and enjoyed a
good night's sleep with the raft tied to the bank.

He was awakened by one of the men who had
invited him aboard and was told that Aaron Burr
wanted to see him. The young Seneca walked a sag-
ging plank to the muddy bank of the river and followed the messenger to a flatboat with a sizable house
astern.

Aaron Burr was at breakfast. He didn't rise when
Little Hawk entered the cabin, but he did look up in
interest. "Ah," he said, "our latest recruit." He
waved a hand toward a chair at the table. "Won't you
join me in this excellent repast?"

"Thank you," Little Hawk said, taking the chair.

"Just help yourself," Burr encouraged.

Little Hawk forked salt bacon and fried eggs onto
a plate, then reached for a hot biscuit.

"I assume you know who I am," Burr said.

"I do, sir. Excuse me for not introducing myself.
My name is Harper. I'm called Hawk."

"You have the look of one," Burr said. "May I
ask, Mr. Harper, what led you to join our enterprise?"

"I heard rumors in St. Louis," Little Hawk replied. "I was going downriver anyhow, so when I saw
your flotilla I remembered the rumors and came
ashore to find out what was going on."

"And, if I may ask, what are your conclusions?"

Little Hawk chewed thoughtfully for a moment. He was hungry, and the bacon and eggs hit the spot. "You have set yourself a very ambitious goal, sir."

Burr chuckled. "Now, the main question is, can you share that goal with me? Can you dream of land of your own in a new country—a country not bound to any of the old powers, nor to the United States? Can you conceive of yourself as a man of position and power—for that is to be the reward of all those who are, shall we say, charter members of this expedition." He patted a napkin against his lips and looked at Little Hawk inquiringly. "What say you, sir?"

"I tied my canoe to your raft, Mr. Burr," Little Hawk said quite truthfully.

"Excellent," Burr responded. "I wish I had a thousand more like you. Have you any experience at the art of war, Mr. Harper?"

Within certain parameters it was permissible for an Indian to lie to a white man. "Not really, sir," Little Hawk said.

" 'Not really'?"

"Well," he said, spreading his hands. "Not at all, really."

"No Indian fighting? Where was it you said you were from?"

"St. Louis, sir."

"Well, we'll whip you into shape once we reach New Orleans," Burr said. "We'll have experienced men to train us. We'll be a first-class fighting force before we move on Mexico."

"If I may ask, sir, when will the rest of the army join us?"

Burr touched the side of his nose with his index finger. "Ah, a worthy question. First we must demonstrate that we are serious. This we are doing at the moment. I can assure you, sir, that our passage down-river is not unnoticed. Soon the men of the West—men who are sick and tired of the unfulfilled promises of the United States, men who have had to fight for everything they own—will come down the river to join us. And there will be others in New Orleans. Never fear! The lack of manpower will not be a problem. You are fortunate, Mr. Harper, in having joined us early. If you desire it and if you are willing to apply yourself, you can command a regiment by the time we go into action."

"That would be an exciting prospect, sir," Little Hawk said.

"Yes," Burr said. He patted his lips again, flung the napkin down, rose. "Well, Mr. Harper, once again let me say that I am pleased to have you with us. Now I must make my rounds. The men like to see me up and about early. Please stay, however, and finish your breakfast."

"Thank you, sir," Little Hawk said. He helped himself to two more eggs and a few more rashers of salt bacon.

He made it back to the raft to which he had tied his canoe just as the lead boats in the flotilla got under way. Soon the raft, with two men on her big sweep at the stern, was drifting down the Mississippi.

The Seneca spent the day relaxing and forming his opinion of Aaron Burr. He had heard from his father and his grandfather about the attempts of George Rogers Clark to raise an army against Spanish possessions and, more recently, of similar ambitions by General James Wilkinson. Knowing his father, he decided that he would have as much information as possible about Burr's force and his intentions when he reached Huntington Castle and the village.

Men approached Little Hawk in a friendly way to ask what the boss had had to say to him. He repeated Burr's words as nearly as he could.

"Yep," said a lanky man in ragged woolens, "he could talk a rabbit out of its hole, that man."

When there were several men about, no one would say a word against Aaron Burr; but as the day went on and the raft made its slow way down the big river, Little Hawk learned things confirming his first

impression that Aaron Burr was living in a world of
dreams. The young marine had not, of course, ever
entertained any idea of joining Burr's army, but he
was more comfortable riding the raft than paddling his
own canoe. A man traveling with Burr could have
three hot meals a day and a dry place to sleep.

On the second morning aboard the raft, while he
was having breakfast, he was approached by a bear of
a man with a bushy black beard.

"Ain't I seen you somewhere?" the big man
asked, studying his face intently.

"That may be, friend, but I can't place your
face," Little Hawk said. "I am Little Hawk, of the
Seneca."

"Name's Hoss Beaver," the big man said. "Danged
if you don't look familiar. You got a older brother
who looks a lot like you?"

"No older brothers," Little Hawk said.

"Well, I don't reckon your sister would be quite
as ugly as you," Hoss said.

Little Hawk laughed. "Indeed, she is not," he
said. "My sister is, I think, very pretty."

"You got a smart mouth," Hoss said. "And
there's something about the way you talk. . . ."

"It may be," Little Hawk said, easing his hand
to the haft of his tomahawk, "that you have met my
father, the sachem Renno."

"That's the one!" Hoss said, snapping his fingers.
"He was traveling with a mean old cuss named Roy
Johnson."

"My grandfather."

"Mean ole sumbitch."

"He can be."

"Your pa was a sumbitch, too."

"He can be, too, at times," Little Hawk allowed.

Hoss Beaver was one of the biggest men Little
Hawk had ever seen, and most of his bulk was muscle.
His thighs bulged. His fists were huge. He probably
weighed in the vicinity of two hundred seventy-five
pounds.

"You don't think much of yer pa and yer grandpa, huh?"

"On the contrary, I am very fond of both of them."

"Both them sumbitches, huh?"

Little Hawk was poised, although he was seated and the big man was standing up. He looked up. "I can only guess, Mr. Beaver, that you had similar words for either my father or my grandfather, and one of them mussed you up."

"Huh?" Beaver said, his face darkening.

Little Hawk held up one hand. "Now hold on, Mr. Beaver. I'm not finished."

"Huh?"

"So which one of them was it?"

"You think an old man like that Roy Johnson—" Beaver went red in the face, paused.

"So it was my father," Little Hawk said, nodding knowingly. "Obviously it was a bare-knuckle affair, for if weapons had been involved, you wouldn't be alive. And if you had won, you wouldn't hold so much resentment."

"Huh?" The big man shook his head. "You talk too danged much. Jest stan' up so's I can knock you down."

"I don't care to play that game," Little Hawk said. His tomahawk flashed, and the razor-sharp blade sliced through Beaver's buckskins and left a tiny red line across his kneecap. The big man leaped back.

"One half-inch more," Little Hawk said, "and you would have had to walk with a stick for the rest of your life."

Beaver roared and jumped forward. His momentum carried him into the quickly raised muzzle of Little Hawk's rifle. It dug deep into his belly. He halted and roared again. But Little Hawk's cold, blue eyes warned the man of impending death. He backed away, shivering with dread.

"Mr. Beaver," Little Hawk said, looking up at his adversary, "I don't have the experience at bare-knuckle fighting that my father has. I do not enjoy being hurt. Therefore, I won't fight you with my hands. I won't kill you if you try to fight me; but I will cripple you, and I think that might be worse for a man like you than being killed."

"Sure, you talk brave with that rifle pointing at me. Just remember, though, you can't stay awake forever."

"No, that's true. But if you take me by surprise, Mr. Beaver, you'd better kill me, because when I am able to move again, I'll come after you. And when I'm done with you, someone will have to feed you with a spoon."

For long moments Little Hawk thought that he would have to kill the big man. An audience had gathered, and he was afraid that pride would force Beaver to attack. Indeed, Hoss looked around, his eyes squinted, his red tongue darting out to moisten his lips. Suddenly he laughed. "You fellers hear that?" he asked. "Ain't he a pistol?"

"Reminds me of his grandfather, Hoss," a man said, laughing. "The old man talked 'bout the same way, soft and easy, 'fore he kicked you in the cods."

Hoss doubled over with laughter. "Said he didn't want me to git hurt," he roared. "Son, what'd you say your name was?"

"Little Hawk."

"Well, Hawk, how'd you like to join me in a drink?"

"Mr. Beaver," Little Hawk said, "I don't drink, but I'd like to have your hand in friendship."

"You got it," Beaver said.

His huge paw engulfed Little Hawk's hand. His black eyes looked straight down into Little Hawk's blue ones, and under his bushy beard was a wide grin. "You come danged close to my kneecap, Son."

"I meant to."

"Reckon you did." He released Little Hawk's hand. "Look, Hawk, I'm on hunt detail next. Ain't got no partner. How 'bout you throw in with me?"

"My pleasure, Mr. Beaver," Little Hawk said.

* * *

Little Hawk and Hoss Beaver left the flotilla when it tied up for the night. Little Hawk spotted fresh sign immediately and led Hoss to a glade where a small herd of deer were grazing. They dropped one each.

"You're a fair shot," Hoss said.

"You didn't do badly yourself."

"Where'd you learn to shoot?"

"My father and my uncle," Little Hawk said.

"My old pappy teached me, up in them hills in western Virginia."

"Why are you with Burr, Mr. Beaver?"

"Well, my pappy had him some land, but it was so steep you had to have a mule with legs shorter on one side to plow it. I always had me a hankering fer some level ground land. Mr. Burr, he done promised land to all of us once we whup them Spaniards."

"Mr. Beaver, there's land for the taking in the Louisiana Territory—thousands of miles of it. And unless you try to clear your farm and plow it right under the nose of some Indian tribe, you won't have to fight for it. Meriwether Lewis says that in all probability the United States will offer title to lands on the western side of the Mississippi soon."

"Well, them's all maybes," Hoss said. "Mr. Burr's gonna give us land for sure."

"Hoss, how many man are in this batch?"

"Right around five hunnerd, I hearn. I ain't counted 'em myself, you understand."

"But aren't some of them just settlers, headed for Bastrop's Grant, in Texas? That's what I hear."

Hoss moved his lips, trying to find an answer.

"And the others think that Burr's scheme has the approval of the United States government. I'm afraid, Mr. Beaver, that if Mr. Burr does gather enough men on the way down the river to mount an attack on Spanish Mexico, that action will upset the United States. Mr. Jefferson's been doing everything in his power to keep us out of a war with Spain. If Burr starts something and Spain blames the United States, Jefferson won't side with Burr. He'll do everything he can to stop him."

"Huh?"

"You'll end up fighting Spain and the United States, too."

"I'll be danged." Beaver lifted one of the deer, held it easily by its hind legs, then slit its throat to bleed it. "I hadn't thought of it that way."

"There will be regular troops in New Spain, in Mexico," Little Hawk continued.

"Mr. Burr says that all of Tennessee and Kentucky will be with us."

"You know where we are?"

"Well, somewhere on the way to Mexico," Beaver said, laughing.

"We're almost to the Tennessee border with Kentucky," Little Hawk told him. "How many Kentuckians have joined us?"

"Huh?" He scratched his beard. "Well, none."

"Any Tennesseeans?"

"Er, nope."

"I wonder when they are going to join us, don't you? If those are their intentions, then what are they waiting for?"

"Hawk, you worry me."

Little Hawk chuckled. "Hoss, if I ever faced trouble I'd damned well like to have you on my side."

"Do I get the idea you ain't goin' to Mexico?"

"If you haven't yet, I'll make it very clear. I'm going to leave the flotilla at Chickasaw Bluffs."

"Huh?"

"That's the nearest point on the Mississippi to my home," Little Hawk said. "I'll go east from there."

Hoss busied himself with the second deer. When the animals had been bled to keep them from tasting wild, he threw one across his shoulder. Little Hawk made motions to heft the other, but Hoss pushed him aside.

"Little feller like you don't need to carry no

deer," he said, taking the second animal on his other shoulder.

Little Hawk figured Hoss was too big to argue with. He led the way. The big man didn't even breathe hard.

"Hawk?"

"Ummm?"

"What you gonna do back east?"

Little Hawk felt an unexpected surge of emotion. Tears came to his eyes, and he had to wait a few seconds before he could speak. Beaver's question had generated quick, random thoughts of family and home—of his grandmother, his father, of Beth, and—and this was the image that caused his throat to constrict—of a taffy-haired young girl who had become a woman, bruised and weeping . . . a woman who had clung to him, looking for comfort, but who had found only repugnance for something that had happened to her that was beyond her control.

The swift, incomplete thoughts created an image of her face as he had last seen it, her dark golden hair, her eyes made sad by his cold indifference at the parting. He knew discomfort that was almost self hate, for it was painfully clear to him that he should have comforted her sincerely, should have told her that as far as he was concerned nothing had happened, that she was as pure in his eyes as the young girl who had given him his first and sweetest kiss.

"What you gonna do, Hawk?" Hoss repeated.

"First I'm going to eat a lot. My mother and my grandmother are fine cooks."

"You gonna farm, or what?"

In the Seneca and Cherokee societies the women made the gardens, but he couldn't envision Naomi digging in the dirt with a hoe to put fresh vegetables on the table during the fruitful seasons. Neither did he see himself as a dirt farmer. He was a soldier, a marine, but at the moment, he was not willing to plan ahead, to think about the time that would inevitably come when he would have to leave his home again.

"I don't know, Hoss," he said. "Things are different with me."

"How so?"

"I *am* Indian. My father is a chief."

"La de da," Hoss said.

"When he goes to the Place across the River—"

"Huh?"

"When he joins his ancestors, I will be chief."

"Maybe you'll need a 'sistant," Hoss said. "I work cheap, and danged if you ain't jest 'bout talked me out of goin' to Mexico."

"If I were you, Hoss, I'd throw in with those settlers who are going to make their home in Texas. They'll need strong men."

Hoss walked in silence for a long time. They came out onto the mud flats at the river fewer than fifty yards above the flatboat. It was growing dark, so Little Hawk called out identification—sometimes the guards got nervous at night.

"Hawk, you noticed that big widow with them settlers?"

Little Hawk grinned. The woman would have been hard not to notice. She was big-boned and close to six feet tall. "I have."

"Well, I'm jest thinkin' on what you said. You said them settlers could use a strong man, and if they's one thing I am, it's strong."

"In more ways than one, Hoss," Little Hawk said wryly. "If you're going to court that widow, I'd suggest that you take a bath and wash your clothes."

"Huh?" Hoss asked. Then, understanding, he laughed. "I've tromped on men fer less than that."

"Hey, Hoss, I was just trying to be helpful," Little Hawk said.

The flotilla tied up just above Chickasaw Bluffs. Indians crowded around the rafts and flatboats to offer various items in trade for whiskey. Aaron Burr lost a few of his men at the town, for there were Chickasaw widows who knew exactly how to display their wares for men who had been long on the river. Little Hawk went in search of Hoss Beaver and found him carrying firewood to one of the settlers' flatboats.

"I wanted to tell you good-bye, Hoss," Little Hawk said.

"Follow me so's I can git rid o' this wood," Hoss said. His clothes were clean. He smelled a lot less like a bear's den.

Little Hawk trailed him up the plank. Hoss dropped the wood with a thunderous crash near the cook area, straightened his back, and sighed.

The widow to whom Little Hawk had referred had a pleasant face, and now, close up, Little Hawk saw that she was all muscle—a good match for Hoss.

"Hawk, this here's Matty," Hoss said. "I been hepin' her out a little. Gittin' firewood and the like."

"Jonathan has spoken about you, Mr. Hawk," Matty said.

"Huh?" Little Hawk said.

"Or, as you know him, Hoss," the big woman said. "I know that it's not a bad nickname for a man who is as big and strong as Jonathan, but it just isn't dignified, is it?"

"No, ma'am," Little Hawk said, controlling the urge to laugh.

"I figured that I would tag along to Texas with these good folks," Hoss explained. "Matty here says that they'll be plenty of work and plenty of land."

"You can be assured of that, Jonathan," Matty confirmed. She put her hand on Hoss's shoulder. Beside the big man she looked smaller. "Perhaps your friend Mr. Hawk would consider joining us as well."

"Thank you, ma'am," Little Hawk said quickly, "but I'm leaving for home tomorrow."

"Hawk, if you're ever out Texas way and don't look me up, I'll be right mad," Hoss warned.

"I wish you a successful journey," the widow said, holding out her hand.

Little Hawk took the hand. She had a solid grip. "Take care of him, Matty," he said, inclining his head toward Hoss.

She winked at him. "You don't need to concern yourself about Jonathan, Mr. Hawk. He'll be just fine."

Little Hawk traded his canoe, his extra rifle, his cook pots and extra blankets—all of which had been provided to him by Meriwether Clark—for a shaky horse that he hoped would not die of antiquity before he reached the Tennessee River. He set out shortly after sunup. The trails were well used. At first there were Chickasaw villages at short intervals, and then, once more, he was a young man alone in a primeval forest. That condition, however, was no longer as burdensome as it had been when he was thousands of miles away from home instead of a few days' travel. In fact, he found himself singing. He sang the songs that his mother used to sing, songs he thought he had forgotten.

They were sad songs, for the most part, for Emily Johnson had been a woman of the frontier, and life was often harsh for such people. Even when the weather worsened and the old horse shivered with the cold, Little Hawk's heart sang. He was going home.

He swam the horse across the Tennessee, and the beast hauled him to the far bank as he held on to her tail. He himself was shivering before he could build a fire to dry his clothing. When he was under way again, he sang in the language of his father and occasionally in Cherokee, for he was riding past the smokes of his brothers. He was pleased by the number of log cabins and by the extent of the cultivated areas around the villages. The Indians of the West and the Northwest had yet to feel the full shock of collision with the white man's hunger for land and distant places; but here, at least, the transition seemed to be progressing smoothly under the enlightened leadership of his uncle Rusog and his father. As he rode through familiar country, ever nearer home, he was a man content.

Chapter Sixteen

Villagewide commotion and elation welcomed home the sachem and Roy Johnson. Family gatherings celebrating the return of the two errant husbands continued for weeks. Ena and Rusog hosted feasts at their lodge, during which Renno and Roy told the tales of their wanderings to their Cherokee brothers. Toshabe, meanwhile, seemed to be consumed with cooking prodigious amounts of food. By the time her series of dinners were through, she had entertained half the Seneca population in her longhouse, where the tales were repeated. Those who had heard the stories before listened to them again, pleased that the tales expanded with the telling, becoming ever more interesting.

In the days immediately after his homecoming, Renno spent a great deal of time in the village, for he was, after all, sachem. During his absence a number of minor disputes had arisen and had been left "lying on the ground" and waiting for his wisdom.

Beth, meanwhile, was fully occupied at Huntington Castle. During her husband's long absence Beth had expanded her agricultural enterprise, and this required that she obtain more labor. Four new structures had been built on the slope leading down to the creek. The buildings were two-room cottages that housed Negro workers, duly purchased from slave traders in North Carolina. Knowing Renno's unalterable hatred for the institution of slavery, Beth had immediately given the new laborers their letter of manumission. It was, she felt, a moot point that none of the Negroes could read their precious papers, that they did not understand the concept of being delivered from slavery. They were so intimidated by their long trek through the ghost-filled forests that there was not the slightest possibility of any of them deciding to take full advantage of their new freedom to leave the safety and good treatment they enjoyed at Huntington Castle.

At the Castle the chores of autumn included the harvest of a large crop of corn. Beth called it maize, since the English called wheat and other small grains corn. Dry bins had been constructed to store the unshucked ears. Some of the other laborers were building an earthen dam across the creek to form a millpond. Two huge millstones had been hauled in from Nashville by ox cart, and a mill house was already under construction. Soon the stored corn could be ground into meal, and Beth was planning to plant wheat as soon as she could import suitable seed.

There were other year-ending chores to be done—swine to be butchered, sausage to be made, and hams to be salted and cured in the smokehouse. Most importantly for Beth, there was a husband to be spoiled. Having Naomi in the house was a blessing, for the girl was willing and able to supervise most of the work activities, and this left Beth free to sit in the council longhouse and watch with a mixture of bemusement and pride as Renno wrestled with difficult problems.

It was Naomi who came up with the idea to hold a day of thanksgiving. She had become a dedicated reader, and there was material aplenty in Beth's house. At least three times a year new books arrived in Knoxville, to be delivered to Huntington Castle by the first Cherokee or Seneca who ventured into the town on business. Naomi had been reading an account of early colonial times—such information was almost invariably published in England—in a compilation of letters written by those who had made the Atlantic crossing out to the colonies. The letter that triggered her imagination was written by a man named Edward Winslow. Dated December 11, 1621, it said that Governor William Bradford of the Plymouth Colony had ordered a three-day festival to celebrate a good harvest and to give thanks to the Lord. Naomi read it aloud to Beth:

> "Our Governor sent four men out fowling, that so we might after a more special manner rejoice together, after we had gathered in the fruit of our labours. They four in one day killed as much fowl as, with a little help beside, served the Company almost a week. At which time, amongst other recreations, we exercised our arms, many of the Indians coming amongst us, and amongst the rest their greatest king, Massasoit with some 90 men, whom for three days we entertained and feasted."

"The concept of a harvest festival is an ancient one," Beth told the girl. "There are those who disparage the entire body of Christian lore simply because many of our religious observations fall at the time of long-standing pagan festivals."

"I think it was very pious of Governor Bradford to have a day of thanksgiving." Naomi put aside the book and picked up another. "They still have annual celebrations in the New England states, and George

Washington proclaimed November 26, 1789, as a day of thanksgiving."

"What was good enough for George Washington is good enough for me," Beth said. "I would venture to say that it would be a very popular holiday with our men, since it would involve two of their most loved activities—eating and hunting. I think we could persuade any number of them to go fowling."

Beth was proved right. The early fowlers spoken of by the pilgrim Edward Winslow had nothing on the men of the village, and the tables at Huntington Castle were piled high with baked turkey and roasted duck, freshly made sausage, fresh ham, bread hot from the ovens, candied sweet potatoes, baked pumpkin, dried beans and corn cooked with a salty ham hock, a variety of sweets, and collards, a particularly pungent form of cabbage that Beth had begun to have planted in order to have a green vegetable after the summer garden season had ended.

Beth and Naomi did not invite ninety men, as did the organizers of the first thanksgiving, nor was the list limited to men only. By the time the names of all the family were compiled, along with the senior matrons, senior warriors, and Se-quo-i with some who had helped Beth from time to time, the seating capacity of the house was strained beyond practicality. Beth prayed for favorable weather and was rewarded by a magnificent autumn day that was highly unusual so late in the year. Makeshift tables were set up in the garden, an arrangement that suited the warriors exactly, since all they had to do to clean their plates before taking yet another helping was to toss aside the bones.

"It's all right," Beth told a worried Naomi when it appeared as if the entire garden would become a bone yard. "We'll have the workers bury them. They'll make good fertilizer."

When speech time came, as it did following every Seneca feast, Beth was given the honor of speaking first. She told the group the reason for the gathering, and it was agreed with many exclamations and grunts of approval that giving thanks to God and/or the Master of Life for an excellent harvest was a worthy idea.

"But," Beth said, "it was my young friend Naomi who thought of it and did much of the preparation."

In response to the assemblage, Naomi rose shyly and explained how she had read about the first thanksgiving and how President George Washington had once proclaimed the day as one of national prayer and gratitude.

"We eat today until our bellies grumble because the first white faces gave thanks?" Rusog growled good-naturedly. "Were they thanking their God for the bounty of the harvest or for not being struck down for stealing the lands of the Indian?"

"Don't be a bear, Brother," Beth said, laughing. "You'll frighten the girl."

"Well, I am thankful that my sister-by-marriage has a good cook," Rusog said, "and that she is rich enough to feed me in a manner to which I could become accustomed."

"Yes, I could eat like this every day," said El-i-chi.

"Soon you would be fat," Ah-wa-o teased.

"But you would love me even if I were fat," El-i-chi told her.

Ah-wa-o looked doubtful, as if she were considering that possibility, and dragging out the moment, until El-i-chi made a playful threatening gesture and said, "Fickle wench."

The day was a great success. The servants needed only three days to clean up the garden. It was agreed by one and all that thanksgiving should become an annual affair at Huntington Castle.

As if regretting the gift of the unusually mild November day, the breath of the great snows huffed down from the far northern plains. Fires burned in the hearths at Huntington Castle. Naomi, knowing how much Renno and Beth valued their private evenings, made it a habit to go to her room early, to read and to dream. There were times when she fleetingly regretted Renno's return. So long as Beth and she had been alone in the house, Naomi had felt needed, for Beth was obviously sincere in saying that she valued the girl's company. Now that Renno was back, Naomi felt that she was becoming an intruder, although the sachem seemed quite fond of her and was always kind and considerate.

So, in those early winter nights, she considered her future and found it to be bleak indeed. The obvious thing for a young frontier girl to do was to marry—but she was far past the age when that event usually happened. At Huntington Castle she had encountered not one suitor. Oh, a few young Seneca and Cherokee men had looked at her, and, she imagined, a return glance might well have encouraged a few of them to investigate a courtship; but there were—and she knew it well from her eager studies of Seneca traditions—considerable obstacles to such unions. Moreover, although she respected and loved Renno's family and had come to think of the Indian in general in quite different terms from before, she could not think of herself as a good Seneca or Cherokee wife.

If she were to avail herself of the option of marriage, she would have to leave Huntington Castle and travel to where there were available men. During the past summer she and Beth had made a trip to Knoxville, and there she had garnered her share of admiring glances from men, young and old. But what would she do if she went there alone? She had no money. If she found work, it would probably be as a servant in a private home. She couldn't simply walk into a town with a sign stating that she was looking for a husband.

She was still, in spite of the cruel tricks that life had played her, a romantic. She mused away hours remembering how a certain fair young man's hair curled around his ears, how he moved his broad shoulders, how he walked with surety and grace, and how he smiled. And that dream became to her as much a fairy tale as any of the fanciful stories in Beth's books.

It seemed more realistic to build wild dreams of traveling to some faraway place—to New Orleans or New York . . . there to meet a handsome man. But her dream lover was always faceless, for when she tried to envision him in specific terms, Little Hawk intruded rudely—and she became his beloved, pampered, treasured wife.

"You are foolish, foolish, foolish," she fumed at herself one night when an insolent north wind howled threats at her window.

Such silly fancies would not solve her dilemma. She could go on dreaming until she was a dried-up spinster, and she'd still be intruding on the home life and privacy of Beth and Renno. Perhaps, she thought, she should simply walk away from the house and into the cold, dressed only in her nightgown. Her freezing to death would do everyone a favor. Ah, *that* was a sad and romantic picture! They would find her sleeping peacefully, snow lying on her as a downy, freezing blanket, her eyes closed, her dead face pale, peaceful, and pitiful. She shivered and discarded that potential solution. She hated being cold.

Naomi said her prayers, banked the fire in her fireplace, wrapped in flannel the marble foot warmer that had been heating on the hearth, then stuck it between her cold sheets at the foot of her bed, where she could press her feet against it. She sighed, settled in, and fell asleep. . . .

She awoke with a start. The room was pitch black and silent. The wind no longer wailed under the eaves. Chill had invaded. She snuggled deeper into the covers and decided that it was the silence that had awakened her.

"No," she said, sitting straight up in bed, for it had been something else—a dream of a young man riding in the darkness through a veil of huge, drifting snowflakes. She cried out, then, embarrassed, clapped her hand over her mouth. She leaped from the bed onto the cold planks of the floor and rushed to the window. She threw back the curtain to see only total blackness.

The windowpanes were cold to her hands. She tried to open the window, but it was frozen in place.

She saw him then against the blackness. It was more than a dream. She truly saw him, the snow caked on his buckskin-clad legs, his head bent low, his face muffled in a thick scarf. The scene was so vivid that she even saw the horse shiver and toss its head, then lower it in resigned determination to plod onward.

Naomi, heart pounding, lit a lamp and freshened herself with icy water from a porcelain washbasin. She dressed hurriedly in her finest dress, which Beth had helped her to make. It was simple in style, of a glowing sable brown just a bit lighter than her eyes.

Renno had accused Beth of leading him into slothful ways since his return. He had taken to sleeping late, often until two hours after sunrise. On that morning he awoke to a diminished light and saw that snow had drifted on the windowsill. He pulled the covers up to his ears and put his arm around Beth, luxuriating in her warmth, her softness. The house was silent. His breath made vapor in the air.

"It's snowing," he whispered.

Beth made a soft, moaning sound.

He let his hand become naughtily familiar.

"Ummmm," she said, turning to face him. Her lips tasted of sleep.

"It's snowing."

"So," she said, imitating him.

"You like snow."

"Not now."

He moved to get up.

"Don't go."

"Do we just stay in bed all day?"

"Maybe not all day," she said, offering him her mouth.

So it was that his blood had warmed as only a woman can make it happen. Afterward he arose and added tinder to the coals of the banked fire. Soon the room was becoming more comfortable, so he dressed.

Beth was beginning to show signs of rousing from the pleasant sleep that had followed lovemaking.

"Go on," she said. "I'll be along soon."

He smelled tantalizing aromas as he walked down the stairs. Already fires were burning cheerily in the fireplaces in the great room and the sitting room. The aroma of fresh bread and coffee met him as he went into the kitchen. And something else . . .

"Do I smell a cake baking?" he asked.

"That you does, Missa Renno," Cook said. "This chile done gone cookin' up another thanksgiving feast."

Naomi, her golden hair piled attractively, was dressed in a color that complemented her cameo skin and her eyes. She was busy with Cook.

Renno winked at Naomi. "We can't invite as many people this time. Too cold to eat outside."

"Only one," Naomi said.

The girl looked different, Renno thought. There was a glow to her. She had always been attractive, but on that particular morning she was quite beautiful. He cocked his head in question.

Naomi beamed at him. "It's a surprise, Sachem."

"Oh, well, then."

"But you'll know before noon," she said.

"Ah." He would not be skeptical. He had seen proof of Naomi's sight. "I can't ask who is to be here before noon?"

"Do you need to ask?"

"Little Hawk," he said softly.

Naomi blushed prettily.

When night came, a glacial wind blew clouds down from the north. He was within a day's travel of the swimming creek. Two hours before, he had passed a small Cherokee village. The only other villages between him and home were off his line of travel. Unless he cared to detour miles away from the trail to sleep in a cabin, he would have to make camp in the forest.

"What do you think?" he asked the horse who,

in spite of her appearance, had proved to be a brave and noble steed. The horse did not choose to answer him. "Well, old girl, silence means consent, so you're for it."

Both he and the horse regretted his decision to ride through the night. The wind died shortly after midnight, and the snow came. Huge flakes drifted softly through still air to slither icily down his neck and accumulate on his clothing.

"I'm sorry, old girl," he told the horse. "But it's too late for apologies, isn't it? We'll just have to push on through." The horse shivered. He leaned forward and patted her on the shoulder.

Dawn was delayed by the snow and the clouds. The snow changed things, altered familiar landmarks, and made him question his choice when he came to a fork in the trail. But there was the place where he had once saved the traveling party of the duc d'Orléans and his brother, the comte de Beaujolais, from an ambush. Reminded of the Frenchmen, one of whom was now his brother-by-marriage, he thought fondly of Renna. A mother now. *What happens to the years?* he mused. Renna the tomboy, who could hold her own in a game of stickball with the toughest boys of the tribe . . . Renna the bride, lifting her face to kiss a man who was now dead . . . Renna the woman, coming back with a new husband, a Frenchman of royal blood. Well, Frenchmen apparently found the women of his family to be attractive. . . .

Fond thoughts, idle thoughts, thoughts to make him forget the cold as he topped a ridge and saw the smokes of the village. And then there was room in his mind only for thoughts of another blond-haired girl.

She had been standing for over an hour at a window in the great room. Now, with the grandfather clock ticking its slow way toward the noon hour, Naomi was joined by Beth and Renno. She went pale, and her hand flew to her heart when a dark, ragged apparition emerged from the heavy snow. The horse

he rode was cadaverous and looked as if it might col-
lapse at any second.

Before he was visible, he was already halfway up
the tree-lined lane. He was slumped in the saddle. A
moth-eaten buffalo robe covered him. A woolen scarf
hid all but his cold-reddened nose, but each of the
three people standing at the window recognized him,
and to each of them he was a beautiful sight.

Renno started toward the door; but Beth stopped
him with a hand on his arm, and she indicated Naomi
with a tilt of her head. Renno nodded imperceptibly.

Naomi watched until Little Hawk pulled the horse
to a stop at the foot of the steps leading to the front
veranda, then she went to open the door. A blast of
snow blew into the room. She stepped out carefully.
The boards of the porch were slick with ice in spite
of frequent brushings by the house servants.

During the morning as he rode across the cold,
weary miles, his old horse trudging along with her
footfalls muffled by the snow, Little Hawk had begun
to experience doubts. He could not erase the face of
the idiot Tommy Morgan from his mind. Images of
foulness attacked him and left him wondering if he
could ever forget.

As he entered the lane he told himself that Naomi
could very well be gone—married, perhaps, or simply
gone away. After all, he had dumped her, as a
stranger, on his stepmother, then left as quickly as
possible.

As the big house emerged from the dense snow,
another thought sent tendrils of a different sort of
coldness into his heart: Naomi could have become ill,
or in despair she could have decided to take her own
life to end her own memories of the three Morgan
men. So it was that when she stepped out into the
snow, her hair lustrous, her face pinked quickly by
the cold, her eyes wide, that he felt relief and then
wonder. She was more beautiful than he remembered.
A nagging image of Tommy Morgan faded.

For some reason he would never understand he greeted her in Seneca, *"Nyah-weh ska-noh."* I thank thee to know that thou art strong.

She answered in perfect Seneca, *"Doges! Aka-noh nai?"* Truly! Are you strong?

Perhaps she was guided by the manitous themselves in learning to speak Seneca, for hearing the words of his language from her lips seemed to be a sign to him that here before him was a new person. She was not the girl who had been slave to the Morgans.

"I've come back for you," he said simply. "If you will have me."

"With all my heart," she replied.

There was time for no more. Renno, unable to restrain himself any longer, rushed out to give his son the clasp of warriors before enveloping him in his arms.

"I will find a warm stall for the horse," Little Hawk said after the greetings were finished. The three of them were standing on the ice-covered porch with the snow blowing around them.

"Go inside," Renno said. "I'll see to the horse."

"Thank you, but no," Little Hawk said. "She has served me well. She deserves my gratitude."

He would not learn until much later that Naomi had seen his coming home in advance, for he did not question why there was heated water for a good scrub in Beth's large bathtub, nor why a huge and delicious meal was ready for him when he came downstairs in clean clothing, freshly shaved, his pale hair clean and tied neatly at the nape of his neck.

There was so much for him to tell! He began during the meal and continued afterward, in the great room. His audience grew until the entire family was present. It was late that night when he knocked softly on Naomi's door.

She wore a heavy woolen dressing gown over her sleepwear. She came into his arms without words, and her lips were as soft as he remembered, and far, far sweeter.

The city of New Orleans was, for all practical purposes, under martial law. The military commander, James Wilkinson, had not officially issued such an order, but he was quick to override the civil authorities. He talked with an urgency that bordered on hysteria about an army of six to seven thousand men on the way to attack the city. In addition to the hapless messenger from Burr, young Samuel Swartwout, he arrested any man who so much as knew Aaron Burr. This included Erich Bollman, who had once helped the Revolutionary War hero General Lafayette escape from an Austrian prison.

The people of New Orleans either ignored what Wilkinson claimed was a terrible threat or ridiculed it. Writs of habeas corpus were granted for some of the men arrested by Wilkinson, but others had already been sent off to Washington under heavy guard. Still others, freed by the court under the writs, were seized and shipped off in irons before the disbelieving judge could react and countermand Wilkinson's overreaction.

The cause of Wilkinson's histrionics—a small flotilla of ten flatboats carrying a few score people, including the Texas-bound settlers who were not a part of Burr's army—arrived at Bayou Pierre in the Mississippi Territory shortly after the beginning of the new year. Burr had lost more men between Chickasaw Bluffs and New Orleans, not to hardship or war but to desertion or just plain boredom with river travel. Other deserters were afflicted with the walking man's disease, the curiosity to see what lay beyond the next ridge.

When Burr was informed that many new recruits were coming, he saw to the neatness of his dress, brushed his hair, and stepped out to greet the men. He was speechless when he realized that his visitors were territorial militiamen who were there to place him under arrest. Around Burr was his "army," fifty-five men and boys, a few women, children, and black servants. His armament consisted merely of the muskets and rifles without which a man would have felt naked on the western frontier.

After Burr had mastered his surprise at the greeting given to a "hero," he agreed to surrender to the civil authorities. James Wilkinson offered a five thousand dollar reward to anyone who would bring Burr into his jurisdiction. A Mississippi Territory grand jury refused to return an indictment against Burr. Freed, Burr fled in disguise into the Mississippi wilderness. He was captured by federal soldiers near Fort Stoddard and taken overland to Richmond, Virginia, to stand trial for his alleged misdeeds.

On March 3, 1807, Thomas Jefferson received a copy of the treaty negotiated in London by James Monroe and William Pinckney of Maryland. The president was disgusted by their efforts.

"Well, James," he told his secretary of state. "It's even worse than we had feared."

"I find no mention of the primary problem," Madison said, "the matter of impressment of our seamen."

"I suppose you have read the abject apologies by Mr. Monroe and Mr. Pinkney?"

"I think they would have had less to apologize for if they had refused to put their signatures to this paper," Madison said.

"We will say nothing," Jefferson said, "until we receive the official copies. At that time I swear I will send this treaty back to London."

"Without consulting the Senate?" Madison asked.

"It was the Senate," Jefferson stormed, "who coerced me into negotiating a treaty. I will not submit this disgraceful document to them lest they lose all perspective and ratify it."

Madison was silent, but there was a muted roaring in his ears, as if of distant guns.

VOLUME XXIV
in the best-selling series
THE WHITE INDIAN
by Donald Clayton Porter

1807-1808. Renno and Little Hawk, father and son, heed the call of the manitous to rescue Renna from danger in the war-torn hills of Spain and Portugal during Napoleon's Peninsular War. It is a region of ancient superstition, where Renna is held prisoner by a sadistic madman bent on restoring the terrors of the Inquisition. Meanwhile her husband, the Comte de Beaujolais, a French diplomat, is feared dead at the hands of an English officer during the British occupation of Lisbon.

In America, another journey takes the younger generation of Seneca and Cherokee westward, as the twins Ho-ya and We-yo, resentful of the encroachments of the white man, lead a ragged band of followers to a new homeland beyond the Mississippi River.

It is a time of storm and stress for the descendants of the white Indian, as some yearn for a return to the old ways, while others are caught up in the historic struggle against Napoleon's lust for conquest.

You won't want to miss this book, available in late 1993 wherever Bantam Domain books are sold.

EXPEDITION!
by
Dana Fuller Ross

After the Lewis and Clark expedition unlocked the vast wilderness of the American West, an influx of adventurers set out to explore the wonders of the new land. Among them were men and women of science, eager to record for the world the plant and animal life native to the region and to document the strange, awe-inspiring natural formations rumored to exist.

It is just such a group that Clay Holt encounters as he, his Sioux wife Shining Moon, and their companions trap beaver along the Yellowstone River in the spring of 1809. Under attack by Blackfoot are a Harvard professor, his daughter, a Prussian artist, and the buckskin-clad men who have led them there. Stranded on a small island midstream, they futilely try to defend themselves, and only because of the expertise of Clay Holt and his group does the expedition survive. The grateful professor persuades Clay to assume leadership of the expedition—but the outraged buckskinner who held that position before will not rest until he gets revenge.

Clay's brother Jeff Holt is hundreds of miles away, returning to their home in Ohio to resume married life with his bride, Melissa. But when Jeff reaches the house, he is greeted not with kisses but with musket balls, and he comes face-to-face with the disheartening news that Melissa is gone—and he has no idea where to begin his search for her.

Read on for an exciting preview of EXPEDITION!, the second book in the Frontier Trilogy, on sale February, 1993, wherever Bantam paperbacks are sold.

The Indians could not brook the intrusion of the whites on the hunting grounds and navigable waters which they had been in habits of considering as their own property from time immemorial

–from Fortescue Cuming's
Sketches of a Tour to the Western Country

The paddle in Clay Holt's hands bit smoothly into the waters of the Yellowstone River, sending the birchbark canoe gliding over the placid surface. The Yellowstone ran narrow and fast in places, but right here it was wide and peaceful, sparkling with a blue and white shimmer in the midday sun.

Springtime in the mountains was Clay's favorite time of year. The sun was warm during the day, and the nights were still cool enough for a man to sleep well, rolled up in a buffalo robe . . . especially when that robe was shared with a woman like Shining Moon.

Clay looked back at her, sitting in the rear of the canoe and lending her efforts with a paddle to his. Her dark eyes met his, and a smile touched his normally stern mouth. With his lean, hard features and the rumpled thatch of black hair under a coonskin cap, Clay looked rather grim most of the time, but Shining Moon could nearly always draw a grin out of him.

A man could search the whole world over, Clay had thought more than once, and never find a better, more beautiful wife.

They made an impressive-looking couple as they paddled along the clear mountain stream that ran through a thickly wooded valley between rugged, snow-capped heights. Clay was dressed in buckskin shirt and trousers, along with high-topped fringed moccasins and a coonskin cap, its ringed tail dangling on his right shoulder. He had tucked a brace of .54 caliber North and Cheney flintlock pistols behind his belt, and he carried two knives, one in a fringed sheath on his belt, the other sheathed and strapped to the calf of his right moccasin. Resting against his left hip were his powder horn and shot pouch, hung from a strap that crossed his broad chest and right shoulder. His Harper's Ferry rifle, identical to the one he had given his brother Jeff, lay at his feet in the bottom of the canoe, where it would be easy to reach in case of trouble.

Shining Moon, a young Hunkpapa Sioux woman of some twenty summers, also wore buckskins, but her dress was decorated with porcupine quills that had been painted different colors and arranged in elaborate patterns on the garment. In addition, a band of brightly colored cloth was tied around her forehead to keep her long, raven-dark hair from falling in front of her eyes. She wore a hunting knife and like her husband had placed a rifle at her feet. She was not as expert a marksman as Clay Holt, but she could outshoot most male members of her tribe, who had only recently become proficient in the use of firearms. And none of the Hunkpapa, male or female, were as good at tracking and reading signs as Shining Moon. She had been invaluable on the journey, leading Clay and his companions unerringly to creeks and smaller rivers teeming with beaver.

As a result, Clay's canoe was heavily loaded with beaver pelts—plews, as the mountain men called them—as was the canoe being paddled by Proud Wolf, Shining Moon's brother, and Aaron Garwood, the fourth member of this partnership. Their canoe was directly behind the one being paddled by Clay and Shining Moon.

It was still fairly early in spring, but Clay and the others had already trapped enough beaver to make it necessary to visit the fort established by Manuel Lisa at the junction of the Yellowstone and Big Horn rivers, where they could sell the pelts. The previous year, Clay and Jeff had worked for the wily Spaniard; this year, Clay had decided to go it alone except for his wife, her brother, and their friend Aaron. Instead of using equipment and provisions supplied by Lisa, they were responsible for outfitting themselves; but Lisa would provide a market for the furs, and Clay and his companions would keep the profits they realized, instead of working for wages. In the long run, Clay thought, they would make more money, even though they would also have more at stake.

Clay wondered how Jeff was doing and if his brother was back in Ohio by now. Would he bring Melissa back to the frontier with him when he returned? Clay and Jeff had talked about that, but Clay had no idea what decision Melissa would come to. There were worse places to live than these mountains, Clay thought.

The past six months since he and Shining Moon were married in a Sioux ceremony had been like an extended honeymoon for him. Jeff might wind up staying back in so-called civilization, but not Clay. This was his home now, and he would be happy to spend the rest of his life in the Shining Mountains.

It was about time to stop for the noon meal, so he gestured to Proud Wolf and Aaron to head for shore. Proud Wolf, sitting in the front of the second canoe, nodded his understanding.

Suddenly, the sound of gunfire came floating to their ears, followed an instant later by a series of bloodcurdling war cries.

"What in blazes!" Clay twisted around to look at Shining Moon.

She shook her head. "I do not know. The sounds are coming from upstream."

Clay could tell from the excited, anxious looks on the faces of Proud Wolf and Aaron that they also heard the ominous noises. He pointed to the shore again, more urgency in the gesture this time.

The prow of Clay's canoe struck the grassy bank, and he leapt out, rifle in one hand, and reached back with the other to haul the canoe out of the river. Shining Moon had already stepped lithely from the craft. A few feet away Proud Wolf and Aaron beached their canoe and hurried to join Clay and Shining Moon.

The gunfire from upstream continued, sporadic blasts punctuated by shouts and cries. A battle was going on, probably no more than a few hundred yards away.

"What do you reckon that's about, Clay?" Aaron asked as he gripped his flintlock rifle. He was a slender young man with brown hair and a beard that did not totally disguise the surprisingly gentle cast of his features. He had been in the mountains less than a year and was not totally at home here yet; given his nature, he might not ever be completely comfortable in the rugged surroundings. His left arm was thinner and weaker than his right, the result of its having been broken in a fight with Clay back in Ohio, when the Garwoods and the Holts were still feuding. Those days were in the past now, and Aaron looked on Clay with a mixture of friendship and admiration.

Clay shook his head in reply to the young man's question. "Don't know, but I intend to find out before we go any farther. I want you and Shining Moon to stay here, Aaron. Proud Wolf and I will go have a look."

Proud Wolf's chest swelled, and he smiled broadly, living up to his name for the moment. At eighteen the Hunkpapa Sioux was still a young man, and even though his body was still undersized, he had a warrior's heart and spirit. He admired no one more than his brother-in-law, Clay Holt, and to be picked to accompany Clay on what might be a dangerous chore appealed to him.

"You should take me," Shining Moon said quietly. She had never been one to meekly accept a decision with which she disagreed, even it came from her husband. "I can move as silently as the wind and without the exuberance of youth."

"You are only two summers older than me, sister," Proud Wolf reminded her.

"Two summers can sometimes be a great deal of time."

"Proud Wolf goes with me," Clay said. "He can keep quiet enough when he wants to, and I want you and Aaron covering our back trail, Shining Moon."

She nodded, realizing that Clay had made his decision based on logic rather than his feelings for her. He knew all too well that nothing got her dander up quicker than sensing that he was trying to be overprotective of her.

The shooting had died down while they were talking,

but now a fresh flurry of it exploded upriver. Somebody was burning a hell of a lot of powder, Clay thought as he and Proud Wolf began making their way along the shore. Thick brush thronged the bank, in places growing nearly all the way down to the river, and Clay was grateful for the cover it provided. By staying low and moving carefully, he and Proud Wolf were able to cover over a hundred yards without emerging into the open.

Behind them, Shining Moon and Aaron Garwood crouched at the edge of the growth, rifles held ready in case of trouble from an unexpected direction.

The river had been running straight, but as Clay and Proud Wolf made their way along it, they entered a stretch of twists and bends. With the thick growth on the banks, it was difficult to see past some of the turns, and Clay and Proud Wolf were almost on top of the battle before they got sight of the conflict. The gunshots were louder now, and as Clay parted the screen of brush to peer through it, he was not surprised to see that some of the combatants were less than fifty yards away.

In the middle of the river was an island, little more than a sandbar with a few trees and bushes growing on it. On that island, their backs to the shore where Clay and Proud Wolf crouched, were some two dozen white men. They were using the sparse growth on the island for cover as they tried to fight off a band of hostile Blackfoot warriors on the far bank. Clay recognized the Blackfoot markings by the beadwork on their moccasins–a design ending in three prongs, which designated the three tribes that comprised the Blackfoot: the Siksika, the Blood, and the Piegan. The warriors were raking the island with arrows and musket fire, and as Clay and Proud Wolf watched, one of the white men crumpled, bending almost double over the arrow that had been driven through his midsection. Several more of the defenders were lying motionless on the sandy island.

"Damn!" Clay swore. "Those pilgrims are in a bad way."

"They have more guns, but the Blackfoot are many. They will attack the island, I think."

Clay agreed with Proud Wolf. The island was separated from the far shore only by a narrow strip of shallow water. The Blackfoot would wait a little longer, content to thin out the ranks of the island's defenders before charging across those shallows to overrun the white men. Clay searched for any sign of canoes but did not see any. The white men must have been on foot; when they'd been jumped by the Blackfoot, they must have retreated onto the island, pinning themselves down in the process.

"What will we do?" Proud Wolf asked quietly.

Clay looked over at him and saw that the young man was almost jumping out of his skin with eagerness to join this fight. The Sioux and the Blackfoot were ancient enemies, and Proud Wolf would like nothing better than to spill some Blackfoot blood. Clay had no love for the Blackfoot, either. He had first clashed with them during the journey with Lewis and Clark, and he knew them to be a treacherous, horse-stealing bunch.

But when you got right down to it, this was not his fight, and he hated to risk the lives of his wife, brother-in-law, and friend to help a group of white men who had blundered into a bad situation. Out here on the frontier, a man took care of his own troubles, and if he could not, he went under. It was as simple as that.

At least that was what Clay tried to convince himself of for all of ten or fifteen seconds. Then he said, "I reckon we'll pitch in and do what we can to help. The way the river bends here, I think we can get our canoes up to this side of that island almost before the Blackfoot see us coming."

Proud Wolf nodded, looking solemn despite his excitement. Doing battle with an enemy was a serious thing to an Indian, even one full of the exuberance of youth, as Shining Moon had phrased it.

Silently, Clay and Proud Wolf retreated through the brush until they reached the spot where they had left Shining Moon and Aaron Garwood. Clay explained tersely what they had witnessed, and Aaron said, "We're going to help those folks, aren't we?"

"I don't see as we've got much choice," Clay replied. "Don't reckon I could live with myself if we went off and left them there to die."

"Nor could I," Shining Moon said, "not at the hands of the Blackfoot." Her eyes were aflame with the same ancestral hatred of the Blackfoot that her brother possessed.

Quickly, Clay outlined his plan, which was simple. They would approach the island from the deeper channel of the river and throw their four flintlocks into the battle on the side of the whites. There were too many people on the island for Clay and his companions to rescue; if only three or four had been in the party, the canoes would have had room enough to carry them away.

Shining Moon got into the canoe while Clay pushed it into deeper water. Likewise Proud Wolf shoved off from the bank in the other canoe with Aaron. They all made sure their rifles were primed and loaded, then took up the paddles and propelled the canoes toward the bend around which the battle was taking place.

They could not waste any time, Clay knew. The arrows of the Blackfoot probably would not be able to reach them as long as they were in the stream, but musket fire was a different story altogether. They would have to cover over fifty yards of open water before they reached the shelter of the island itself. And since the river narrowed as it passed the sandbar, the current was liable to be stronger there, and paddling against it would slow them down. Still, they could do nothing else.

Hunched forward in the bow of the canoe, Clay dipped the paddle deep into the water, the corded muscles in his arms and shoulders working smoothly. Shining Moon was also strong, and together their efforts sent the canoe shooting through the current. Behind them, Proud Wolf and Aaron followed along as best they could.

The island came into view as they rounded the bend. A haze of black-powder smoke hung in the air over it, as well as along the shore. Flintlocks still boomed and arrows hummed in the air. Clay bent his back even more to the task of paddling, sparing only a brief glance toward the bank. Though he could see only a few Blackfoot warriors, he figured they outnumbered the defenders on the island two to one.

Four more rifles would not make a great difference, or

at least one would not think so. But Clay had confidence in his own marksmanship, along with that of Shining Moon, Proud Wolf, and Aaron. If they could reach the island and make every shot count, the Blackfoot might decide the price they would have to pay to continue the attack was too high.

Ten yards slid under the canoes, then twenty, then thirty. They were more than halfway there, and so far the Blackfoot had paid no attention to them. That changed abruptly, however. Over the gunfire and the splashing of the paddles, Clay heard a sudden cry of alarm that was echoed seconds later by several more of the warriors. He saw a splash just ahead to the right and knew it was a musket ball hitting the water.

As long as the aim of the Blackfoot stayed that far off, Clay was not worried. If they had a chance to get the range, though, he and the others might be in trouble.

Then the tip of the island was only ten yards away. More lead missiles peppered the surface of the river near the canoes. Clay ignored them and kept paddling. A few seconds later, the humped back of the sandbar loomed up to the right, between the canoes and the far shore where the Blackfoot were hidden in the trees. Clay dug down with the paddle and sent the canoe grating onto the sandy beach. He and Shining Moon leapt out of the birchbark craft with their rifles as Proud Wolf and Aaron arrived nearby, also unhurt by the gauntlet of musket fire.

Some of the island's defenders had seen them coming. Buckskin-clad bearded men jumped up and ran toward the newcomers. They would have been better off fighting the Blackfoot than greeting the reinforcements, Clay thought.

Then he realized that a greeting was the last thing these men had in mind. Without slowing down, one of them slammed into Clay, knocking him off-balance. Clay caught himself before he fell, but he had no chance to regain solid footing before another man slashed at him with the butt of a rifle. Clay blocked the blow with a forearm, but this time he went down under the impact. A few feet away Shining Moon cried out in surprise and alarm as one of the other man knocked her roughly aside and sprang into the canoe.

"Hey!" Aaron yelled as he and Proud Wolf were the

victims of a similar assault. "What the hell are you doing?"

One of the bearded men paused long enough to throw him a hideous grin. "Gettin' out o' here, sonny!" he called as he threw himself into the second canoe.

Clay came up on his knees and saw at least half a dozen men trying to pile into each of the canoes, fighting with one another for space. They were making a desperate attempt to escape, stealing the canoes and abandoning the others to their fate. Clay's instincts cried out for him to put a shot in the middle of the ungrateful lot of them, but out of the corner of his eye he saw one of the Blackfoot emerge from the shelter of a deadfall on the shore–and train his musket on the fleeing men.

Throwing himself down on his belly, Clay brought his rifle to his shoulder, thumbed back the cock on the flintlock, and settled the sight on the chest of the Blackfoot warrior. He fired at the same instant as the Blackfoot. There was no way of knowing where the ball from the Indian's musket went, but Clay's shot caught the warrior in the chest and sent him sprawling backward, blood gushing from the mortal wound.

Clay glanced over his shoulder and saw that both canoes were back in the river now, riding low in the water because too many men had clambered into them before pushing off. They were not even trying to paddle but were content to let the current carry them downstream.

A smaller band of Blackfoot detached themselves from the main party and raced along the shoreline, firing arrows and muskets toward the canoes. The men who were trying to escape soon discovered they had left the sparse shelter of the island for something even worse. A couple of them toppled from each canoe, arrows protruding from their bodies. Others sagged, wounded by musket fire, but managed to stay aboard.

The crude boats were awash within moments, however, not only overloaded but also perforated by balls from the Blackfoot muskets. From the island, Clay saw them sinking and uttered a heartfelt curse. When the canoes went down, they would take all the supplies and a season's worth of pelts to the bottom of the river.

He could do nothing about it, Clay realized bleakly. The supplies and pelts meant nothing if he and the others were killed by the Blackfoot. Shining Moon was still on the ground where she had been spilled by the rush of men trying to escape. Clay caught her wrist, hauled her to her feet, and together they ran toward a clump of small trees where several of the defenders were clustered. Aaron and Proud Wolf hurried toward a brushy thicket several yards away.

Clay and Shining Moon threw themselves to the ground beside the other defenders. Musket fire still rattled and popped around them. Clay's eyes widened in shock as he realized that one of the whites was a woman. A young woman, at that, with strawberry-blond hair underneath a hooded cloak. An older, round-faced man hovered beside her, one arm over her protectively. Neither of them seemed to be armed, but the other men with them, all buckskin-clad frontiersmen, were firing toward the shore with a mixture of pistols and rifles.

Debris was clumped at the base of the trees, and Clay guessed it had caught there during the spring floods, when the river had run higher. The driftwood and brush provided some shelter from the Blackfoot attack; it was unlikely to stop a musket ball, but it would prevent many arrows from getting through.

Clay reloaded with fast, practiced ease, then rose up to get a bead on one of the Indians. The Blackfoot was showing only a few inches of shoulder behind a tree, but that was enough. Clay's rifle roared, and the warrior went staggering, his right arm dangling uselessly from a shattered shoulder.

"Good Lord!" cried the round-faced man who was sheltering the young woman. "That's quite some shooting!"

Clay put the rifle on the ground and jerked out his pistols. They did not have the range of the long gun, but in his hands they were accurate enough to down a couple more Blackfoot. Beside him, Shining Moon fired her rifle and sent another attacker spinning to the ground. From the nearby clump of brush, Proud Wolf and Aaron added their firepower to the efforts of the defenders, spacing their shots so that they would be firing while the others were reloading.

As he crouched down and reloaded the rifle and pistols, Clay glanced toward the river and saw that both canoes had sunk, leaving the would-be escapees floundering in the water. Some of them were floating facedown, while others struggled back toward the island. The current was too strong for any of them to reach the far shore and escape that way.

Clay swallowed the revulsion he felt for those men. There would be time later to deal with them—if he came out of this mess alive.

His weapons reloaded, he fired again. This time one of the pistol shots missed, but the other one, as well as the ball from the rifle, hit their targets. Another Blackfoot died, and one more staggered away badly wounded. Clay had put five of the warriors out of the fight already, and Shining Moon, Proud Wolf, and Aaron Garwood were taking an impressive toll with their fire, too.

"Pour it into them!" Clay shouted, his voice booming out over the island. "Keep firing!"

Leading by example as well as words, Clay rallied the defenders over the next few minutes, and although two more of the white men were killed by the Blackfoot, the casualties suffered by the Indians were much greater. Rifle fire raked the shoreline, the defenders shooting in volleys now, rather than offering the scattered, disorganized resistance they had before Clay's arrival. He was not surprised when the attackers suddenly broke and ran.

A cheer went up from the men on the island as they saw the Indians retreating, but Clay leapt up and shouted, "Give 'em a hot send-off, boys!" He had his pistols in his hands, and he fired both guns after the fleeing Blackfoot. The other men followed his lead, sending more balls whining through the forest after the Indians.

One man let out an exuberant whoop, slapped Clay on the shoulder, and cried, "We showed 'em, didn't we? We really taught them redskinned bastards a lesson!"

Clay looked over at the man, saw that his buckskins were soaking wet, and savagely backhanded him. Only the fact that Clay had tucked away the pistol he had been holding in that hand saved the man from a busted head. As it was he staggered back a couple of steps, tripped, and fell heavily to the ground.

"Touch me again and I'll kill you," Clay said coldly.

The man's face twisted with rage, and he started to scramble to his feet, his hand reaching for the knife sheathed at his waist. He stopped short as he saw Shining Moon, Proud Wolf, and Aaron ranging themselves beside Clay.

"Here now, there's no need for fighting among ourselves!" exclaimed the heavy-set, middle-aged man who had been hovering over the young woman. He pushed himself to his feet, helped the girl up, and said, "We've just saved ourselves from those savages. We should be celebrating."

Clay did not look at the man who had just spoken but nodded toward the buckskin-clad man on the ground. "No thanks to this son of a bitch and the others like him who tried to save their own skins. They stole my canoes and ran out on the rest of you."

"The hell we did!" flared the man in the wet buckskins. "We were just . . . just tryin' to get around behind those redskins, so that we could catch 'em in a cross fire." He folded his arms across his chest and glared at Clay. "That's what we were doin'."

"Sure," Clay said, his voice filled with contemptuous disbelief. He turned back to the older man, who seemed to be in charge of this group, and said, "Name's Clay Holt. This is my wife, Shining Moon; her brother, Proud Wolf; and our friend Aaron Garwood."

"I'm exceedingly pleased to meet you, Mr. Holt. I am Professor Donald Elwood Franklin, and this is my daughter, Miss Lucy Franklin. We're from Cambridge, Massachusetts. Harvard, you know. I'm an instructor in botany there."

Clay greeted this announcement with some surprise. What the hell was a botany professor from Harvard doing out here in the middle of the wilderness, especially dragging a teenaged daughter along with him?

"Let's get off this island," he said. Explanations would have to wait.

FROM THE PRODUCER OF WAGONS WEST
AND THE KENT FAMILY CHRONICLES COMES
A SWEEPING SAGA OF WAR AND HEROISM
AT THE BIRTH OF A NATION
THE WHITE INDIAN SERIES

The compelling story of America's birth against
the equally exciting adventures of an English
child raised as a Seneca.